I0577258

George H. Filian

Armenia and her People

The story of Armenia by an Armenian

George H. Filian

Armenia and her People
The story of Armenia by an Armenian

ISBN/EAN: 9783337287542

Printed in Europe, USA, Canada, Australia, Japan

Cover: Foto ©Andreas Hilbeck / pixelio.de

More available books at **www.hansebooks.com**

ARMENIA AND HER PEOPLE

OR

𝕿𝔥𝔢 𝔖𝔱𝔬𝔯𝔶 𝔬𝔣 𝔄𝔯𝔪𝔢𝔫𝔦𝔞

BY AN ARMENIAN

A description of the land of Armenia:
its ancient and modern history; its
physical features; its people, their religious beliefs, customs, etc., from the
oldest dates, as recorded in Armenian
Histories and Church Records. A
presentation of the true causes of the
recent atrocities and a detailed account
of the massacres ✄ ✄ ✄ ✄ ✄ ✄

By

Rev. George H. Filian

A native pastor, banished by the Turkish Government
from the City of Marsovan, Armenia

✄ ✄ ✄

HARTFORD, CONN.
AMERICAN PUBLISHING COMPANY
1896

Dedication

IN REMEMBRANCE OF THE MARTYRS OF ARMENIA WHO
SACRIFICED THEIR LIVES FOR CHRIST THIS
VOLUME IS AFFECTIONATELY INSCRIBED

CONTENTS.

(v)

ILLUSTRATIONS.

PREFACE.

The problem of Armenia and the Turkish atrocities there, is in the very forefront of the world's burning questions at the present time. In every civilized land it is ranked alongside their own pressing local issues; everywhere there is not only sympathy and indignation, but a feeling of real responsibility. We are a group of Christian nations, and the first Christian nation is being exterminated. Within a few months the unspeakable Turks and barbarous Kurds destroyed more than a thousand villages and towns, murdered a hundred thousand Armenian Christians,—men, women, and innocent children,— and left 500,000 others without homes, clothing, or food, thousands of women shamefully defiled, and thousands of men put to horrible tortures. Dying in the streets, in the fields, on the mountains; dying of hunger, of cold, of storm, and of diseases bred of all these; dying of broken hearts and despair, even more, of shame and mental torture. Yet all these Armenians who thus suffered and were driven forth to starve and die like deserted animals, were absolutely peaceable,— indeed, they were totally unarmed and could not have been otherwise if they wished,— perfectly respectable, most of them comfortably off, and some of them rich. One who was last week a banker is to-day a beggar; yesterday a merchant, to-day a tramp. Why? For the main reason that he is a Christian, and the Sultan has resolved to have no more Christians in his dominion; the doom of Islamism is hanging over their heads. "If you accept Islam," they are told, "well and good; if you do

not, you shall be killed — or worse — as your fellows have
been."

These are all facts, proved to superfluity, though the Sultan denies them and instructs his ministers everywhere to
deny them. How often has the Turkish minister in Washington, Mavroyeni Beg, officially (?) declared the Armenian
atrocities to be fiction, giving the papers lying statements
(which come from the Sublime Porte), and asserted that the
Armenians were the aggressors ! It is precisely as though
one should account for a devastated sheepfold, with the
wolves raging about in it, by alleging that the lambs had
wantonly assailed and slain the wolves first. Some pretended to believe this rubbish; but most people, to their
credit, are only the more angered and disgusted by it. The
Turkish proverbs, occasionally good, are generally evil,—
a significant index to the race; one of the commonest is this:
" Yalan yigitin kullesi dir " (A lie is the fortress of the
brave). Kill, plunder, ravish, and then deny it; not simply deny it, but charge those very things to your enemy,
and make them an excuse for all you do to him or his. Such
are the principles of the Sultan, the false successor of the
false prophet of Arabia. At the very time when noble
American and European Christians are sending help to the
survivors of his massacres, to the half-million homeless,
naked, starving, heart-broken beggars he has made from
prosperous citizens, he coolly denies that anything has happened but the putting down of a few local riots. He writes
to Queen Victoria sympathizing with her expressions of
humane sentiment, but declaring that the reports were invented by evil-disposed persons; that on the exact contrary,
it was the Turks who were first attacked while praying in
the mosques. He assures the Queen that his measures
have succeeded in restoring order.

And this same Sultan a few months ago, before the greatest of the recent massacres, wrote to Lord Salisbury as follows:— "Take the words of my honor, I will make reforms in Armenia. I will keep before me every article of the desired reforms, and will order the governors of the provinces to carry them into effect." He at once began to put this pledge of his "honor" into effect, by sending orders from Yildiz Kiosk to the provincial governors in Armenia to root out or convert the accursed infidels. Since that promise of his "honor" months have passed away; and during the time at least eighty thousand more Armenian Christians have been killed, and even death has been the most merciful "reform" he has bestowed on the land. The word in his mouth means beggaring, burning, ravaging, violating, mutilating, torturing, and assassinating. When all the leading Armenians are slain and their helpless families forced to become Mohammedans, after the women have been dishonored,—in a word, when all the Armenian Christians are exterminated, then Armenia will have been reformed. A special chapter is devoted to the person and doings of this eminent reformer.

THE AUTHOR.

A SKETCH OF HIS LIFE AND BIRTHPLACE.

I was born January 20, 1853, in a suburb of Antioch; twelfth child and youngest son of a family of nine boys and four girls, and therefore considered the Joseph of the family, and as a small boy went to a missionary school with my elder brothers. My father was a banker and merchant. His partner in the former business was Mr. Edward Barker, English consul at Aleppo; in the latter a Greek, Jabra Antaki, their traffic being in raw silk, for which and for silkworms Antioch is a great center. Millions of dollars passed through his hands, and he was considered one of the wealthiest men in the city. A common saying was, "If you can drain the Mediterranean dry, you can drain Filian's money dry." This saying roused the cupidity of the local governor; he imprisoned my father, and proposed to torture and kill him, and confiscate his property. Americans would relish living under this sort of government. His partner, the consul, saved him, however, and won his undying gratitude; and when Mr. Barker died, my father gave his son a part of his own orchard for a burial ground. The son erected a beautiful $25,000 monument there, which still stands, the ground being owned by my brother, Moses Filian.

When I was fourteen or fifteen, my father lost all his money through the failure of others, became hopelessly bankrupt, and was too old to regain his position, and sank into a poor and broken-hearted old man: his Mediterranean was not inexhaustible. He often patted me and said, "My dear boy, I am sorry — I helped your brothers and gave them good educations, and I meant to do the same by you; but I cannot, for I am too poor. You will have to make your own way." He was a devoted friend of education, himself highly educated, master of three languages,— Ar-

(xii)

Yours most sincerely
Geo. H. Filian.

menian, Arabic, and Turkish,—and of strong reasoning powers, logical, imaginative, profound, and far-sighted. Moreover, he was a zealous Christian, greatly respected and liked. In person he was tall, and very stout, with large, bright eyes, and full, rosy cheeks; built like my great-grand-father, from whose elephantine figure the family took its surname. Filian means "Son of an elephant," and his de-scendants — about 150 in all, one of the largest single fami-lies in the Orient — have been mostly large-framed men and women.

At about fifteen I had to go to work. One of my brothers being a weaver, I learned that trade from him, and kept at it for three years, weaving both cotton and silk, and not only supporting myself, but helping support my father. Then I took up shoemaking, which paid better, but neither my father nor myself was satisfied to have me remain a common workman. He wanted me to become a banker and merchant, as he had been, and his old friends, who re-spected him, would have given me a chance to start; but I had always been devout from a little boy, and felt that I had a call to be a minister. While making shoes, I prayed the Lord. to open the way. I often thought, "Suppose I become the richest shoemaker or even the richest banker in Antioch, what then? Shall I ever be happy? No. Then Lord, what is my call?" I believed I heard the answer-ing voice of God in my soul saying, "I have created thee to become a minister of the gospel." So I went to a missionary of the American Board in Antioch, and consulted him; by his encouragement I went to the Theological Seminary at Marash, in Armenia Minor, and studied there three years in the preparatory course.

Before taking my theological lessons I was sent by the missionaries to Caesarea (Kayserieh) to teach in a town near by. On reaching the city the pastor of the Protestant Church invited me to preach to his congregation the fol-lowing Sunday morning. I did so; the missionaries heard me, changed their minds, said I was better fitted for a preacher than a teacher, and sent me to preach at a vil-lage named Chomakli, near Mt. Argaeus. The Lord seemed to fill me with eloquence, and crowds flocked to hear me.

Then the missionaries called me to a larger field, Talas, their central town; the same fortune attended me there, and steadily followed me in the other places to which I went. I will not make a long story of it. Enough to say that I always felt utterly helpless before preaching, empty of matter and words; I went to my room and cried to my Heavenly Father, and always overflowed with things to say when the time came. There was no limit to my imagination; illustrations thronged upon me by hundreds; I felt inspired from Heaven. I never wrote a sermon before preaching it, but wrote it down literally as soon as I had finished, — I wrote every Monday, — and they are all ready to be published in both Armenian and Turkish.

I was a successful preacher, but I had no theological education (though I studied my Bible hard), and felt that I needed one. I decided to go to America for it, but the missionaries opposed the plan bitterly. One of the ladies told me plainly it was a sin; that I had no right to give up a successful and useful ministry to go there. I replied that giving up the ministry would be a sin, but not going away to prepare for higher usefulness, and coming back to carry it out. Then she said I had no money to go, and did not understand English. I answered that I had faith that God would create the means. She laughingly bade me give her best regards to her friends when I came. She meant it for a joke, but I carried it out in earnest.

How I finally came to this country would take too long to tell. I will only say that I crossed the ocean by faith. When I reached New York in July, 1879, I had only 15 cents in my pocket. I worked hard day and night in a rag felt factory in the Bowery, and slept on the rags on the floor, covering myself with a piece of flannel. But the Lord opened the way. I went to Oberlin, Ohio, and studied there, supporting myself by sawing wood for the professors of the Theological Seminary. In six months I could talk English well enough to lecture, and after that time I supported myself by lecturing. Finally I was sent to Nebraska as a home missionary during the summer vacation. On my return I entered the Chicago Theological Seminary, and graduated there in 1882, after which I lectured rather widely through the country. Then I went home, and for a time was pastor of the Constantinople Evangelical Armenian Church. Later I had a call from Marsovan, accepted it, and had so large a congregation there that a church with a capacity of 2,000 was needed. I returned to this country, raised the money, left it in a Chicago bank (where it still lies in trust), and went back to build the church. That very success aroused the jealousy of some wicked men, and they falsely charged me with being the leader of the revolutionary societies in Turkey. On this charge I was banished, and now I am here again,— free and happy with my family, but full of sorrow for my dear people daily martyred by the Turks.

ANTIOCH.

The city of Antioch, where the disciples were first called Christians, (Acts xi. 26,) was built by Seleucus Nicator, 300 B. C., and enlarged by Antiochus Epiphanes. All the civilized world was then under Roman rule; Rome, Antioch, and Jerusalem were the leading cities. Jerusalem being a Jewish city, and Rome being a Roman heathen city, there was no room in either to preach the gospel freely; nor indeed in any other — the disciples were persecuted and martyred everywhere. There was just one exception — the city of Antioch; that was as free as any American city is to-day. This arose from the fact that when in the Asiatic campaign of Pompey the Great, he came about 65 B. C. to Antioch, he was received by the people with great honors; and was so charmed with the city, and his treatment, that he made it an absolutely free city for all, for every nation and for every religion, and the Roman emperors continued its privileges. When Stephen was martyred in Jerusalem the disciples were scattered; some of them reached Antioch, 300 miles north, and began to preach freely, making many converts. Barnabas was in Jerusalem, but hearing of his brethren's success, he also went to Antioch and began to preach; as he was a great orator, full of enthusiasm and faith, thousands were converted. But he was not satisfied. Crossing the Bay of Iskenderoon, about eighty miles off, he went to Tarsus, where Paul, now a convert, was living, and induced Paul to return with him to Antioch that they might preach the gospel together.

Only scholars have any idea of the greatness and beauty of Antioch at this time; it was second only to Rome, and was the second largest city in the world, with nearly a million people; so rich and luxurious as to be called the Golden City; so lovely and architecturally imposing as to be called the Queen City. The finest street ran east and west for several miles; it was of great width, paved from end to end with vari-colored marble blocks, and with marble pillars on both sides along its whole extent, on which were magnificent marble palaces of the Roman officers. In that same grand avenue were theaters, singers of both sexes, fortune-tellers, great heathen orators and philosophers, and throngs of people passing along. Paul and Barnabas stood on the marble pavement month after month for a year, full of the Holy Ghost, and proclaimed the everlasting gospel. Crowds gathered to hear them; even the officers and their wives, stretching their heads from the windows of their palaces, listened to them; they gained disciples from every rank for Christ and His religion, and the converts there first received the name of Christians.

This was my birthplace and my relatives still live there. Since the time of Christ and his disciples, Antioch has been ten times destroyed by earthquakes. In the fourth century the whole city was destroyed, and 250,000 people were buried under the ruins. That beautiful street and its magnificent palaces are now buried two or three yards below the surface of the ground. In 1872, when I was there, an earthquake destroyed the whole city, and almost in a moment several thousand people perished. Several of my own relatives and many of my friends were killed. The city has now only 25,000 people, most of them Mohammedan Turks. There are many Fellahin, and perhaps 2,000 Greeks, and 500 Armenians, but in the suburbs the Armenians are more numerous, and are the intellectual heads of the whole.

Antioch is still a beautiful and stately city, and a great center for licorice, raw silk, wheat, and soap. The finest soap is manufactured there. About thirty factories make it, from pure olive oil and daphne oil, the latter giving it a sweet fragrance. The daphne groves are very numerous. The city has excellent orchards and vineyards, orange trees, olive trees, fig trees, yenidulnya trees, palm trees, pomegranate trees. All sorts of fruits, in every season of the year, are fresh on the branches. But for occasional earthquakes, it would be a queen city yet; none could surpass its beauty or fruitfulness.

GEORGE H. FILIAN.

CITY OF ANTIOCH.

Translation of a letter (see opposite page) written in 1842 by the District Catholicos at city of Sis to Kevork F'llian (father of the author) in Antioch :

Red Seal of Catholicos.

Symbol in colors representing an Altar.

Symbol in colors representing the name Jesus Christ.

Michael Catholicos, The servant of Jesus Christ by the grace of our Lord, the supreme father of all Armenians who live in Great Seleucia. I the servant of St. Gregory's right hand and most Holy throne of the Holy Mother Church. Greetings of love and blessings upon my spiritual son Kevork F'llian esteemed and honored and to all who belong to his family, perpetual happiness through Jesus Christ.

Honorable Gentleman. You will be informed through my letter of spiritual greetings and blessings that truly and earnestly, more than a father, I am willing to bestow upon you my blessings and praises, and in order to show my respect practically, I feel it my duty to thank you for your hospitality, when I came to your blessed home, as a spiritual father, where I was entertained and received proper honors. The Lord bless your valuable soul and keep you prosperous and happy through the mediation of Jesus and St. Gregory. The Lord give you and to all those who belong to you, power and ability in doing good. For a long time I have desired to send to you this letter of blessing; but I have not been able. Now I am glad to send to you one of my spiritual sons Rev. Sarkis Vartabed (a preacher). When he comes he will see your good deeds and enjoy your hospitality. May 4. 1842.

(xix,

AUTHOR'S EXPLANATION.

The author feels that it is due to both his Armenian readers and himself to explain why, in some points, he has deviated alike from the Armenian historians and his own conviction. It is because on these points, the Armenian records are in irreconcilable conflict with those of Rome or Persia, or both, and in a book mainly for Anglo-Saxon readers it is not possible to defy the general consensus of western scholarship, which, in my judgment, has not given proper weight to Armenian sources. I will specify only two or three items; if my Armenian friends notice other contradictions of their accepted history they will be safe in setting them down to the same cause.

It is a commonplace of Armenian history that St. Gregory, the Illuminator, the Christianizer of Armenia, was the son of Anag, the murderer of King Chosroes (see page 72) born about the time of the murder, and made himself the companion of Chosroes' son, Tiridates, partly in order to atone for his father's crime. I am very reluctant to omit this fact; but the birth of Gregory and the death of Ardashir will not fit according to western dates, though they are coherent from Armenian.

I have also given twenty years' rule and a good character to King Artavasdes, who reigned three and was a coward.

Most unwillingly of all, I have changed a very full and eulogistic account of Moses Khorenatzi, the great national historian of Armenia, for a meager and depreciating one. That he lived in the fifth century and wrote as an eye and ear witness, instead of being a not wholly veracious compiler of two centuries later, and that his history is sound and consistent, is my firm belief. That his work is better known than all other Armenian works together, and is the one native book that has become a standard western classic, shows the powerful genius of the man.

GEORGE H. FILIAN.

(xx)

I.

THE LAND OF ARMENIA.

PHYSICAL FEATURES.

Where is Armenia ? It seems a simple question, yet during my lecturing in the United States I have met far more people who did not know than who did. That is natural enough, for until the late horrors, it seemed little more than a name of old history, of no present importance; but there is a further reason. The present Sultan forbids the use of the name altogether, and insists on the district being termed Kurdistan, or called by the names of its vilayets, Diarbekr, Van, Erzroom, etc. Many maps do not have the name Armenia at all. A few years ago, when the missionaries of the American Board were organizing the college at Harpoot, now so bloodily famous, they named it Armenia College; but the Sultan forbade it on the ground that there was no longer an Armenia, and the use of the name would encourage the Armenians*
to revolt. The missionaries were forced to change the name to Euphrates College. If any Turkish subject uses the word, he is fined and imprisoned; if it is used in any book, the book is confiscated, and the author banished or killed. The study of Armenian history

---

* The word "Armenian" is not altogether indicative of race, it refers more particularly to those who are Christians. Any who have forsaken the faith and become Mohammedans are no longer regarded as Armenians, but are Turks.

is forbidden to the Armenians; they must be kept in
ignorance about their own land, so that many of them
do not know where Armenia was or what Armenia is.
A letter directed to any person or place in Armenia
will never reach its destination; for the Turkish pos-
tal authorities recognize no such address. There is
still another cause for the widespread ignorance
concerning Armenia. It has been partitioned between three different powers, Turkey, Russia, and Persia. The northern part, from Batoum on the Black
Sea to Baku on the Caspian,— the river Araxes being
the boundary to near Mt. Ararat,— belongs to Russia; the southeastern course of the Araxes from near
Mt. Ararat, to Persia; the largest and most fertile part,
the western, from Mt. Ararat to the Black Sea and
the Kizil-Irmak to Turkey. But at the time of its
greatest extent and power, when its people were great
and its kings were great, long before Alexander's conquest, — Armenia covered about 500,000 square
miles, and stretched from the Black Sea and the Caucasus on the north to Persia, and Syria on the south,
from the Caspian and a much smaller Persia on the
east, to Cilicia and far beyond the Halys (Kizil-Irmak) on the west, but including also old Media and a
part of Mesopotamia.

It is one of the most picturesque of countries; travelers call it the Switzerland of Asia. Its general
character is that of a plateau some 4,000 feet above
the sea, a natural garden watered by noble streams
and studded with beautiful lakes; but the mountain

MOUNT ARARAT.

ranges are 7,000 to 8,000 on the average, while that historic land-mark, the superb snow-capped Mt. Ararat, is about 18,000,— towering toward Heaven nearly in the center of Armenia, piercing and ruling over the clouds and the storms.

Armenia is the mother land, the cradle of humanity, and all other lands are her daughters; but she is fairer than any other. Even her mountain tops of perpetual snow are a crown of glory; the sun kisses her brow with the smile of morning; and she supplies the beautiful rivers, Euphrates, Tigris, Pison, Araxes, and many others from the jewels of her crown. These rivers penetrate to every corner of the land; traverse many hundreds of miles to give life to the fields, the vineyards, and the orchards, to turn the mills, and finally close their course in the Caspian Sea, the Black Sea, and the Gulf of Persia, carrying the bounty and good-will messages of the mother land to her children in remote parts, to Persia, India, and Russia. From the same inexhaustible reservoir she feeds her noble lakes; Sevan (Gokche), Urumiah, Van and the rest. Lake Sevan is the only sweet-water lake; the others are salt. The most important is Lake Van, probably the most elevated of any large-sized lake in the world; it is 5,400 feet above sea level, and its area is 1,400 square miles. A few words from the author's respected teacher, Professor Philip Schaff, will not be amiss. Schaff's Bible Dictionary, page 68, "Physical Features of Armenia;" says: "It is chiefly an elevated plateau about 7,000 feet above

the level of the sea, the highest peak being Mt. Ararat.
The lower portions of the plateau are broken by valleys and glens, including the fertile valleys of the Euphrates and Tigris. It is watered by four large
streams, the Araxes, the Kur, the Euphrates, and the
Tigris; also by numerous lakes, one of the largest, the
salt Lake Van, being over 5,400 feet above the sea."

NATURAL RESOURCES.

The mineral wealth of Armenia is very great; but
like the other potential riches of the Turkish Empire, it profits nobody, not even the greedy despot
whose word is death. Gold, silver, copper, iron, and
minor metals, besides marble and other beautiful
stones, are present in abundance. About three miles
from Marsovan, where I preached, is a mountain called
Tarshan Dagh (rabbit mountain), rich in gold; another
called Goomish Dagh, about eight miles west, is laden
with silver; and they are likely to remain so, for no
one will rifle them of their treasures while Turkey en-
dures. ·The Sultan, it is true, sends an officer from
Constantinople under large salary, to take out the precious metals, but that person does very little work.
He lives like a lord, lets things go as they will, bribes
the palace officials, and all the gold and silver extracted
does not pay his wages. The Sultan will not permit
Christians to work mines, and if they did, he would
rob them of the proceeds. Everywhere the condition
is the same. Though Armenia is the oldest inhabited
country, she is, in utilization, the newest; much newer

than the United States, for indeed she does not exist yet. She is a virgin land, her mines not open, her soil not half tilled. The Turks and the Kurds are lazy and stagnant; they will do nothing, and they will not permit the industrious Armenian Christians to do anything of importance.

The country has all the old fertility which made Asia Minor under the Byzantine Empire the garden of the world, till the Turks half turned it into a desert, as they do every spot accursed by their presence. The grain, the fruit, the vegetables are hardly, if at all, to be equaled. The watermelons raised on the banks of the Euphrates and the Tigris are the largest and sweetest of their kind; two melons are sometimes a camel's load. It is impossible for a family to use the whole of such a melon, which has to be cut up and sold in pieces. The grapes, either fresh or in the shape of wine or raisins, are of the first rank. Many varieties when cured and dried as raisins exceed in size the plumpest grapes of other lands. Nearly everything is raised or grows wild in Armenia which is to be had in the Northern or Southern States of America, though of course each country has some things peculiar to itself. The products of the North are paralleled by those of the rugged picturesque highlands of North Turkish and Russian Armenia, with their cold, snowy winters, short, hot summers, and mild intervening seasons; those of the South find their counterparts from the rich upland valleys, or the lowland plains needing irrigation, of Kurdistan and Persian

Armenia (Azerbijan), with its semi-tropical climate, and alternations of wet and dry seasons. The grain crops are wheat, Indian corn, barley, and oats. Cotton is one of the main products; a great deal of tobacco and rice are raised; and sugar is made in the Persian part. In the fields and gardens you can find not only the wonderful melons I have just spoken of, but pumpkins and squashes, lettuce and egg-plant, and indeed most of the vegetables that come to an American table. As to fruits, all that you know we know also, only of finer flavors. Asia Minor is the original home of the quince, the apricot, and the nectarine, and I believe of the peach too; while our apples, pears, and plums are incomparable. The Muscat apples of Amassia are exceptional even there. After eating them, one hardly wonders that Adam and Eve could not resist the temptation of doing the same, at the cost of innocence and Eden. The pears of Malatia keep them company; and the quince grows sometimes as large as a man's head. Another fruit equally important is the mulberry for silk-worms. The olive and fig are cultivated and also grow wild, and filberts and walnuts can be gathered anywhere in the woods, as well as orchards; of course not the American " hickory nuts," but the " English walnuts " of the groceries.

In spite of the dreadful roads, and the lack of protection for travelers, the Armenians manage to send a good deal of grown or manufactured stuff to the ports on the Black and Caspian seas,— Trebizond, Batoum,

Poti, Baku,— silk and cotton, and fabrics made from them; hides and leather, including lambskins; wine, dried fruits, raisins, tobacco, drugs, and dyestuffs, wax, and other things.

Methods.of cultivation are probably much like what they were in Abraham's time; there are no very modern machines or even tools. The plough is not quite the mere scratching-stick of the savages, to be sure; but it is only a crooked piece of wood with a bit of iron fastened to the end that touches the ground, drawn by oxen and held by the farmer. The fields of grain are reaped by the sickle as of old; it takes as long to cut down one acre so as fifty by a common mowing machine. The sheaves are carried to a gal or thresh-ing floor near the house, an open platform, not shel-tered from the weather; and there the grain is sepa-rated from the straw by a process so curious that I doubt if any American, save a missionary to Armenia, has ever heard of it. It is not treading it out under the feet of the cattle, as pictured in the Bible, nor beating it out with a flail; both these methods kept the straw whole. A threshing board is made by fastening hundreds of sharp flints into a wooden frame; the grain is placed between this and the threshing floor, the oxen attached to the board, and the farmer sitting on it drives them round and round in a circle until the straw is cut fine, and the grain well rubbed and shaken loose. Then, on the first windy day, he takes the old hand fan or winnow, and separates the grain from the straw, keeping the latter

to feed the animals in winter; for the long grass of
American plateaus, and the barns of hay from them,
are seldom seen in Armenia.

The wheat crops are extraordinary; not only great
in yield, but the grains often double the size of ordinary American wheat, as compared with specimens
from the large and representative fields of Minnesota
and Nebraska.

TAXATION.

But when this wheat is threshed out, the farmer
cannot shovel it up and grind, or sell, or put it into
bins; no indeed ! He cannot take up a quart of it
without permission from the government; for the government claims one-eighth of it as a tax,— it was
always a " tithe " or tenth from the oldest historic
times down to the present Sultan, but he raised the
percentage to an eighth,— and it must stay on that
exposed threshing floor, in rain or winds, or any sort
of weather, till the tax-gatherer comes and measures
it, which may be a week, or two weeks, or a month,
and will be forever unless he is bribed to come. Nor
is even this double tax all; the tax-gatherer is a tax
farmer,— that is, he pays a lump sum to the government for the taxes of a district, and all he can get
above that is so much profit to him; so if the grain
on a threshing floor actually measures ten bushels, say,
he will write it fifteen. After the farmer has paid
first the tax on the land to the government direct, then
the double, or rather treble, tax to the gatherer on the
crops, more than half the income he can get from the

land has gone to the government. I do not know an Armenian farmer who is not in debt; they work hard, but the products of their labor go to the government and the Kurds, and any one who complains is considered a revolutionist, and imprisoned or killed. The simple unvarnished truth is that an Armenian Christian has no rights of life or property whatever; and all he keeps of either (not very much) is what the regularly appointed officials or the self-appointed Kurdish fleecers choose to leave him.

This, however, is anticipating. I have only begun on the catalogue of taxes which strip most Armenians, and are intended to strip them, of everything but the means of sustaining life and perpetuating their race. When a boy is born, a poll-tax is laid on him,— two dollars on the average,— which must be paid every year as long as he lives, whether he remains in Armenia or leaves it. Of course, during boyhood the parents have to pay this tax on every male child; if a woman is widowed, she has to go on paying these capitation taxes just the same. They are assumed to be taxes in lieu of military service; the Sultan takes no soldiers from the Armenians,— does not dare,— and this poll-tax is used to raise and pay that very Turkish army which in return butchers the Armenians, just as the old tribute of Christian children was used to butcher their parents. (That the Armenians are unwarlike and would not make good soldiers is ridiculously untrue; many of the best soldiers and best officers, even commanders-in-chief, in the Russian service are Armenians.) When the boy has attained manhood he pays his own tax,— he must have a paper of citizenship, which must be renewed every year, and for which he must pay; but he is not allowed to leave the country without providing absolute security, either in property or bondsmen, for paying that tax through life, wherever he may be. Of course this is utterly impossible in most cases,— men of property do not often migrate, and men without property do not easily get people to be responsible for lifelong obligation to let them emigrate; which is one chief reason why so few Armenians, except banished ones, or runaways, are seen in foreign countries. Furthermore, as I have said, he must pay for a passport every time he stirs from home. Land, houses, cattle, crops, are all separately taxed. Suppose an Armenian owns a vineyard. First, the land is taxed; there is a separate tax for irrigation, a third for the grapes, a fourth if you make wine from them. In all, a vineyard pays five taxes, and the government gets more than the owner.

Why don't they emigrate? ask my American friends. I have given one explanation. Pharaoh would not permit the Hebrews to go away, nor will the Sultan permit the Armenians. Another reason is that even if one has property, it is very hard to sell it. Turks have no money and Armenians no confidence. And to run away to a foreign country, whose language you do not know, wholly without money, is so desperate a remedy that most of them shrink from it.

THE CLIMATE.

Armenia, in my belief, is the healthiest country in the world; I do not say one of the healthiest, but the very healthiest. The climate is excellent all the year round, and, though the winters are severe, and much of the country is covered with snow, yet on account of the elevation — being several thousand feet above sea level, and in latitude 36° to 42°, or say from North Carolina to Massachusetts — the air is dry, pure, and agreeable, a preventative of disease, and conducive to longevity. The dread disease, consumption, does not exist there, while dyspeptics, if any are to be found, must have been imported. The perfect type of physical vigor is to be seen there. Generally the Armenians are tall, powerful, and ruddy cheeked, full of endurance and energy. Shrewd and enterprising they are, as reputed; but pure and honest too. They are longer lived than any other people. I have known Armenians of 115 and even 125 years of age; one old lady of my acquaintance at 115 was full of life and fun; I have seen her dance at wedding festivities like a girl of 15. An old gentleman of 125 was my neighbor; he worked on his farm as if he were not over 25. He could run and jump and was as gay as a boy, and greatly enjoyed children's society. If the people of Armenia could have the same government, the same encouragements, the same freedom from horrible fears, as the people of the United States, they would live many, many years longer than they do, till it might be necessary to kill the old folks in order to get rid of them. The most of the American missionaries in Armenia would be sure to echo these words. A returned missionary gave a striking testimony to this effect. He was addressing the students of the Chicago Theological Seminary, and spoke as follows:—" Before I became a missionary I had very poor health; most of my family died of hereditary consumption, and I was attacked by it. My physicians strongly protested against my becoming a missionary, saying that if I went to a foreign land I would grow worse, and probably die there. I paid no attention to this; I presumed they were right, but I was determined to go anyway, and if I must die, to die in my chosen work. When I offered myself to the American Board, I was allotted to Armenia, and thither I went; my disease disappeared and now I am as healthy as any missionary in the world. You see how stout and vigorous I look, and I do not expect to die soon. But I feel sure that if I had stayed in America to save my life, I should have lost it before this time." He is still living in Armenia, and I hope will live to be over a hundred, as many of the natives do.

The reader will smile at all this as the patriotic boastfulness of an Armenian, and say perhaps that he can make as fabulous declarations for his own land, wherever he may be; but such claims cannot be substantiated by records and personal observations as these for Armenia can. Take the Bible; some of the Patriarchs lived to be 700, 800, one even to 969, if

indeed he ever died a natural death; some were taken
up to heaven without knowing death; and all these
long lives, as will be shown, were lived in Armenia.
God's judgment was good. He did not create man
in America, Europe, or India, or anywhere but in
Armenia. He came down there from Heaven, planted
the Garden of Eden there, and from the dust of that
land created the first man. When the race had become sinful and only Noah's family were preserved, the
ark was not brought to rest on the Rockies, the Alps,
or the Himalayas, but on Ararat in Armenia.

Where was the Garden of Eden? In my belief,
around Lake Van, the highest lake, the largest lake,
and the most picturesque lake in the Bible lands; its
surrounding country, mountains, plains, flower gardens, and orchards, make it a most charming spot, and
quite worthy to have been the seat of Paradise on
earth. As the wickedest cities, Sodom and Gomorrah,
were on the lowest, ugliest, and nastiest lake, the Dead
Sea, it is natural that Paradise should be on the highest
and loveliest one. A certain very learned Gospel
minister, who desired to change my views respecting
the Garden of Eden, declared that when the North
Pole was discovered the Garden of Eden would be.
Some think it was in India, and there are about as
many opinions as there are countries on the earth.
The Bible, however, seems to be pretty clear about it
and settles the question to the Armenian mind; we
feel, therefore, that we cannot be far from the Scrip-
tural descriptions.

3

TRAVEL AND TRANSPORTATION.

Both are as hard in Armenia as they can be, short of impossibility. In the Russian section the roads are as good as in any part of Russia, and there are railroads; but in Persian and Turkish Armenia there are none of the latter, and the roads are very poor bridle-paths. A few years ago the government levied an extra tax to build "Shosse Yolou" or macadamized roads for carriages; but most of the money was spent as usual, in a good time for the Turkish officials; the roads built were wretched, and riding over them in the springless carriages of the country is weariness and torture. Most of the traveling is done on horseback or muleback, while the transportation of goods is almost entirely by camels and donkeys.

An hour's journey in America in distance is a two days' journey in Armenia, and it must be accomplished on horseback, muleback, or foot; or perhaps in a wagon without springs. Almost all the horse and mule keepers are Turks, Kurds or Circassians, all Mohammedans and of the lowest types,— which does not increase either the comfort or the security of a journey. The tenders and drivers of animals are never of a very high order of men in any country; in Armenia they are specially vulgar, dirty, and sometimes dangerous brutes. If you wish to travel with your family, you must arrange with the horse-keeper several days or even weeks beforehand; if he is ready when the time comes, he calls at your house and tells

KURDISH BANDITS.

ORIENTAL THRESHING FLOOR.

you. If animals are used and the family large, baskets will be needed to put the children in; they are put on the animals like panniers, one on each side with the mother between. This is attended with more or less danger from accidents of various kinds, liable to occur on the unkept paths, which, rough in some places and horribly muddy in others, are used for roads. As in the case of the writer, who, when an infant, nearly lost his life before he could be pulled out of the mud into which he had fallen from his mother's arms, she being thrown from the stumbling horse she was riding.

A more modern way of travel is in springless carriages; which on the rough roads means racking your body horribly, bones, nerves, and all, into outright and often severe suffering, a pain and fatigue which the traveler feels for a long time. At evening all travelers must go to a caravanserai or khan; often they are all huddled into a single room, men, women, and children, and the room is invariably filthy, and full of every kind of vermin. Such getting about is constant torment.

There is no safety in traveling; Kurdish, Circassian, or Georgian brigands may meet you on the roads anywhere, and plunder, torture, or perhaps kill you. A few years ago, when traveling in Armenia with a company of about forty persons of both sexes, we came to a forested pass between two mountains. Suddenly three men leaped out in front of us; they were Georgian brigands (Mohammedans), armed from top to toe. They stopped the caravan, picked out the rich persons and the Christians, and robbed them of all their valuables. They did not search the writer, probably supposing that as a minister he was too poor to be worth troubling. The women were dreadfully frightened, for the robbers declared that if they did not give up their earrings their ears would be cut off, and if they did not give up their bracelets their hands would be cut off. It can easily be imagined that they made haste to relinquish all their valuables. Such robberies take place every day in Armenia, for there is no protection or redress whatever; it is a matter of indifference at best, and probably of satisfaction, to the Sultan and his governors.

The brigands are not the only robbers. Bear in mind that before any one in Armenia can travel at all, the government officials plunder him. He must get a passport first; I do not mean when he goes to foreign countries, for an Armenian is forbidden to go there at all,— all who are in other lands reached there by bribing the police and running away,— but when he goes to another place or town in Armenia itself, even if it is not over fifteen or twenty miles off. This passport will cost him from two to five dollars in bribes to the officials to let him have it. When he reaches his destination, the officials of the latter place must examine his passport, and they force him to pay for the examination, else they will not let him enter the town. So the Armenians are robbed at every step whether they travel or stay at home.

Transportation of goods is even harder. Nearly all goods are carried on camels or donkeys which never go more than ten miles a day, and of course much less in bad spots; it takes months and even a year to get goods if they have to come very far, or may never be received. If an Armenian merchant orders goods from Constantinople, say 500 miles away, it takes five or six months at best from the time of sending the order to the time of receiving the goods, even if he ever gets them, no matter what condition they are in.

The difficulties of transportation prevent the export, to any extent, of Armenian products to foreign countries, and even between neighboring cities exchange of supplies is well-nigh impossible. As all through the East, there is often famine in one part of Armenia, while there is plenty in other parts; one city may be hungry while another is feasting; one willing to pay any price but unable to buy, another eager to sell but with no one to sell to; because there is no way to transport the grain or produce. Yet good highways are not built because the officials embezzle the funds, railroads are not built because it would hinder the Sultan from crushing the people.

It may be asked, Are there no railroads in Turkey? and will not the Sultan permit them, and are there not Armenians in the places along their route? Yes, there are a few short lines; one from Constantinople to Adrianople, one from Constantinople to Angora, one from Smyrna to Aiden, one from Mersina to Adana, one from Joppa to Jerusalem. I think there is also one lately built from Beirout to Damascus. The length of the whole system is not over 1,000 miles, one of them is in Europe, part of them are tourist lines, along routes that streams of Europeans would traverse anyway. Some of them were built before the time of the present Sultan; some of them are near the seashore, where there are some Armenian emigrants; but none of these roads are in Armenia.

Plenty of money has always been available from European and even Armenian sources to build railroads; syndicates and private capitalists have tried again and again to get permission to build them; but the Sultan will not grant it, for it runs counter to his fixed policy of isolating the Armenians, to make their oppression or destruction easier. Railroads would mean not only prosperity and strength for the people, but easy gathering and sending out of news to the world, easy bringing of help from the world, lighting up the dark places, and exposing the horrors of the hell now existing. When they are built, commerce will follow; Europeans will flock in, and a new era dawn. Who are the commercial class ? The Armenian Christians or Europeans; not a Turk or a Kurd among them. Commerce means, then, the increase of the Christian population; wealth, greatness, security for the Armenians; finally freedom from the Ottoman power. Therefore that power forbids any improvement of the backward conditions.

II.

THE PEOPLE OF ARMENIA.

Who are the Armenians? The average American knows very little about them, while few even of the educated classes have much knowledge of the race or its history. Many people regard them as barbarians, partially Christianized. Some think them of Chinese type; most often they are considered as Turks because the chief portion of Armenia is part of the Turkish Empire; every Armenian feels justly indignant at the latter classification. The old story applies of the Irishman who refused to consider himself an American though born in America, on the ground that "being born in a stable did not make one a horse"; we know that the Scotch and English in Ireland do not consider themselves Irish; we know it would be worse than absurd to call the English children born in India Hindoos. When the missionaries of the American Board first went to Turkey, the people there supposed from the name American, that they must be Indians, and crowded to see them out of curiosity, but they were much surprised and probably somewhat disappointed when they found them very like themselves. In the same way, being born in Turkish Armenia does not make one a Turk. The Turks are one race,

the Armenians a totally different one, and different in
the very foundation type. The Turks are Turanian,
the Armenians Aryan. The Turks belong to the
Turko-Tataric stock; they are kinsmen of the Tartars.

The primal origin of the Armenians will be found
in Genesis, Chapter 10,— from Togarmah, the son of
Gomer, the son of Japheth; the Armenians are sometimes called the Sons of Togarmah. Togarmah had
a son named Haig (the Armenian records tell us), and
Armenians call themselves Haigian or Haigazian from
him; and the land of Armenia is called Hayasdan or
the land of Haig. He was a powerful warrior and
the founder of the Armenian Kingdom, which began
2350 B. C., and ended with Levon VI., 1375 A. D.;
thus lasting 3725 years, though with intervals of extinction. Their own kings did not always reign in
Armenia; sometimes other nations ruled over it;
by way of compensation, sometimes the Armenians
ruled over other nations. The people never call themselves Armenians, or their country Armenia; they use
the name simply for the sake of foreigners. But
where did the name come from ? Of course as with
many very old ones, the origin is somewhat a matter
of guesswork. Some derive it from the great King,
Aram, the seventh from Haig; some from Armerag
or Armen, the eldest son of Haig,— the more probable
supposition of the two; still others connect it with the
Hebrew Aram (Aramea), the district of Mesopotamia
and North Syria, and derive both from a word meaning " man," most old names of nations having meant

that originally. Whatever its origin, it is certain that the Armenians are a very ancient nation,— as ancient as the Assyrians or Persians.

The people belong to the stock formerly known as Japhetic, later as Caucasian (from the Caucasus Mountains on the north of Armenia), then as Indo-European, now as Aryan; the most advanced type of mankind, and the most physically beautiful. And what are the people of the United States ? Hamitic or Negroid ? Of course not. Semitic (Arab, Jew) ? Certainly not. They are Japhetic or Aryan too — exactly the same as the Armenians. Indeed, the type of face is the same, and the type of character. The Armenians are often called the Anglo-Saxons of the East; they are the same blood, features, religion, and civilization as those of the West, and are true brothers and sisters, though the opportunities of the latter have been greater; however, the ancestors of the former were Christians in Asia before those of the latter were in Europe, and they kept the mother land faithfully while the others ran away.

THEIR LANGUAGE.

The tongue spoken by the Armenians is one of the great family now known as the Aryan languages; certainly one of the oldest of them if there is any difference in the ages of the different branches, though that really means nothing. It has no relation whatever to the Semitic tongues like Chaldee or Phoenician, nor the Tataric tongues of Scythia, though those were

in the earlier ages its nearest neighbors, while it is
blood brother to languages so widely separated as Irish
on the west and Hindoo on the east, to Gothic and
Greek, Lithuanian and Latin. Linguists think the
whole Aryan family much younger than the Semitic
or the Turko-Tataric or the Mongoloid, but this would
not be granted by the Armenians without much more
solid proof than has yet been brought forward. They
claim first that Noah and his sons lived in Armenia,
which has been shown must be true; second, that they
spoke the Armenian language, which therefore was
the very oldest. Some of the arguments in favor of
this are as follows:— In Armenia, near Mt. Ararat,
are places with Armenian names, which have preserved
the same names from the time of Noah till now.
North of Ararat is a city named Erivan, which in
Armenian means " appearance "; after Noah's ark
rested on the mountain, the first place he saw was Erivan. Another city southeast of Ararat is called
Nakhichevan, which in Armenian means " the first
station "; it was the first stopping-place of Noah when
he came out of the ark. The first chief or King of
the Armenians, Haig, built a village and called it Hark,
which means " fathers," as he was the father of the
Armenians; and when Haig fought with Belus and
killed him, the place was called Kereznank, meaning
" grave " or " graves." There are many such places
in Armenia, where the names have always been the
same and are certainly Armenian now, indicating that
the language has always been the same; here are a

few: Arakaz, Armavir, Shirag, Ararat. The latter took its name from Ara, the Armenian king who was the son of Aram, that great King who ruled in Armenia for fifty years; the name means " lofty " or " holy." These instances show the antiquity of the language; but even if they were not sufficient, it would not affect the antiquity of the race. Many very old races speak languages much less old. The mass of people in Tuscany are Etruscans, a race which some people hold to be much older than the whole Aryan family; but they speak Italian, a very modern tongue. A large part of the Basques, believed by many scientists to be the oldest race in Europe, older even than the Tuscans, speak Spanish, much more modern even than Italian. So that it does not follow that the Armenian race, aside from the language, may not be the oldest in the world.

The old Armenian classic language is very difficult, from the number of particles and participles in it; but modern Armenian is one of the easiest of languages to learn, very regular in inflection and the spelling entirely phonetic. There are no exceptions or anomalies; for instance, to pluralize a noun, you invariably add the particle ner or er. Thus, doon means " house;" the plural is dooner. Manch is " boy"; plural mancher; mannugh is " child," mannughner " children." The irregularities of English in these forms are too well-known to need illustration. The Armenian tongue is not only very regular, but very sweet, as well to the ears of foreigners as of natives.

The testimony of "Sunset" Cox of Ohio is worth citing on this point. He was United States minister to Turkey some years ago, and as such presided at the Commencement Exercises of Robert College in Constantinople, that being the rule of the college. In his address on this occasion, he said he did not like Bulgarian (which is a Turkish tongue), because it had no sweetness;— indeed, there is none in any of the Turkish languages, which are strong and emphatic, but harsh. But he said he liked Armenian; it was the " sweetest language he ever heard." He went on to say that Adam talked Armenian in the Garden of Eden, proposed to Eve in that language, and succeeded in winning her heart; in any other language he might not have done it. "It is the loveliest of tongues to make love to a woman in, and sure of success if the lady knows Armenian." I think he was right; but I think too, that next to Armenian, if not equal to it, is English. It sounds as sweetly to my ears as Armenian. I am an Armenian and my wife is an Armenian; but I proposed to her in English and was successful; not a sure test, perhaps, for any language is beautiful when words of love are uttered in it to ears that are willing to hear; and true love may be successful without any words at all.

Coat of Arms and Flags of Ancient Armenia.

1. The House of Haigh.
2. The Dynasty of Arshagounian.
3. The Dynasty of Pakradounian
4. The Kingdom of Roubinian

III.

THE ARMENIAN DYNASTIES.

According to the histories written by native historians from the old Armenian records.

1. THE HAIGAZIAN DYNASTY.

This dynasty began 2350 years before Christ, and ended in the time of Alexander the Great, 328 B. C. No other recorded dynasty has so long an unbroken succession.

2. THE ARSHAGOONIAN DYNASTY.

This dynasty began 150 years B. C. and ended 428 A. D.

3. THE PAKRADOONIAN DYNASTY.

This dynasty began 885 A. D. and ended 1045 A. D.

4. THE RUPENIAN DYNASTY.

This dynasty began 1080 A. D. and ended 1375 A. D.

I shall try to show the condition of the Armenians under the rule of these different dynasties.

1. THE HAIGAZIAN DYNASTY.

As already mentioned, Haig was the founder of the Armenian kingdom. He can scarcely be called a king, because in his time there was not a great Armenian nation; it was rather a tribe, and Haig was chief or governor. His position was like that of Abraham; what would now be called a sheikh; and like Abraham, he was a worshiper of the true God.

Haig went from the highlands of Armenia to the plains of Shinar to help build the Tower of Babel. During the progress of the work, Belus, a warlike giant, descended from Ham, assumed to direct the enterprise; Haig would not submit to this, and so returned to his own country. When the undertaking failed, all the tribes became scattered. To wreak vengeance on Haig, Belus resolved to go to Armenia, kill him in fight, and reign over his land. When he reached Armenia with his men on his errand, Haig went with a force to meet him; a great battle took place and Haig was victorious, killing Belus and saving his country from being overwhelmed by the Hamites. His spirit was inherited by his posterity, though recent irresistible force and refusal of permission to bear arms may seem to make them submissive. They have battled stoutly against awful odds and with insufficient means for liberty and for freedom of thought and conscience; and millions have lost their lives for those principles; if they could now have arms and help, they would fight and die again for them.

After the repulse of this Hamitic invasion, the Armenians increased so rapidly that Haig became a real king and took that title, thus actually founding the Armenian Kingship. They were free, lived long lives, and married only one wife each,— all favorable conditions for growth of population,— it need not be pointed out how slavery and polygamy check national growth. And they kept their faith in the one true God, as their ancestor Noah did.

Haig's son Armen succeeded his father, and greatly enlarged the kingdom. He subdued a large district northeast of Mt. Ararat and built cities and towns there. It is most likely the name Armenia comes from him. Some recent foreign writers have the impudence to say that there was no such king, but that his name was made up to account for that of Armenia; but the same records which tell us of Haig, tell us of his son. After Armen we find his son Arma-iss, who built the city of Armavir.

I will not enumerate all the names of the dynasty; it would only be a tedious catalogue without profit. I will only mention the most noted ones, and those most interesting from their relations with the Jews or the heathen nations.

One of the notable kings is Aram, the seventh in succession, and the greatest of Armenian conquerors. He raised and drilled an army of 50,000 men, whose efficiency and his own military skill and energy are proved by his invading and conquering Media. He then invaded Assyria and conquered a part of that

country.   Next he marched westward and subjugated
some of the eastern portion of Asia Minor inhabited by
the Greeks,— the later Cappadocia, along the Halys
or Kizil-Irmak.   Aram named this district the Hayasdan, translated by the Romans as " Armenia Minor ";
which, oddly enough, in later times became Greater
Armenia or Armenia Proper.   Aram set over this
province a governor named Mishag, with instructions
to compel the Greeks to speak Armenian.   Mishag
built a city which exists in Cappadocia (Karamania)
to-day, frightfully familiar from recent events.   He
called it by his own name; the Greeks mispronounced
it as Mazag; the Roman emperors afterwards named
it Caesarea, which the Turks corrupted into Kayseri,
and several thousand Armenians were massacred there
some months ago, which will be described further on.
The richest and most enterprising Armenians in the
Turkish Empire are from Kayseri, and it is a leading
missionary station of the American Board.   The
writer preached there and in that vicinity for four
years.

The enormous growth of the Armenian Kingdom
under Aram, and its conquest of part of Assyria,
excited the alarm of the Assyrian king, Ninos.   Not
feeling strong enough to engage in open warfare with
him, he thought to compass his destruction by winning
his friendship and then putting him out of the way,
and, as a first step, sent him a costly jeweled crown.
The intrigue failed, however, and Aram lived to a
great age, reigning fifty years.

Aram was succeeded by his son Ara, called "Ara the Beautiful." The fame of his beauty went abroad through the world; the Assyrian queen Semiramis was so enchanted by the sight of his person that she fell madly in love and proposed marriage to him, but he refused her. This military Amazon was not to be balked so. She resolved to marry him by force, and came with a great army to Armenia to capture the prize; but he was killed in the war, and she took possession of the country, with which she was so charmed that she decided to remain; she removed the capital of the enlarged Assyrian Kingdom to the lovely shores of Lake Van, erecting a palace there for herself, and building on the eastern side a city named "Shamiramaguerd" (built by Semiramis). Many years later, a king of the Haigazian Dynasty whose name was Van rebuilt it and called it after himself. This was the present city of Van, another great center of the American Board and of Turkish horrors.

The next great interesting event was in 710 B. C. when Sennacherib of Assyria was assassinated by his two sons, Adramelich and Sharezer, who escaped into Armenia. The king of Armenia at this time was Sgayorti, which means "son of a giant." He received the sons of Sennacherib with great kindness; they married Armenian women, and remained in the country till their death. Their descendants were great Armenian princes, bearing the titles Prince Arziroonian and Prince Kinoonian.

Armenia comes to view again in connection with

4

Biblical history in the capture of Jerusalem by Nebuchadnezzar, 600 B. C., and the deportation of the Judean people; the Armenian king, Hurachia, was one of his allies in the siege, and on returning to Armenia carried with him a Hebrew prince named Shampad. This was a very intelligent man, and made himself greatly loved and esteemed by the Armenians; a sort of Daniel or Joseph. He, too, married an Armenian noblewoman, and his descendants became the very foremost of the noble families and ecclesiastical functionaries of the country, crowning the kings on occasion. They were called Pakradoonian Princes, and at last one of them founded the third dynasty of Armenian kings, the Pakradoonian. Though the nation is Aryan, there is noble Hebrew (Semitic) blood mixed with it.

Perhaps the most interesting part of the Haigazian Dynasty comes just before the end; the time of Dikran or Tigranes I. In him both wisdom and valor were combined to an eminent degree. As soon as he succeeded his father, Yerevant, he instituted great reforms to improve the state of the country. He not only enlarged it by conquest, but he greatly improved public education and morals, removed obstructions to international commerce, introduced navigation on the lakes and rivers, encouraged cultivation; trade flourished, every acre of ground was tilled, the country was alive with energy and hope. This vigor and prosperity aroused the envy of Ashdahag, King of Media; he resolved to kill Dikran, and to throw

him off his guard married his sister, Princess Dik-
ranoohi.   A plot to murder Dikran was then set on
foot; the princess learned of it, warned her brother,
whom she loved, and ran away.   Dikran collected an
army, made a rapid march to Media, surprised and
slew Ashdahag, and brought back a vast amount of
spoils in captives and goods.   He built a fine city on
the banks of the Tigris, and called it Dikranagerd, the
city of Dikran; it was afterwards the residence of the
sister who had saved his life.   It is now called by the
Turks Diarbekr, and was the scene of a frightful massacre a few months since.   The most important political achievement of his life was assisting Cyrus in the
capture of Babylon 538 B. C.; the two monarchs
were very friendly, and Dikran's Armenian army was
a chief factor in the conquest.   In Jeremiah's prophecy of the capture, about a century before it occurred,
he mentions the Armenian Kingdom as one of the
actors: " The Kingdoms of Ararat, Minni, and Ash-
chenaz." (Jer. li. 27.)

After Dikran's death his son Vahakn succeeded
him; he was considered a god by the people, and worshiped as such through a monument after his death.
Thus far the people had mostly worshiped the one true
God, but from this time they relapsed into heathenism
for a while on account of the influences pressing on
them from outside.   The last king of the Haigazian
Dynasty was Vahe.   When Alexander the Great invaded Persia, Vahe went to Darius' help with 40,000
infantry and 7,000 cavalry; but Alexander conquered

first Darius and then Vahe (328 B. C.), and annexed
both Persia and Armenia. Thus came to an end the
first Armenian dynasty, after an existence of 1922
years.

ARSHAGOONIAN OR ARSACID DYNASTY.

This dynasty began not far from 150 B. C.,—
close to the time when Carthage was utterly destroyed,
and Greece was finally subjugated; it ended 428 A. D.,
about half a century before the extinction of the Western Roman Empire, and about the time Genseric and
his Vandals conquered Africa. It is by far the most
famous of the Armenian royal houses; for it embraces
the very heart of the classic times with which all educated people are familiar, it brings us perpetually in
contact with the most brilliant and best-known of
classic names, it is sprinkled itself with names towering up familiar and powerful, even among the Greek
and Roman magnates; and, in spite of political ups and
downs, it covers a time of immense expansion for the
Armenian people, of a firmly rooted growth in numbers, wealth, and consciousness of national unity,
which has enabled the nation to survive and keep its
united being through many centuries of dismemberment, impoverishment, massacre, and attempts at outright extermination again and again. More than all,
it covers the time of Jesus Christ, and the conversion
of Armenia to his religion, first of all the nations of
the earth, as by its history and traditions it ought to
have been.

During the time between the disappearance of the line of Haig and the rise of the line of Arshag, Armenia was not by any means wholly without kings of its own; but it was mostly a dependency.

Alexander the Great, after his conquest, put a native governor named Mihran over it; but on Alexander's death, five years later (323 B. C.), his generals partitioned the Macedonian Empire among themselves, and Armenia fell to Neoptolemus. His government was at once so oppressive, and so contemptuous of native feeling (he and his court were Greeks, and despised all Asiatics), that the people rose and drove him out in 317, under the lead of one Arduat (Ardvates), who remained their king for thirty-three years; but he left no successor, and Armenia was conquered by and became part of the great Syrian Empire founded by Seleucus. It remained so in the main for about three quarters of a century, though the eastern part (Kurdistan), fell under the Parthian kings. Armenia was never a very quiet province, however, and its revolts against the Syrian satraps kept it much of the time in a half-anarchic state. About 210 B. C. Antiochus the Great quelled one of these uprisings, and divided the country into Greater and Lesser Armenia (whose boundaries I have described), putting a separate deputy over each. But after his crushing defeat by the Romans at Magnesia in 189 B. C., and having to buy peace by giving up everything beyond the Halys, each governor proclaimed his province an independent kingdom. Zadriades (Zadreh), in Lesser Armenia founded a family which kept their hold for almost exactly a century, when Tigranes II once more united the two Armenias. Artaxias (Ardashes), in Greater Armenia was powerful as long as he lived, and sheltered Hannibal at his court when the Romans had set a price on the head of their great foe; but about the middle of the century his family was dispossessed by Mithridates of Parthia, who conquered the country. The family name of this Parthian house was Arshag, rendered by the Greeks Arsakes, spelled by the Romans Arsaces. Mithridates made Greater Armenia a kingdom for his brother Wagh-arshag (Val-arsaces), whose family remained in succession to the throne, though sometimes eclipsed for long periods from actual occupation of it, for six hundred years. The new king had the great hereditary ability both in war and statesmanship which characterized the whole Arsacid line, and the Mithridates in particular, and its great knowledge of men. He knew an able man when he saw him, and liked to raise him up; he promoted industry and built cities; he reformed the system of laws and their administration as well.

The new line did not escape the usual fate of Eastern dynasties, of having disputes over the succession, in which their neighbors interfered. In 94 B. C., Dikran or Tigranes II (great-grandson of Wagh-Arshag), owed his possession of the throne of Greater Armenia to his third cousin, Mithridates II (the Great), of Parthia, who exacted seventy Armenian valleys as the price; probably part of Kurdistan. Ti-

granes, however, paid no more blood-money to anybody when once on the throne. On the contrary, he
began at once to overrun and annex the neighboring
states. He first conquered Lesser Armenia, and made
it one with its sister again; then part of Syria, so long
the mistress of his own state; then, in a series of wars
with the weak successors of Mithridates, he half destroyed the Parthian Empire itself, not only recovering
the seventy valleys he had paid for his throne, but conquering Media, and annexing Mesopotamia and Adia-
bene. After these conquests he called himself " King
of Kings " (that is, emperor, king with other kings
under him), which title the Parthian kings had
claimed theretofore. He would probably have ended
by mastering and restoring the unity of the old Seleu-
cid Kingdom in its widest extent, the whole heart of
Western Asia, had he not in an evil hour been induced by that reckless old fighter, his father-in-law,
Mithridates of Pontus, to join him in war against the
Romans. Tigranes' own son had quarreled with him,
and taken refuge with the King of Parthia, whose
daughter he married; and now offered to guide his
father-in-law into Armenia if he would invade it as the
ally of the Romans. This was done, and Tigranes
the elder had to fly to the mountains; but the Parthian
king grew tired of the siege of rock castles, and went
home, leaving his son-in-law to carry on operations with
part of the army. The great Armenian king at once
broke loose and annihilated the forces of his son, who
fled to Pompey, just invading Armenia with the Ro-

man army. Even the great Tigranes was no match for
Rome, and had to surrender. Pompey was not harsh
with him, but left him Armenia (except Sophene and
Gordyene, which were made into a kingdom for his
son), and his Parthian conquests; even going so far
as to send a Roman division to wrest these from the
Parthian king, who had re-conquered them on Tigranes' defeat, and restore them to the latter. On the
departure of Pompey the Parthian once more re-
claimed them, but a compromise was finally made.
Phraates of Parthia, however, resumed once more the
title of "King of Kings." Tigranes remained the
ally of the Romans till his death in 55 B. C.; a reign
of thirty-nine years, on the whole of great glory and
usefulness.

He was succeeded by his son, Artavasdes (Ardvash)
II, who inherited that most dreadful of legacies, a
place between the hammer and the anvil. For the
next quarter of a century the Romans, and the steadily
growing and consolidating power of the Parthian Empire were alternately irresistible in Eastern Anatolia;
it was impossible to avoid taking sides, for neutrality
meant invasion by one party or the other; and whichever side he took he was sure to be punished for as soon
as the other came uppermost. If Artavasdes had been
as dexterous as Alexius Comnenus himself, he could
hardly have escaped ruin; that he kept his throne for
over twenty years is proof that he was not unworthy of
his father. First came the invasion of Parthia by
Crassus; Artavasdes, faithful to his father's Roman

allegiance; asked him to make the invasion by way of Armenia, and offered to help him. Crassus refused, but the Parthian king, Orodes, invaded Armenia; however, he made peace, and betrothed his eldest son, Pacorus, to Artavasdes' daughter, just before news was brought him of the annihilation of Crassus' army, guaranteed by Crassus' severed head and hand. The civil wars at Rome for years to come broke the Roman power, and the Parthians (with the good-will of the inhabitants, who detested the Roman proconsuls), swept westward, compelled submission or alliance from all the countries to the Taurus, and even annexed all Syria for a time, just as seven centuries later the Syrians, from hate of the Byzantine governors, gave up their cities to the Saracens. But the Roman power once more rallied; the Parthians were driven out of Syria, and Pacorus was killed; the aged Orodes, under whom the Parthian Empire proper reached its pinnacle, died, leaving the throne to one of those jealous murderous despots so familiar in Eastern history, who made a general slaughter of his brothers, and even murdered his son, to remove any possible leader of a revolt, and Artavasdes once more returned to the Roman alliance. In the year 36 A. D., Mark Antony undertook the task Crassus had so terribly failed in seventeen years before, of striking at the heart of Parthia; but this time the invasion was by way of Armenia. It was almost as frightful a disaster as the former; a third of the army of 100,000 men was destroyed by the enemy, 8,000 died of cold and storm in the Armenian mountains, the wounded died in enormous numbers; but that Artavasdes let the army winter in his country it would have perished as completely as Crassus' did.   In spite of this, the Romans, wanting a scapegoat, laid the whole blame on Artavasdes, without a shadow of reason that can be shown.   It was the last time for a century and a half that the Romans attacked Parthia. In default of that plunder, they resolved to have Armenia, and a couple of years later, in the year 33 A. D., they seized Artavasdes by treachery, and occupied the country.   The Parthians at once took up the cause of his son, Artaxes, and made war on the Romans to seat him on the throne; and when the Roman troops were withdrawn to help Antony's cause, which was lost in the battle of Actium, the Parthians overran Armenia, and killed all the Romans in the country, and made their candidate king as Artaxes II.   This was in 30 B. C., and in the same year his father, Artavasdes, who had been carried to Alexandria by Antony, was beheaded by Cleopatra.   But the very next year the worthless tyrant Phraates of Parthia was driven from the throne by a rebellion, and Artaxes made peace with Rome.

The history of Artavasdes' reign is in essence the history of the next four centuries, save that the results were incomparably worse.   We have been dealing with a time at least of steady, single-handed government, of able rulers either inside or outside, of some sort of ability to keep the civil structure of the country from breaking to pieces; but even that disappears over long periods in the early centuries of the Roman Empire. One great secret of Armenia's misery during these ages of woe — indeed, to a large extent during all the ages since — lies in the fact that she is a borderland; a buffer between great states, and indeed between great natural divisions of climate and society. She is the boundary between semi-tropic Central Asia and temperate Eastern Europe, touching the land of the fig and the silk-worm on the one side, and that of the apple and the mountain goat on the other; between Scythian steppes and Syrian deserts. In these earlier ages she was fought for between east, west, and south,— Parthia, Rome, and a Syro-Egyptian power of some sort; in these days divided between east, west, and north,— Persia the successor of Parthia, Turkey the successor of Rome, while the southern power is ages dead, and a great northern power, Russia, has grown up in the steppes. Had Armenia been smaller, or more level, she would have perished without a struggle, perhaps rather would never have existed; but her territory is so large and so defensible that her history could have been predicted,— final dismemberment between great states surrounding her, yet not without ages of desperate struggle. She was not large enough to be permanently the seat of empire; she was far too large for either rival to let pass wholly into the hands of the other — so she was pulled to pieces. But she wanted to control her own destiny, and made a long and heroic fight before being dismembered.

To write the history of the next few centuries would tire out all my readers, and would not do any good; it was a long duel between Rome and Persia for the ownership of Armenia, in which the prosperity and happiness of their unhappy foot-ball nearly perished. Almost the whole foreign policy of Parthia was to control, or to have a paramount influence in Armenia; almost the whole foreign policy of Rome in the East was to do the same thing. For nearly a century following Artavasdes' deposition, though the Romans professed to govern the country and the Parthians sometimes held it, and both sides repeatedly put kings on its throne, it was actually in a state of pure anarchy. Every great family, seeing it must depend on its own strength for preservation, extended its rule over as wide a district as would submit; nearly two hundred houses acted with perfect independence of each other, and of the nominal government, and some of them established principalities of considerable size. After this, though the country was for century after century just the same shuttlecock between the rival states, the feudal anarchy was somewhat reduced, the turbulent nobility better held in check, but it was impossible that there should be really firm and orderly government when a king could not be secure of his throne for a year on one side or the other, and dared not render his powerful subjects disaffected by making them obey the laws. We may be sure that the government was really an oligarchy under the forms of a monarchy, and even the title " King of Armenia " during this period must not be taken to mean too much. There were sometimes separate kings of Upper and Lower Armenia, one under Roman, and one under Parthian influence; the independent princes often made head against both, and outlying principalities, like those of Osrhoene and Gordyene probably got hold of more or less Armenian territory in the melee. No king of Armenia after Tigranes ever held sway over all of old Armenia for any length of time, if at all. But any king who got an acknowledged position at all was invariably an Arshagoonian; the people considered that line the only rightful kings. Artavasdes III, whom the Romans seated in power just before the birth of Christ; Tigranes IV, who expelled him by Parthian aid the year of Christ's birth; Vonones, a deposed Parthian king, who got himself chosen king as the Roman favorite in 16 A. D., but was persuaded by Tiberius to retire; Arsaces, son of the king of Parthia, assassinated by the king of Iberia whose brother was the Roman candidate, about the time of the crucifixion; Ervand, who made himself master of the land after a fashion, in 58; Dertad (Tiridates), set up by the Parthians in 52, and acknowledged by the Romans in 66; Exedarus (Eshdir ?) son of the Parthian king, given the throne with Roman consent about 100, pulled down by his uncle in 114, resulting in the conquest of the country by Trajan; Sohaemus, set up by the Romans about 150, dethroned by the Par-

thians in 162 in favor of another Arsacid, restored by
the Romans in 164; and the other fleeting monarchs
of this long nightmare were all of the same line of
Arshag, which in Armenia survived for over two
centuries its brother line in Parthia, the last of whom,
Ardvan (Artabanus), was slain in battle in 224 by Ardashir (Artaxerxes), first of the Sassanian house, and
founder of the Persian Empire. But I must go back
a little.

The most important event in the history of any nation is its conversion to Christianity, and therefore we
wish to know when the Armenians first came to believe
in Christ, and how it came about. Of course it did
not come all at once; but it came very early, and the
story of the first converts is very curious. According
to the Armenian church history, and also the great
Christian father Eusebius, it came through King Abgar or Apkar (Abgarus), the fifteenth king of the little
kingdom of Osrhoene, in northern Mesopotamia, whose
capital was the flourishing city of Edessa, now Oorfa;
it lay next the southern border of Armenia.

The church history gives the following account:

" The origin of Christianity in Armenia dates
from the time of its king Abgar, who reigned at the
beginning of the Christian era; he had his seat of government in the city of Edessa, and was tributary to the
Romans.

" Herod Antipas, the tetrarch of Judea, was hostile
to king Abgar, but was unable to injure him except by
exciting the Romans against him. He therefore accused him falsely, to the Emperor Tiberius, of rebel-

lious projects. King Abgar, on being made acquainted with this accusation, hastened to send messengers to the Roman general Marinus, then governor of Syria, Phoenicia, and Palestine, for the purpose of vindicating himself. During their stay in Palestine these messengers — among whom was Anane, Abgar's confidant — hearing of the wonders that were wrought by our Saviour, determined to visit Jerusalem, in order to gratify their curiosity.

" When, therefore, their mission was concluded, they proceeded thither and were filled with wonder at witnessing the miracles performed by Jesus our Lord.

" On returning to Armenia they related all the particulars to their master. Abgar, after having listened to their narrative, became satisfied that Jesus was the son of God, and immediately wrote to him as follows:

" ' Abgar, son of Arsham, to Jesus, the great healer, who has appeared in the country of Judea at the city of Jerusalem — greeting Lord,— I have heard that thou dost not heal by medicines but only through the Word; that thou makest the blind to see, the lame to walk; that thou cleansest the lepers and makest the deaf to hear; that thou castest out devils, raiseth the dead, and healest through the word only. No sooner had the great miracles that thou performest been related to me, than I reflected, and now believe that thou art God and the son of God, descended from heaven to perform these acts of beneficence. For this reason I have written thee this letter, to pray thee to come to me, that I may adore thee and be healed of my sickness by thee, according to my faith in thy power. Moreover, I have heard that the Jews murmur against thee, and seek to slay thee. I pray thee, therefore, come to me; I have a good little city, which is enough for both of us, and there we can peaceably live together.' "

The messengers sent with the letter were instructed to offer sacrifices for the King at the temple in Jerusalem; and one of them was a painter, who was to make a portrait of the Saviour, that if he would not come, the king might at least have his features. Jesus received the letter joyfully,— as it was the day of his triumphal entry into Jerusalem, the messengers did not venture to approach him, and it was taken to him by the apostles Philip and Andrew,— and dictated the following answer to the apostle Thomas:

" Blessed be he who believes in me without having seen me; for thus it is written of me: Those who see me shall not believe in me; and those who do not see me, they shall believe and be saved. Inasmuch as you have written to me to go to you, know that it is necessary I should fulfill here all for which I have been sent. And when I shall have done so, I shall ascend to Him who sent me; and then I will send you one of my disciples, who shall remove your pain, and shall give life to you and those around you."

The painter could not execute his order on account of the multitude; the Saviour at last noticed him, and causing him to approach, passed a handkerchief over his face and miraculously imprinted on it a perfect likeness of his countenance, and then gave it to him, and bade him take it to his master as a reward for his faith. The king received the letter and portrait with great joy, and put them in safe custody, and awaited the fulfillment of our Lord's promise.

After the Ascension, Thomas, the disciple, sent Thaddeus, one of the seventy, to Abgar, as our Lord had directed. Thaddeus went to Tobias, a prince of the Pakradoonian tribe, and consequently a Jew by blood, who received the apostle into his house, and became a believer. Thaddeus then began to perform many miracles upon sick people, and his fame being spread throughout the city, reached King Abgar, who sent for Prince Tobias and desired him to bring the apostle to him. This was done, and Thaddeus healed the king in his sickness, and instructed him in the faith. He did likewise to all the people of the city, and baptized them, together with the king and his court. All the temples dedicated to idols were shut up, and a large church was built. Thaddeus then created a bishop to rule the new congregation, selecting a silk-mercer, the king's cap-maker, for that office, and giving him the name of Adde. It is related that upon the principal gate of Edessa was the statue of a Greek idol, which all who entered the city were obliged to reverence. King Abgar ordered this to be taken away, and placed in its stead the sacred portrait of our Lord, with this inscription: " Christ God, he who hopes in thee is not deceived in his hope;" at the same time ordering all those who entered the city to give it divine honor. This conversion of King Abgar and of the Edessians took place in the thirtieth

5

year of the Vulgar Era, or in the thirty-third year after the birth of Christ.

Shortly after, Thaddeus, desiring to spread the light of the Gospel in other parts of the country, went to Inner Armenia to visit Sanadrug, who then resided in the province of Shavarshan or Ardaz. Sanadrug soon became a Christian and was baptized, together with his daughter Santukht, and a great number of the chiefs and common people. Here Thaddeus also consecrated a bishop, named Zachariah, and then proceeded to Upper Armenia; but finding the people there unwilling to listen to his preaching, he left them and went to the country of the Aghuans.

Abgar, in his zeal for the faith he had just embraced, wrote to the Emperor Tiberius in favor of Christ, informing him how the Jews unjustly crucified him, exhorting him at the same time to believe and command others to adore the Saviour. Many letters passed between the two monarchs on the subject of his divine mission. He also wrote to Ardashes, king of Persia, and to his son Nersch, the young king of Assyria, exhorting them to become believers in Christ. However, before he received replies to these, he died, in the third year of his conversion to Christianity.

His death seemed at first to have undone all his work. His son Anane apostatized and tried to make his people do the same; he reopened the heathen temples, resumed the public worship of the idols, and ordered the sacred handkerchief removed from the city gate. Adde the bishop walled up the latter. The king ordered the bishop to make a diadem for him as he had for his father; the bishop refused to make one for a head that would not bow to Christ, and the king had the bishop's feet cut off while he was preaching, causing his death,— the first Christian martyr on record. By a just retribution, the savage king met his own death by a marble pillar in his palace falling on him and breaking his legs.

Meantime Abgar's nephew, Sanadrug, had set up his standard in Shavarshan or Ardaz, proclaiming himself king of Armenia,— one of the countless chieftains who took advantage of Armenian anarchy to carve out principalities for themselves. On the death of Anane he marched to Edessa, claiming it as his own inheritance. The people admitted him on his oath not to harm them; but once inside he massacred all the males of the house of Abgar. He spared his aunt, Queen Helena, Abgar's widow, who became widely famed as a Christian philanthropist, and was buried with great pomp before one of the gates of Jerusalem, where a splendid mausoleum was erected over her remains. He himself had apostatized, and ordered all his people to do likewise; but most of them refused to obey, and Thaddeus, hearing of it at Caesarea, in Cappadocia, started for Edessa to reconvert him. On his way he fell in with a Roman embassy to Sanadrug, composed of five patricians headed by one Chrysos; he converted and baptized them all, conferred priest's orders on Chrysos, and they gave up all their property

and became preachers of Christ. They were known
as followers of Chrysos, and all eventually obtained
the crown of martyrdom.

On the news of these conversions, Sanadrug invited Thaddeus to Shavarshan; on his arrival he put
him to death, and with him his own daughter, Santukht, who would not give up her faith in Christ. At
her death various miracles were wrought, which caused
many conversions to Christianity; among them a
notable chief, who was baptized with all his family,
was renamed Samuel, and was put to death by the
king's order.

A princess named Zarmantukht also became a convert, with all her household, two hundred people in
all; the whole of them suffered martyrdom in consequence.

Dr. Philip Schaff says: "It is now impossible to
decide how much truth there may be in the somewhat
mythical stories of correspondence between Christ and
Abgarus, and the missionary activity and martyrdom
of Thaddeus, Bartholomew, Simon of Cana, and Judas
Lebbeus. But it is certain that Christianity was introduced very early in Armenia." I, however, consider what I have told to be true.

After this time, Christianity spread in Armenia as
it did in other parts of the Greek Empire; rapidly in
the cities, where intelligence was quick, and new ideas
were welcomed; slowly in the country districts, where
people did not readily change. Its first result everywhere was not so much to make people believe in it

as to make them disbelieve in Paganism; for every person who actually came to believe in Christ, there were fifty who ceased to believe in Jupiter, or Bel, or Thoth, Venus or Astarte. There would be a flourishing Christian church in a great city when most of the people did not have any faith in any religion. But everybody who had a family came gradually to think very well of a religion that gave them the power to teach children righteousness, and enforce it by the command of God; and the respectable classes became more and more Christian. But the fact that till two or three centuries after Christ there was no general attempt on the part of the pagan governments to put down the Christians by persecution, shows that not till then did they become so numerous as to frighten the governments for fear they would before long have a majority; persecution means fear. The governments let the Christians pretty much alone, except for little fits of anger now and then, till they were afraid the growth of the sect would overthrow themselves or bring on civil war. The Christians had become well established in Armenia within a century or so after the death of Christ; but it was over a century and a half before they seemed an imminent menace to the ruling class. Then a furious persecution began, about the same time as that of Diocletian in the Roman Empire, and indeed, part of the same movement. Diocletian had set the persecuting King Tiridates on his throne, and Tiridates had passed his life from boyhood almost to old age in the Roman service, and had the same ideas as the pagan Roman upper classes. Yet in the providence of God this same Tiridates made Christianity supreme in Armenia, fifteen years before Constantine made it supreme in the Roman Empire, thus making Armenia the first Christian nation.

GREGORY THE ILLUMINATOR AND KING DERTAD.

In the continual struggle between Rome and Parthia for the control of Armenia, the Parthian kings had one great advantage; they were Arsacids, and could put their sons or brothers on the Armenian throne with the good-will of the people, thus strengthening their dynastic position without much cost in military force. Often, too, the Armenian kingship was obtained by Parthian princes, who fled after a family quarrel, or after deposition or other misfortune. One of these Armenian kings was Chosroes, who reigned in the time of Ardashir, the first king of Persia, before spoken of. It is not certain just who he was; some say a brother of Ardvan, the last king of Parthia; some say the son of Ardvan, who fled after his father's death. Anyway, he was a mortal enemy of Ardashir, and was at first supported by the Romans. Ardashir invaded Armenia, but was beaten later. Chosroes quarreled with the Romans, who withdrew their support, and assailed him, but he defeated them; and when Ardashir again invaded the country, Chosroes again drove him back. The old days of Tigranes seemed to have returned, and Armenia to be on the road again to unity and independence; and Chosroes was called the Great. Ardashir was furious at being

baffled, and is said to have offered his daughter's hand
and a share in the kingdom to any one of his leading
nobles who would assassinate Chosroes. An Arsacid
named Anag accepted the offer, though he had a
wife already, and went with his family to Armenia,
pretending to be in flight from Persian troops. Chosroes gave him a military escort into the province of
Ardaz, where he lived for a time in the very place
St. Thaddeus' bones were deposited. Later on, Anag
removed to Vagharshabad (the present city of Etchmiazin, where the Armenian Catholicos resides), Chosroes' royal city. Here Anag seizing his opportunity,
stabbed Chosroes to the heart. In his flight he was
drowned in trying to cross the Aras, and his family
were massacred by the soldiery.

Ardashir had gotten rid of his unconquerable enemy, and without having to pay the stipulated price.
He at once entered Armenia and put to death every
member of Chosroes' family save a boy and a girl,
Tiridates and Chosrovitukht, who were somehow smug-
gled away, and the old game of Perso-Roman foot-ball
over Armenia went on as before. Tiridates entered
the Roman army, when grown up, and became distinguished there, evidently inheriting his father's military ability; and remained in the Roman service certainly to the age of over 45, and perhaps till over 50.
That the Romans waited all this time before using
him as a candidate for the Armenian throne seems
strange; but the reason probably is that the early
years of his manhood fell in a time when Rome was

weak and Persia strong. The great Shahpur, Ardashir's son, reigned in Persia till about 272; the imbecile Gallienus of Rome reigned from 260 till 268, and was succeeded by a crowd of emperors able indeed, but too short-lived to carry out any steady policy, or drive the Persians out of their strong places. The first emperor who found himself in a position to restore the Roman power in the East was Diocletian, who came to the Roman throne in 284, and it is significant that he made Tiridates king of Armenia only two years later. As Diocletian was a soldier of fortune, probably he had known and respected Tiridates long before. Anyway, in 286 Rome once more had her turn in Armenian affairs, and with one short interval, kept absolute control of the country for over half a century.

Now there had been born in Armenia about 257 a child who had early been taken to Caesarea by Christian relatives, baptized, named Gregory, and reared in the Christian faith. On reaching maturity he married a Christian girl by whom he had two sons; but after three years they separated by mutual consent. The wife entered a convent. Gregory, hearing of Tiridates' renown in the Roman army, went and obtained service near the prince's person, to be able to have influence with him if he ever regained his kingdom. They became fast friends. When Tiridates was proclaimed king, he went first to Erija, in the province of Egueghatz, where was a temple of Anahid (Diana), whom the Armenians worshiped as guardian goddess of the country; and making offerings to her of garlands and crowns, asked Gregory to join him in his idolatry. Gregory refused to worship anything but the one God. Tiridates ordered him imprisoned for a while, thinking the loathsome dungeon of that time would change his resolution; finding him still firm, he had him tortured in a dozen frightful ways, and at last taken to the fortress of Ardashad and thrown into a deep pit, where criminals were left to starve. There Gregory remained fourteen years, supported all that time by the charity of a pious Christian woman. After about ten years of reign, Tiridates was driven from his throne by Persians, and once more became a wanderer; but two years later he was reinstated by the Romans, and finished his life on the throne. In gratitude for this second restoration, he had daily offerings made to the heathen gods all over his kingdom; and on being told that the Christians refused to comply, ordered all recusants to be tortured, and their property confiscated.

About this time Diocletian determined to find and marry the handsomest woman in his empire, and sent officers all over in search of noted beauties. One party, hearing that a nun named Ripsime was very beautiful, entered her convent by force, had a portrait made of her, and carried it to the emperor. Diocletian was enchanted with it, and ordered preparations made for the nuptials; but the abbess, Kayane, to save the nun from sin, and the community from danger, broke up the convent, and the inmates with sev-

eral priests — seventy in all — went to the East, and
scattered themselves in different localities. Ripsime
and Kayane, with thirty-five companions, reached Ardashad in Armenia, and took refuge in a building
among the vineyards, where wine vats were stored.
Diocletian had search made for his flown bird, and,
hearing that her company had gone to Armenia, commanded Tiridates to send her back to him unless he
wished to keep her for his own wife. Tiridates had
her hunted out, and the officers bringing a report of
her extraordinary beauty, so great that people flocked
to admire her, he ordered her brought to him, intend-
ing to marry her. Kayane exhorted her not to deny
Christ for the sake of earthly honors, and she refused
to go. She was carried by force, however, and the
king undertook to gain a husband's rights at once; but
the virgin, strengthened by divine power, resisted him
successfully. Tiridates then had the Abbess Kayane
brought to him to overcome the girl's scruples; but
instead, she once more exhorted Ripsime to keep herself pure in spite of all offered grandeur. The king
once more endeavored to deflower the maiden, and
was once more beaten; and Ripsime, opening the doors
and passing out through the astonished guards, walked
out of the city, to her companions in the vineyard,
went to a high place, and knelt down in prayer. The
incensed Tiridates sent a body of guards to put her to
death by the most dreadful tortures, which was done,
and her body cut into small pieces. Her companions
gathered to bury her remains, and were at once

butchered by the soldiery, as well as a sick one, who had stayed behind in the wine press. The bodies of the thirty-four martyrs were thrown into the fields as food for the beasts of prey. The next day Tiridates had Kayane and two other companions put to death. These events occurred on the 5th and 6th of October, 301.

Shortly after, God visited the king and many of his household with a dreadful disease for his persecution of the saints. They ran around like mad people or demoniacs. While they were in this state, the king's virgin sister Chosrovitukht had a divine revelation that she should go to Ardashad and release Gregory from the pit, and he would heal them all. As he had been thrown there fourteen years ago, and was believed to be long dead, no attention was paid to it; but the next day it was repeated five times with threats, and a chief named Oda was sent, who brought him back alive, to their great amazement and joy. They prostrated themselves before him and asked forgiveness, but he told them to worship only their Creator. Then he demanded to be shown the bodies of the holy martyrs lately just slain for belief in Christ; they were found after nine days and nights untouched, and he gathered them up and put them into the wine press, where he also established himself. First he ordered the king and all the people to fast five days, and commended them to the mercy of God; and after that for sixty consecutive days he preached the word of God, instructing them in all the mysteries of the

Christian religion. On the sixty-sixth day they again besought him to heal them, but first he made them build three chapels for the relics of the martyrs, each in a separate coffin, wall in the place where he had seen a vision of the Son of God coming down from heaven, and erect a crucifix before which the people should prostrate themselves. Finally, seeing that they all believed in the true God, St. Gregory bade them kneel down and pray to Him for healing; he himself prayed for them at the same time, and a miraculous cure was at once effected on all the sufferers.

This done, Gregory and Tiridates set about exterminating idolatry; they smashed the idols and demolished the temples, the new converts joyfully assisting them. The work of conversion went on rapidly, under the wonderful preaching of the Saint, and the zeal of the king; all the people converted were baptized by immersion. In eight years the majority of the Armenian nation, many millions in number, had become Christians. That religion was made the State creed of Armenia in 310, while the Council of Nice, which did the same work for Rome, was not held till 325.

Gregory deserves every credit for this magnificent work; but I cannot help wishing he had been less zealous in destroying the pagan literature, which is a very great loss to the world. However, Christianity is worth it, if we could not have it at a less price.

Schools, as well as churches and benevolent institutions, were organized in great numbers under

Christian auspices during the next two or three centuries, and a brilliant band of scholars and preachers
went out from them, the equals of any in their age,
and perhaps in any age. I will give sketches of some
of the principal figures, but first let me briefly tell the
history of Armenia during that period.

The rivalry between Rome and Persia grew fiercer
than ever with the introduction of Christianity, for
now religious hate was added to political ambition;
and on the side of Persia the Armenian difficulties
were doubled, for a considerable part of the Armenians
were still Zoroastrians, and sympathized with the Persians against their own government, while many of
the Persians had become Christian, and opposed their
pagan rulers. Thus the Persians felt that they had a
civil war on their hands as well as foreign wars, and
persecuted their Christians horribly. On the other
hand, they had the help of the pagan part of the Armenians in invading or controlling that state; still
again, the Armenian Christians now favored the Romans much more strongly than they had before, because Rome was now Christian; while on top of all were
the great barons, almost independent of the nominal
kings, and who favored neither party but wanted their
feudal independence. Yet the Roman control of the
kingship, for what it was worth, lasted without a break
for over half a century after the victory of Christianity, and over three-quarters of a century from the accession of Tiridates; which was due largely to the
great ability of the Roman emperors Diocletian and

Constantine, and the excellent administration and military organization they left, which saved the eastern provinces from Persia for over a quarter of a century after Constantine's death. Shahpur II, of Persia, won many victories, but he could not hold even the places he captured, and he gained no territory till the death of " Julian the Apostate " in his Persian campaign of 363. His weak and frightened successor Jovian surrendered a great section of the Eastern Roman territory, and still more disgracefully agreed that the Romans should not help their ally Arshag (Arsaces), king of Armenia, against Shahpur. Armenia was at once invaded, but she felt her national existence at stake, and fought with desperation. Though Shahpur had the help of two apostate Armenian princes, Merujan and Vahan, and other native traitors, who ravaged the country and fought their king because he was a Christian, Arshag held out four years, aided by his heroic though unprincipled wife Parantzem, and his able chief commander Vashag. Vagharshabad, Ardashad, Ervandshad, and many other cities were taken and destroyed; finally Arshag and Vashag were captured. Arshag's eyes were put out, and he was thrown into a Persian dungeon in Ecbatana; Vashag was flayed alive, and his skin stuffed and set near the king. Queen Parantzem still refused to surrender, and with 11,000 soldiers and 6,000 fugitive women held the fortress of Ardis fourteen months, till nearly all of them were dead from hunger or disease; then she opened the gates herself. Instead of honoring her,

Shahpur, who was a worthy predecessor of the Turks, had her violated on a public platform by his soldiers, and then impaled (368). Meantime, her and Ashag's son, Bab (Papa), had escaped to Constantinople and asked the help of the co-Emperor Valens. That emperor hated to break the treaty, and involve Rome in a new eastern war; but he could not suffer Persia to be strengthened by the possession of all Armenia, and the Roman statesmen had determined to end the long struggle over Armenia by dividing it between Persia and themselves. Bab was secretly helped by the Romans; he kept up a guerrilla warfare in the mountains, and a large part of the Armenian people were prepared to welcome him back to his rightful throne. The Romans tried to keep within the letter of their treaty by not letting him assume the title of king. The Persians considered his support by Greek troops a breach of the treaty, none the less, and Valens alternately aided and disavowed him. The matter was not mended by the worthless character of Bab himself, who murdered his best friends on the least suspicion, and had the incredible baseness to hold a secret correspondence with Shahpur, the worse than murderer of his parents. Finally the Romans, convinced that he must be under their watch if they were to have any security of him, tolled him down to Cilicia, and prevented him from returning by guards of soldiers. He made his escape, and professed his allegiance to the Romans as before; but Valens resolved to be rid of him, and had him murdered by Count Trajan, the Roman commander in the East.

Meantime a powerful Roman army under Count Trajan, and the chief Persian host, had actually camped opposite each other on the borders of Armenia (371); but neither side wanted a general war just then, —Rome must have her hands free for the Goths, and Persia hers for the Mongols. Finally, in 379, Shahpur died, and there was an instant and entire change in Persian policy toward Rome, and even toward Christianity for a while. His brother and successor, Ardashir, was an old man, and reigned but four years; his successor, Shahpur III, at once sent embassies to Rome, and made a treaty of peace (384). Finally, on the succession of Bahram IV (Kirman Shah), in 390, that monarch arranged a treaty of partition with Theodosius, the Roman emperor, by which Armenia ceased to exist. The western portion became a Roman province; the then reigning sovereign, Arshag IV, was made governor to keep the people contented. The eastern, and much the larger section, was annexed to Persia, under the name of Persarmenia; and to please the people, an Arsacid, Chosroes IV, was made governor, and the dynasty was continued in its rule over the Armenians till after the great Perso-Roman war of 421-2, and the persecution of Christians by Persia, which was the pretext of it. The persecution and the war led to a movement for Armenian independence; after it was over, Bahram V of Persia (Gor, the Wild Ass, " the mighty hunter ") put a new vassal, Ardashes IV, into the governorship; but the great Armenian barons would not give up the struggle, and this last of the Arshagoonian dynasty was removed in 428 and Persian governors substituted.

Thus ended the rule of the line of Arshag. It was a mighty race, and swarms with brilliant names; but in Persia it was justly displaced by one of better public policy, and in Armenia the position of the country was fatal to it.

THE INTERREGNUM.

PROMINENT MEN; LITERATURE; THE CHURCH AND THE CLERGY.

From the time of the partition to the succession of the Pakradoonian dynasty there was not in name an Armenian kingdom; but it must not be supposed that there was not an Armenian nation. No matter how its neighbor nations changed, that country was always called Armenia, and the people held to their Armenian ways and feelings. The national feeling was as strong as before, and above all the feeling of church unity was very intense. No one will ever understand Armenian history, or indeed any Oriental history at all, who does not realize that religious questions come first, and political questions second. The Armenian church was, it is true, a Christian church; but it was the Armenian Christian church, not the Greek church, and the Syrian and African churches had their separate creeds and preferences, and the Greek church, which was the official church of the Greek Empire, was always trying to root out their
6

" heresies " and make them Greek.   That was one reason why the Mohammedans conquered those countries
so easily.   The Africans would rather be ruled by
the Mohammedans than by the Greek church, the
Syrians were angry because the Greek church wanted
to take away their own church and give them the
Greek.   But the Armenians would not take either
the Greek or the Mohammedan or the Zoroastrian;
they wanted their own.   So they were persecuted terribly by the Greek Christians and the Persian fire-
worshipers alike.   Just as before the partition, each
country invaded the other's part of Armenia whenever they got into war; and whichever won, the Armenians were the losers.   When the Greeks won, they
tortured the Armenians; when the Persians won, they
tortured the Armenians; later, when the Mohammedans won, they also tortured the Armenians.   The
mediaeval history of Armenia is that of a battle-
ground between contending races — Greeks, Persians, Scythians, Arabs, Seljuk Turks, Ottoman Turks,
Mongols, and so on.   Millions of its people were slain;
millions died of famine and disease; millions of its
women were forced to embrace Mohammedanism and
become the wives and mothers of Mohammedans,—
half the blood of those who are called Turks at this
day is Armenian; millions of its boys were forced into
the Turkish service, so that many of the best-known
names in Turkish history, and in the Turkey of to-
day, are Armenian names.   Yet through all these ca-

lamities and decimations Armenia has kept its national life and national religion.

From 390 to 640 the history of both sections of Armenia is little more than an account of religious persecutions and their results; the persecutors on the one side were Christians, and on the other side Zoroastrians, but the results to the Armenians were much the same. The Persian atrocities, however, were on the larger scale, and the outcome was a chronic state of revolt, which will be alluded to in the sketch of Vartan the defender. But the rise of the Saracen power changed Armenia's greatest foe from the Persian to the Arab, from the fire-worshipers to the Mohammedans. Persia was invaded by the forces of the caliph Omar in 634, and about 640-2 the decisive battle of Nehavend annihilated the last great Persian army, though scattered places held out much longer. The Armenian highlands at once resumed their independence, and their chiefs, with those of the western section belonging to the Byzantine Empire, fought for their own hand in lack of a true national chief whom all could look up to, but allied themselves mainly with the Greek power against the barbarians; and for two entire centuries, and more, Armenia was a furious and bloody battle-ground between Greeks and Saracens, while internally in a state of feudal anarchy. Then a prince of the family of Pakrad or Bagrat (well-known to students of the last century's history in the form of Bagration), of Jewish descent, as has already been mentioned, which had obtained power over the

central and northern parts of Armenia, was recognized
by the caliph as an independent monarch; and thus
founded the Pakradoonian dynasty, which lasted till
Armenia's independence was once more extinguished
by the Byzantine Empire,— a crime almost immediately punished by the overwhelming of Asia Minor by
the Seljuk Turks.

PROMINENT MEN OF THE PERIOD.

NIERSES THE GREAT.

This was the great creator of Armenian scholarship. He was a descendant of St. Gregory; studied
in the Greek schools of Caesarea during boyhood; later
in those of Constantinople, where he became famous
for learning, married a Greek princess of a distinguished house, and on his return to Armenia was made
pontiff. (All the clergy were married then, as the
Greek priests are now.) He founded over 2,000
schools, and benevolent institutions, as well as great
numbers of churches, was a powerful and persuasive
preacher, and a considerable writer, part of the Church
history being his. From these schools went forth a
very brilliant band of scholars, preachers and orators,
the equals of any in the world.

It was during his pontificate that the affairs of
Arshag and Bab took place, and he was intimately con-
nected with them till his death at the hands of the latter. Previous to the desertion of Armenia by the
Romans in 363, they had quarreled with Arshag, and
sent an army to punish him; but on Nierses' intercession with Valens it was recalled, and the Saint obtained

high favor with the emperor. Arshag's conduct, however, grew too bad for endurance; he had his father and a relative named Kuenel (or Gnel) killed, and married Kuenel's wife, Parantzem (who afterwards met such a horrible fate), though his own wife, Olympias, was still alive. Nierses, finding admonition of no avail, quitted Vagharshabad and went into a convent. But Arshag, getting into fresh difficulties with the emperor and his own rebellious vassals, besought the saint to assist him once more, and once more Nierses complied. He first pacified the turbulent nobility; then interceded with the Roman commander to such effect that the general withdrew his army and went to Constantinople to justify himself to the emperor, taking a letter to him from Arshag, and hostages for the latter's loyalty, and also inducing Nierses to accompany him. But Valens was enraged at the withdrawal, would neither read the letter nor see the saint, and ordered the hostages killed and Nierses banished. The former sentence was revoked on the general's intercession, but Nierses was shipped for his place of exile; on the way a storm wrecked the vessel on a desert island, but he and the crew were saved. It was winter, and they could find no food but the roots of trees, but in a short time the sea miraculously cast abundance of fish on shore, and for eight months they never suffered for sustenance. At the end of that time the saint was set free.

After the restoration of Bab to the land, though not the acknowledged throne of his fathers, Nierses

convened an assembly of Armenian princes and ecclesiastical heads, with the king, and swore them all to
mutual concord and good behavior, to unite the land
against the Persians; but Bab, like so many Eastern
potentates and indeed his father, cared for nothing but
to indulge his own passions, and would have sold his
country to Shahpur if he could have got his price.
Nierses in vain tried to turn him from his evil ways;
Bab merely hated him for it, and finally had him poisoned, in the village of Khakh in the province of Eghue-
ghiatz. Nierses had been pontiff eight years, but they
were crowded with labors of immense variety and usefulness. He left one son (Isaac), who eventually became pontiff also.

SAHAG AND MESROB.

Isaac was educated at Constantinople like his
father, and had at first no thought of being a great
churchman, but only of leading the life of a noble.
He was always, however, of a very pure and lofty character, a marked contrast to the proud and dissolute nobility around him; and after the early death of his
wife, devoted himself to religious seclusion, into which
he was followed by sixty disciples. In 389, a few
years after his father's death, he was called out to fill
the pontificate, once more vacant. This was the year
before the partition of Armenia; but even after that,
though the country was divided, the church was not.
The Armenian Church was still one, with a single
head; but the appointment of that head was of such

immense political importance that, as the king had before claimed the deciding voice in it, so now each power insisted on being satisfied,— no easy matter. Some of the nobles who opposed Chosroes of Persarmenia now complained to the king of Persia that the appointment of the new pontiff had been made without his consent, in order to foment a rebellion, and make Armenia independent again; and the king deposed Isaac. Shortly after, however, a new king reinstated him; and a new vassal king being put in Chosroes' place, and the country more quiet, St. Isaac began to repair the churches, which had fallen into decay,— entirely rebuilding that of St. Ripsime, destroyed by Shahpur, in the course of which he discovered St. Gregory's urn sealed with his cross-engraven signet.

About this time St. Mesrob began to be famous for sanctity. He was a scholar well versed in Greek, Syrian, and Persian, as well as his native tongue; had been secretary to St. Nierses, and after his death remained at court under the patronage of a prince named Aravan, where he became chancellor. Finally he became wearied of earthly glory and court corruptions, and entered a convent, whither many disciples were attracted by his learning and sanctity. Hearing of St. Isaac's beneficent deeds, however, he left the convent and attached himself to him; and under his authority preached and taught in all parts of the province. We are told that by the aid of the chief of Koghten he extirpated a diabolic heathen sect in that province. But his fame is chiefly as having begun

with Isaac the Golden Age of Armenian literature; I
shall speak of this a little later.

BAROUYR OR BROYERIOS.

We must not judge the ability and reputation of
men in their own ages solely by the familiarity of
their names to us; those that have come down to
us are a mere handful, and not by any means always
the greatest of their time. Much depends on chance
— the preservation of certain works, and the loss
of others, or certain men happening to do something
dramatic. Great orators are especially likely to be
forgotten; they leave no written works of their own,
and not being in political life, the common histories
do not mention them. The name of Barouyr is wholly
unknown to this age; but we have the testimony of a
contemporary writer, Eunapius of Sardis,— not a
countryman of his, and therefore free from all suspicion of patriotic brag, and most unlikely to make out
an Armenian greater than he was,— that he was the
most wonderful orator of his time, famous all over the
Roman world, and greatly admired even by the emperors. He was one of those men to whom all languages
seem alike to come by nature, and his oratory was as
easy and as perfect in one as in the other; in Latin or
Greek as in his national Armenian. The only comparison I can give in modern times is Louis Kossuth.
That Barouyr has not the fame of Cicero or Demosthe-
nes, Kossuth or Gladstone, is probably because under
the circumstances of the time he could not engage in

political life; military service or high birth were about the only avenues to that. I will quote in substance what Eunapius says of this brilliant orator, whom he probably knew all about, as our boys know Gladstone, — for he was born in 347, and Barouyr was certainly alive in the time of the Emperor Julian, who came to the throne in 361:—

Barouyr lived to be ninety, and was beautiful even in old age, having the vigor of youth in his looks. He was eight feet high. When a boy he left Armenia and went to Antioch, the first seat of the Christians, and entered the school of oratory under the celebrated Albianos, where he shortly became the foremost pupil. Thence he went to Athens and studied under Julian, the greatest of the teachers of oratory there,— supporting himself by working meantime, as he was very poor; in no long time he was recognized as the leading orator of Athens, and taught the art to the Athenians. The other teachers were so angry that they bribed the governor to banish him; but on the governor's removal some time after, he was permitted to return. The new governor instituted an oratorical competition; whoever could deliver the best extempore oration on a subject to be given out on the spot, should receive great honors. Barouyr took part on condition that the auditors should take careful notes, and should not cheer; but they were so fascinated that they broke both conditions, listening in rapture and applauding repeatedly. The governor offered him his chair, and honored him as the greatest orator in Athens.

Later, the Emperor Constans was so struck with his wisdom and oratorical power that he called him first to Gaul and then to Rome, where he delivered his greatest orations, and the Romans erected a bronze monument in his honor, inscribed "Regina Rerum Romae, Regi Eloquentiae" (Rome Queen of Affairs, to the King of Eloquence). From Rome he returned to Athens, and taught there many years with great repute, up to the time of the Emperor Julian, who honored him, and spoke as follows of him: "Barouyr was a flowing river of oratory, and in power and persuasiveness of speech was like Pericles." And I must add that with all this he was a thorough Christian man, — not a priest, but a great Christian layman and teacher.

VARTAN, DEFENDER OF THE FAITH.

Vartan Mamigonian is the most esteemed and beloved name in Armenian history. Tiridates founded the Christian kingdom; but when the religion was in danger of extermination throughout Persian Armenia at the hands of the fire-worshipers, Vartan saved it, and died for it, a faithful servant of God and his Saviour. It was said of him that he was an honest, modest, wise, brave, true, pure, childlike, and Christlike Christian commander, a great soldier of the Cross. He was a lamb in nature, but when he came to defend his religion he was a lion. As a little boy he was so full of grace that the Pontiff Sahag adopted him as his son; and through this companionship of the aged ecclesiastic and the religious boy, the latter developed into a great spiritual light. In 421 he went to Constantinople with St. Mesrob, and was much loved and esteemed by the emperor (Theodosius II) and the court; then to Persia, where the king honored him and gave him the title of prince.

In 439 Yazdegerd II of Persia succeeded his father, Bahram V, the destroyer of the Arsacid dynasty, and began a furious persecution of both Jews and Christians, which lasted a dozen years, and ended in a complete victory for religious freedom. The king, like James I of England, fancied himself a great theologian, and could always be victorious in a debate by killing his opponent. One specimen will suffice. He called a convocation of Armenian priests and noblemen, and commanded them to embrace fire-worship on pain of death. " Your Christ cannot save you," said he, " for He is crucified and dead." " Oh my gracious king," replied a young nobleman, " why did you not read further about Christ ? He was indeed crucified, but rose again, ascended to Heaven, and is living now and our Saviour." The king in a rage had his head struck off.

Finally in 450 the people of Persian Armenia rose in revolt, and determined to fight for their religion. Vartan took command of them, and showed himself the ablest commander of his time. For a year he held at bay the overwhelming forces of the Persian Empire, and was victorious in every battle, even to the last,— a striking parallel to Judas Maccabaeus in historical

position, as well as military ability. Finally the forces were arrayed for battle on the banks of the Dughmood river, in the plains of Avarayr, near the present city of Van. Vartan had 66,000 men, the Persians several times as many. Vartan prayed to God for help, and to Christ for his own salvation; then he made a speech to his soldiers, in substance as follows:—
" Soldiers, as Christians we are averse from fighting; but to defend the Christian religion and our own freedom we have to fight. Surely our lives are not as valuable as Christ's, and if he was willing to die on the cross for us, we ought to be willing to die in battle for him." Then, with his troops, he crossed the river, fell on the enemy's center, and scattered the huge army in rout, killing 3,544 men besides nine great princes, and losing 1,036 of his own; but alas ! one of these was himself, dying from a mortal wound not long after. Nevertheless, he had won the victory he was striving for. Yazdegerd saw it was impossible to conquer the Armenians in a war for religion, and granted entire liberty to the Christians to believe and preach as they pleased.

ARMENIAN LITERATURE.

FIFTH CENTURY.

The Armenian schools and universities and their outpour of great scholars and writers have already been spoken of, but of course Armenian youths, eager for the best of the world's learning, did not confine themselves to their own country; they studied in Constantinople, Athens, Antioch, Alexandria, and wherever great teachers were located. All were zealous Christians, and the books they have left behind were Christian literature, not works of mere enjoyment. A very rich and valuable literature it is, too, in my judgment the most so of any single body that exists; though much of it has perished in the recent destruction of everything Christian the Turks can reach. My readers will not credit my opinion of it, because most of it has never been translated, but that makes it all the more valuable now, it has so much that is new to add to the stores of the world. It is not necessary to give them all, but to point out the chief writers.

The fifth century is called the Golden Age of Armenian literature. First in point of time as well as importance comes the Armenian Bible. The furious opposition of the Church in the Middle Ages to letting the people have the Bible to read in their own tongues seems perfectly ridiculous, when we remember that in the early Christian church every people had it in their own language, and it was thought to be the greatest work for a heathen people that could be done, to translate the Bible for them. It was not thought needful then to keep the word of God in a strange tongue, so that the people could neither read it for themselves nor understand it when it was read to them.

There were probably some books of popular tales and songs in Armenia before the fifth century, for we are told that there was an Armenian alphabet to write them in as early as the second, but if so they have

all perished, and the alphabet was doubtless a poor
and meager one.   Armenian scholars and writers read
Greek or Latin books, and occasionally Hebrew or
Syriac ones, and wrote in Greek or Latin themselves;
if it was necessary to write Armenian, as in letters,
they made the Greek, Syriac, or Persian characters,
which of course were insufficient to give the Armenian
sounds.   They would have got along with this, however, if it had not been for the eagerness of Christian enthusiasm which made them wish to give the
Bible to Armenia; it was to spread the word of God,
not to write books, that they were anxious.   St. Mesrob set to work and invented a very perfect alphabet
of thirty-six letters, to which two have been added
since.   According to one of his disciples, having
vainly sought help from the learned, he prayed to God,
and received the new alphabet in a vision.   This was
about 405.   He and Sahag the Pontiff at once began
to translate the New Testament and the Book of Proverbs from a poor Greek version, the best they had,
with the assistance of two pupils, John of Eghueghi-
atz and Joseph of Baghin.   This was finished in 406.
Many years later (seemingly about the time Persian
Armenia was made a satrapy), they undertook the
translation of the Old Testament; but as the Persians
had destroyed all the Greek MSS., it was necessary to
use a Syriac version.   The same two assistants aided
them; but being sent to the Council of Ephesus in 431,
they brought back copies of the Greek Septuagint, and
the old translation was at once dropped, and a new one

put under way. But all found their knowledge of Greek too imperfect to rely on, and the pupils were sent to Alexandria and Athens to complete their education; on their return they seem to have brought a new Alexandrian version, and corrections were made from that, and the work completed, most likely about 435.

The Bible completed, they turned to other labors. The Saints Sahag and Mesrob are said to have written six hundred books themselves, all in Christian theology and instruction; and the pupils from the schools St. Nierses and themselves had founded — the chief of their own were at Noravank, Ayri, and Vochkhoroz — wrote great numbers besides. The first original work of Sahag was one on Pastoral Theology, setting forth that the Church of Christ is the Bride of Christ, and the ministers must therefore be holy, pure, and obedient. He wrote many epistles to kings and emperors, all of whom reverenced and were greatly influenced by him. He wrote a large part of the Armenian Church History, composed many hymns, and translated many commentaries and theological works from the Greek.

Fortunately during this period the government of Armenia was very good, with the exception of one period of two years or so; even after its partition, for close on forty years it had practically self-government in internal affairs, and for another decade the Christians enjoyed full rights of worship. Bahram IV of Persia (389-399), who helped divide it, was a monarch who loved peace above all things, both with forcign countries and his own people; his successor, Yazdegerd I (399-420), went even further, employed the Catholicos or Pontiff on embassies to Constantinople, and as mediator with his own brother, and made his son, Shahpur, governor of Persian Armenia, continuing the Arsacid dynasty. He was murdered by his nobles, instigated by the Zoroastrian priests, for being too tolerant to the Christians, and his successor Bahram V, who got the throne by favor of the rebellious elements, tried to please them by persecuting the Christians; this involved him in a war with Rome, as I have said, and after a couple of years he made peace and gave toleration again. The turning of Persian Armenia into a satrapy in 428 I have already told; but no fresh persecution was undertaken till that of Yazdegerd II, in 439, ending in Vartan's revolt just detailed. Shahpur of Armenia was a prince of great wisdom, generosity, and public spirit; he patronized men of learning, founded schools, made large grants from the treasury for scholarship, and sent scholars to all the great seats of learning to teach and acquire the languages, literature, and history of other nations, after which they wrote and translated hundreds of volumes. Among them were Tavit, Khosrov, Mampre, and Zazar; a great historian, Eghishe (Elisaeus), author of the Life of Vartan; and a great philosopher, Yeznic. These are only a few out of scores worthy of mention.

Dr. Philip Schaff says:— " In spite of the unfavorable state of political and social affairs in Armenia during this epoch, more than six hundred Greek and Syrian works were translated within the first forty years after the translation of the Bible; and as in many cases the original works have perished, while the translations have been preserved, the great importance of this whole literary activity is apparent. Among works which in this way have come down to us are several books by Philo-Alexandrinus, on Providence, on reason, commentaries, etc.; the Chronicle of Eusebius, nearly complete; the epistles of Ignatius, translated from a Syrian version; fifteen Homilies by Severianus; the exegetical writings of Ephraim Syrus, previously completely unknown, on the historical books of the Old Testament, the synoptical gospels, the parables of Jesus, and the fourteen Pauline epistles; the Hexahemeron of Basil the Great; the Catechesis of Cyril of Jerusalem; several homilies by Chrysostom, etc. The period, however, was not characterized by translations only. Several of the disciples of Mesrob and Sahak left original works. Esnik wrote four books against heretics, printed at Venice in 1826, and translated into French by Le Vailliant de Florival, Paris, 1853. A biography of Mesrob by Koriun, homilies by Mambres, and various writings by the Philosopher David, have been published; and the works of Moses Chorenensis, published in Venice in 1842, and again in 1864, have acquired a wide celebrity; his history of Armenia has been translated into Latin, French, Italian, and Russian."

Sixth Century.

The leading authors in this century are Abraham Mamigonian, who wrote on the Council of Ephesus; and Bedross Sounian, who wrote on the Life of Christ. There are, however, many others of merit.

7

SEVENTH CENTURY.

By far the greatest name in this century, and indeed the best-known and most important name in Armenian literature altogether, is the writer who calls himself Movses Khorentzi, well known to all historical scholars as Moses of Chorene, author of the History of Armenia. For more than a thousand years, up to this century, indeed, this was practically the only source of Armenian history to the world; the other writers were inaccessible. And it is still very valuable, though not in just the way it was once thought to be. It preserves a vast amount of Armenian tradition, stories and ballads, and real history, which have perished except for this work; but he seems not to have had the Greek and Latin histories to draw from, and makes a great many mistakes. He gives a life of himself, and says he is writing in the fifth century, and knew Sahag and Mesrob when he was young; but he really lived in the seventh, and wrote history about the year 640. But still he is a great writer, and one of Armenia's literary lights; and we do not need to claim for him anything more than he deserves.

Besides Movses, the chief authors were Gomidas, Yezr, Matossagha, Krikoradour, Hovhannes, Vertanes, and Anania. They wrote chiefly religious books; but Anania Shiragatzi is the author of a valuable work on astronomy.

EIGHTH CENTURY.

The leading authors were: Hovhan Imassdasser,

Sdepannoss Sounetzi, and Levont Yeretz. They wrote hymns, books on oratory, etc.

NINTH CENTURY.

Zakaria Shabooh, Tooma, Kourken, etc.

TENTH CENTURY.

The chief authors were Anania, Khasrov, and Krikor Naregatzi. The latter wrote a prayer book in ninety-five chapters, which one of the missionaries of the American Board thinks the best in the world. He says that only Beecher was able to offer such prayers as Krikor Naregatzi.

ELEVENTH CENTURY.

The leading writers were Hovhannes, Krikor, and Aristagues. In this century some of the best commentaries were written on the Bible.

TWELFTH CENTURY.

Leading authors: Nerses Shinorhali is the foremost of Armenian poets, and a thoroughly converted and consecrated man of God. His hymns were intensely spiritual, and the Armenians still chant them in their churches. They are worthy to be translated into English. Nerses Lampronatzi, the greatest scholar ever born in Armenia, was a distinguished commentator on the Old Testament, and wrote many other books. Another is Yeremia.

Again I quote from the Schaff-Herzog Encyclopaedia:— " Another flourishing period falls in the twelfth century, during the Rubenian dynasty. Nerses Klagensis and Nerses Lambronensis belong to this period; also Ignatius, whose commentary to the Gospel of St. Luke appeared in Constantinople in 1735 and 1824; Sargis Shnorhali, whose commentary on the Catholic Epistles was published in Constantinople in 1743, and again in 1826; Matthew of Edessa, whose history, comprising the period from 952 to 1132, and continued by Gregory the Priest to 1163, contains many interesting notices concerning the Crusaders; Samuel Aniensis, the chronologist; Michael Syrus, whose history has been edited with a French translation by V. Langlois, Paris, 1864; Mekhitar Kosh, of whom a hundred and ninety fables appeared at Venice, 1780 and 1812. A most powerful impulse the Armenian literature received in the eighteenth century by the foundation of the Mekhitarist monastery in Venice, from whose press the treasures of the Armenian literature were spread over Europe, and new works, explaining and completing the old, were added. The Armenian liturgy was published in 1826, the breviary in 1845, the ritual in 1831."

THIRTEENTH CENTURY.

Leading authors:— Krikor Sguevratzi, Kevork Sguevratzi, Mukhitar Anetzi, Vanagan Vartabed, Vartan Vartabed, etc. They wrote histories, commentaries, etc. As the Armenian dynasties ended in the fourteenth century, I will reserve my notes on the later literature till towards the end of the book.

The peculiar value of the Armenian literature is not realized as it should be, by European and American scholars; the language is well worth learning for what it can give the student. Not alone is the original

ST. MARY'S IN ATCHIMIATZIN.

work that comes from the first Christian nation especially valuable for its bearing on primitive Christianity, but the Armenian scholars translated great numbers of works from other languages, and these translations are preserved in Armenian monasteries when the originals have been irretrievably lost in the wars, and burnings, and devastations of other countries. Six hundred volumes of this old literature are known to exist now, two hundred in Europe, and four hundred in different places in Armenia.

THE ARMENIAN CHURCH.

The first thing to remember about this is, that it is an independent and separate body as much as the Greek or the Roman Catholic church, and older than either of them. I often hear such expressions as "the Armenian Catholic Church," and many people think it simply a "branch" of the great Eastern or Greek Church. It would be just as sensible to consider the Greek a branch of the Armenian Church. Each of them represents a form of church organization and body of doctrine which best satisfied the representatives of certain races or nations; the advantage of the Greek was that that race — or at least its speech and thought — happened to be dominant in the Roman Empire at the time when Christianity won the battle, and so had the official backing of the empire, and was able to outgrow and crush down the others. It was not any truer, any more the real Church of Christ, than the Syrian or African or Ar-

menian; it was not the earliest, for the very first
Christian churches sprang from the Jews; it was not
even the earliest great national church body, for the
Armenian church has that distinction.   It had the
most soldiers back of it to put down its opponents, that
is all.   I have already told the story of the foundation
of the Armenian church by St. Gregory and Tiridates.
That church has its own head — the Catholicos or Pontiff, who is no more a subordinate of either the Pope
or the Greek Patriarch than the Grand Llama is, or
Dr. Parkhurst — and its own self-subsistent being.

As to the differences between them, in the first
place the Armenian is a purely Trinitarian.   There
is no room for Unitarianism within its lines.   When
Gregory the Illuminator was preaching his sermons
on the hills and plains of Armenia, he laid the foundation of the national church in the Trinity.   His first
sermon was on the Trinity; his last sermon was on the
Trinity.   In all his sermons he asserted the Trinity,
— the Father, the Son, and the Holy Ghost.   Jesus
Christ being a perfect Man and a perfect God; in his
person we see God in man and man in God; a perfect
Emmanuel, God with us.   We see in him that man can
be united with God.   The only possible way of salvation is through Jesus Christ.   He is the Saviour of
the world and none else, and whosoever believeth in
Him shall be saved.   This is the belief and the only belief of the Armenian Church.   Its members repeat
the Apostolic Creed and the Lord's Prayer every day
in their churches.   I say every day because Armen-

ians go to church every day,— twice, morning and evening, and three times on Sunday.

Secondly, the Armenian has never been a persecuting church, and every other one of the great Christian churches has been. The Armenian church, as befits the first and most Christ-like of all the bodies that professed Christ before Luther's time, has always been the broadest, the most inclusive, the most untechnical of churches. It fellowships with all other churches. It demands only that men shall profess and believe in Christ, and live Christian lives; not that one shall belong to its own church body. Its canons are conversion and regeneration, purity, holiness, being born again from the Holy Spirit and becoming Christ-like. It holds that Christianity is brotherhood through Jesus Christ, and gives no warrant for oppression or persecution, curses or anathemas. I need hardly say that it is alone in this of the older churches. The others hold that no one can be saved outside of their own bodies; hence they fulminate anathemas against all others, and have the anathemas read in their churches, and they persecute others to compel them to join themselves, or rid the world of a possible danger that their own members may be tolled outside. The Greek Church, where it has full power, will not even allow people of other creeds to come into its country; for example, in Croatia a Protestant is not allowed to live there at all, and the people said in the Hungarian Diet that "intolerance was the most precious of their rights." The Russian Greek Church will not

permit a Protestant missionary in Russia. Where the
Roman Catholic power is complete, it is just as intoler-
ant. The Armenian church has been repeatedly persecuted by both, and has always protested against the
principle of it, as well as' against the pretensions of
the Popes to universal sway. It is fairly entitled to be
called the first Protestant Church.

That the Armenian contention is for freedom of
will, freedom of conscience, freedom of worship, and
political freedom, is the cause of their being hated
both by the Mohammedans and by their so-called Christian neighbors; but it ought to be also a reason why
Americans, who believe in these things themselves,
should sympathize with us. If the Armenians would
accept Mohammedanism, would the Turks persecute
them ? No. If they would accept Roman Catholic-
ism would the Turks persecute them ? No, for the
Catholic states would not permit it. If they would
accept the Greek Church, would the Turks persecute
them ? No, for Russia would not permit it. But as
they are an independent church the others are interested in persecuting them, and nobody is interested
in defending them. If there is any help to come to
them it will not be from the old churches of Europe,
but from Protestant Anglo-Saxons helping their spiritual brethren, the Anglo-Saxons of the East; and it
will be found, when the great battle comes, that the
Slavonic, Greek, and Catholic churches will be on the
side of the Mohammedans against the Armenian Chris-

tians. But that battle will come, and the victory will be on the side of freedom and righteousness.

As to theological questions, the Armenian Church fathers did not pay much attention to them. Not because they were not able, but because they were too able, and very far-sighted. They knew well that such questions can never be solved, no matter how many centuries pass away, no matter how great scholars the world produces; therefore they would not enter into the debate. And so every Armenian scholar has his own theology. I confess that the Armenian Church has not a theology, or an especial official doctrine; and this is a very fortunate thing for the Armenians. They care more for righteousness of life than for particular beliefs about the way of getting it. When there was a great controversy in the Council of Chalcedon, 451 A. D., about the nature of Christ, Armenians did not care about it. Some of the great theologians said Christ had two natures; some said he had only one nature; the Armenian bishops would not give any opinion. They believe in Christ as their Saviour, that is the essential thing; but whether He has two natures or one nature is not essential. Then came the controversy about the Holy Spirit. Whence does the Holy Spirit proceed ? Some say from the Father and the Son, some simply from the Father. When the question came before the Armenian bishops they replied that they did not care whence He proceeds. They know that they need the Holy Spirit for guidance in spiritual life, for regeneration; they know that the Holy Spirit is one of the persons in the Trinity; and that is enough for them.

Now I would ask, do the theologians of the nineteenth century agree on such questions, or any other theological question ? Are the theologians of the coming centuries going to agree on them ? I leave this to the scholars of Europe and America. I simply state that I studied in three different theological seminaries in America; first in Oberlin, in 1880; second in Union Theological Seminary, New York, in 1881; and finally I was graduated from the Chicago Theological Seminary. But I never saw a theologian who could agree with any other, and have no hope ever to see any such. President Fairchild of Oberlin differed from Professor Shedd of New York, and Professor Boardman of Chicago did not agree with either of them; and I never agreed with any of them, and as an Armenian I have my own theology. So every reader of this book will see that the Armenian scholars had the best judgment, far-sightedness, and common sense of those in any or all the communions. Instead of theological controversies, they preached the gospel and reached the masses, for the Kingdom of Christ.

THE ARMENIAN CLERGY.

The Armenian clergy are divided into three classes: the pastor, the preacher, and the presiding bishop. The pastor is called Yeretz, the preacher is called Vartabed, and the presiding bishop is called Yebisgobos (Episcopus). The presiding bishop ordains the preacher and the teacher. The Armenians believe in apostolic succession, and they believe in immersion. Baptism can be administered both to grown people and to children, if they are the children of members of the church; but always by immersion, and in the name of the Father, the Son, and of the Holy Ghost. If you unite the present Episcopal church with the Baptist, you will make an Armenian church. All the clergy of the Armenian church, bishops, preachers, and teachers, were married in the early centuries. Gregory the Illuminator, the first bishop of Armenia, was married. His sons were bishops, and were married. There was no church law whatever against marriage of the clergy. At present the bishop and the preacher, or the Yebisgobos and the Vartabed, cannot marry, but the pastor or Yeretz must be married. No Armenian pastor can be ordained if he is not married.

Of course I am not writing here an Armenian church history; the main object in writing this book is to inform the American public about the causes of the atrocities, and the atrocities themselves. Therefore I consider the above information about the Armenian church enough; but I will add that the Armenian church until the twelfth century was as simple in ceremonial as any American Protestant church is to-day. But when their kingdom was coming to an end, and they were in a life-and-death struggle with the Mohammedan powers, Popes Innocent, Benedict, and others promised to help them if they would accept some of the Roman doctrines and ritual; and since that time — the twelfth century — there has been more or less similarity in the ceremonial of the two churches. But Armenians have never believed in the Pope, and now they are getting rid of the Roman ritual also, as it is foreign to them.

Before I finish this subject, I must give a little information about the Armenian Patriarch in Constantinople, and the Armenian Catholicos of Etchmiazin. There are many people in this country who do not know the difference between the Patriarch and the Catholicos. The difference between them is as follows: The Patriarch at Constantinople has nothing to do with religion, though he is a bishop. As a personal bishop, he goes to the church, and occasionally preaches and leads the pastors, but his duty is political. He is the political head of the Armenians in Constantinople, and responsible to the Sultan for the Armenian nation who live in Turkey. The Armenians are not anxious to have such a political head; it is simply the wish of the Sultan, or it has been the wishes of the Sultans in centuries gone by. The present Patriarch, Right Rev. Bishop Izmirlian, is a very learned, experienced, and eloquent bishop. He is very popular; the whole Armenian nation love and esteem him; but the Sultan hates him, because he is brave, honest, and true. The Sultan ordered him to send out false reports, alleging that the Armenians were not being massacred, but were safe and prospering under Abdul Hamid's reign; but the Patriarch refused to issue any

THE ARMENIAN PATRIARCH.

such documents while in fact the Armenians were being plundered, tortured, outraged, and killed. The Patriarch's life is consequently in great danger, but the Patriarch says that if it is necessary to sacrifice his life for his beloved nation, he is ready to die.

The Armenian Catholicos is the spiritual head of the Armenian church; he has nothing to do with politics. He is considered to be fallible, and he is elected both by bishops and laymen; and if the nation is not satisfied with him, they may remove him and elect another. He is a presiding bishop. He lives at Etchmiazin (the former Vagharshabad) north of Mt. Ararat in Russia; it has been the seat of the Pontiff since the time of St. Gregory. The present Catholicos is Rt. Rev. Bishop Mugurditch Kirimian. He is very much esteemed and loved by the Armenians throughout the world. Before he became Catholicos, he was Patriarch in Constantinople, and was the most popular and the ablest of Patriarchs, but the present Sultan of course hated him, and according to stories I heard from good authority, when I was in Constantinople, tried repeatedly to kill him. One day he was summoned to the palace to see the Sultan; but on arriving there, was instead locked into a room with a brazier of burning charcoal, and left to die. Before it was too late, however, the Russian Ambassador, being informed of the attempt, saved his life. Failing to get rid of him that way, the Sultan banished him to Jerusalem, but sent false reports to the newspapers, that he thought highly of the Patriarch, and had given him money to go to Jerusalem that he might improve his health and enjoy himself. The Sultan lives and breathes falsehood.

While in Jerusalem, Kirimian was shadowed by the Sultan's detectives; but about three years ago he was elected Catholicos by the Armenians, and the Russian Czar (not the present one, but his father, Alexander), sanctioned his election. The Armenians are proud of him, for he is worthy of his office. He is a great scholar, and the author of several books which are worthy of translation into English. His book Traghti Endanik (the family of Paradise), is the best book I ever saw or read in any language on family life. In it he describes the first holy family, which was created in the Garden of Eden, in Armenia, and then goes on to describe a holy family, the ideal family, a true home. It is full of the Holy Spirit. Catholicos Kirimian was married and had a family, and really his family was a holy family and he had an ideal home,— therefore Armenians call him Kirimian Hayrig or "father," and he is worthy of the title; but his wife died. He is also a great orator, preaching fiery gospel sermons as our greatest revivalists preach them. He loved the American missionaries in Constantinople, and they returned the feeling. Kirimian was born in Van April 16, 1820; therefore he is now 76 years old, but full of life and vigor. I hope he will live longer, to see his beloved nation and country saved from the oppressions of the cruel Turkish Sultan. I could

write a book on the life of Kirimian and his great
deeds in Armenia, for the Armenians; how he opened
schools and established printing presses; how he went
to the Congress in Berlin and championed the Armenian cause; and all his noble works.   But this is not
the place.

THE PAKRADOONIAN DYNASTY.

For a century after the Mohammedan conquest
of Persia, the fortunes of Armenia were apparently at
their lowest ebb, and as a country it almost disappears
from history; but by one of the compensations of nature, which provides that human force, like other
force, cannot be extinguished, but if suppressed will
find an outlet elsewhere, its people began a career of
brilliancy and power unequaled in its history, and
broadened from the rule of a tormented buffer-state
to that of the great Byzantine Empire itself.   The
Saracen torrent flowed over Armenia's lowlands and
up to the base of its mountain fortresses, but never
overcame them; generation after generation the contending forces battled together, surging back and forth,
and filling the beautiful valleys with fire and blood,
but Armenia proper was never added to the list of
Saracen conquests, never made a part of the Mohammedan Empire or strengthened Mohammedanism
till four centuries later through Byzantine greed and
folly.   Internally it was all in feudal anarchy again
so far as concerned any one central focus of government.   Even the Persian satraps had gone from
the Persian side, and with them the half-control they

had kept over the turbulent baronage; on the Roman side from early in the seventh century to early in the eighth, the throne of Constantinople was filled with weak and unstable monarchs, fighting for Anatolia against the Saracens, and unable to exercise any effective control over Armenia, to which indeed they looked as a frontier defense against those very foes.

But let us not attach too harsh a meaning to " anarchy." There were a hundred rulers, it is true, great dukes and barons, each supreme in his own district; but because they held power by the sword against a savage enemy, their subjects had to be a strong, independent race, with arms in their hands, which they would use against their chiefs as well as the foreigners if there was great oppression. In this fiery school, Armenia learned the sternest lessons of self-help and discipline. With no interference from outsiders to fear, and no help from them to be got, it became even more confirmed in its own independent isolated ways, a world to itself as it has been ever since. Its cultivators tilled their fields as they had done for so many centuries, and its scholars read such books as they had, and wrote such as their own minds furnished. But vast numbers of its hardy sons took service in the Greek armies, and became the bone and sinew of the defense of Asia Minor against the caliphs; not only so, but they rose by hundreds to the highest commands in the empire, both civil and military. They formed the best " society " in Constantinople itself; and to crown all, a score of emperors and empresses in four different lines, including the most illustrious ones that ever sat on the throne from Constantine down, and who ruled the empire for two hundred and seventy-seven years, were Armenians.

It is within the truth, and can be justified from the greatest of English historians, to say that for four centuries the Byzantine Empire was not a Greek but an Armenian empire. Armenians by blood filled all the great offices of state, commanded the armies, occupied the throne for nearly three hundred years, preserved the empire from external invasion and internal disintegration. It was the accession of an Armenian dynasty that turned it from a decaying power to one that expanded steadily for two centuries, from one falling into anarchy to one the glory of the world for scientific organizations; and it was the final overthrow of Armenian influence that ruined the empire, being followed almost at once by the loss of half its territory and the richest part, and the break-up of its system of civil administration. Everywhere in the time of Byzantine glory you find the list full of Armenian names. The appearance of " Bardas " as the name of generals or civil magnates is always proof of Armenian blood, and that name is monotonously common; it is the Greek form of " Vartan," though now and then they make it " Bardanes." One of the greatest conquerors in Byzantine history, John Kurkuas, was an Armenian, from a family which supplied three generations of statesmen and generals, and two great emperors. And this is part of what the

8

immortal historian of " Greece Under Foreign Domination," George Finlay, has to say:—

" At the accession of Leo III (717), the Hellenic race occupied a very subordinate position in the empire. The predominant influence in the political administration was in the hands of Asiatics, and particularly of Armenians, who filled the highest military commands. Of the numerous rebels who assumed the title of emperor, the greater part were Armenians. Artabasdos, who rebelled against his brother, Constantine V, was an Armenian. Alexios Mousel, strangled by order of Constantine VI, in the year 790; Bardan called the Turk, who rebelled against Nicephorus I; Arsaber [Arshavir] the father-in-law of Leo V, convicted of treason in 808; and Thomas, who revolted against Michael II, were all Asiatics, and most of them Armenians. Many of the Armenians in the Byzantine Empire belonged to the oldest and most illustrious families in the Christian world; and their connection with the remains of Roman society at Constantinople, in which the pride of birth was cherished, was a proof that Asiatic influence had eclipsed Roman and Greek in the government of the empire. An amazing instance of the influence of Asiatic prejudices at Constantinople will appear in the eagerness displayed by Basil I, a Sclavonian groom from Macedonia, to claim descent from the Armenian royal family." (But I shall show that he was an Armenian.)

Let us note the Armenian sovereigns of the Byzantine Empire. First the great Iconoclast house, of Leo the so-called Isaurian, the saviour and restorer of the empire, which reigned from 716 to 797. Leo considered himself an Armenian, and he ought to have known best, and he married his daughter to an Armenian. He saved Constantinople from capture by the Saracens, causing the destruction of the finest Mohammedan army ever got together; of its 180,000 men only 30,000 got back home, according to the Mohammedan historians. Twenty-two years later another great Moslem army was annihilated by Leo, and for two centuries the Saracens scarcely troubled the empire again. But not only so, he remodeled the whole administration so effectively that no serious break-down occurred for three centuries, and he put new life into the whole society, so that it began to outgrow its enemies, as well as outfight them. After his able dynasty ended, another Armenian, Leo V, reigned seven and a half years, from 813 to 820. About half a century later began the Basilian dynasty, under which the laws were codified, and Bulgaria destroyed. Basil was born in Macedonia, but the name of his brother, Symbatios, Armenian Simpad, shows that he was of an Armenian family, the colonies of Armenians having spread all over the civilized world. His line reigned without a break from 867 to 963, when the beautiful widow Theophano was pushed aside for sixteen years by another Armenian house, Nikephoros Phokas and his nephew John Zimiskes, two of the ablest generals and statesmen ever on the throne, descendants of a brother of the great commander, John Kurkuas, before spoken of; then Theophano's son, Basil II.— Boulgaroktonos, the Bulgarian slayer, and the ultimate destroyer of Armenia as well — took the throne, 979, and the dynasty continued till 1057, when it had run to dregs, and had just before finally ruined Armenia, and by so doing ruined the empire.

To go back to Armenia itself. The reason a feudal anarchy always ends in a military monarchy, no matter how able or self-willed every one of the separate chiefs may be, is that this very class most interested in perpetuating it grow weary of it. The stronger barons oppress and plunder the weaker, who are always superior in numbers, and in united strength if they will act together. A small lord may like to be free from control by the king's officers as well as a great one; but if he can only have that privilege by letting his overbearing neighbor be free from it too, and rob him, he finds it does not pay, and sighs for a law that will control everyone alike, and a strong ruler to enforce it. So if a chief in such a community comes to be known as having a hard hand and letting no one be above the law but himself, the small landholders flock under his banner; he grows into a prince, and eventually some prince of such a family will make himself king, with the goodwill and help of all but a few great houses, who feel able to take care of themselves and desirous of taking care of others.

This happened in Armenia. In 743, a century after the battle of Nehavend and four years after Leo's crushing defeat of the second great Saracen army, we find that a chief named Ashod, of the family of Pakrad or Bagrat, claiming descent from the ancient Jews (see the Haigian dynasty in this book), had managed to win control over central and northern Armenia; how long it had been exercised, or what it grew from, no one knows. Ashod I is the first known founder of the Pakradoonian dynasty, though it is counted as beginning from the recognition of its independence by the caliphs over a century later. He recovered some parts of Armenia proper, and fought hard for Lesser Armenia. The family had vigorous blood in it, and somewhere in the ninth century — 885 is the date fixed — it was recognized by the caliphs as an independent house of kings, and Armenia as a kingdom. But it had really been so for over a hundred years before.

Ashod II, " the Iron," gained his title from his stern military power; he beat back the Arabs and gave the land peace for a considerable time. He left no son, and his brother Appas succeeded him; another brave and wise ruler, who brought back the Armenian captives held in bondage by the Saracens. He made the city of Kars his capital. It is now owned by Russia, having been captured by her forces in the Russo-Turkish war of 1878. He greatly improved the city, and built a beautiful cathedral there. After a reign of twenty-four years he died in peace, and his son succeeded him as Ashod III.

This was the glory of the line in prowess and generosity; he reminds one of Alfred the Great, in England. He was the terror of his country's enemies; not one of them — Arab, Greek, or Persian — dared to invade Armenia, and they sent presents to conciliate his friendship. It was under him that the country became formally independent again. He filled it with fortified places. He gave all his personal income in charity, and established almshouses and state charities. He was so benevolent and so interested in the destitute that he was called The Merciful. He ruled over Armenia twenty-six years, and was succeeded by his son Simpad. This was neither a good man nor good ruler; corrupt, cruel, and ambitious only for selfish purposes. He made the city of Ani, on the north side of Mt. Ararat, the royal capital, built strong walls and lofty towers around it, and is said to have erected 1001 churches in it — which he might do, and still be a bad man. The extent of its still existing ruins of palaces, churches, towers, and castles testifies that it was one of the great cities of the world, like Babylon and Antioch.

For more than a century Armenia flourished and grew rich; then it disappeared once more under the hammer and anvil of Byzantine and Saracen, aided by internal disruption — the traitorousness of its great nobles, who hated the kings for controlling their lawlessness. Let us take in just its situation. It included the heart of the Armenian highlands; but it had not the extent of old Armenia, several Armenian districts being independent of it, and either free or tributary to the Byzantine Empire. Ani was its seat; but the district around Kars, fifty miles northwest, had split off into a separate principality, the boundary between the two being the Aras; on the east was Vaspourakan, another princedom; on the west Sebaste, another; on the north Iberia, and Abkhasia or Abasgia or Albania, the realms of the Georgians; and one or two others not quite certain,— but all these ruled by Armenian princes, mostly of the Pakradoonian house. Though Armenia was in fragments, therefore, the pieces formed a sort of family confederacy, and often acted together, as they did to their eventual ruin. Their folly paved the way for the destruction of Armenian national existence, and the worse folly of a Byzantine emperor accomplished it. About 1020 the Seljuk Turks were pressing so hard on Vaspourakan that the prince, Sennacherib, was unable to hold out, and ceded his dominion to Basil II of Constantinople in return for the sovereignty of Sebaste, which he agreed to hold as a Byzantine governor; great numbers of his subjects went with him. Something about this transaction roused the Armenian national feeling to resentment; for John Simpad, king of Armenia (known at this time as the Kingdom of Ani, from its capital), joined with George the Pakradoonian king of Iberia, to promise help to a couple of discontented generals, one at least an Armenian, who were to raise the standard of revolt in Cappadocia and call on all Armenians to rise. It was to have been a general revolt of all eastern Asia Minor. But the mighty Basil, conqueror of Bulgaria, and nearing the end of his half-century's reign, first crushed the rebellion by buying up one of the generals and getting him to assassinate

the other (the Armenian), and then crushed the league
of Bagratian kings. The king of Armenia, as the
price of retaining his throne, was compelled to sign a
treaty ceding the kingdom to the Byzantine Empire
after his death.

John Simpad was succeeded by his nephew Kakig,
an able ruler and good general. But in 1042 there was
placed on the Byzantine throne the fourth husband
of the despicable old female (Zoe), whose male creatures, married or not married to her, misgoverned
the empire for nearly thirty years. The reign of Constantine Monomachos stands out black in the history
of the world; it not only destroyed Armenia, but it
fatally wounded the Greek Empire; it gave Asia
Minor to the Turks; it was the first great step towards
subjecting Eastern Christianity to the Mohammedans;
it began the Eastern Question. The sack of Constantinople by the Turks, four centuries later, was directly
due to it. Almost never has sheer contemptible neg-
ative good-for-nothingness produced such awful results. He was a worthless man and an utterly incapable statesman; a libertine without decency, a spend-
thrift without generosity or taste, a ruler without sense
of responsibility. Having spent on debauchery or his
favorites, or diversions, or palaces in Constantinople,
or other selfish, short-sighted gratifications, or on the
church to win its indulgence for them, all the money
he could wring from his subjects without risking his
throne, he bethought himself of another resource.
The provinces on the frontiers of Iberia, Armenia,

and Syria, were exempted from taxation, and the small dependent states in that region from tribute, in consideration of maintaining bodies of militia to defend their territories, and save the central government from keeping regular troops there.   The emperor ordered the militia disbanded, and the taxes and tribute collected and remitted to Constantinople as from other places.   This monstrous piece of imbecility laid the southeastern frontier open to the Turks at once; and the money was quickly wasted in the emperor's pleasures.   But even this was not enough, and he cast his eyes on Armenia as a rich country to squeeze taxes out of, and sent word to Kakig to fulfill his uncle's will, and yield up his kingdom.   Kakig refused.   Constantine formed an alliance with the Saracen emir of Tovin (on the east flank of Armenia), and sent an army to attack Ani; and a number of the great Armenian nobles turned traitors and joined the Byzantine forces.   Kakig could not make head against the three allies with the slender forces left him; and choosing to yield to Christians rather than Saracens, though Constantine evidently had no such scruples, surrendered Ani to the imperial forces (1045), and went to Constantinople to plead his cause with the emperor. Constantine would not yield, and Kakig resigned his kingship for a magistracy, and large estates in Cappadocia.   The emperor forced the Catholicos to leave Ani and live at Arzen, then at Constantinople; finally the Comnenian house allowed him to settle in Sebaste among his people.   The princedom of Kars alone preserved its independence against both Christians and Saracens, and thus the Armenian life still beat; but as a kingdom, Armenia perished and the Pakradoonian dynasty with it when Ani surrendered.

This piece of wanton foolishness and criminality had its immediate reward; it laid all Asia Minor open to the Turks — for the Armenians after they had lost their independence would not fight for their oppressors as they had fought for themselves; and the Turks were ready. Three years before the capture of Ani, a Turkish chief, cousin of Togrul Beg, flying after a defeat, had asked the Byzantine governor of Vaspourakan to let him pass through that district; on being refused, he attacked the imperial troops, routed them, captured the governor, and on reaching Turkish ground sold him as a slave, and urged Togrul to invade the Byzantine territories, as they were of matchless fertility and wealth, and the troops not formidable. Togrul sent his nephew Ibrahim to do so in 1048; the timid Byzantine commanders, after defeating a detachment of his troops, waited for reinforcements before encountering the main body, and Ibrahim, finding the movable wealth mostly stored up in fortresses, assailed the rich, unfortified city of Arzen, with 300,000 people, who had neglected to transfer their possessions to Theodosiopolis, the nearest fortress. It was one of the chief seats of Asiatic commerce, full of the warehouses of Armenian and Syrian merchants. They defended themselves for six days with such desperation that Ibrahim, giving up the hope of plunder, and wishing at once to secure his rear from attack while retreating, and to injure Byzantine resources, set fire to the city, and reduced it to ashes. Few such conflagrations have ever been witnessed on earth; perhaps Moscow and Chicago are the only things comparable. It is said that 140,000 persons perished in the fire and in the massacre by the Turks that followed, and the prisoners taken were such a multitude that the slave markets of Asia were filled with ladies and children from Arzen. This was the first of the many such calamities that have dispersed the Armenians all over the world, like the Jews, have reduced one of the richest and most populous countries on the earth to a poor and thinly populated one, and turned Asia Minor practically into a desert. The next year Kars was overrun; but in 1050 an attack on Manzikert failed, and after an unsuccessful invasion again in 1052, the Turks retired for a while, but only for a more terrible onslaught.

Before going on to the next dynasty, I will finish the story of Kakig. In his Cappadocian magistracy he was still called King Kakig and honored as a king. One day he heard that a Greek bishop had called his dog " Armen " to insult the Armenians, and went to his house to make sure, and to exact vengeance if it were true. They drank heavily together, and Kakig ordered the bishop to call his dog; the bishop, too drunk to know what he was about, called him " Here, Armen." Kakig, in a rage, ordered his retainers to put the bishop and his dog into a bag together, and then beat the dog till he bit his master to death. The church was too powerful for even a king to murder a bishop with impunity, and Kakig was hanged on a castle wall. This gave rise to the Turkish proverb, " Kart Giavour musliman almaz, Room Ermenic dost almaz " (An infidel never becomes a Moslem, a Greek never loves an Armenian). The Turks have always acted on this, and used the Greeks against the Armenians; but the old hate has died out now under common oppression.

THE RUPENIAN DYNASTY.

The imbecile policy of the Byzantine Court continued after the suppression of the line of Pakrad, and with even worse results. Having destroyed the interest and even the right of Armenia to keep up an army of her own, and confiscated her revenues applied to that purpose, the loss of defenders should have been made good as far as possible, by keeping a large regular army there in their place; but the same corrupt and profligate court avarice which had caused the one, prevented the other. Not only did Constantine X (1059-67) actually reduce the number of his army, leave it unprovided with arms and ammunition and other supplies, let the frontier fortifications fall out of repair, and leave the garrison unpaid, to save money for his overgrown court of costly favorites (the Byzantine court a little later cost $20,000,000 a year by itself), and let the officers put civilians on the rolls, and made artisans and shop-keepers of their real soldiers to pocket fraudulent pay for themselves, as the Persians do now, but he used to disband most of his army after every campaign to save paying them, letting them have free quarters on the citizens.   The Seljuks were prompt to take advantage of this.   In 1060 Togrul sacked Sebaste.   In 1063 his greater nephew Alp Arslan began a series of raids that soon reduced Iberia and Northern Armenia almost to a waste.   The systematic policy of the Turks was to make any country they invaded impossible of civilized habitation again, by obliterating all the results and " plant " of civilization which many ages of labor and money had enriched it with.   They deliberately cut down all the vineyards, orchards, and olive groves, wrecked the aqueducts, filled up the wells and cisterns, broke up the bridges, and in short made the land (except for a few fortresses) a mere desert pasture ground to feed their cattle on.   They were only nomad shepherds and cattle-men, despised cities as at best necessary evils, and did not care for tilling the soil.   Whatever spot the Turk has set his foot on, he has blasted like a breath from hell, turning to naught the labors of thousands of years at a blow; and he has never put anything of his own in place of what he has destroyed. Where are the Turkish great cities developed by them, the Turkish flourishing agricultural regions, the Turkish manufactures, the Turkish literature or art ?   At most they have not quite been able to exterminate others' progress, because they must perish themselves in doing it.

The Armenian king of Iberia had to submit; the

Armenian prince of Lorhi close by had to give his daughter's hand to Alp Arslan; and at last the royal city of Ani, though strongly situated on a rocky peninsula and protected on two sides by a rapid river and a deep ravine, was left without help by the Byzantines, and in spite of a heroic defense, was taken by storm, June 6, 1064. This convinced the Armenian prince of Kars (another Kakig), that he could not hold out; he surrendered his province to the Byzantine Empire for the appanage of the district of Amassia. This removed the last Armenian prince from the old seats of the race, which were now all occupied by the Turks; and the Armenians emigrated in vast numbers to the districts west and south (old Cappadocia and Cilicia), where their native princes were living as great Byzantine dukes and governors. A number of semi-independent vassal principalities were soon formed, making as before an Armenian wall between the Turks and the empire; but only part way, and far weaker, having left its impregnable mountains, and being much poorer, and having lost heart. The upper part, through Old Armenia, was left wholly open; and the Seljuks poured into Asia Minor like a flood, ruining the country beyond reparation as they went. Within a dozen years from the capture of Ani, the Seljuk dominion reached to Nicaea, fifty miles from Constantinople, and the seat of the first Christian church council. Its lands could be seen from St. Sophia; the Byzantine Empire retained only a strip of Asia Minor along the sea-coast.

But the Armenian courage and national spirit, and the political and military ability which had governed the Eastern Empire so many centuries, were not extinct. The heart of the nation, forced out of its immemorial lands, still beat strongly, and animated their mass of dukedoms, now forming a compact body in the center of Asia Minor, with a common life and national instinct, which was soon to weld them into a new Armenian kingdom, as true and real a one as the old, Armenians under an Armenian prince, but in a wholly different territory, south and southwest of the former. Among the great barons of this district was one Rupen (Reuben), a relative of the slain Kakig; it is said that he saw him hanged. At any rate, no sooner was the deed accomplished than he retired to the mountains of Northeastern Cilicia, and raised the standard of Armenian independence, with himself as king. There was absolutely no reason why it should not be gained; the Seljuk conquests had cut the Armenian districts wholly off from the Greek Empire, so that a Greek army could not come upon them to punish them for revolt without traversing at least a hundred miles of Turkish or other Mohammedan territory. The Armenian settlements were an island in a sea of Mohammedanism. The new kingdom of Cilicia or Lesser Armenia grew with a rapidity that would seem miraculous, only it was a mere coalescing of the fragments of Armenia into their old unity; in no long time it had spread east to the Euphrates, taking in Melitene (Malatia), and

Samosata, north fully half way to the Black Sea, and south to the Mediterranean, occupying the coast from Tarsus almost to Antioch. This kingdom played a part of the first importance in the history of Asia Minor for close on three centuries; its territories were gradually whittled away by Turks and Mongols, but it kept the Eastern Mediterranean open for Christian action against the Mohammedans to the last. To their shame, the Byzantine emperors were much more hostile to it than to the Turks, with whom they often allied themselves against it; for some years it was vassal to the Byzantine Empire; later it was overwhelmed by the Mameluke deluge from Egypt, and allied itself with Jenghiz Khan's Mongol hordes against them; but the Mongols passed and the Mamelukes remained, and exacted a terrible vengeance, putting an end to the kingdom with the usual horrors of Oriental conquest in 1375.

Rupen's son Constantine succeeded him. It was by his help that the leaders of the first crusade captured Antioch. Constantine was succeeded by his two sons, Leo and Theodore jointly, but finally Leo reigned alone; he was an able prince, fought the Saracens with success, and much enlarged his kingdom, and at last made a naval attack on Isaurian Seleucia, the frontier fortress of the Byzantine Empire in this part, and an important seaport. This brought "Handsome John," the ablest of the Comnenian line of Byzantine Emperors, into the field; he stormed the Cilician seaports, and then reduced the chief interior fortresses; Leo fled to the Taurus Mountains, but was captured, and died in captivity at Constantinople. His son Rupen had his eyes put out on a charge of treason, and died of it; but his other son, Toros, escaped, and after John's death restored the Cilician kingdom, which had temporarily been made vassal by John.   Toros is the glory of the whole Rupenian line; he was of the first rank, both as a general and a statesman.   He scarcely ever suffered a military reverse.   He beat the Byzantine armies in campaign after campaign, and the Seljuks as well; under him the new Armenia was almost a match for all its enemies combined, and no one of them dreamed of attacking it single-handed.   Levon was another able ruler, who maintained the power and prosperity of the kingdom; he was an ally of the great Emperor Frederick Barbarossa in the Third Crusade, assisted him in capturing Iconium (1190), and both Frederick and the Greek Emperor Alexius III sent him crowns,— the second no great honor, as Alexius was one of the most contemptible of human beings.   In Levon's time the capital of the kingdom was Cis, where there is now a great Armenian monastery with rare manuscripts, the residence of a Catholicos.   The changes in the extent of the kingdom are very curious; perhaps most curious of all (since the Armenians were always a race of inland and highland farmers, not seamen), the new kingdom was gradually crowded down on the north and lost two-thirds of its territory in that direction, but steadily extended along the coast until it came to include not only all

9

Cilicia but all of old Isauria clear to its western mountain barrier; hundreds of miles of seaboard, from close
to Antioch on the one side, to far west of Cyprus on the
other, being indeed a strong maritime power. At the
end it had lost these western coast extensions, but still
had an area larger than that of the Crimea now, a very
considerable power to hold the northeast corner of the
Mediterranean.

It was during these times that the hard-pressed
Armenians received promises from the Popes to help
them against their enemies if they would use the
Roman ritual and ceremonial, and submit themselves
to the papacy. The country never did accept Ro-
manism, though some churches introduced the ritual
and images, and conformed to the Roman fashion;
and of course it never did get any help from the popes,
who had nothing to give but recommendations, which
the temporal powers paid no attention to.

Levon VI was the last of the line. He was a weak,
easy-going man, handsome and popular, but not of
much ability; perhaps he could not have saved his
country if he had been. I have told of the Mamelukes
and their invasion; they overran the country, and
treated the people as the Turks have done lately,
striking terror to them by terrific massacres, satiating
their lust on the women, and carrying off many thousands of captives for wives or slaves. Levon was taken
captive also; after some years in Egypt, he was permitted to go free, wandered through Europe for a
dozen years, and finally settled in Paris, where he died

iu 1393.   He was buried by the high altar of the
Church of the Celestine; the following epitaph is on
his monument, which still exists to-day:

Here lies Levon VI, the noble Lousinian Prince,
the King of Armenia,
who died 1393, A.D., Nov. 23d, in Paris.

I have been dealing here with the special kingdom
of Armenia, under a regular king; but it must not
be forgotten that the older sections, ruled by Greek
or Turk, were Armenia still, inhabited largely by Armenians, in spite of emigration and Turkish settlement, and their fortunes really part of this history.
Under both Jenghiz Khan and his successors, and
Timour, every horror was let loose on the unhappy
lands.   For nearly a century the first Tatar invasion
cursed and devasted it; hundreds of villages were
destroyed, the inhabitants slain or at the mercy of
the savages, and vast numbers emigrated in despair.
Among others, the cities of Ani and Erzeroum were
captured, and every inhabitant put to the sword, each
soldier being given his portion to kill, so that none
should escape.   Timour compelled all whom he
spared to become Mohammedans.   When he took the
city of Van, he threw the inhabitants from the castle
walls until the dead bodies reached to the height of
the walls.   A great famine followed, and many thousands died of it; the starving wretches sometimes ate
their children or parents to sustain life a little longer.
The reader will see later whether the modern Turks
have any superiority over the hordes of the thirteenth
or fifteenth century.

IV

RULERS OF THE OTTOMAN EMPIRE.

SULTANS OF THE PAST.

The Ottoman Empire begins with Othman, born 1258 A.D.; the dynasty is usually counted from the time of his being given a local governorship by the last of the Seljuk Sultans, in 1289. The tribe was simply one small group of families when we first hear of it; Othman's father Ertogrul entered the Seljuk dominion not many years before that date with only four hundred tents, say two thousand people in all, counting women and children. They had been driven from their homes in Central Asia by the Mongols. The Seljuk Sultan Ala-ed-din III made Othman governor of Karadja-hissar (Melangeia). Now Othman, though a plundering marauder like other tribal chiefs, turbulent and cruel, knew some things that better men never find out. He knew that impartial justice is a greater strength to a state and a greater lure to draw others to it than anything else; he made the fair at Karadja-hissar a model of business equity for all races and religions, it was thronged with traders, and other Turkish tribes soon flocked to the banner of the man who never broke his promises and dealt out even-handed justice. The lying Greeks never learned the lesson in all their history. In a dozen years he was able to collect an army of 5,000 soldiers, beat a Byzantine force sent against him, overrun a large province of Asia Minor, and with the plunder greatly increased his following. He realized too that education and thorough practical training and moral discipline were the foundations of success; most of us know that now, but few understood it then. But the wild and barbarous Turks could not be educated and disciplined as he wished,— would not stand it and were incapable of profiting by it,— and so he or his son Orkhan developed the terrible system which for centuries made the " Turks " irresistible, which made the " Turks " seem to increase rapidly, and makes the " Turks " today appear numerous while in fact not one drop in ten of the blood in their veins is Turkish at all. This was to exact from the Christian population — Greek or Armenian chiefly — a regular tribute of boys as well as money. These were taken from their parents at about eight years old, educated and trained in the household of the Ottoman Sultan himself, of course drilled in the Mohammedan religion, and gradually inducted into the highest posts, civil or military, if fit for them, or made into a special body guard for the Sultan. These were called " yeni cheri " (new soldiers), which is familiar to everybody in the form " Janissaries." From that day to this, the Turkish system has been built up by foreign blood, and outside of the Sultanate pretty much entirely by foreign brains; it was the constant infusion of fresh civilized Christian ability and moral character into it that kept.

its inherent defects and vices from bringing it to an
end long ago.   Finally the system partly rotted out
and partly became impossible to enforce for fear of
revolution (Sultan Mahmoud ended it in 1826); but
never outside of this has a tribe of barbarians ever
succeeded so completely in impressing into its own
service the powers of a higher race.   It is as though
horses should have regularly broken and driven teams
of men for centuries; even more usefully to the Turks,
because intermarriage (largely by force on their part)
has filled their own veins with civilized Armenian
and other blood.   As soon as this reinforcement
stopped, the Turks began to decay.

I cannot enter even in outline into the political
history of the Armenians during the next few centuries.   The country has been torn into fragments,
and each fragment has a history so separate that there
would be no unity between them.   One section of
what was once Armenia would be governed by Persian officials; another occupied by the savage Kurds;
another mis-governed and oppressed by the Turks;
another under the rule of Russia; and so on.   Persia,
when she recovered her national being, held and still
holds a small part of the eastern section, as I stated
earlier in the book, Russia the north; but the heart
of old Armenia is in Turkish hands.   The Sultans
have succeeded in mixing themselves with the natives
and occupying their confiscated lands till the Armenians are put in a minority in their own country.

I must correct here a notion fostered by historical

writers, that the Turks are very brave.   They may
have been once, though I doubt it and there is no proof
of it; but they certainly have gotten over it now.   In
the last Turko-Russian war (1878), they ran by thousands to Christian houses for protection.   They are
just like wild dogs: savage and ferocious, but not
brave.   Nor are they wise: they have some low cunning, but no practical sagacity — that too is a thing of
the past.   As to industrial talents they have simply
none whatever; they depend on foreigners for everything: they will not learn and indeed cannot learn, and
never try to learn.   They have never made a cannon
or even a gun, they never built a war vessel and very
few if any other kinds, they make neither powder nor
shot; all come from Europe or America.   Nor have
they even decent military talent, the very thing they
pretend is their special business: their best generals
are Germans, their admiral for a long time was the
Englishman Hobart, I think the Englishman Woods
is so now.   As to civil ability, their best administrators
have always been Armenians.   Bezjian Amira was
Sultan Mahmoud's adviser; Haroun Dadian, another
Armenian, is the chief adviser in foreign affairs of the
present Sultan.   His personal treasurer is an Armenian, Portucalian Pasha.   Is this inconsistent with
what I have said of his hating the Armenians for their
intelligence ?   Not in the least: he employs them in
spite of his hatred, because he can trust no others: the
Turks are too stupid and all others too unsafe.

LIST OF OTTOMAN SULTANS AND DATE OF ACCESSION.

		A.D.
1.	Othman I, gazi,	1299
2.	Orkhan I, gazi,	1327
3.	Murad I, gazi,	1360
4.	Bayazid I, yelderim,	1389
5.	Mohammed I, chelebi,	1413
6.	Murad II, gazi,	1421
7.	Mohammed II, fatih,	1451
8.	Bayazid II, gazi,	1481
9.	Selim I, yavouz,	1512
10.	Suleyman I, kanooni,	1520
11.	Selim II, gazi,	1566
12.	Murad III, gazi,	1574
13.	Mohammed III, gazi,	1595
14.	Ahmed I, gazi,	1603
15.	Mustafa I,	1617
16.	Othman II, guendj,	1618
17.	Murad IV, gazi,	1622
18.	Ibrahim I,	1640
19.	Mohammed IV,	1648
20.	Suleyman II,	1687
21.	Ahmed II,	1691
22.	Mustafa II,	1695
23.	Ahmed III, gazi,	1702
24.	Mahmud I, gazi,	1730
25.	Othman III,	1754
26.	Mustafa III, gazi,	1757
27.	Abdul Hamid I, gazi,	1773
28.	Selim III,	1789
29.	Mustafa IV,	1807
30.	Mahmud II, adil,	1808
31.	Abdul Mejid I, gazi,	1839
32.	Abdul Aziz I,	1861
33.	Murad V,	1876
34.	Abdul Hamid II, gazi,	1876

Some of the above Sultans have special titles, like our " William the Conqueror," " Charles the Bold," " Henry Beauclerk," etc.   Thus, gazi and fatih mean conqueror; adil, righteous; guendj, young; yavouz, brave; kanooni, law-giver; yelderim, lightning; che-lebi, gentleman.   Most of them have the title gazi, or conqueror; the present Sultan bears it because he fought with Russia.   He was beaten, to be sure, but he took the title all the same.

Sultan Mohammed II, who captured the city of Constantinople, established an Armenian Patriarchate there in 1461 A. D.   The first Patriarch was Hova-guem, the Bishop of Broosa, a friend of the Sultan. Mohammed II had two motives in this: first, to have an Armenian ecclesiastical center in Constantinople for the nucleus of a strong Armenian settlement there, to play off against the Greeks from whom the city was taken and who might be dangerous, whereas the feud between Armenians and Greeks would make each weaken the other; second, to have a hostage for the Armenians, responsible for their not breaking into revolt; not at all for the benefit of the Armenians, but for that of the Sultan.   The same reason obtains to this day.   If there was no Patriarch, their cause would be much better off.   After the establishment of this Patriarchate the Armenians had no more kings or princes; their political head was the Patriarch. Even after the Patriarchate was established they were not safe.   They yielded to the Sultans, they became slaves to the Sultans, but the Persian Mohammedans were foes of the Turkish Mohammedans, and Armenia, as of old in Roman times, was the battle-ground. In the time of Sultan Ahmed and Shah Appas, the latter overran Armenia and carried away the people to captivity, besides killing hundreds of thousands. Then it was retaken by the Turks. Then a part of it was captured by the Russians. Historians write of the Huguenots and their sufferings; of the conflicts in Europe between the Catholics and the Protestants. How many centuries were the Protestants persecuted and martyred? How many millions were killed by the Roman Catholics? Do all the Protestant martyrs in Europe number as many as the Armenian martyrs ? I doubt it.

And let it not be said that these were not religious martyrs, but merely victims of the fortunes of war or political conflicts. The wars were three times out of four based on real if not nominal grounds of religious antagonism, — Mohammedan or Zoroastrian against Christian, — or claims of religious protectorate, as Russia over the Armenian Christians; the political exigencies which called or formed a pretext for the massacre of myriads of men and old women, the outrage of the young brides and maidens, the enslavement of the children, were without a single exception created by the resistance of Christians to forced conversion, or the fear of Mohammedan rulers that as Christians they meant to revolt, or sheer blind hatred to men of another creed. The victims were truly martyrs to Christianity.

THE SULTAN, FROM A RECENT PORTRAIT.

(By permission of "The Youths Companion.")

THE PRESENT SULTAN, HAMID II.

This is the thirty-fourth Sultan in the Ottoman line, and probably the worst, the least, and the last. It is not likely the Turks will ever have another Sultan, for this one is pretty sure to bring the Sultanate to an end. His days are numbered, he knows it well, and the Turks know it well too. Before his life and his kingdom are finished, he has resolved to end the Armenian nation; that, however, will not be ended, the people will not be exterminated; when the Turkish Empire is abolished the remaining Armenians will have freedom.

Hamid II was born September 22, 1842, second son of Abdul Mejid, and wrested the throne from his brother Mourad August 31, 1876. He is not a legitimate Sultan, but a usurper. When but a little boy he manifested a savage and cruel spirit. While the Dalma Bagsh Palace, the largest in Constantinople, perhaps in the world — was going up, he went to visit it; seeing it unfinished, he called the Armenian architect and told him it must be finished by the next day. " My dear prince and lord," said the architect, " I wish I could finish it, but it is impossible; and especially not to-morrow, since it is Sunday, and we Christians do not work on Sundays."   " You heathen dog, you Armenian," said the boy Hamid, " if I grow up, and some day become a Sultan, I will force all the Armenians to break the Sabbath, and if they do not, I will order the soldiers to kill them all."   He is carry-

ing out his threat.   He grew to manhood without becoming any milder, and is morally corrupt besides.
He has drunken bouts with worthless associates,
and spent his time in all sorts of monstrous debauchery and brutality.   He was such a miserable wretch
that it is impossible to describe his beastly life on
paper.   There is no humanity in him, no grace, no
sympathy, no brains, no strength; he is pale and sick,
well worthy to be called the " sick man of Turkey."

    This is a very different description of him from that
given by General Lew Wallace and Mr. Terrell.   I
can only say that I know what I am talking about, and
they do not.   I lived in Constantinople, as a native of
Turkey, and with means of knowing, seeing him often,
and hear authentic stories of his doings day by day.
General Wallace was invited to the palace, feasted
and flattered, and his wife decorated with jewels;
naturally, he thinks no ill of a man who treated him so
well, and with whom he hopes for more good times
when he goes back.   He has done infinite harm to the
cause of Armenia by his popular lectures, declaring
the atrocities " exaggerated " (he evidently thinks that
if a newspaper report gives ten thousand men murdered when there were only five, and all the women of
a city violated when a dozen of them got away,
you are entitled to dismiss the whole thing from your
mind as of little account), and the Sultan a good man,
incapable of such things.   People are bewildered, and
ask, " How can we doubt a good American who was
minister there ? "   Why, good people, what has his

ministry got to do with it ?   He was hundreds of miles from Armenia, and did not know any of the chief languages of Constantinople,— either Armenian, Turkish, or Romanic; and what could he tell of his host, except of the quality of his hospitality ?   A man usually shows his best side to those he entertains; did he suppose the Sultan was going to amuse his guests by having one Armenian disemboweled, and another emasculated or impaled on red-hot iron rods, and a couple of women ravished, as a light and playful interlude between the main dishes and the dessert ?   His praise of the Sultan is as valuable as his praise of the Grand Llama would be,— he knows nothing of either; and his inference from the Sultan's pleasant talk that he could not order a nation extirpated with hideous cruelties, is simply imbecile.   And since he has given all this loose talk, the consular reports, from English residents among the very scenes, have been published, showing that the atrocities have not only not been exaggerated, but are even worse than reported.   In this case, even the newspapers were unable to come up to the truth; their rhetoric fell short of the full measure of the awful truth.

To go back a little: Twenty years ago Abdul Aziz, uncle of the present Sultan, was the ruler of the Ottoman Empire.   He cared little for the country or the people; he wanted only to eat and drink, and have good times.   He was a very strong and hearty man, and I was told he could eat a whole roast lamb for dinner, and think it probable.   He had the innate cruelty of his family, their love of blood for its own sake. He had tigers and lions fight together; he would order a live lamb flung to a lion, and laugh to see the lion tear and devour it. He married all the handsome girls he could find, but for pure animality; he cared nothing for their education or virtue, and his several hundred wives were what you might expect. One of them fell in love with the commander-in-chief, or Minister of War, Heussein Avni Pasha, a very ambitious and daring adventurer, who had gained the confidence of the Sultan, and went often to the palace. The Sultan heard of the intrigue, went to the woman's room, kicked her fatally, and threw her out of the window. But before her death, she sent word to Heussein to avenge her on the Sultan. Heussein's position was very critical; evidently it was a race between him and the Sultan which should kill the other first. He went to Midhad, the Grand Vezir, and to Kaysereli Ahmed, the admiral, both liberal-minded pashas, in favor of establishing a constitutional (or even if they could, a republican) government, and without telling them his relations to and fears from the Sultan, persuaded them that now was the time to depose the Sultan, and establish liberal institutions, and told them it must be done that night, or the Sultan would get wind of it, and then good-by to all of them. And he clinched the argument by telling them he would order his soldiers to kill both of them if they refused to join him, and then depose the Sultan just the same; " as commander-in-chief," he said, " I can

PRESENT SULTAN, HAMID II.
From an early portrait.

compel obedience, and I am in earnest." They consented, and while the Sultan was asleep that night the commander's soldiers and the admiral's sailors surrounded the palace by the land and sea. This was the Dalma Bagsh, the largest and handsomest palace in Constantinople. Heussein entered, saying he had important news for the Sultan. Going to the chamber where Aziz was sleeping, he awakened him, and said, "In the name of your nephew, Sultan Murad, I depose you." Then he compelled him to go down-stairs to a boat in waiting, filled with soldiers, carried him to Cheragan Palace, and imprisoned him there; after which he informed the Sultan's nephew, then Prince Murad, that his uncle had been deposed because the people would not endure him, and added, " As the oldest in the royal family you succeed him, and I, as commander-in-chief, have the honor and privilege of humbly serving my master, and leading your majesty to the throne of the Ottoman Empire."

Murad was too astonished to know what to do or say; but Heussein was resolute, and Murad reluctantly followed him to the Dalma Bagsh; there the commander ordered the soldiers to cry out three times " Padishahum chock yasa " (Long live the Sultan). All this was about midnight; and meantime printed notices were prepared and scattered throughout Constantinople that Sultan Aziz was deposed and Sultan Murad was on the throne. After a few days the commander-in-chief sent a eunuch and a physician to Cheragan Palace, with orders to put Aziz to death.

They did so by chloroforming him and cutting his blood-vessels with scissors. Heussein prepared a false report stating that he had committed suicide, and brought it to Sultan Murad. The latter did not believe it, and said, " you killed my uncle." Heussein left the Sultan's presence in great anger, and went to Midhad's palace to confer with him, calling in also Kaysereli Ahmed and other officers. While they were together, another officer, Cherkez Hassan by name, brother-in-law of the dead Sultan, came to the palace, informing the guard that he had a message from the Sultan to the pashas, who were in conference. . The guard admitted him, and he went to the parlor. After the usual salutations the commander asked him, " Hassan, why did you come here ? " Hassan replied, " I came to kill you, dog," and fired three shots at him from his revolver, stretching him dead on the floor. Then, before the others could assail him, he killed every one present, except Midhad, who escaped. Hassan was finally captured and hanged, but Murad was established on the throne. He was a good-natured and liberal-minded man; he believed in constitutional government, and organized a working system. There was to be a parliament, one-third Christians and two-thirds Mohammedans, elected by the people of the provinces or vilayets. Each vilayet furnished three members, two Mohammedans and one Christian, all indorsed by the clergymen. During the elections I was pastor of Adana in Armenia Minor, and had to endorse our members. The Adana member was an Armenian named Krikor Bizdigian, the richest man of that city, perhaps in Turkey; if still living, he must be ninety. When the parliament was opened in Constantinople, Sultan Murad presided, and told the members to discuss any questions freely.   He said, " We are here for the good of the country, and the empire needs to be reformed; how can we reform it ? " This was an entire novelty; " government by discussion " is not the Oriental way, and not the Oriental liking either.   The Mohammedan members were astonished, and they were wrathful at the Christian members when the latter began to make free and able speeches.   They said, " Are we going to be governed by these heathen dogs, the Christian hogs ?   We will have no parliament where every dog is free to open his mouth.   We want the good old ways of Mohammed."   They were like mad dogs, ready to bite.   They hated the Christians, and they hated the Sultan.   They went to his younger brother, the present Sultan, and told him his brother Murad was insane.   " He makes Christian dogs equal to Mussulmen; he will ruin the country; you must become Sultan to save the Turkish Empire."   This suited Abdul Aziz exactly; he headed a revolt, deposed his good brother, dissolved the parliament, imprisoned Murad in the palace where his uncle was assassinated, and since then has been carrying the country to destruction.   He is a perfect devil in all respects.   A devil can take the guise of an angel, and the Sultan has the cunning to make himself appear a perfect gentleman, a benevolent and humane person.   The devil

10

can cheat most people, and so can the Sultan, all but the native Christians in Turkey, to whom he shows his horns, and hoofs, and tail.

The nauseous praise of the Sultan from travelers and ministers reminds me of a Turkish brigand named Guro, who infested Asia Minor a quarter of a century ago. He robbed year after year all travelers who had anything worth taking; but when he met tramps he gave them money, and even a roasted lamb to eat now and then. The tramps all praised him; he was a benevolent, humane, kind-hearted man; they had never seen anything cruel or dishonest about him. So the Sultan robs the Armenians, and uses their money to feast the American ministers and decorate their wives. Oh, but the Sultan sent money to the sufferers from famine in the Western States of America; so generous of him ! I am glad to say the money was refused. All Americans who praise the Sultan are like the tramps and the brigand. They are either ignorant or in effect bribed. And then there is the affectation of impartiality, so easy a cover for ignorance, coldness, and laziness. You must say some good things about a scoundrel, and some ill ones about a saint, or you will be considered a partisan. You must not tell even the truth, if the truth is all on one side. If the Sultan massacres all the Christians in Turkey, why, there are two sides to the question; perhaps the Christians were not agreeable people, and if so, you cannot wonder he has them exterminated by sword, and fire, and torture, and rape; it is really the only way he could get rid of them.   And then, he is king, and has a right to do what he pleases with his own; nobody has any business to interfere.   Of course a President could not order three millions of people put to death by letting loose all the savage Indians of the West on them to do as they pleased with them, for the sake of making them worship the Big Manitou; but a Sultan — that is different, even though a Kurd is exactly as bad as an Indian, and an Indian's knife does not cut throats any more effectively, nor an Indian's tortures inflict more unnamable horrors of suffering, nor an Indian's torch burn houses any better, nor an Indian's beastly lust defile women any worse.   Are all the writers, then, who have praised him ignorant or silly ?. Yes; the Sultan's deeds, proved by countless thousands of witnesses, set forth in the consular reports, show that they are.

As soon as Abdul Hamid had seized the throne, he girded on the sword of Osman, which I will explain later is equivalent to coronation.   The keys of the palace where Murad was imprisoned he keeps in his pocket.   The nominal ground of his imprisonment is insanity, but he was not insane; it was his liberality of mind, his greatness of heart, and his mild and kind spirit.   He was an exceptional Turk.   Then Hamid called Midhad Pasha to him, gave him $25,000, and told him to leave the country and never come back. The country was thus left without a single man of any force of character and a large position combined. After the death of Aziz the two greatest Turks were

Sultan Murad and Midhad Pasha, and had Murad not been imprisoned, and Midhad banished, the Turkish Empire would be an entirely different country, and have a different future.

Midhad was finally recalled, but only to be murdered. As the Sultan felt his position secure, he began to get rid of all men of superior character and education. Some he banished, some he imprisoned, some he killed. But Midhad, as the greatest, was the most obnoxious. He was of course not dispatched at once. He was invited back, made governor of Smyrna, given the highest emoluments, paid the greatest honors; then one night he was suddenly summoned to Constantinople by the Sultan. He knew it was the death-call, and fled to the French consulate for shelter, but the consul was afraid to protect him. Finally he was taken by force to Constantinople, tried before a tribunal of course packed by the Sultan, and condemned to death. But the kind-hearted Sultan commuted the death sentence to banishment and hard labor for life, and quietly ordered the officers who were going to take him to banishment to kill him instead, which they did.

After he had got rid of all the great Turks, he appointed a host of ignorant and cruel ruffians as governors, sub-governors, and generals; like Hadjii Hassan Pasha, governor of Beshick-Tash near the Sultan's palace, and whose business is to watch over the Sultan, and who cannot read or write. He prefers ignorance, because it means fanaticism, and he thinks cannot plot against him.   He dreads and hates education and the educated, though he makes a show of encouraging them.   He taxed the people for public schools and put up magnificent buildings, but there are few if any scholars in them; they were not built for educational purposes, but for a show, and if necessary, for barracks in the future.   All the same, he has his agents in Europe and America chant his praises as a lover of learning.   Parents will not send their children to them anyway, for there are not competent teachers in them; there are a very few ignorant Mohammedan teachers, but even they are so corrupt morally that no one dares trust his boy or girl with them.   The Sultan professed that people of all nationalities and religions would have equal privileges in his public schools, therefore he ordered all to contribute money for them.   He raised the farmers' tax from one-tenth to one-eighth of the crops on pretense of supporting the public schools.   Of course he got most of it from the Armenians, but there is not an Armenian teacher or child in them.

Abdul Hamid is a stupendous hypocrite and charlatan; he makes a great pretense of wisdom, religion, and morality, and he has not a spark of either one. His wisdom is only the animal cunning of a jealous, cruel, suspicious brute, his morals simply do not exist, and his religion is pure sham.   It is often reported that he is very religious.   All that it amounts to is that every Friday (the Mohammedan Sunday) he goes to the mosque to worship (a ceremony called selamlik), with several thousand soldiers lining the roads from the palace to the mosque to prevent his assassination, of which he is in hourly fear; that once a year he goes to the old Seraglio and pays tribute to the mantle of Mohammed and other relics, kissing the slipper, coat, and beard of the prophet; and he worships in the mosque of St. Sophia as a conqueror. All this is merely for show, to please the fanatic Mohammedans. He advertises himself as a temperance man, too, but he drinks to excess privately. In a word, he is thoroughly false from top to bottom, pretending all good, and doing all evil.

His officers of course imitate him; most of them are absolute infidels, believing in nothing, but professing great devotion. I knew a governor of this stamp. He used to worship at the mosque, and even ordered a hair of Mohammed's whiskers to be brought from Constantinople to please the Mohammedan population. He never drank a drop of liquor in public, but privately drank all he could hold. He had plenty of fellows. For instance, Khalil Rifat Pasha, the present Grand Vezir, appointed a few months ago, has been governor of several different provinces, and notorious in all as a great hypocrite and a thoroughly corrupt man, full of lust and profligacy. When a European or a native Christian of high position called on him, he would treat the visitor with great politeness, promise anything he asked, say, "take my word of honor," and assure him of his entire sincerity; as soon as he was gone, Khalil would curse him, and call

:

him a heathen dog, say to another Mohammedan, " See how that Christian hog believed what I said ! " and keep not a word of his promises.

The Sultan is just the same. He is outwardly very pleasant, very gentlemanly, very humane. He will promise almost anything, but he will do nothing, and he calls his enraptured guests dogs and hogs behind their backs. Who knows how many times he has called Lord Salisbury, the German Emperor, or the Russian Czar, who are helping him to kill the Armenians, heathen dogs ?   See the promises of the Sultan in 1878, in the Berlin Treaty, Article 61:— " The Sublime Porte undertakes to carry out without further delay the improvements and reforms demanded by local requirements in the provinces inhabited by the Armenians, and to guarantee their security against Circassians and Kurds.   It will periodically make known the steps taken to this effect to the powers, who will superintend their application."   These promises were made eighteen years ago, and the reforms were to be made " without further delay."   His reforms have consisted in ordering Circassians and Kurds to murder and plunder them.   Since the Berlin Treaty, the Sultan, calling the European kings, emperors, and princes heathen hogs and Christian dogs, directly and indirectly has killed 200,000 Armenians.   That was his reform.

When he seized the throne, Turkey had 40,000,000 people, and the Sultan thought his power was irresistible.   He let loose a horde of Circassians to massacre the Bulgarians, just as he has let loose the Kurds to massacre the Armenians. But the Bulgarians are Slavs, and belong to the Greek Church, and the Russian Czar, Alexander, grandfather of the present Czar, interfered in their favor. This excited the fears of the other powers, and a Congress was held in Constantinople to settle the question. Lord Salisbury came from England, Count Ignatieff from Russia, and others from other parts of Europe, gathered in a beautiful palace (now the admiralty) on the shores of the Golden Horn of sweet waters, discussed the question, and decided that the Bulgarian atrocities must stop, Bulgaria be reformed and allowed to govern itself internally, and that Turkey must not fight Russia because it was too weak. This decision was communicated to the Sultan, and he was furious: he would not grant freedom or a government to Bulgaria, and he was quite able to fight Russia. Finally he refused flatly to accept the decision, and called a Turkish Congress to give their "opinion." Of course they gave what was wanted, and pronounced in favor of a war with Russia. A few were bold enough to disfavor it, and the Sultan punished them. One of these was Hagop Efendi Madteosian, the representative of the Protestant Armenian community. Another was a thoughtful, experienced Turk, and when the Sultan asked him his reason for opposing the war, he related the following parable:

" There was once a miser whom the king gave his choice of three things: to eat five pounds of raw onions without bread at one meal, to receive five hundred lashes on the bare back, or to pay $5,000. The miser could not bear to lose so much money; he could not endure such a flogging; and he chose to eat the onions. After eating a pound or so their bitterness and rankness nauseated him, and he concluded to take the whipping. He stood about a hundred lashes, and saw that he should die under it; and decided to pay the $5,000 after all." " Now," said the wise Turk, " this illustrates what I mean. If you go to war with Russia, you will sacrifice many thousands of soldiers, which is a very bitter thing to digest; then you will lose European Turkey, and finally you will have to pay millions of dollars indemnity and ruin the country. I cannot approve the war." The Sultan cried out in rage, " Begone, you old crank! I will not listen to any more foolish words from you. I shall conquer the Czar, enlarge the country, and strengthen my kingdom." He did go to war in 1876, was whipped by the Czar, and lost almost the whole of European Turkey and other parts of the empire, with 22,000,000 people: Roumania, Bulgaria, Servia, Bosnia, Herzegovina, part of Macedonia, part of Armenia, Cyprus, and afterwards Egypt. He lost many thousands of soldiers and millions of dollars, and besides has had to pay millions of dollars indemnity to Russia. And the Sultan is called an " able man " and " wise ruler " ! These things look like it.

After the war and the loss of the provinces, he encouraged the Mohammedan population of European

Turkey to emigrate to Asiatic Turkey, that they might not live under Christians, and that they might increase the number of Mohammedans in the Asiatic part. The slaughter of the Armenians and the confiscation of their property forms part of the scheme to make room for them. Before his time the Armenians in Armenia outnumbered the Turks; but the massacres, the occupation of the farms and houses by the savages let loose on them, and the emigration of many more Armenians to Persia and Russia, have greatly diminished their numbers. Of course they are not permitted to emigrate, they simply fly. About 200,000 have actually perished. As to the forced conversions, the Sultan does not care a particle for Islamism, but wants to please the Moslem and finds this an agreeable way to do it. As to the converts from Islamism to Christianity, they are ordered to go to Constantinople and are killed there. Hundreds and thousands of the Mohammedan Turks are Christians in secret, but do not dare to confess it. These are the ones who helped and protected the Armenians during the recent atrocities. Some six years ago a number of such professed the Christian religion publicly; they were at once ordered to go to Constantinople and every one of them was murdered by order of the Sultan. When the representatives of the Christian powers asked about them the Sultan denied that they had come there at all. This was the method of their assassination: The Sultan has several pleasure boats, and in one of these boats he fitted up an air-tight room with an air-pump; each night one of the converts was taken from prison and put into this room, the air was pumped out, and he was suffocated; then an iron chain was hooked round him, and he was thrown into the Bosphorus. One by one all of them were so murdered. How did the author of this book discover the secret ? Well, when in Constantinople, I had an intimate friend among the engineers; the engineer of this death boat told my friend about it, and he told me.

And the Sultan is not simply a murderer by proxy and official order; he is a murderer himself personally. When in Constantinople, I learned from several authoritative sources that he killed with his own revolver several of his servants, for no cause whatever, but merely from suspicion or rage. He always keeps a revolver in his pocket, and whomever in the palace he suspects, he shoots. He is a great coward. I heard there that he has more than 10,000 detectives, at a cost of several hundred thousand dollars a year. He lives in Yildiz Palace, about two miles from the Bosphorus, on a hill on the European shore; he has built new barracks, and keeps a large army around the palace to protect him from assassination. His " wisdom " is merely care for his skin. He cares nothing for the prosperity of the country; it is steadily growing poorer, while he is personally growing very rich. That is one reason why he keeps an Armenian treasurer, that the Turks may not know his secrets. Even the Turks are disgusted with him. I often used to hear the Turks say, " God deliver us from the Sultan

and send another master, even if he is the Czar of
Russia." His immense family costs him from $10,-
000,000 to $15,000,000 a year; it is the largest in the
world. I was told that it consists of 5,000 persons,
counting the eunuchs, the servants, and all. He has
about 500 wives; he did not marry them all; he inherited most of them. When a Sultan dies, his successor has everything that belonged to him, including
his wives. And besides, he has to marry a new wife
every year, by the Mohammedan and governmental
law; he has no choice in the matter. That makes
twenty wives in the twenty years of Abdul Hamid's
reign. This is the system: He has at present nearly
one hundred young girls in the harem, supposed to be
the most beautiful in the world; they are presented to
him by the governor-generals, who get them from the
local governors, who get their offices by sending their
superiors the finest looking girls, or the best Arabian
horses, and the governor-generals get theirs by passing the gifts on to the Sultan. That is the way to get
office in Turkey. You may be a murderer, a thief,
or an ignoramus, but you can be sure of an office
if you can furnish a handsome girl, or a fine stallion,
or a few thousand dollars. When I was pastor in
Marsovan, the local governor, Suddue Bey, bought a
very pretty girl, and sent her to the governor-general
of Beshick-Tash in Constantinople, Hadji Hassan
Pash, the Sultan's special guard; he had got his office
from that functionary. As to how the girls are got,
it depends; if they are Mohammedan, they are bought;

if they are Christian they are seized by force, for the Christians will not sell their daughters. Several months ago Bahri Pasha, the governor-general of Van, carried off several Armenian girls and presented them to the Sultan, who decorated him for the service, and appointed him Vali or governor-general of Adana, in Armenia Minor. These girls are kept in the harem of the Sultan. When the time comes to marry another wife, he has the girls stand in a row, and chooses one of them by covering her face with a silk handkerchief; then she is taken by the eunuchs to the quarters allotted to the Sultanas, and can have separate servants, carriages, and eunuchs. The life of the Sultan and his big family is the most miserable in the world. The palace is a focus of discontent, quarrels, jealousy, lust, and cruelty; in a word, it is a perfect hell. The women have nothing to do, and nothing to think of; they do not read, they have no work, and no share even in household management; they are idle, and unspeakably bored, and they do what most idle people of both sexes do all over the world — excite their nerves with sensual cravings, and then try to satisfy them. They often manage to bring boys to their quarters by stealth, and keep them there for weeks for purposes of lust, and the Sultan knows nothing about it; often they bribe their eunuchs, and go to other places to satisfy their desires, and the Sultan never hears of it. Aziz lost his life through an intrigue of one of his wives. With so large and exacting a family, it is no wonder the Sultan has no time or energy left for improving his administration. He only finds a little time to send telegrams to the governors to exterminate the Armenians.

THE SULTANATE AND ITS POWERS.

There is no coronation in Turkey; instead the Sultans gird on the sword of Osman, the founder of the Ottoman Dynasty, which is kept in the mosque of Ayoob, in Constantinople. When a Sultan is proclaimed, he goes to that mosque with great pomp, and all the members of the Sublime Porte, the civil officers, the generals, commanders, soldiers, patriarchs of different religions, and the Sheik-ul-Islam, the Mohammedan religious head, follow him. But no Christians enter that holy place, as it is forbidden them. After impressive service, the chief of the dervishes of the order of Mevlair girds the Sultan with the sword; then he is officially recognized as emperor. Then, as God's will be done, Sultan's will be done, because the Sultan represents God in heaven, Mohammed in Paradise, Osman on the earth. He has three offices, God's office, Mohammed's office, Osman's office. He is as infallible as the Pope of Rome, and temporally everything belongs to him without exception, men, women, children, money, property, just as everything belongs to God. A Turkish proverb says, "Mal, jan, erz, Padishahin dir" (Property, soul, and virtue belong to the Sultan). He can claim any man's wife for his enjoyment at any time; his son, or his daughter, or his money, or his property of any sort; there is no use refusing — a man does not own himself, or his wife, or his children; the Sultan owns them all, and it is only by his grace that he permits his subjects to have anything, and he can resume it at any time, for half an hour, or forever. Besides, anybody's head would come off that refused. If the Sultan asks a millionaire in Constantinople to send him half his wealth, the millionaire must not refuse; he himself is simply a steward; if the Sultan wants it all it must go to him, and the millionaire must beg bread for a living. At the same time he must praise the Sultan, because the Sultan is God on earth. If he refuses to send his wife or daughter to the Sultan's bed, or his son or money for whatever uses they are wanted to supply, the Sultan has a right to kill him, and take all his possessions by force, because the man was not a faithful slave.

"But I cannot believe this," says the American in his free, peaceful country. "It is not natural. How can a man be considered as God, owning everything, not in a spiritual sense, but in a very material, pecuniary, and male sense?"

Go to Turkey, get naturalized there, become a Turkish subject, and you will understand it fully, and perhaps shockingly. Of course, if you go as an American citizen, with plenty of money, travel under the escort of soldiers, or Zapties, get presented by the American minister to the Sultan, are entertained in the palace, and receive handsome presents, you will not understand it at all; very likely not believe it; you may come home and praise the Sultan like the rest.

The natural question is, I know, " Do the Sultans,
any of them, carry this theory into practice ?   Has
the present Sultan ? "   Yes; and not once or twice,
but thousands of times.   To be sure, they do not go in
person on such errands; they depute their officers and
soldiers to do what they wish.   I have shown how the
history of the Armenians illustrates it, in the
seizure of their property, the forced conversion
of their boys into troops to fight against their parents,
the appropriation of their wives and daughters, to be
given to the Sultan.   As to the present Sultan, I have
already spoken of Bahri Pasha's exploit in carrying off
by force several Armenian young brides, and girls,
and presenting them to the Sultan, and his being decorated and promoted for it.   While on his way, he
had to pass through Trebizond, and the Armenians
fired on him to rescue the women, but failed.   They
forgot that all women belong to the Sultan, and they
made a mistake in firing on one of his officers.   He
at once ordered all the Armenians in Trebizond to be
slaughtered.   Some of the richest of the nation lived
there; every penny was taken from them, most of
them were killed, and their wives and children,
and those of them who survived are begging bread.
And all through Armenia the girls and young brides
are being looked over to pick out the best looking ones
for the Sultan's harem.

Once for all, Armenia is not America. The
Turks, the Kurds, the Circassians, the Georgians,
though they may be like Americans, are like

American Indians only. The Sultan is not a president, and his divine right to kill any man, appropriate any property, or enjoy any woman, is not like the Constitution of the United States. People who think that the Sultan would not do or be allowed to do such things because no ruler they are familiar with does them, that it is impossible they can happen in Armenia because they could not happen in America, that the Armenians must have provoked them in some way, because it is hard to believe any ruler could do so in pure wantonness or from deliberate policy, are reasoning from wrong premises. They did happen, and are happening,— see the consular reports; were perfectly unprovoked,— see the plentiful proofs that the Armenians carry no arms, and cannot even defend themselves from murder, or their wives from dishonor before their eyes. Why it is done, and how much more is to be done, I have explained repeatedly.

THE SUBLIME PORTE AND THE MOHAMMEDAN RELIGION.

The Sublime Porte, or in Turkish Babi-Ali, is the cabinet of the Turkish government, as follows:—

1. The Grand Vezir, or Prime Minister.
2. The Minister of the Interior.
3. The Minister of Foreign Affairs.
4. The Superintendent of the Cabinet Council.
5. The Commander-in-chief, or Minister of War.
6. The Minister of the Navy.
7. The Minister of Finance.

11

8. The Minister of Commerce and Public Buildings.
9. The Minister of Sacred Properties.
10. The Minister of Education.
11. The Sheik-ul-Islam, or religious head.

There is no election in Turkey; all officers are appointed by the Sultan, who can dismiss any of them at any time, and appoint some one else, and I have already explained why he almost always appoints bad ones. The Sublime Porte has no power to decide anything; it is simply a farce council to cheat the European powers; a dumb tool in the hands of the Sultan. For instance, the Sultan calls the Grand Vezir, the president of the Sublime Porte, into his presence, and tells him such a question is to be discussed in such a way, and this or that conclusion reached. " Very well, my Lord and Master," says the Grand Vezir; he goes to the Sublime Porte palace, and says to the council: " To-day I was permitted to come into the presence of His Majesty the Sultan, and he instructed me that I must bring such a question before you, and after we discuss it in such a manner, we must come to such a decision." Then all of them stand up and say, " Sultan's will be done," and that is all; their " decision " is announced to the Sultan, and he " sanctions " it. There is no discussion for days or weeks, as in England or here; it is all cut short. The Sublime Porte can decide any question in a few minutes. This is the sort of thing Mr. Carlyle wanted. You have seen the beautiful effects of it.

The question naturally arises, Why does the Sultan keep a Sublime Porte, since he decides everything himself?

There are three reasons.

First, it is the old custom.   All the other Sultans have had one, and he might offend the Turks if he abolished it.

Second, as the Sultan can do no wrong, there must be somebody else to lay blame on.   He is the representative of God and Prophet Mohammed.   If there is any mistake in any decision, he is not responsible for it; the Sublime Porte is responsible.

Third, because he has relations with the European powers, and if any decision needs to be reversed, it can be if it is that of the Sublime Porte; but if it were the personal decision of the Sultan it could not be changed, because he is considered immutable, just as God is.

When people read about the Sublime Porte after this, I hope they will understand that there is not really any Sublime Porte; that it is a mere name, an echo, a farce, a show to bunco the world with.

Some newspaper and other writers think it is " impartial " to say that the Sultan means well, but he has a " corrupt ministry "; that it is the Sublime Porte that ruins the Turkish Empire; if it were left to the Sultan, he would reform the country; he would not let the Armenians be massacred.   Put no faith in such ignorant rubbish.   The Sultan dictates everything; and if any minister has the sense and courage to suggest any improvement, the Sultan dismisses him, say-

ing that it is his own business to consider the improvements of the country and not that of any one else. The
governors would not dare to order the Kurds and the
Turks to wreak their worst and vilest will on the Armenians without direct orders from the Sultan. The
Sultan originates all these cruelties. The recent
Grand Vezir, Said Pasha, at one time was a very
decent Turk. When he differed with the Sultan
about massacreing the Armenians, the Sultan threatened to kill him, and he had to fly to the English
embassy for protection. Murad Bey was another
good Turk who remonstrated against the cruelties; his
life was threatened, and he fled to Europe; now he is
in Egypt, denouncing the Sultan in the press and in
letters. The Sultan sentenced him to death, and
asked the British government to hand him over to
the Turkish officers; but the representative of the British government in Cairo refused. Just before the
Armenian atrocities in Constantinople, the members
of the Sublime Porte tried to have the Armenian
grievances redressed, and the people pacified; the Sultan would have no such pottering, and ordered the soldiers to kill the Armenians in the streets. But this
was a rare piece of virtue in the Porte. Mostly they
are as bad as the Sultan himself, for he appoints men
of his own stripe. Good men would not be useful
tools. The Sultan has another trick of management;
before making any one a member of the Porte, he
tries to find out whether he is a friend to any of the
ministers already in; if so, he will not appoint him.

On the other hand, if the man happens to be an enemy to one of the members, he is almost sure of appointment. The Sublime Porte, therefore, is a group of mutual enemies, hating one another, and ready to betray one another at any time. He thinks if they are friendly, they may unite and depose him some day. Besides this, there are more detectives in the Sublime Porte, watching the ministers on behalf of the Sultan, than there are members. They keep the Sultan informed about the situation. If any minister or officer acts contrary to the wishes of the Sultan, he is marked for death.

THE SHEIK-UL-ISLAM.

Sheik-ul-Islam means chief of Islam — the Mohammedan religion. His office is solely religious; he has nothing to do with politics. He sees that the mosques and priests are kept in order, and the religious services properly conducted; and there are many questions among the Mohammedans which are settled without going to a magistrate, by the Sheik-ul-Islam, or by his deputies, called Muftees. These Muftees can be found in every city in Turkey. The Sheik-ul-Islam and his representatives issue Fetvas (religious decrees) according to the Koran.

There is no inconsistency between this and what I have said before about the Sultan being the representative of Mohammed, and therefore the chief of his religion. Both the Sultan and the Sheik-ul-Islam are the heads of it, just as the Greek emperor and the Patriarch were of the Greek church, and the relative position is about the same. The Sheik-ul-Islam is the special head of the ecclesiastical organization. The Sultan appoints him, but once appointed, if he is insubordinate and opposes the Sultan, the latter cannot suppress or replace him without grave scandal to the Mohammedan world. It is like Henry II and Becket; it is easier to make a head of a church than to rule him afterwards. It is like the Emperors and the Popes in the Middle Ages; and as with them, sometimes the Sheik-ul-Islam joins with political officers to depose the Sultan, and his fetva, or decree, makes it legal. When Abdul Aziz was deposed, the then Sheik-ul-Islam, Khairollah Effendi, issued the fetva for it, reluctantly, for Heussein Avni Pasha forced him to do it under threat of death. As Heussein's own head was in immediate peril, he had no scruples about the Sheik-ul-Islam's. Every fetva has two questions and one answer. A case is set forth; after a brief discussion the question Olourni (To be ?) and Olmazmi (Not to be ?) are asked, and the answer is given as either Olour or Olmaz (To be, or Not to be). The fetva which Heussein forced the Sheik-ul-Islam to sign was something like this:— "If a Sultan should prove to be unworthy to govern his people, is it necessary to uphold him or not ?" The answer was Olmaz, and Abdul Aziz was deposed.

MOHAMMEDANISM AND THE INTERNAL STATE OF TURKEY.

Nobody who has not lived in Turkey can realize how hopeless, almost self-contradictory, it is to talk

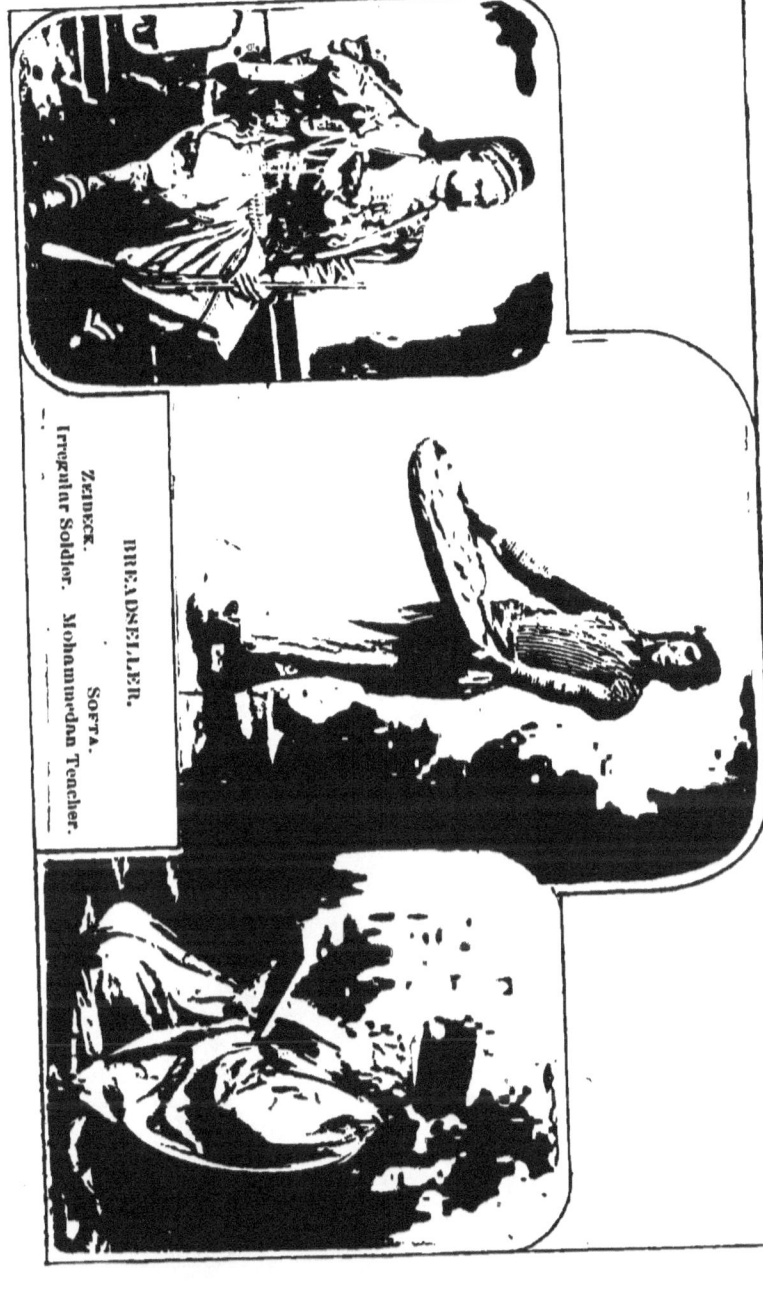

BREADSELLER.

ZEIBECK.
Irregular Soldier.

SOFTA.
Mohammedan Teacher.

of " reforming " Turkey. It could not be reformed and be Mohammedan Turkey; the lack of reform or power of reform is just what makes it what it is. The root of the evil is Mohammedanism itself; it is embodied social stagnation, corruption, ultimate ruin. Neither the Sultan nor the Turks can improve the state of the Empire, even if they wished. The usual " broad-minded " statements about Mohammed and his religion are simply elaborations of ignorance, made up out of men's own minds, and what they think must be true. It is customary for writers to talk in this fashion:— " Mohammedanism is a half-way house to Christianity; Mohammed converted the heathen Arabs to a belief in the true God. Mohammed established a great religion and a great Empire," etc., etc. There is no truth in this, for all its plausible sound. Mohammedanism is not even on the road to Christianity; and Arabia, Asia Minor, and Palestine were all much better off before the Mohammedan conquest than after it. Buddhism and Brahmanism are better religions than Mohammedanism. The Chinese, the Japanese, the people of India are much better than the Turks. The Chinese Emperor and the Japanese Mikado are far better men than the Mohammedan Sultan. The heathen religions rear better men than Mohammedanism. The Mongols are more humane and sympathetic than the Turks. Heathenism at its worst, though a low form of religion, is really a form of religion; but Mohammedanism is not a religion at all. Then what is it ? It is a system of imposture and false pretense, and of lives of human lust and cruelty. Mohammed practiced all these, and his successors have done the same, and taught the same ever since; and the system means just that now, and nothing else. There is neither love nor sympathy, manliness nor humanity in Mohammedanism. Can a system lacking all these be considered a religion? This is the substance of Mohammed's teachings:— " Love your fellow believers, hate and slay all who refuse to accept your religion. Marry as many wives as you can afford; if you can afford but one do not repine, for you shall have seven thousand to enjoy in Paradise. If you conquer a country, show no mercy to the people unless they embrace Islam; if they refuse, either kill them or make slaves of them." What sort of reforms can you expect in Armenia, or in Turkey, when the very religion that is to make people better, inculcates such principles ? If one does not know a language he cannot speak it; if he has not a principle he will not practice it; how can the Sultan, a vicious man to begin with, trained in a religion calculated to make a cruel and licentious animal even out of a decent man, reform anything ? His very religion forbids it; he cares nothing for the religion when it stands in his way, but he will follow its injunctions to please the Mohammedans, especially when they gratify and justify his worst passions.

I shall be asked if the Mohammedans do not believe in one God, and the same God as the Christian; and if that does not make it a religion, and very near

that of Christians.   Yes, they do; and so do the devils.
That is what Mohammedanism is, the religion of
devils.   Most of the Turkish conversation consists of
oaths and smut.   I do not mean among the common
people — theirs is nothing else — but of the educated
upper classes, their scholars, teachers, governors, and
priests.   I came in contact with them for years, and
I hated to listen to them, their talk was so full of cursing and filth.   You never see the fruits of the spirit
in them; only the fruits of the flesh.   They do not
understand what spiritual life is; with them all is sense,
— eating and drinking, finery and lust,— lust above
all, everywhere and always, like cattle.   They seem
never able to forget sex and its uses.   Some people
think the climate makes the Turks lazy; it is
enough on that point to say that Constantinople is
almost exactly in the same latitude as New York, and
Smyrna as St. Louis.   The Turkish climate is a temperate and salubrious one, with no greater extremes of
temperature than the United States; not tropical or
enervating.   Nor is it their race that makes the Turks
lazy; they were not so at the outset.   It is their religion and the habits it breeds.   Their minds and
bodies are enervated by the unwholesome nervous
excitation of lust, their energies further sapped by a
falsehood that leaves no room for aspiration, their
vanity as a military caste in not working takes all the
spirit of manly enterprise out of them.   If the climate enervates the Turks, why does it not the Christians ?   In the very same cities you find the Chris-

tians rich, enterprising, full of energy; the Turks poor, ignorant, unambitious, and lazy. The religion makes all the difference. Christianity teaches purity, sympathy, and industry; Mohammedanism teaches impurity, hate, and sloth. The pure life of the Christian conserves all the energies; the hopes of Christianity give vigor and endurance. The promise of each for the future gives the clue to the history of each; the Christian heaven of unity with God, the Mohammedan heaven of a lot of street dogs and sluts.

Here I must comment on the extraordinary statement of Alexander Webb, at the Parliament of. Religions in Chicago. Mr. Webb was an American consul in the East, and became a convert to Mohammedanism, or professes to have done so; it is not very hard to guess what part of that so-called religion attracted him. He said the religion of Mohammed teaches the Fatherhood of God, and the Brotherhood of Humanity. Now, as a fact, Mohammedans believe in neither one. As to God, they believe he is a monarch, and that no one can approach him; they have the same idea the Jews had. " Our Father who art in Heaven " is a purely Christian aspiration, not that of any other religion on earth; it is Christianity alone that teaches the Fatherhood of God. And Mohammedans directly ridicule the idea of God the Father, or of a Son of God. They say God is not married, and cannot be a father; and that when they go to heaven they will not be in his presence, nor wish to be, but will have a separate heaven, to enjoy their wives in. They look at everything from a sexual or sensual stand-point. As to brotherhood, there is no such thing in Mohammedanism; even sons of the same mother are not brothers in feeling. A Mohammedan has not confidence enough, even in his brother, to show his wives to him, and even in heaven they will have to live in different places on account of their wives. How can there be brotherhood without love or purity ? And we have seen and know what the " brotherhood " of Mohammedans to other nations and religions is; there can be no relations whatever but of master and slave, or murderer and corpse, or violator and victim. The impudence of this talk of brotherhood is fathomless.

And then he said he was proud to be a convert to Islam, because that meant believing in purity ! This is more outrageously impudent still. His ideal of purity must be a curious one if he finds more in Mohammedanism than in Christianity; in a religion with a heaven stuffed with concubines than in one where even earth is sprinkled with nuns; in one that makes Titanic lust its crowning reward, as if men were so feeble in sexual desires that they needed to be stimulated, than in one which makes chastity its key-note, and pronounces the very coveting of more than one wife a spiritual adultery; in one that prescribes polygamy (that is, keeping erotic turbulence stirred up much oftener and longer than it naturally would be), than in one that allows but one wife, and smiles on getting along without that; in one whose devotees are ashamed of foul language, and even of foul thoughts, than in one whose devotees are rank and rotten with lustful ideas and talk to correspond.

The whole Mohammedan system is designed to make the gratification of lust as easy and plentiful as possible short of a promiscuity that would lead to civil anarchy. A Mohammedan can divorce his wife any time he pleases by paying back her dower, and marry another and do likewise; every week, or day if he sees fit, and he can remarry and redivorce the first one as often as he pleases. It is like trading horses; as little sentiment or morality in one as the other; the slightest possible regulation of sheer animal desire. There is, however, one form or divorce which is complete, and does not allow of remarriage until another marriage has intervened; that is called the achden docuza (three to nine) divorce, from the terms the husband uses in doing it, "I divorce you three to nine." Nobody knows what it means or meant. After this, if he wants his wife back, he must get somebody else to marry and divorce her regularly; and as this is perilous, because the second husband after marrying her may take a notion to keep her, or anyway keep her much longer than the first one relishes, or demand a large sum of money, the usual plan is to fix on a very poor man, or a blind beggar (preferably blind, so that he cannot see the wife, and be so charmed by her beauties that he will wish to keep her), get him to become the woman's husband for a few days, and then pay him something to divorce her. Then the first can marry her again if he chooses.

There are many more specimens of Mohammedan " purity " too shameful to write, and too shameful to read; I cannot soil the paper with them. Doubtless they are part of Mr. Webb's pride in being a Mohammedan. But I must mention one more engine of corruption which lies at the very root of Mohammedanism itself: the pilgrimage to Mecca, to the birthplace of Mohammed in Arabia. Once a year Mohammedan pilgrims from every quarter of the world go to Mecca to pay homage to their beloved prophet; averaging a million a year. It is their duty to sacrifice animals there, and about a million are so sacrificed. This is done on the hills which surround the great temple, the greatest mosque in the world. It is a square building, which covers several acres of land. Just in the cluster is the Holy Well, called Zemzem. Mohammedans believe that if they drink of that water, hell-fire cannot burn them, and every pilgrim does so; then they begin to die from cholera to the tune of fifty thousand a year or so, for the well is a mere cesspool. You see, after cutting the throats of the animals, they leave the filth and blood just as they are, for the Mohammedan religion does not allow the sacrifice to be touched. The sandy soil absorbs this putrid filth, which leaches into the well. But it is a great merit to die on the spot where Mohammed was born; one goes straight to heaven if he does. That is not the worst, however; they fill bottles with that water, and carry it to their families, and friends throughout the Turkish Empire, Persia, and India, from which cholera is spread abroad over the world.

The pilgrims do not take their wives as far as the birthplace of Mohammed, but leave them half-way, and on reaching Mecca they marry temporarily. About 20,000 prostitutes there make a business of being short-term wives of the pilgrims, getting $5 to $25 from each, and being his wife for anywhere from a day to a fortnight, so that each woman marries from fifty to a hundred pilgrims a year. This is not prostitution; it is religion — and Mohammedan " purity." Mecca is considered the most holy spot on earth by Mohammedans; but it is the most corrupt spot. It is a hell. And the Mohammedan Paradise is worse than Mecca.

In one word, Mohammedans have no right to exist, politically, socially, or religiously. In the first they have wrought nothing but ruin; in the second nothing but corruption; in the third nothing but devilishness. They are working nothing else now in either of the three. They have never built up anything; they are pure destroyers. Anything which is built in any Mohammedan country is built both by Christian money and by Christian architects; Mohammedans have neither the money, the architects, nor the sense. The day one becomes a Mohammedan he loses his intellect, his skill, and his common sense. Mohammedanism is a poison fatal to any good gifts or graces; it cultivates in him falsehood, cruelty, and lust. It was sent by God for a curse to the Christians; as a punishment, just as the Philistines were sent to the people of Israel.

V.

THE GREAT POWERS AND THE ARMENIAN QUESTION.

There was no Armenian question till the time of the present Sultan; under Abdul Aziz, whatever his faults as a ruler or a man, the Armenians prospered well, and though the whole system of administration is bad, corrupt, and uncertain, they had no special grievance as a race to complain of. I have already referred to Abdul Hamid's usurpation, his Bulgarian atrocities, his famous war against Russia, and the Congress in Berlin in which the powers ordered him to execute reforms in Armenia, and report to them, and the Sultan signed the treaty promising to do it. This was in 1878. The Sultan lost no time in violating the treaty, and not only so, but in acting grossly contrary to it. He called in Circassians and Kurds to settle in the midst of Armenians, and confiscated Armenian lands for them to settle on. The Armenians were far worse off than before the treaty; but foolishly depending on the powers, they did not try to arm themselves for the future. They have had plenty of chance to repent in blood and tears, agony and shame, their faith that Christian nations would not ignore a solemn obligation, voluntarily entered into, to save a whole people from being exterminated by fire and sword. England was the worst of these sinners, for she had taken on special obligations by a separate treaty, and forced those who would have taken the Sultan by the throat to let go.

THE ANGLO-TURKISH CONVENTION.

This took place at the same time as the Berlin Congress; it was simply between Turkey and England.

Article I. "If Batoum, Ardahan, Kars, or any of them shall be retained by Russia, and if any attempt shall be made at any future time by Russia to take possession of any further territory of His Imperial Majesty, the Sultan, in Asia, as fixed by the Definitive Treaty of Peace, England engages to join His Imperial Majesty, the Sultan, in defending them by force of arms.

"In return, His Imperial Majesty, the Sultan, promises England to introduce necessary reforms, to be agreed upon later between the two powers, into the government and for the protection of the Christian and other subjects of the Porte in these territories; and in order to enable England to make necessary provisions for executing her engagement, His Imperial Majesty, the Sultan, further consents to assign the Island of Cyprus to be occupied and administered by England.

Article VII. "If Russia restores to Turkey Kars and the other conquests made by her in Armenia during the last war, the Island of Cyprus will be evacuated by England, and the convention of the 4th of June, 1878, will be at an end." ·

When England was preparing this private treaty, the English fleet was on the Sea of Marmora, at the gate of the Bosphorus, threatening Russia, to make her withdraw her soldiers from the gates of Constanti-

nople, for the conquering Russian army had reached
the suburbs, and encamped at San Stefano, only eight
or ten miles away.   But for England, Russia would
have captured Constantinople, and kept it.   But England backed Turkey, and the other powers backed
England, and Russia reluctantly withdrew her troops.
But Russia has never forgiven England for it; and if
England wishes to help the Armenians, no matter
how many are massacred, Russia will help Turkey,
while the others side with neither.   As to there ever
being a European concert to reform Armenia, a pleasant dream which has deluded many thousands, I have
always laughed at it, and I laugh at it still.   The
powers will never act together for any such purpose.
It is not " practical politics " to think of it.   The real
center of action is not Germany or Russia, but England, for several reasons.   One is that London is the
money capital of the world.   Money rules; money
buys force.   The richest nation is the strongest.
What does Lombard street say ? is the vital question.
The second is her navy, the strongest in the world;
stronger that that of any other two nations combined;
perhaps in actual fight a match for all combined.   The
third is that her possessions are everywhere; she is a
local power in every quarter of the globe; she has to
pass by everybody's doors in managing her colonies.
So I will begin with England.

ENGLAND AND THE ARMENIAN QUESTION.

If England had wished to solve this question, she
could have done it long ago; but she never cared to.

12

When Mr. Gladstone was in power, he tried to do it, but his Cabinet overbore him. He did, however, show by isolated cases what power England had if she chose to exercise it. After I was banished by the Turkish government, two native Christian ministers supplied my pulpit. They were sentenced to death on a false charge, but Gladstone threatened the Sultan, and the latter commuted the sentence to banishment. These ministers were Professors Thoumaian and Kayayian, who are now in England with their families. What could be done on a small scale could be done on a large one. I will give here some of the speeches of Gladstone on the Armenian question; then compare Lord Salisbury with him and his policy.

W. E. GLADSTONE.

He assails Turkey's Intolerable Misgovernment and Emphasizes the Value of Impartial American Testimony.

[By Cable to The New York Herald.]

London, Aug. 6, 1895.—A pro-American meeting, presided over by the Duke of Westminster, was held at Chester this afternoon. Mr. Gladstone was among those present, and upon entering the hall was received with great enthusiasm.

In addressing the meeting, Mr. Gladstone said he had attended rather to meet the expectation that he would be present than because he had any important contribution to make to the discussion of the subject under consideration. The question before the meeting, he said, was not a party question, neither was it strictly a religious question, although the sufferers, on whose behalf the meeting was called, were Christians.

The evil arose from the fact that the sufferers were under an intolerably bad government — one of the worst, in fact, that ever existed.   A resolution would be proposed presenting, with justice and firmness, the true view of the matter.   Mr. Gladstone added that as America had no political interest in the Levant her witnesses were doubly entitled to credit.

Important Treaty Provisions.

The treaty of 1856, Mr. Gladstone continued, gave the powers the right to march into Armenia and take the government of the country out of the hands of Turkey, and under the treaty of 1878 the Sultan was bound to carry out reforms.   The ex-Premier made three proposals:— First, that the demands of the powers should be moderate; second, that no promises of the Turkish authorities should be accepted; and third, that the powers should not fear the word " coercion."

" We have reached a critical position," said Mr. Gladstone, in conclusion, " and the honor of the powers is pledged to the institution of reforms in Armenia."

A resolution was then proposed expressing the conviction that the government would have the support of the entire nation in any measures it might adopt to secure in Armenia reforms guaranteeing to the inhabitants safety of life, honor, religion, and property, and that no reforms can be effected which are not placed under the continuous control of the great powers of Europe.   The resolution was seconded by the Rev. Canon Malcolm MacColl, and was adopted.

Says Baseness and Villany Have Reached a Climax in Turkey's Treatment of Armenia.

[From The New York Herald.]

London, Dec. 27, 1895.—Murad Bey, formerly Ottoman Commissioner of the Turkish debt, who recently fled from Constantinople to Paris, sent to Mr. Gladstone a few days ago a pamphlet which he had published in Paris, entitled " The Yildiz Palace and the Sublime Porte," with a view to enlightening public opinion on Turkish affairs. In the course of his reply acknowledging the receipt of the pamphlet, Mr. Gladstone disavowed any feeling of enmity toward the Turks and Mussulmans generally. He said:—"I have felt it my duty to make it known that the Mohammedans, including the Turks, suffer from the bad government of the Sultan. I have heartily wished success to every effort made toward ending the great evil. Still, Turks and other Mohammedans are not, so far as I know, plundered, raped, murdered, starved, and burned; but this is the treatment that the Sultan knowingly deals out to his Armenian subjects daily. There are degrees of suffering, degrees of baseness and villany among men, and both seem to have reached their climax in the case of Armenia."

His Masterly Speech in Chester Re-enforced with a letter to a Turk.

[From The New York Sun.]

London, Aug. 10.—Once more have the wonderful power and the true greatness of England's Grand Old Man been demonstrated in the remarkable revival of popular interest in the fate of Armenia. The whole nation is marveling over his great speech at Chester, and there are no words, even among those who have always been his political opponents, save those of sympathy and admiration. Nobody is any longer foolish enough to deny the main features of the fearful atrocities in Armenia, and there is no possible doubt of the accuracy of the latest reports that thousands near the scene of the massacres are perishing of starvation.

The only protest against Mr. Gladstone's speech has been a long letter from Khalef Khalid, a conspicuous Turk, who asks the Grand Old Man why he hates and denounces the Turks so indiscriminately, when as many and as great outrages against the Mohammedans have been perpetrated by Christians as were ever committed by the subjects of Islam.

Mr. Gladstone's reply was made public to-day. It is one of the most pointed epistles the old man ever wrote. He says:— " I entirely disclaim the hatred and hostility to the Turks, or any race of men, which you ascribe to me. I do not doubt that you write in entire good faith, but your statements of facts are unauthenticated. I proceed only upon authenticated statements. I make no charge against the Turks at large, but against a Turkish government. I make the charges which they have been proved guilty of by public authority. In my opinion, I have been a far better friend to the Ottoman Empire than have the Sultan and his advisers. I have always recommended the granting of reasonable powers of local self-government, which would have saved Turkey from terrible losses. This good advice has been spurned, and in consequence Turkey has lost 18,000,000 of people, and may lose more. Pray weigh these words."—

The birthday of the Ex-Premier was made the occasion for an anti-Turkish demonstration.

Outrages and Abominations of 1876 in Bulgaria Repeated in Armenia in 1894.

[From The New York Herald.]

London, Dec. 29, 1894.—Mr. Gladstone celebrated his eighty-fifth birthday to-day, and was the recipient of hundreds of letters and telegrams of congratulation and parcels containing birthday gifts. Mr. Gladstone was in remarkably good health and spirits, and, despite the stormy weather, drove through the village of Hawarden to the church, where he met a deputation of Armenian Christians from Paris and London. The deputation presented a silver chalice to the church. The chalice was presented to the Rev. Stephen Gladstone, son of the ex-Premier, and rector of the Hawarden church, in recognition of the interest his father has taken in the Armenian outrages. Mr. Gladstone, in his reply to the deputation's address, said that it was not their duty to assume that all the allegations of outrages were true, but rather to await the result of the inquiry which had been instituted. However, he said, the published accounts pointed strongly to the conclusion that the outrages, sins, and abominations committed in 1876 in Bulgaria had been repeated in 1894 in Armenia. Continuing, Mr. Gladstone said: "Don't let me be told that one nation has no authority over another. Every nation, aye, every human being, has authority in behalf of humanity and justice." He had been silent, he said, because he had full confidence that the government knew its duty. If the allegations made should prove to be true, it was time that the execration of humanity should force itself upon the ears of the Sultan of Turkey, and make him sensible of the madness of such a course as was being pursued. Mr. Gladstone, in conclusion, said:—"The history of Turkey is a sad and painful one. The Turkish race has not been without remarkable, even fine qualities, but from too many points of view it has been a scourge which has been made use of by a wise Providence for the sins of the world.   If these tales of murder, violation, and outrage be true, well, then, they cannot be overlooked, nor can they be made light of.   I have lived to see the Empire of Turkey in Europe reduced to less than one-half of what it was when I was born. And why ?   Simply because of its misdeeds, and the great record written by the hand of Almighty God against its injustice, lust, and most abominable cruelty. I hope and feel sure that the government of Great Britain will do everything that can be done to pierce to the bottom of this mystery, and make the facts known to the world.

"If happily (I speak hoping against hope) the reports be disproved or mitigated, let us thank God.   If, on the other hand, they be established, it will more than ever stand before the world that there is a lesson, however severe it may be, that can teach certain people the duty of prudence, and the necessity of observing the laws of decency, humanity, and justice.   If the allegations are true, it is time that there should be one general shout of execration against these deeds of wickedness from outraged humanity.   If the facts are well established, it should be written in letters of iron upon the records of the world that a government which could be guilty of countenancing and covering up such atrocities is a disgrace to Mohammed the prophet, a disgrace to civilization at large, and a disgrace to mankind.   Now that is strong language, but strong language ought to be used when the facts are strong. But strong language ought not to be used without the strength of facts.

"I have counseled you to be still and keep your judgment in suspense; but as the evidence grows, the case darkens, and my hopes dwindle and decline, and as long as I have voice it will be uttered in behalf of humanity and truth. I wish you heartily every blessing, and also wish with every heartiness prosperity to your nation, however dark the present may seem."

LORD SALISBURY.

Now we come to the present Prime Minister, Lord Salisbury. He is reputed a great statesman. That should mean that he has accomplished something great. Well, what ? I know of nothing, have heard of nothing. Has he saved any country ? Has he elevated any ? Has he done any public action that can be set down to his credit ? He has hindered some good ones, that is all. On the Armenian question he has done enormous harm. If he is not a great hypocrite, there is no use comparing a man's words with his actions. I have always told my friends that nothing good could be hoped for from him, for morally he is worse than the Sultan. An eminent English clergyman told me that Lord Salisbury is another Sultan, and I believe him. Here are a few of Lord Salisbury's deliverances; see how they agree:—

[From The New York World, August 16, 1895.]

Lord Salisbury to Sir Philip Currie, the British Ambassador to Constantinople:— "The Porte must accept the proposals of the Powers unconditionally, or England would use sharper means than those adopted by Lord Rosebery to settle affairs in Armenia."— [July 30, 1895.

Lord Salisbury, in a speech in London about the time of the above, said, "The concert of Europe on the Armenian question is complete, and England has the loyal support of other powers to reform Armenia."

At another time we note:— "There is every reason to believe that the Chinese government is sincerely desirous of punishing the perpetrators of the outrages and those who connived at them. Should any lukewarmness become discernible, it will become our duty to supply its defect.

"With respect to Armenia, we have accepted the policy which our predecessors initiated, and our efforts will be directed to obtaining an adequate guarantee for the carrying out of reform. We have received the most loyal support from both France and Russia. The permanence of the Sultan's rule is involved in the conduct he pursues. If the cries of misery continue, the Sultan must realize that Europe will become weary of appeals, and the fictitious strength which the powers have given the empire will fail it. The Sultan will make a calamitous mistake if he refuses to accept the advice of the European powers relative to the reforms." The House of Lords adopted the address in reply to the Queen's speech.

After the above strong words, Lord Salisbury backed down and sneaked out of his bold attitude in this way. (Jan. 31, 1896.) See how he asserts, first that England cannot do anything for the Armenians, and second that it is not her duty to do anything:—

[From The New York Tribune.]

"The Prime Minister expressed sympathy with the Armenians, but denied that Great Britain was under obligation to declare war against the Sultan of Turkey in order to compel him to govern justly, and cited the treaties in proof of his contention. He ascribed the atrocities to the passions of race and creed.

He believed that the Sultan's government was wretched and impotent, but there was no ground for imagining that the Sultan had instigated the massacres. It might be asked why Europe did not interfere. He could only answer for England. She had lacked the power to do the only thing necessary to end the troubles, namely, to militarily occupy Turkish provinces. None of the powers wished so to occupy them.

"Lord Salisbury said he concurred in the belief that the only authority, albeit it was an evil one, in that country was the prestige of the Sultan's name. Patience must be exercised, and time must be given to His Majesty to enforce the reforms he had promised. He remarked upon the gradual return of order in Anatolia during the last few weeks, although he admitted that these signs should not be trusted too much. He concluded by declaring that if Great Britain did not co-operate with the other powers, she must act against them, which would lead to calamities far more awful than the Armenian massacres."

Ambassador Currie instructed not to exert Undue Pressure on the Sultan.

[From The New York World, 1895.]

London, Nov. 23, 1895.—It can be authoritatively stated that Lord Salisbury's instructions to Sir Philip Currie, the British Ambassador to Turkey, who left England a few days ago on his return to his post of duty, are to refrain from exerting undue pressure on the Sultan for the execution of the reforms in Armenia, and to give the Porte time to recover from the existing administrative anarchy, and appoint authorities through whom the reforms must be effected.

Sir Philip has taken with him an autograph letter from the Queen to the Sultan. This is supposed to be a reply to a letter the Sultan sent to her with the communication he sent to Lord Salisbury, which the latter read at the meeting of the National Union of Conservatives at Brighton, on Tuesday night last.

It is reported that the Queen will invite the Sultan to visit England, when the time shall be auspicious. The anxiety at the Foreign Office in regard to the East has greatly lessened during the week.

England possessed the Island of Cyprus, and it became her duty to look after the reforms in Turkey. But now Salisbury denies it, saying that it is not her duty, and meantime says that time must be given to the Sultan of Turkey; as if all the time had not been given him since the Berlin treaty of 1878.

Salisbury used another silly trick, persuading the Queen of England to write a letter to the Sultan and appeal to his good nature; as if the Sultan had a good nature; but the Queen wrote the letter.

A strong criticism by the editor of the New York "Press" on Lord Salisbury's speech.

February 3, 1896.

" We confess that we are at a loss to comprehend the meaning of Lord Salisbury's Armenian speech. We do not know what to make of it when he says that the Berlin Treaty " bound the signatory powers, that, if the Sultan promulgated certain reforms, they would watch over the progress of these reforms. Nothing more." We cannot understand him when he declares that the Cyprus Convention ' contains no trace of an understanding to interfere in behalf of the Sultan's subjects.' When Russia made, in March, 1878, a treaty with Turkey, called the treaty of San Stefano, Great Britain became alarmed lest Russia should se-

cure too much influence in Constantinople. Russia
then held some Armenian provinces bordering on her
territory, and it seemed clear that it was her purpose to
seize others. England protested to the Sultan against
the treaty of San Stefano, but the government of the
Ottoman Porte was helpless against the Czar, and the
Sultan declared that he must adhere to the treaty.
Great Britain then secretly bound herself to aid Turkey by force of arms in preventing Russia from ap-
propriating further Armenian provinces, Turkey
agreeing, on her part, to reform her local administration in her remaining Armenian provinces and as-
signing the island of Cyprus to be occupied and administered by Great Britain.

"Great Britain, meanwhile, had incited the other
powers of Europe to take action against the treaty of
San Stefano. Austria was induced to suggest a European Congress. Russia at first refused to go into this
Congress; but, seeing that all the great powers were
uniting against her, she consented to attend. The result of this Congress was the Treaty of Berlin, signed
by the six powers,— England, Russia, Germany,
France, Austria, and Italy. By this treaty Turkey
was stripped of Bulgaria, Servia, and Roumania, and
Russia was deprived of all she had won during
the Turko-Russian war, except the Armenian provinces which she still controls. By this treaty, also,
the signatory powers became guardians and trustees of
the Ottoman Porte, pledging themselves that religious
freedom should be secured in the Turkish Empire, and
that Armenian Christians should be protected against
the Circassians and Kurds.

"We are puzzled, therefore, to understand Lord
Salisbury when he says that all these promises did not
mean anything. Certainly he ought to know, for, as
the agent of the Disraeli government, it was Lord

Salisbury who drafted the agreements and drew up the promises. For eighteen years Christian civilization has supposed that they did mean something. But Lord Salisbury says not. He says that all the powers agreed to do was to ' watch over the execution of those reforms ' if they were promulgated.

"What does that mean, anyway ? Does it mean, as the Christian world has all along supposed, that the six powers would engage themselves to see that these reforms were carried out by Turkey, or does it mean that if the reforms were carried out they would simply look on; and if the reforms were not carried out, if ten thousand Armenian homes were destroyed, and four times ten thousand Armenian citizens were butchered, they would still simply look on ?

"Nor do we understand Lord Salisbury when he pleads that it requires time for the Turkish government to carry out the reforms ' which the Sultan recently has accepted.' Why the Turkish government ? There is no Turkish government. There is a Mohammedan administration, but the government of the Ottoman Porte expired with the Treaty of Berlin. The Turkish government is vested de facto in the six signatory powers of the Berlin Congress. Even the local government of Constantinople itself lies in the hands of these powers. The capital is divided into six sections, each controlled by a treaty power. Each has its own courts, its own military, even its own police. When Englishmen wish a wrong to be righted in the Turkish Empire, or a reform to be executed, they do not request the ' Turkish government ' to listen to their appeal. The British Minister summons the Grand Vezir and orders him to do what is wished. And he does it forthwith, so far as he is permitted by the orders of the representatives of the other treaty powers. It is in London, in Berlin, in St. Petersburg,

in Paris, in Vienna, and in Rome that the Turkish
government rests.

"It is for these reasons that we are unable to understand what Lord Salisbury means when he says
that the Berlin Treaty and the Cyprus Convention
impose no responsibility for Armenian reforms upon
any one save the Sultan.   The Cyprus Convention
specifies:—

"Treaty of Defensive Alliance between the British
Government and the Sublime Porte, signed on June
4, 1878:—

Article I. If Batoum, Ardahau, Kars, or any of them
shall be retained by Russia, and if any attempt shall be
made at any future time by Russia to take possession of
any further territories of his Imperial Majesty, the Sultan,
in Asia, as fixed by the definitive treaty of peace, England
engages to join His Imperial Majesty, the Sultan, in defending them by force of arms.   In return, His Imperial Majesty,
the Sultan, promises to England to introduce necessary
reforms, to be agreed upon later between the two powers,
into the government, and for the protection of Christian and
other subjects of the Porte in these territories; and in order
to enable England to make necessary provision for executing
her engagement, His Imperial Majesty, the Sultan, further
consents to assign the Island of Cyprus, to be occupied and
administered by England.

"Why, then, does not Lord Salisbury carry out
England's pledges, for which he is directly responsible, since he made them in her name ?

"England must be held to an accounting for the
disorders in Armenia.   There are no such disorders
in the provinces administered by the Czar, provinces
adjoining those where for the last six years pillage,
destruction, and murder have swept away every sign
of government.   In the provinces controlled by the
Czar the Armenians have been so well treated, enjoy-

ing unquestioned religious freedom and rights, that there have been not the slightest disorders.   But in the provinces where England pledged reform, the Armenian is butchered daily.

" Does Lord Salisbury mean that so long as Great Britain occupies Cyprus, pending the execution of reforms, it is better for England that the reforms should not be executed and that England should ' watch over them; nothing more ' ? "

Note carefully what Salisbury says first; then what he says afterward.   First he says there is complete concert among the powers, then he says there is not; first he threatens the Sultan, then he is friendly. First he seems to be a brave and noble statesman, then a cowardly politician.

Sir Philip Currie, the British Ambassador at Constantinople, is a brave and noble gentleman.   He was sent there by the Liberal government, before Salisbury's accession.   He has done a great deal for the Armenian cause.   But after Lord Salisbury became Prime Minister, he called him to London and instructed him to have cordial relations with the Sultan, and now he can do nothing.

Finally there appear to be two Englands, conservative England and liberal England, slave England and free England, selfish England and noble and sympathetic England, false England and true England.   The head of conservative, selfish, false, oppressive England is Lord Salisbury.   The head of liberal, free, noble, and true England is Mr. Gladstone.   Therefore nothing for Armenia can be expected from the Conservatives, while much may be hoped from the Liberals. Gladstone is an old man, but God will raise a Joshua to succeed Moses; Gladstone will see the Armenian nation free, and then he will die.

GERMANY AND THE ARMENIAN QUESTION.

Listen to what the haughty young ruler of Germany says:— " It is better that the Armenians be killed than the peace of Europe be disturbed." The explanation is easy enough. When he visited Constantinople half a dozen years ago, the Sultan presented him with Arabian horses, jewelry of massive gold, and many other valuable articles, worth in all several hundred thousand dollars; and last summer sent him a beautiful and valuable sword made in Constantinople by Armenians, which was carried to him by Shakir Pasha, the butcher who was afterwards appointed by the Sultan to reform Armenia,— the commander of the " Hamidich Cavalry," whose work I tell of later on. This embassy was to secure the alliance of Germany against molestation by Russia.

The German Emperor has three motives in his present action. One is to show gratitude for the Sultan's generosity — as though it were not the easiest thing in the world to be munificent when it all comes out of other people. The second is to punish Lord Salisbury for not getting England to join the Triple Alliance, when the Emperor asked him in person on his journey to England. When Salisbury threatened the Sultan in the interest of Armenia, the German Emperor said, "The English government has no right to interfere with the Turkish Empire. Every sovereign must have the right to govern as he thinks necessary, or he is no sovereign." He afterwards sent his Chancellor, Prince Hohenlohe, to the Czar to arrange united resistance to England, and afterwards sent Count Von Moltke on the same errand. And the Czar instructed his Ambassador at Constantinople, M. Nelidoff, to inform the Sultan that he would not support the English government in coercing Turkey. The Sultan therefore refused Salisbury's demands, and he dared not go on alone. The Emperor's third motive was to gain the friendship of the Czar against France, which had lately been taking up the Russian alliance with great fervor. Another reason is that he hates the Armenians for having bought the German factories and property in Amassia. He is very anxious to plant German colonies in Turkey, of all places in the world, for profit. There are about fifty families in Amassia, near Marsovan, and they had started various kinds of factories there; but the shrewd and wealthy Armenians bought them out. The Emperor is angry because his colony was not successful.

For all these reasons the German Emperor refused to send gunboats to the Bosphorus when the other powers did; he said he saw no need of it. He was right so far as Germans were concerned; the Sultan was not going to allow his ally's subjects to be slaughtered and the ally turned into an enemy. And if he

13

could stop the massacre of one sort of people, he could of another; nothing shows the Sultan's deliberate purpose in the massacres better than the fact that when he chose not to let any particular sort of people be harmed, that sort were not harmed. But as to Germany, what hope for Armenia is there from it ? The Emperor has his own interests, and the Armenians might be tortured or outraged to death, and he would not stir a finger.

RUSSIA AND THE ARMENIANS.

The present Czar, Nicholas II, is a corrupt weakling, who is on the throne by the law of heredity, against the will of his father. Morally he is as bad as the Sultan; not so cruel yet, though he may develop that in time, but fully as sensual and devoid of principle. I have had it from good Russian authority that his life before his marriage was so bad that it has rendered him entirely impotent. "Birds of a feather flock together." No wonder he helps the Sultan. His political aims and character are wholly selfish. He, too, like the German Emperor, is continually exchanging presents with the Sultan. Here is a press notice of Feb. 26, 1896:—"M. Nelidoff, the Russian Ambassador, has presented to the Sultan a pair of jasper vases from the Czar, together with an autograph letter from His Majesty thanking the Sultan for the gifts sent to him." Not only so, but they have concluded an alliance. Read the following dispatch of Jan. 23, 1896:—

" London, Jan. 23, 1896.—A dispatch to the Pall
Mall Gazette from Constantinople, dated yesterday,
says that an offensive and defensive alliance has been
concluded between Russia and Turkey. The Pall Mall
Gazette correspondent adds that the treaty was signed
at Constantinople, and that the ratifications were ex-
changed at St. Petersburg between Arifi Pasha and
the Czar.

" The basis of the treaty is declared to be on the
lines of the Unkiarskelessi agreement of 1833, by
which Turkey agreed, in the event of Russia going
to war, to close the Dardanelles to war-ships of all
nations. The Pall Mall Gazette's correspondent then
says the treaty will soon be abandoned, owing to the
refusal of the powers to recognize it. He also says
that the French Ambassador, M. Cambon, conferred
with the Sultan yesterday, and that it is probable
France will be included in the new alliance.

" The Pall Mall Gazette says: ' We regard the
news as true, and the result of the treaty is that the
Dardanelles is now the Southern outpost of Russia,
and Turkey is Russia's vassal. We presume the
British government will protest against the treaty for
all it is worth.

" ' The information is plainly of the very gravest
importance. The first intimation reached us four
days ago; but we withheld it until the arrival of strong
confirmation, which we received this morning. This
brings Russia into the Mediterranean with a vengeance, and may necessitate the strengthening of our
fleet in those waters. Politically, the effect will be
far greater. The treaty means that Turkey has realized her own impotence against disorders both from
within and without, and has decided to throw herself
for safety into the arms of Russia. She is now Russia's vassal, and Russia is entitled to dispatch troops

to any part of the Sultan's dominions whenever there is the least breach of order — and when is there not ?

" ' We presume the arrangement will give the keenest satisfaction to the Anglo-American section of our people.   With them lies the chief blame for the complete alienation of Turkey, though it must be owned that it has been sedulously fostered by a long term of weak policy at Constantinople.' "

For the present the Czar will do no more mischief, because he is to have his coronation in May, and prefers to put on the smoothest outside to every nation; but after that is over he will show his hand. His father and his grandfather favored the Armenians in Russia, and they prospered wonderfully, but this one proposes to persecute them to please the Sultan.   The two will join in a common policy toward the unhappy race, till not less than a million are slain.   The Czar's motive is not love of the Sultan, whom he hates in spite of their community of character; it is simply that he wishes to get Constantinople peaceably if he can.   The Sultan knows this quite well, but he is too weak in military power, and too poor, and owes too large an indemnity to the Czar to be able to help himself.   He is compelled to throw himself on the Czar for protection.

Will the Czar succeed in getting Constantinople ? No; the attempt will ruin and break up the Russian Empire.   All the European powers would resist it; some of them may seem friendly to the Czar now, but when he comes to seize Constantinople every one of them will be against him.   He will try it, none the

less.   The famous " will " of Peter the Great, though
a patent and notorious forgery of Napoleon's,— never
seen till 1812, just before the Russian campaign, and
circulated then to influence Europe against Russia,—
was the most magnificent piece of forgery ever committed, for it has actually become a guiding policy to
the country it was aimed against, just as if it had
been real.   Nothing in history equals this for impudence and success combined; it is a true Napoleonism.
This bogus " will " has become the " Monroe doctrine " of Russia; I am not entitled to say whether
the latter is as mischievous as the former.   That most
Russian of all Russian journals, the " Ruskija Vja-
domosti," has lately been having one of its periodical
spasms of hysterical hatred toward all policy not
" good Russian," and boldly proclaims that Russia
must follow the precepts laid down in this will !
Since, therefore, it is just as important as if it were
not the greatest of all " fakes," I give it here that the
reader may know what Russian policy is to be:—

WILL OF PETER THE GREAT.

In the name of the most holy and indivisible Trinity,
we, Peter the Great, unto all our descendants and successors to the throne and government of the Russian nation; the
All-Powerful, from whom we hold our life and our throne,
after having revealed unto us his wishes and intentions,
and after being our support, permits us to look upon Russia
as called upon to establish her rule over all Europe.   This
idea is based upon the fact that all nations of this portion
of the globe are fast approaching a state of utter decrepi-
tude.   From this it results that they can be easily conquered
by a new race of people when it has attained full power
and strength.   We look upon our invasion of the West and

East as a decree of divine providence, which has already once regenerated the Roman Empire by an invasion of "barbarians."

The emigration of men from the North is like the inundation of the Nile, which, at certain seasons, enriches with its waters the arid plains of Egypt. We found Russia a small rivulet; we leave it an immense river. Our successors will make it an ocean, destined to fertilize the whole of Europe if they know how to guide its waves. We leave them, then, the following instructions, which we earnestly recommend to their constant meditation.

I. To keep the Prussian nation in constant warfare, in order always to have good soldiers. Peace must only be permitted to recuperate finance, to recruit the army, to choose the moment favorable for attack. Thus peace will advance your projects of war, and war those of peace, for obtaining the enlargement and prosperity of Russia.

.II. Draw unto you by all possible means, from the civilized nations of Europe, captains during war and learned men during peace, so that Russia may benefit by the advantages of other nations.

III. Take care to mix in the affairs of all Europe, and in particular of Germany, which, being the nearest nation to you, deserves your chief attention.

IV. Divide Poland by raising up continual disorders and jealousies within its bosom. Gain over its rulers with gold influence and corrupt the Diet, in order to have a voice in the election of the kings. Make partisans and protect them; if neighboring powers raise objections and opposition, surmount the obstacles by stirring up discord within their countries.

V. Take all you can from Sweden, and to this effect isolate her from Denmark, and *vice versa*. Be careful to rouse their mutual jealousy.

VI. Marry Russian princes to German Princesses; multiply these alliances, unite these interests, and by the increase of our influence attach Germany to our cause.

VII. Seek the alliance with England on account of our commerce, as being the country most useful for the development of our navy, merchants, etc., and for the exchange of our produce against her gold. Keep up continual communication with her merchants and sailors, so that ours may acquire experience in commerce and navigation.

VIII. Constantly extend yourselves along the shores of the Baltic and the borders of the Euxine.

IX. Do all in your power to approach closely Constantinople and India. Remember that he who rules over these countries is the real sovereign of the world. Keep up continued wars with Turkey and with Persia. Establish dockyards in the Black Sea. Gradually obtain the command of this sea as well as of the Baltic. This is necessary for the entire success of our projects. Hasten the fall of Persia. Open for yourself a route toward the Persian Gulf. Re-establish as much as possible, by means of Syria, the ancient commerce of the Levant, and thus advance toward India. Once there you will not require English gold.

X. Carefully seek the alliance of Austria. Make her believe that you will second her in her projects for dominion over Germany, but secretly stir up other princes against her, and manage so that each be disposed to claim the assistance of Russia; and exercise over each a sort of protection, which will lead the way to a future dominion over them.

XI. Make Austria drive the Turks out of Europe, and neutralize her jealousy by offering to her a portion of your conquests, which you will further on take back.

XII. Above all, recall around you the schismatic Greeks who are spread over Hungary and Poland. Become their center, and support a universal dominion over them by a kind of sacerdotal autocracy; by this you will have many friends among your enemies.

XIII. Sweden dismembered, Persia conquered, Poland subjugated, Turkey beaten, our armies united, the Black and Baltic seas guarded by our vessels, prepare, separately and secretly, first the court of Versailles, then that of Vienna, to share the empire of the universe with Russia. If one accept, flatter her ambition and vanity, and make use of one to crush the other by engaging them in war. The result cannot be doubted; Russia will be possessed of the whole of the East and a great portion of Europe.

XIV. If, which is not probable, both should refuse the offer of Russia, raise a quarrel between them, and one which will ruin them both; then Russia, profiting by this decisive movement, will inundate Germany with the troops which she will have assembled beforehand. At the same time two fleets full of soldiers will leave the Baltic and the Black Sea, will advance along the Mediterranean and the ocean, keeping France in check with the one and Germany with the other. And these two countries conquered, the remainder of Europe will fall under our yoke. Thus can Europe be subjugated.

But aside from this, no help could be expected from Russia in any event, because she needs all her strength to save herself from destruction by her own internal decay. She is a great tree, hollow in the inside. The Nihilists and the Constitutional Reformers are both against her, and, in my belief, she will go to pieces in the present Czar's lifetime. The Sultan's days are numbered, but the Czar's and the Emperor's are too; their own people will rise and depose them. It is against Socialists and Nihilists that they are massing such great armies. How can they spare any service for a people being murdered off the earth ?

FRANCE AND ARMENIA.

Of the other powers, little need be said. France has lost all her great men, and become a tail to Russia, and is ready to be moved blindly, as Russia may direct. And as part of the people are infidels, and the rest fanatical Catholics, there is no religious motive to prompt them to come to the rescue. France, in a word, can or will do nothing directly; all it can do is to threaten the haughty Emperor of Germany.

Italy is bankrupt, and even the throne of King Humbert is in danger, and that country will follow in the wake of Austria.

THE POPE OF ROME AND THE ARMENIANS.

Pope Leo XIII sent 70,000 lire to the Armenian sufferers; probably to the Catholics alone, for there are about 100,000 Catholic Armenians in Turkey. But the Armenians can expect no help from the Pope; he has no troops; he has no great fund of spare money, and he would be very unlikely to use either if he had them. The motive of all the Popes has been to convert the Protestant Armenian Church to become a part of the Roman Catholic Church,— to acknowledge the Papacy. I say Protestant, for before Martin Luther was born, the Armenian Church protested against the popes of Rome age after age, and was persecuted by them. The Armenians offer their thanks to the Pope for his gifts, but they cannot accept his dominion.

[Press dispatch, N. Y. Herald.]

Rome, Dec. 16, 1895.—The Pope has sent 20,-000 lire for the relief of the sufferers from Turkish misrule in Anatolia, in addition to the 50,000 lire previously given by him for the same purpose."

The European edition published recently in a dispatch from Rome the following passage dealing with the Eastern question in the allocution delivered by Leo XIII at the consistory on November 29:—

" The whole of Europe in anxious expectation looks toward its eastern neighbor, troubled by griev-

ous events and internal conflicts. The sight of towns
and villages defiled by scenes of blood and of vast ex-
tents of territory ravaged by fire and sword is a cruel
and lamentable spectacle.

" While the powers are taking counsel together
in the laudable effort to find means of putting an end
to the carnage and restore quiet, we have not omitted
to defend this noble and just cause to the extent of
our power. Long before these recent events, we voluntarily intervened in favor of the Armenian nation.
We advised concord, quiet, and equity.

" Our counsels did not appear to give offense. We
mean to pursue the work we have begun, for we desire
nothing so much as to see the security of persons and
all rights safeguarded throughout the immense empire.

" In the meantime we have decided to send help
to the most tried and the most needy of the Armenians."

AMERICA AND ARMENIA.

Now we cross the ocean and come to the United
States. Everywhere here the people have shown the
greatest sympathy for us; and the Armenians are
deeply moved and exceedingly grateful for it. The
newspapers have almost uniformly been on our side
also; the only exception of any moment has been the
New York " Herald," which has steadily favored the
Sultan. The reason is the same as for General Wallace's like opinion of that worthless animal,— mis-
taking his entertainments and gifts for proofs of good
character, humanity, and statesmanship. Mr. Ben-
nett, too, knows the taste of the dinners at the palace,
and perhaps the weight of the golden ornaments he

gives out.   Fortunately his paper has very little influence on public opinion; and the real leaders of it have remained true.

I believe it will be the Americans who will finally put an end to the Armenian atrocities; but the time has not come yet.   It will take two years more, then this 70,000,000 of people will be aroused as one man and stop them.   I should like here to give an account of the many mass meetings held here for our cause; but I can only take space for two, one which I organized in Baltimore, and one held in New York, at which I was present.

MASS-MEETING AT LEVERING HALL, BALTIMORE
[Report from Baltimore Sun.]

December 11, 1894.—An enthusiastic meeting of Baltimoreans was held last night at Levering Hall, Johns Hopkins University, to make an emphatic protest·against the Turkish outrages upon Christian Armenians, and to urge the United States government to do all in its power to remedy the existing evils.

The meeting was called by a committee of Baltimore ministers.   It was presided over by Attorney-General John P. Poe, and the Rev. T. M. Beadenkoff was the secretary.

Addresses were made by Mr. Poe, Rev. George H. Filian, an exiled Armenian Christian Minister, Rabbi Wm. Rosenan, and Rev. Dr. F. M. Ellis.

Cardinal Gibbons and Judge Harlan sent letters regretting their inability to be present, and expressing sympathy with the object of the gathering.

Mr. Poe, in taking the chair, said:— " The accounts which have reached us of the indescribable atrocities recently committed upon the Christians in

Armenia have stirred the indignation and aroused the sympathy of the whole country.

" At first the nameless outrages inflicted upon them were received with incredulity, for it seemed almost impossible that they could be true. But there is now no reason to discredit the harrowing details. Indeed, denial is hardly any longer attempted, nor is it claimed that the reports of the cruelties of which these helpless people are the victims have been exaggerated.

" Conscious that the facts cannot be suppressed or belittled, the representatives and apologists of the ruthless perpetrators of these atrocities are endeavoring to palliate and excuse the enormities which they cannot truthfully deny. In order to shield themselves and their governments from universal execration, the world is asked to believe that the Christians of Armenia were themselves the aggressors, and that the horrors of massacre and rapine which have been visited upon them with such relentless fury were but necessary and pardonable measures of punishment and repression. The long record of the patient and submissive sufferers is a silent yet unanswerable refutation of this falsehood.

" In their misery and woe these sufferers lift their eyes to us, and ask us to extend to them such sympathy and assistance as will rescue them from total ruin.

" We are met here to-night to express these feelings — to declare that we cannot look unmoved upon the calamities of our Christian brethren, though separated from us by thousands of miles, and to recommend to Congress the adoption of such measures as, without departure from the well-settled policy of our government, will bring to them speedy and effectual deliverance, safety, and peace."

Cardinal Gibbons' letter sent to the meeting was as follows:

" I regret my inability to attend the meeting to protest against the alleged outrages recently committed in Armenia.

" The reports of these outrages have been published with harrowing details throughout the civilized world, and I am not aware that these circumstantial details have been successfully denied.

" The Christians of Armenia have been conspicuous among their Oriental co-religionists for their enlightened and progressive spirit.

" It is earnestly to be hoped that these alleged deeds of lawless violence will be thoroughly investigated in a calm and dispassionate spirit, so that the whole truth may be brought to light, and that outraged law may be vindicated. The recital of these inhuman cruelties is calculated to fill every generous heart with righteous indignation.

" The commercial and social ties that now bind together the human family quicken our sympathy for our suffering brethren, though separated from us by ocean and mountains, and this sympathy is deepened by the consideration that many of their countrymen have cast their lot among us, and that they and their persecuted brethren are united to us in the sacred bonds of a common Christian faith.

" It is gratifying to note, from recent publications, that a mixed commission, to make thorough investigation, has been appointed by the Sublime Porte."

Dr. Cyrus Hamlin of Lexington, Mass., whose article on the outrages in Armenia, published in the "Congregationalist," has been used by the Turkish government as a defense of the recent actions of the soldiers of the Porte, was asked to be present at the meeting, and was also asked to define his position as to the probable accuracy of the reports from Armenia, and as to the responsibility of the Sultan for the occurrence of the massacre.

His letter of reply was read at the meeting. He stated emphatically that he believed the accounts of the horrible atrocities to be in the main true, and added that he believed the Sultan of Turkey was perfectly cognizant of them, and should be held responsible for them.

Extracts were also read from a letter from some Congregational missionaries now near the seat of the massacres. The stories which they told, having been written nearly a month after the occurrences, showed that the earlier dispatches did not enlarge upon or exaggerate the horror of the scenes.

Much interest was manifested in the address of Mr. Filian, who feelingly described the pitiable condition of his country and his countrymen, and graphically portrayed the extent of the recent massacres, illustrating his talk with references to a large map of Turkey and Armenia.

" Armenia," he said, " was mentioned in the Bible 700 years before Christ. It then had an area of 1,-000,000 square miles, and it was in that land that the Garden of Eden was situated. Adam was created there, and within its confines, upon Mt. Ararat, the ark of Noah found a resting place after the flood. Armenia was named after Armen, the great-grandson of Japhet, one of the three sons of Noah. In the time of Christ the population of the country was 40,000,-000. It was fully Christianized in 310 A. D., and was not only the first Christian nation of the earth, but the first civilized nation. And now, from all these glories, the people of Armenia have dwindled to 4,000,000."

He concluded by citing the cause of the massacre

as the desire of the Turks to check the rapid growth and improvement of the Armenians.

The following resolutions, which had been prepared by a committee composed of Rev. Dr. Conrad Clever, Rev. W. T. McKenney, Rev. F. T. Tagg, and Rev. C. A. Fulton, were, after some discussion, passed:

"It has come to our knowledge through sources that cannot be disputed that an outrageous massacre of Armenians has been executed within the boundaries of the Turkish empire.

"These outrages have been committed by soldiers who are in the employ and under the direction of the Sultan at Constantinople.

"The thousands who have been murdered were Christians and peaceably disposed citizens.

"We, representatives of the citizens of Baltimore, prompted by motives of Christianity and common brotherhood, do call upon our government to use every power in its control, in harmony with that international law which governs nations in their relationship with each other, to aid these sufferers, and if possible to bring such influence to bear upon the Turkish government as will render justice to those who have been deprived of their rightful liberties as honest and industrious citizens of one of the recognized empires of the earth."

It was also resolved that a committee of five, with Mr. John P. Poe chairman, should be appointed to present the resolutions to the president at the earliest opportunity, and " to gratefully acknowledge the steps already taken in the appointment of an American member of the committee of investigation."

MASS MEETING IN DR. GREER'S CHURCH.

[Report from N. Y. Tribune.]

The interest which the American Christian feels in the Armenian question was shown by the large attendance at St. Bartholomew's Church, last night, when a special service was held under the direction of Rev. Dr. David H. Greer.   The object was to express indignation at Turkey's acts of violence toward Armenians, and to enter a protest against a course of conduct which is not in keeping with the spirit of the nineteenth century.

The main body of the church was reserved for Armenians, of whom there were about 500 present.

After the processional hymn, "The Son of God Goes Forth," had been given, the full choir sang the anthem, "I Will Mention the Loving Kindnesses of the Lord."

Dr. Greer then spoke of the outrages committed last September in Armenia, the particulars of which had only recently become known. He said in part:

"The purpose of this meeting is not only to express sympathy with those who have suffered, and are suffering now from the atrocities and barbarious cruelties inflicted by Turkish soldiers, but for protesting against the further infliction of such atrocities. What has been done is done, and cannot be undone; but if it is possible to prevent in any measure a repetition of it in the future, it should become everyone who is not a Christian merely, but a man, to exert himself to the utmost in that direction."

The speaker told of the untrustworthiness of reports from Turkey, and said that letters recently received from good sources give the following details:

Early in September some Kurds — the brigands of that region — robbed some Armenian villages of their flocks. The Armenians tried to recover their property, and about a dozen Kurds were killed. The authorities then telegraphed to the Sultan that the Armenians had killed some of the Sultan's troops. The Sultan on hearing this ordered the army, infantry, and cavalry, to put down the rebellion; and not finding any rebellion to put down, they cleared the country so that none should occur in the future. A number of towns and villages — the estimate varying from twenty-four to forty-eight — were destroyed. Men, women, and children were put to the sword, and from six to ten thousand persons massacred in the district of Sassoun. As the result of this wholesale butchery and slaughter, an epidemic of cholera has broken out, which is still ravaging the country.

The Turk has always been a cruel force, and has practiced his cruelties hitherto with impunity. But he cannot do so now. An enlightened public opinion is to-day the governing power of the world. It is to that we have to trust to accomplish moral reforms, not only here, but everywhere. It is stronger than states; it is mightier than empires, and the most arbitrary and autocratic of despots feel its controlling force. It is the force that moves the world. If meetings similar to this are held in different parts of the country and public sentiment aroused, even the Turkish authorities will not be impervious to it.

Dr. Greer read a letter from Bishop Potter, in which he expressed his regret at being unable to be present at the meeting. "I am," he wrote, "A Monroe-doctrine disciple, first, last, and all time, but I am a human being also, and while I think our competency as a nation to send a commissioner to Turkish-Armenia is open to question, I am quite clear that our duty as something else than savages is to protest against barbarism wherever it is to be found."

The Rev. Abraham Johannan then spoke in Armenian, and was followed by the Rev. Dr. George H. McGrew, who, during years of missionary work in Armenia, had become familiar with the people and their customs, and gave vivid pictures of the hatred of the Turks toward any who acknowledges Christ as the Son of God.

14

Mr. Depew's Speech.

Chauncey M. Depew was then introduced, and made an eloquent appeal for the Armenians. He said in part:

" The closing days of 1894 could not be passed more appropriately than in a protest by the Christian peoples of the world against the outrages upon humanity which will be the ever-living disgrace of the dying year. The industrial and financial disturbances which have convulsed the world, and caused such widespread distress during the last twelve months, are of temporary and passing importance compared with the merciless persecutions of a people because of their religious faith.

" It is a criticism upon the boastfulness of the nineteenth century that there should be any occasion for this meeting, but it is also a tribute to the spirit of the century that this meeting is held. There have been religious wars and persecutions, and bloody reprisals, in all ages of modern times. They arouse our indignation and our horror, but they excited little attention beyond the countries where they occurred from the twelfth to the nineteenth centuries. The distinguishing feature of our period is an international public opinion. It came with steam and electricity; it is the child of liberty of conscience. The Turkish government, founded by the sword of Islam, is a hierarchy and a creed, and not a government of liberty and law."

Mr. Depew then described the disadvantages under which Christians dwell in Turkey, and how their standing before the law amounts to nothing.

" It was the atrocities incident to such institutions," he said, " which aroused Europe and liberated Greece, which caused the other nations to stand still and risk the balance of power, while Russia freed Bulgaria,

Roumania, and Servia, and made them practically independent states. It was to assure religious liberty that the treaty of Berlin recognized the autonomy of the states, and bound the Christian nations of Europe to protect the Christian people still within the Turkish dominion."

After holding up to ridicule the European "peace" which is being maintained with continually growing armies, Mr. Depew said: "The Armenians are the New Englanders of the East. Their intellect, industry, and thrift make them prosperous." He spoke of their being the oldest Christian people, and of the sacrifices which they have made and which they daily make in the cause of their faith. The horrible outrages committed against the peasants in Armenia were graphically described, and in this connection Mr. Depew said:

"The story of the attacks of these savage hordes and no less savage troops reads as if fourteenth-century conditions, repeated with all their horrors in 1894, were the means adopted by Providence to shame the civilized world into the performance of its duty, and to stir the Christian conscience to a sense of its neglect of it."

Mr. Depew's description of the heroism of the Armenian women who, rather than be captured by the Turks and suffer defilement, threw themselves into the ravine which surrounded their village, moved the audience deeply. He went on:

"The world has taken little note of this supreme tragedy. Fifty years from now, and some painter will become immortal by putting it upon canvas. A few years, and some novelist will mount to enduring fame by a romance, of which it will be the center. A few years, and some poet will embalm it in verse which will stand in literature alongside of the battle lyrics of Campbell, Macaulay, and Tennyson. Some orator will give to the narrative and its lesson a setting and an inspiration, so that from the stage of the school and the academy, from the lips of the boys and the girls, it will teach down the centuries the triumphs of patriotism and faith.

"Yesterday an old man of world-wide fame celebrated his eighty-fifth birthday. He had been the ruler of the British Empire — he is a private citizen. Among the utterances which he deemed appropriate, in reply to the congratulations which came to him from every land, was an indignant protest against the outrages against the Armenian Christians, and a demand upon the Christian people of the earth to compel their governments to call upon Turkey for a halt.

"This warning and appeal from the lips of Mr. Gladstone was flashed across continents and under oceans; it penetrated cabinets, it thundered in the ears of sovereigns, and through the great journals it thrilled every household and every church of every race and of every tongue.

"To-morrow — aye, to-day — Rosebery is consulting with the French Premier, and France and England are speaking to the Emperor of Germany, and the young Czar and the King of Italy, and the Emperor of Austria for united action, which will bring the Turk to mercy, peace, and liberty for the Armenian Christian without destroying the equilibrium of Europe.

"We seek no foreign alliances, we court no international complications, but we claim the right under the Fatherhood of God to demand for our brother and our sister in the distant East, law, justice, and the exercise of conscience."

Dr. Greer then read resolutions expressing sympathy for the Armenians, and protesting against further outrages.   The document closes as follows:

" *Resolved*, That we hereby extend our deepest sympathy to the Armenian people who, for their Christian faith, have repeatedly suffered unspeakable cruelties from their Turkish rulers and Kurdish neighbors;

" *Resolved*, That we hereby express to our Christian brethren in England and on the continent, who are endeavoring to investigate these outrages and to bring the perpetrators of them to justice, our hearty good-will and godspeed. We hope and believe that they will not pause until the extent of these atrocities is clearly ascertained and the responsibility for them finally fixed;

" *Resolved*, That in their efforts to provide against the recurrence of similar acts of oppression in the future, they shall receive our hearty and unwavering moral support;

" *Resolved*, That we earnestly call upon our Christian fellow-citizens everywhere throughout the country to organize and express an indignant and universal protest against the continuance of a state of affairs under which it is possible for women and children to be murdered simply because they are Christians."

The resolutions were adopted by a rising vote, and the Rev. Dr. Tiffany, Archdeacon of New York, pronounced the benediction.

Very many such mass meetings were held in different cities of the United States.   The U. S. Senate discussed the question and made similar resolutions. Mr. Call submitted the following as a substitute for the committee resolutions:

" 'That humanity and religion, and the principles on which all civilization rests, demand that the civilized governments shall, by peaceful negotiations, or, if necessary, by force of arms, prevent and suppress the cruelties and massacres inflicted on the Armenian subjects of Turkey, by the establishment of a government of their own people, with such guarantees by the civilized powers of its authority and permanence as shall be adequate to that end.' "

All these resolutions, both of the people and the Senate, went to President Cleveland, but he has not seen fit to act on them.   It would be absurd to impute this to weakness or unwillingness to decide a new question: Mr. Cleveland, whatever his limitations, has never lacked firmness or decision. Doubtless it is because he thinks this country ought not to break away from its old traditions and involve itself with European concerns. But this is not a European concern; it is European, Asiatic, American, the world's; the concern of all humanity, not to say Christianity.

It concerns the lives and result of sixty years' work of American missionaries; the government cannot wash its hands of all concern or responsibility for them, and alone of all great powers declare that its Christian citizens may not spread Christianity. And a great and rich nation has no more right to go off with its hands in its pockets, and declare that it has no obligation to the well-being of the world, than a great, rich man has a right to declare that he has no obligation to society. The rich man only keeps his money because there is a civilized society with laws and policemen to protect him in it; this nation only keeps at peace because other nations' civilization and international law prevent a great combination to plunder it. It ought to accept its share of the general social duty — man the fire pumps, and do police work if needed; and not let a thug murder one of its companions — nay, relatives — before its eyes. It is bound as a Christian state not to let a bloody and sensual Mohammedan barbarism extinguish the light of a sister Christian community; it is bound as a nation of civilized beings not to let a horde of savages like its own Indians stamp out a civilized nation mil-

lions in number by horrors unspeakable, every atrocity of butchery, and rape, and torture that ever sprung
from the cruelty or the lust of man.   These things
are as awful, as hideous to the Armenians as they
would be to you if fifty thousand Indians overflowed
Colorado and inflicted them on your American families.   What would you feel and do if most of that
State were turned into a burnt desolation, with here
and there a cabin standing, Denver half obliterated
and ten thousand of its inhabitants slaughtered in
cold blood, hundreds impaled, or burnt, or flayed
alive, the sisters and daughters of your own house-
holds by thousands violated over and over, thousands
made slaves and concubines in the wigwams of dirty
Indian brutes, and others wandering as naked beggars
in the wintry snows about the ruins of their once happy
homes ?   Yet this is a picture of what happened over
part of Armenia; can you think it is of no concern to
you ?   Ought Congress and the President to think it
of no concern to them ?   Surely there are some things
where national lines ought not to count.

Mr. Cleveland has been unfortunate in his advisers,
partly chosen by himself, and partly inherited.   Minister Terrill has taken the word of the Sultan and the
palace clique, and made no attempt to investigate for
himself; consequently he is full of respect for the
Mohammedans, and scorn for the Armenians.   Admiral Kirtland visited a few seaports, found the Armenians there working as usual (of course — the massacres were carried on where news could be inter-

cepted and suppressed by the Turks), and reports that
he didn't find any evidence of outrages or disorders,
and considers the stories false, or much exaggerated.
And such lazy or prejudiced negatives as these are
to be counted as outweighing the sworn official reports of consuls on the spot, and of pitiful letters from
the survivors among the very victims themselves !

I have said that Mr. Cleveland does not lack firmness.   He does not in internal policy, but he certainly did not show enough in the matter of these
atrocities.   The Sultan asked him to nominate a commissioner to join those of other powers in inves-
tigating the Sassoun massacres.   He appointed Milo
A. Jewett, consul at Sivas; but Mr. Jewett was much
too keen and forcible a man for the Sultan, who refused to let him take his place on the commission.   Mr.
Cleveland did not insist, as he ought.   The very fact
that the Sultan did not want it, was the best of reasons
for persisting.

Again, last year, the Senate voted to send two
more consuls to Armenia; Mr. Cleveland appointed
Messrs. Chilton and Hunter to go to Erzeroum and
Harpoot respectively, but the Sultan refused to accept
them, and they had to come back.   To consent to this
was wrong and weak; the American government
should firmly declare its right to protect its own interests in its own way.

But the President will act if the American people
will stand at his back.   When will they send forth
a mandate that these horrors must stop ?

CIRCASSIANS.

GEORGIANS.

VI.

THE CAUSES OF THE ATROCITIES.

THE GREAT QUESTION.

The Armenian atrocities can never be fully understood by those who may be born in a free land, where there are no Turks, no Kurds, no Circassians, no Georgians, no Zeibecks, and no Mohammedan religion, with its oppressions and persecutions.

Why the Sultan orders the Turks, Kurds, or other followers to destroy the Armenians, whereby more than 100,000 of them have recently been killed, and 500,000 been rendered homeless and left to die of starvation in the streets and fields, or why the Sultan ordered all who are spared to accept the Mohammedan religion, is never referred to with any sort of correctness by the newspapers or periodicals in their accounts of the dreadful atrocities taking place in Armenia, and therefore the people are left in ignorance and doubt respecting the true situation both as to the causes and the atrocities themselves.

FIRST CAUSE.

The first cause is a very simple one. That the Armenians are Christians, and the Turks, Kurds, Circassians, and Georgians in Turkey are Mohammedans, and the Mohammedan religion urges brutality. It

(217)

has already been shown to be not a religion, but a
system of falsehood, hatred, cruelty, lust, and sensuality; of course, these things combined can only result
in corruption. It would seem that Mohammed must
have taken his inspiration from both the domestic fowl
and a bull. A rooster is a polygamist; he has his hens
without limit. So Mohammed, the professed prophet,
had wives without limit. He claimed to have received
a revelation from Heaven directing him to take to himself any woman he pleased, no matter whether she was
married and had a husband or not; that made no difference with Mohammed. He took any woman he
wanted, and if her husband objected he was sure to
be put to death. Mohammedans cannot differ from
their prophet, they follow him, they strive to imitate
him just as much as true Christians strive to follow
and imitate Christ. Further, cocks, as a rule, have
crowing spells five times in twenty-four hours, and generally mount a high place and do their screaming there.
So the Mohammedan priests, who are called Moezzins,
ascend a minaret, or a tower, and five times in twenty
four hours they call the people to worship. There
is so little confidence placed in the priests or criers
that the people prefer to have a blind one go on the
minaret to give the calls, so that he may not see their
women unveiled in their houses.

From a bull, because he is not only immoderately
lustful, but fierce and destructive; and the farmers
say that the older he grows, the worse he is in both respects. It is certainly so with Mohammedans,—

naturally enough, for nothing is so lickerish as an old
man who has been sensual all his life, and cruelty is a
trait which grows with indulgence.   The Sultan grows
more of a beast, and more of a fiend as he grows older,
and all the Mohammedans are of the same stripe.
Armenian men and Armenian women alike dread the
approach of an old Turk far more than of a young
one.   Unless one has witnessed a fight between bulls,
he can have little idea of Turkish warfare.   No animal
fight can approach it in ferocity or insatiability; when
a bull conquers another, he never leaves him until he
gores him to death.   So when Mohammedans conquer
a nation, be sure they will exterminate it.   To them
mercy means apostasy; to leave a man alive or a woman
unravished is to be false to the precepts of Mohammed.
They cannot help it, it is their religion; a religion
for wild animals.   Their priests go to the mosques and
preach to them thus: " Believers in Mohammed, love
your fellow believers, but hate and kill all others; they
are Giaours, heathen dogs, filthy hogs."   To kill a
Christian and to kill a hog is all the same to a Mohammedan; there is as little sin in one as the other.   The
priests say, " Ask them to accept our religion; if they
do, you must not harm them; but if they will not, kill
them, for they have no right to live in a Mohammedan
country.   It is not only no sin, but a great virtue; the
more Christians you kill, the greater reward you will
have from Allah and his prophet Mohammed."   The
Turks are slaughtering the Armenians to earn this reward.   Of course if the men apostatize they are

spared; but the Turk has no notion of losing the gratification of his lust on the women in that way. A woman who falls into their hands need not hope to keep her virtue on any terms, even by abjuring her religion; they violate her first, and force her to become a Mohammedan afterwards.

Let it be fully understood throughout the Christian world that the massacre is a religious demand; the Turks have to comply. As a Christian tries to be faithful to Christ and his teachings, so the Turks are trying to be faithful to their prophet and his. They go to the mosques and pray, " Allah, help us; strengthen our hands and sharpen our swords to kill the infidel Armenians." Then they come from the mosques and begin to kill, and plunder, and outrage, and commit every sort of indescribable atrocities on the peaceable and defenseless Armenians. And it will grow worse instead of better, since so-called Christian nations have given the Sultan public notice that they will not interfere with him. Do not be deceived by his lying reports; there was no Armenian rebellion; they could not rebel; they did not kill the Turks, they never dreamed of such madness. This awful fate has fallen on them purely and simply for being Christians.

SECOND CAUSE.

This seems frivolous and incredible, but it is true; namely, a dream of the Sultan.

Some six years ago, a report was circulated in Constantinople about this dream. It was, that in his sleep the Sultan saw a little tree planted in the center of his kingdom. It began to grow larger and larger, till it covered the whole Turkish Empire, and overshadowed even the mountains. All the nations of Turkey dwelt under its glorious and majestic shade. Still it grew, till the branches crossed the oceans and covered all the other kingdoms, finally the whole world. He woke, but the dream troubled him deeply, and he called some of the ulemas or wise men, of whom he always has a number in his palace, to interpret it for him. They explained it by saying that the tree was Christianity; Christian missionary work in the heart of his empire. It was a menace to his throne and country, and would grow till it covered the world. The Sultan, alarmed and angry, asked what he should do. The ulemas advised him to cut it down while it was small, and he has been doing his best to follow their advice. He did not dare to kill the missionaries, but he is accomplishing the same result by destroying their churches and schools and forbidding any more to be built, confiscating all religious books, and killing the native Christian ministers. He has employed every device to force the missionaries to depart by paralyzing their work; if they chose to stay, he would accuse them of inciting the natives to revolt. He has succeeded so far; plunder, burning, torture, murder, violation and forced conversion of Christian women, have practically put an end to missionary work. Now the time has come to kill the missionaries; and he will very likely find some excuse for doing it — he has an arsenal of falsehoods always at his command. Quite likely he will say the Armenians killed them, and then murder more Armenians in reprisal. His cunning is as infinite as his cruelty. He gives a charter to a missionary institution and destroys ten others. He invites Minister Terrell to the palace, gives him grand receptions, and loads him with promises and flatteries, and all the time goes on obliterating the schools and churches and killing the native pastors. He creates a ruin; when the European powers protest, he says he will make amends, and he does it by perpetrating a greater one, in which the first is forgotten. He massacres hundreds in a city; when the powers protest, he says he will restore order, and does it by ordering thousands killed in another city, and the first is again forgotten. His atrocities increase as he finds that he is to be unmolested; he is resolute to cut down that spreading tree, and has already cut thousands of branches from it. And the Christian nations look on and say they cannot help it. They know perfectly well what is going on, but their "interests" of one sort or another will not permit them to remove that awful blot on civilization.

THIRD CAUSE.

The Mohammedan population in Turkey is decreasing, and the Christians are increasing. When the present Sultan captured the throne from his brother Murad, Turkey had 40,000,000 people; as soon as he girded the sword of Osman, he began the great battle with Russia, and after the Turko-Russian war he found himself with 18,000,000. Who are the lost ? Roumania, Bulgaria, Servia, Montenegro, Bosnia, Herzegovina, a part of Macedonia, Cyprus, and a part of Armenia. Practically the whole of Europe was lost for Turkey except Constantinople and the district Edirne or Adrianople. Turkey is not an empire any more, but it is a little kingdom; rather a little feudal system, or more accurately still, a little anarchy. If it were not for mutual European jealousy, the Sultan could not keep his anarchism. Yet many still think that the Ottoman Empire is a great one, a powerful government. They look at the Sultan and his dominion through a magnifying glass. This shows ignorance. The Turks are decayed and are decaying. The sick man of Turkey is the dead man of Turkey, and ought to be buried, but the European powers do not bury him because there are precious stones and jewelry in the coffin; no matter how bad the corpse smells, they will endure it. And the bad smell of the Sultan is killing hundreds of thousands of Christians; but the dead stays where it is, and may stay for some years, but the end will come before many have gone by. When I say that the days of the Sultan are numbered, and the brutal Turkish mis-rule will cease, many Americans will rejoin "that the same has often been said long years since, though the empire remains to-day, and seems likely to remain." The fact is, however, that during my own life more than half of it has gone to pieces, and the fragment which remains will go to

pieces soon.   Permit me to say that all former prophecies have been mistaken because those who made
them have judged and misjudged the situation from
an occidental standpoint; I judge it from that of a
native, who knows the realities as only a native can.
What can an English ambassador or an American minister in Constantinople, staying perhaps two or three
years, and entertained and decorated by the crafty
Sultan, know about the internal state of Turkey ?
Having traveled through the country, lived and
preached for years at a time; preached in different
cities, including Constantinople, I can see signs of a
break-up that a foreigner would not notice.

The reason the Turkish population does not increase is this: The army has to be made up of Mohammedans, partly because the Sultan does not put
arms into the hands of the Christians, for obvious reasons, since they have no motive to uphold and every
motive to fight him, and partly because to be a soldier
in Turkey is a holy service, the privilege of Mohammedans alone.   As there is a large standing army, nearly
all the Mohammedan youths have to become soldiers.
Their service begins when they are about twenty years
old.   The shortest term is five years; for many it is
ten; and even after that, there are many who cannot
escape.   If a young Mohammedan is not married at
twenty, obviously he cannot marry until twenty-five
anyway, and perhaps thirty,— very late for a country
population; if he is married his wife is virtually a
widow for five to ten years.   Now the reader can

see my drift.   With marriages so late, and husbands so long absent, Turkish families are small; they do not make good the deaths.   And there is a still plainer cause: The soldiers being very poorly fed, and constant fighting going on, ninety per cent. die in the army, and so never have any families; the flower of the nation perishes barren.   Those who survive and return are pale and sick, good for nothing, a burden to their families and to the nation.   The Armenians have to support the Sultan's army, since they do not furnish it, but they rear families, and are drowning out the Turks.

Another cause of decrease is the pilgrimage to Mecca, where Mohammed was born.   On an average, a million pilgrims go there every year,— of course not all from Turkey, but most of them, and every year about 50,000 of them die of cholera before reaching home, from the Holy Well (Zemzem sooyi), which is full of unholy foulness; even those who live and return home take that water to their families, and many of the latter die too.   Cholera is perpetual in Turkey, and it originates at Mecca.   When I was in Marsovan twelve at one time went on the pilgrimage and only four returned.   It is a great virtue to die where Mohammed was born, or to drink that water and die, and they are going to him at a rapid rate.   Last year, when the English, Russian, and French consuls at Jiddeh, the seaport of Mecca, established a quarantine to detain those coming from Mecca and bringing cholera, they were murdered by the Mohammedan

15

Arabs, who said they were interfering with the sacred religion, and the Sultan had to pay the indemnity.

Still another reason is the shocking increase of abortions among the wealthy town dwellers. The Mohammedan women are growing to love selfish indulgences better than the duties and delights of motherhood. They do not wish to be " bothered " by children, and they take medicine to prevent having them. Where the women come to this, it is better for a race to die out; they have outlived their purpose.

A fourth cause is polygamy. People naturally think that marrying more than one wife should increase the number of children; but the facts emphatically prove the reverse. The polygamous Turks do not increase as fast as the Christians who have but one wife.

For the fifth, the Turks are an exceedingly sensual race, by nature and education, as I have shown. The very religion that should help to make them pure, helps to make them vile. Lust leads them, and they follow; nature prompts, and their religion requires it. I am truly ashamed to tell it, but even when they go to their mosques to worship, they manifest their sensuality. Not only the relations of male and female are very rank, but between male and male they are worse; between the old Turks and young Turks, the very boys, the relations are too disgusting to describe. All such moral corruptions not only weaken a people's forces morally, but physically as well; they substitute barren lusts for legitimate gratifications, selfish passions for mutual ones.

Hence the Mohammedans are fast decreasing in Turkey, and the Sultan is terrified, and hopes by killing a large part of the Christians, and forcing the survivors to accept Mohammedanism, that their power of multiplication may be the boon of a Mohammedan people. Out of the 18,000,000 inhabitants of Turkey, 6,000,000 are native Christians, about half of them Armenians. This leaves only 12,000,000 for the whole Mohammedan population in the present Turkish dominion; and it grows less, while the Christian part grows greater. To check this increase, the Sultan a few years ago made the obtaining of a marriage certificate compulsory, and the Turkish authorities have understood that they are to make it as hard as possible to get; it has cost great sums of money to obtain it. But for many months now, there have been no marriages at all in Armenia; the authorities will not grant certificates on any terms, and to prevent any more Christians being born, the daughters and young brides of the murdered thousands are made mothers through violation by the Turks and Kurds.

The Christians have been increasing not only from within, but from without. Europeans have begun to go wherever railroads go. Hence another reason for massacre and forced conversion. That the Sultan has been planning this massacre ever since the Turko-Russian war is evidenced by the fact that after the war he encouraged or ordered a number of Mohammedan tribes — Circassians, Georgians, Kurds, and Lazes — to emigrate from Russia to Armenia, confiscated masses of Christians' property, and gave it to them, and directed them to reduce the number of Armenian Christians by any way they saw fit, giving them full license to do what they would with Armenians, without penalty. You know what that means with fierce tribes of human wild animals, cruel and foul, and he knew what it meant too, and intended it to mean that. Before his time the Christians far outnumbered the Mohammedans in Armenia proper; but under his " government "— his deliberate policy of extermination — great numbers fled the country, numbers were killed and their women made concubines to Mohammedans, and now the Mohammedans are more numerous in Armenia than the Armenian Christians. And if the Sultan is permitted to go on, he will kill a million more, the rest will be " converted," and then he will call the attention of the European powers to this fact, and say, " See here, you ask me to reform Armenia; Armenia is reformed. There is no Armenia; there are no Armenians; the people in that part of my empire are Mohammedans, and they are satisfied with my government. What do you want from me ? What right have you to interfere with my country and religion ? " That is his plan. When the Berlin Congress was held, the Armenians were the majority in their own country, and the Congress decided on reforms for it; the Sultan promised them, with the full intention of depopulating and converting it, and then telling the powers there was no need of reform there. He is doing this now incessantly, and as remorselessly as a fiend.

FOURTH CAUSE.

The Armenians are rich and educated, and the Mohammedans are poor and ignorant. The Turks have never cared for money or education. They have always said, " Let the Christians make the money, and we will take it from them whenever we choose. We will be the rulers, the soldiers, the police; we will have the sword in our hands. Then their property, and their women too, will be ours at will, and we can force them to become Mohammedans." Such being their reasoning, they took good care of their swords and their guns, which were furnished to them from Europe and the United States. The Christian Armenians believing that the great Christian powers would never permit the Turks to wreak their murderous and shameful will on them, did not risk the vengeance of the Turks by secretly buying weapons, nor train themselves in the use of arms. They trained their minds, got education, traveled in Europe and this United States, enlightened themselves in every way they could; they sharpened their intellects rather than their swords. They learned to make money also; they established all the business houses in Turkey; all the Turks that get employment in the cities get it from the Armenian merchants. As far as Turkey has any finances, they are in the hands of Armenians. Go

where you will in Turkey, seaboard or interior, all the
money and education belong to the Armenians, poverty and ignorance are the portion of the Turks.
Ninety per cent. of the Armenians know how to read
and write, while ninety per cent. of the Turks do not.
Sixty per cent. of the Mohammedan property has
been sold to the Christian Armenians within twenty
years. When I was in Armenia, the Mohammedans
were always selling and the Christians always buying.
One day a Turk was going to sell his field to an Armenian, and they went to the government office to make
the transfer. The officer in charge said he could not
transfer the property of a Mohammedan to a Christian. This was something new. "Why is that?"
they asked. "The governor forbids it," said the officer, "he told me that hereafter it should not be
done." Finally both went to the governor and asked
him why he forbade it. The governor replied, "Of
late the Armenians have bought up the fields of the
Mohammedans, till they own the greater part of them;
if we let them go on they will own everything, and the
Mohammedans will be left without property. Therefore I forbid it; no Mohammedan shall hereafter sell
any property to a Christian." He told the Turk he
might sell his field to another Mohammedan, but not
to a Christian. "All right," said the Turk, "I will
sell it to you, then, at the same price, or maybe a little
less; will you buy it? I need the money to support
my family." "I cannot buy it," said the governor; "I
have no money." "I know that," replied the Turk;

" and not only you, but all the other Mohammedans
have no money either.   They are all poor.   I cannot
find any Turk who has the money to buy my field, and
I need money, and I have to sell it to that Christian."
Finally the governor was forced to give the permission,
and the Armenian bought the field.   This is only one
case, but it is typical.   There are thousands of just
such.   And this is another cause which aroused the
jealousy of the Sultan and his subordinates to order
the massacre of the Armenians, and the seizure of
their property.

I often hear it said in this country, " Let us help
the poor Armenians "; and I feel very indignant.
Poor Armenians !   There are poor among the Armenians, as among all nations; but the Armenians as
a body are not poor.   They are the richest people in
Turkey.   That is one reason why they are plundered
and killed.   I do not want the American people to
help the Armenians as a poor, ignorant, miserable people, but because they deserve help as a rich, noble,
Christian nation being rooted out by plunder and
murder, for the benefit of, and by means of a horde of
savages.   I will illustrate by a very little story.

When Alexander the Great reached the mountains of Afghanistan on his way to India, the Afghan
king refused to let him pass through his country.
After a great battle, and the slaughter of thousands
on both sides, Alexander was victorious.   The king
himself was captured, and brought before Alexander,
who said to him, " You are my captive; how shall I

treat you ? " " As a king," said the prisoner. Alexander was charmed with the dignity of the answer, and replied, " You shall be treated as one, and a brave one. I leave you on your throne; but permit me to pass on to India." So the king kept his royalty as before, and Alexander continued his conquests.

Such is the Armenian question. They are a noble people, an enterprising people, but captives in the hands of the Turks. But the Turks have not the magnanimity of Alexander. We need a nation which does have it, to say to the Armenians, " Remain where you are, in your ancient home, and rule there; govern yourselves freely as a Christian nation. You have fought centuries after centuries for home and honor, and now we come to your help, to establish you on the old Armenian throne." Do not help the Armenians merely as a poor people, but help them because they were rich, and now they are stripped and poor, without fault of their own, from hate of their (and your) religion, and envy of their superiority.

FIFTH CAUSE.

This is perhaps the greatest of all. It is the American missionary work in Armenia. It was in 1831 that the American Board of Foreign Missions established the first Protestant mission there. Their purpose was to send missionaries, not simply to the Armenians, but to all classes and sects in Turkey. Those pioneer American missionaries were among the noblest of men, and greatest of teachers, preachers, and organizers. I will name a few: Dr. Goodell, Dr. Dwight, Dr. Schaffler, Dr. Cyrus Hamlin, founder of Robert College, living now at Lexington, Mass., 86 years old, one of the greatest missionaries ever born, Dr. H. Van Lennep, another great missionary, greatly beloved by the Armenians. Books could be written about these Christian chiefs, to whom, and to the American people who sent them, we Armenians are grateful. When Dr. Van Lennep died at Great Barrington, Mass., about six years ago, the author was raising money here to build a church in Armenia, as already told. He went to condole with Mrs. Van Lennep, and told her not to put any monument over the doctor's grave. He would see the other Armenians, and as a grateful people they would erect him a beautiful one. He kept his word, and his faith was justified; they raised the funds and put up the monument. It stands in the cemetery at Great Barrington, with the following inscription:—

HENRY JOHN VAN LENNEP, D.D.
1815 — 1889.
FOR THIRTY YEARS MISSIONARY IN TURKEY.
This monument is erected by his Armenian friends in grateful appreciation of his heroic virtues, and endearing services rendered to their people.
The beloved Missionary
VAN LENNEP.

When the noble missionaries went to Turkey, the Turks hated them, the Jews hated them, the Greeks hated them, and these three peoples hate them still.

But the Armenians welcomed them; they loved and esteemed them, and they love and esteem them more than ever now. The question is often asked " Are not the Armenians a Christian people ? Then why did the missionaries go there ? " Yes, they are; but still they needed the missionaries, and need them now more than ever. Why ? Well, for two reasons. Their churches and schools having been destroyed by the long oppression by the Turks, they needed help from a sister Christian church to help them educate themselves, and build up churches, schools, and colleges, benevolent institutions, printing offices. The missionaries have done that great work in Armenia, but I am sorry to say that some of their creations have been destroyed by the Turks during the recent atrocities.

The second reason is that the Armenian church stood in great need of reformation. I have already explained in this book (see " The Armenian Church ") how in the last desperate struggle for national existence, a part of the people reluctantly accepted help from the Pope of Rome, at the price of uniting with the Roman church, and using its rituals, images, etc. Hence, in many of the Armenian churches there was no pure gospel preaching; rituals were the leading element of the services. There was therefore great need that such preaching should be introduced; the missionaries did so, and the Armenian church has been greatly reformed. My purpose here is not to write a church history, nor to give an account of missionary work in

Turkey.   I mention it incidentally as a chief cause of the atrocities.

The missionaries have trained both boys and girls in their schools for sixty-five years now; many thousands of them.   The Turks have not been permitted to go to them, the Greeks are too proud to send their children, but the Armenians were hungry for education, especially for an American education.   The new-born baby of the time when the missionaries arrived is now sixty-five years old, with his American education, which has wonderfully elevated the Armenians, and turned Armenia almost into a second America, educationally.   The American colleges in different parts of Turkey are great centers of light; about ninety per cent. of the students and the leading native professors and teachers are Armenians.   I will mention a few: Robert College and the Woman's College in Constantinople; the Ladies' Seminary in Smyrna; Anatolia College, the Ladies' Seminary, and the Theological Seminary in Marsovan; the writer's pastorate, Central Turkey College and the Ladies' College at Aintab, Euphrates College (first called Armenia College, but the name is forbidden by the Turks, as encouraging Armenian independence) and the Ladies' Department at Harpoot; the Academy and the Theological Seminary at Marash, where I studied three years; the colleges both for girls and boys at Beirut; and many high schools and primary schools throughout Armenia.   The American Bible House is a great depot of Christian literature.   These

are all American Christian institutions, and nine-tenths
of their inmates are Armenians.

The reader can clearly see how the Armenians
have become a wholly new race; they have had the advantage of American education, and it has revolution-
ized the nation. It has elevated, refined, and prospered them. This great improvement among the Armenians aroused the jealousy of the Sultan and his
underlings. He first began to close the schools; then
to imprison the native Armenian teachers and preachers; then to kill the Armenians and destroy the missionary institutions, that no Armenian may be left to go
to any American school, and that if any escapes, there
may be no American school to receive him. I consider this missionary education the very greatest cause
for the atrocities, and the Armenian bishops agree
with me. Here is what the Armenian bishop of Oorfa
(Edessa), where about 8,000 Armenians were massacred, has to say:

TO THE AMERICANS.

March 12, 1896.

" We have been strenuously opposed to your mission work among us, but these bloody days have proven
that some of our Protestant brothers have been staunch
defenders of our honor and faith. You at least know
that our crime, in the eyes of the Turk, has been that
we have adopted the civilization you commended.
Behold the missions and schools which you planted
among us, and which cost millions of dollars, and hundreds of precious lives, now in ruins. The Turk is

planning to rid himself of missionaries and teachers by leaving them nobody to labor among."

It is very significant that wherever there was a missionary institution, and especially a missionary Theological Seminary to train Armenian ministers, there has been the greatest atrocity. This shows how the Sultan hates Americans, and American education. There are nearly two hundred American male and female missionaries in Turkey. They are in great danger. The Turks have determined to kill them, and the Sultan can no longer control them, for he gave the order and put the sword into their hands. The Kurds and the Turks say, " The missionaries have better things than the Armenians had. We killed the Armenians and got their valuables, and we enjoy them. We are richer now, and we did not work for it; we did not waste time in hard labor; the only thing we had to do was to obey the Sultan and kill the Armenians and get their property. Why not kill the Americans and get richer ? " Reader, keep in your mind that the Turks will kill the missionaries also. The horrible time is coming, in spite of what your minister to Turkey says, and partly because he believes Turkish lies, and says there was no need of sending missionaries there.

Another point worthy of consideration is this: Russia and Turkey made an alliance. Russia is as much opposed to the missionaries as Turkey is, and perhaps the Czar is secretly encouraging the Sultan to get rid of them. Undoubtedly Russia is trying to get rid of Protestant influence in Turkey, and therefore sacrifices the old Protestant Armenian nation to Turkey. In my belief, the time is coming when the Protestant nations will unite and protest practically against the outrages of Turkey and Russia. They have no right to persecute Turks or Russians, but they have a perfect right to protect an old Protestant church and the American missionaries. No matter how much it costs, it pays to protect them, and, pay or no pay, it is the duty of America and England to unite and protect them. And if England and America should really unite, Turkey and Russia will yield. I do not at all concur with Americans who favor Russia and hate England. Lord Salisbury is too timid to do it, but Lord Salisbury is not England. The English people are a noble people, and if the American noble people unite with them, they can accomplish a great work for God and humanity, for peace and liberty, for freedom and happiness in Armenia.

As far as I can judge, the foregoing are the causes of the atrocities in Armenia. Perhaps there may be other minor ones, but they are not worthy of discussion.

KURDISH HOME.

KURD CHIEFS.

KURD WOMAN.

THE TURKISH ATROCITIES IN ARMENIA.

THE BEGINNING.

Turkish atrocities in Armenia are no new thing; they have gone on for centuries, and left but a fraction of the population it once had. But let us disregard old history, and come to the subject of to-day. Practically that begins with Hamid II, the present Sultan. He began his persecutions nearly twenty years ago, but on a small scale. He has continually devised new methods of getting rid of the Armenians without responsibility; finally he hit on the plan of arming the Kurds and letting them loose with full power to do their worst. When I was in Constantinople he summoned the Kurdish chiefs, hundreds of them — I have seen them with my own eyes — entertained them in the palace, armed them with modern rifles, and sent them to Armenia on their mission. The pretense under which he did it was worthy of him: he called them the "Hamidieh Cavalry," and pretended that they were a sort of mounted police, who were to keep order and protect the Armenians. This was exactly as though a regiment of red Indians should be armed and sent to Oregon to protect the inhabitants, and called, say, the Presidential Guard, and the Armenians knew well what they were for. But the European travelers and newspaper correspondents took it all seriously, and talked of his "civilizing the Kurds," etc. Now these were only the chiefs; each chief had a large following of tribesmen, so that about 30,000 Kurds in all were given arms and ordered to go to work exterminating the Armenians. This work began in 1891, but on a small scale, and in a very crafty way, so that it should not have the appearance of a premeditated massacre; then it was stopped till about sixteen months ago, when they were encouraged to begin again, publicly, and with full swing. It was decided to begin in Sassoun, a district far from the sea, with no roads and a sparse population; if successful in escaping report there, he could carry out the massacre through all Armenia, for which "reforms" were asked and promished. He ordered Zekii Pasha to have his soldiers ready, and meantime to have the "Hamidich Cavalry" the Kurdish chiefs and tribesmen, ready to attack and kill all the Armenians in Sassoun. This city lies between Moosh and Bitlis, in a mountainous country, and the Sassounites are a brave people, as much so as the Zeitoonlis are. The district had about sixty villages and towns, and about 20,000 people sixteen months ago, but it has none now. The regular soldiers and the armed Kurds surrounded the district from all sides, and in about a month had slaughtered the entire population. It was reported that Zekii Pasha carried on his breast an order from the Sultan as follows: "Whoever spares man, woman, or child is disloyal." After he had finished his task, he received great rewards from the Sultan, and is now one of his most esteemed commanders.

Zekii Pasha is said to have had 40,000 Kurds and regular soldiers under his command when he began the massacre. The people of Sassoun, knowing that they were doomed, fought desperately. They repulsed the Kurds several times, and killed many of them; but finally the regular soldiers took part, pretending to come in aid of the Armenians, and overbore them, killing all without quarter. The Sultan's order was to spare neither man, woman, nor child; but as the men met the enemy first, they were killed first. When the women's turn came, the Turks and Kurds abused all they could get hold of, and then told them that if they would deny Christ and accept Mohammed and become their wives, they should live; but if they refused, every one of them, according to the Sultan's order, should be killed. "Now," said they, "choose between Islam and death." These noble Armenian Christian women said:— "We are Christians, we can never deny Christ. Jesus Christ is our Saviour. He came down from Heaven and died on the cross for us. For that dying and loving Christ we are Christians; we are ready to die for Him who died for us." And they added further, "We are no better than our husbands were; you killed them, kill us too." Then the horrible butchery began on those defenseless women. Thousands of them were slaughtered, and thousands ran to different churches, hoping that perhaps they might find protection in some way in those holy walls,

16

or hoping that God in his great mercy might shelter them. But the ferocious Kurds and Turkish soldiers pursued them, sword in hand, violated them, even in the churches, and cut their throats there until the floors were streaming with blood. Then they poured kerosene on the buildings and burned them.

They went to one village and killed every man; the women of course, knowing their fate was soon to be worse than their husbands'. One of the leading women, named Shaheg, perceiving that the Turks and Kurds were getting ready to seize and ravish them, called the other women and said, " Sisters, our husbands are killed, and you know what is in store for us and our children. Don't let us fall into the hands of these savage beasts; we have to die anyway, and can die easier, and without being defiled first, and perhaps tortured. Let us go to the precipice and jump off." So saying, she took her baby on her arm, ran to the rock, and threw herself over; the others followed her, and thus all were killed. The Turks captured many boys and girls, six, or eight, or ten years of age, held them by an arm or foot, and hacked them to pieces with their swords. Sometimes they stood the boys in a row and shot them, to see how many could be killed by a single bullet. They wrenched babies from their mothers' arms, cut their throats while the mothers shrieked and pleaded, and boiling them in kettles, forced the mothers to eat the flesh. They cut open women about to become mothers, tore out the unborn babes, and marched triumphantly with the

ghastly trophies on their spears — something almost
surpassing the savagery of the Apache Indian.   Even
their worst horrors they made worse yet by the way
they did them; they took a gloating delight in doubling
the cruelty or the shame by making it torture others
too.   The husband was forced to look on while his
wife was violated, and she in turn while he was mutilated, tortured, and murdered; the father while his
daughters, even little girls of ten or twelve, were deflowered and their throats cut, the son while his parents had every form of shame and torture inflicted
on them, and were killed before him, or saw him killed
first.   They tortured their victims like Indians or
Inquisitors, in every fashion of lingering death and
torment that makes the heart sicken and the blood
run cold to read of.   Crucifying head downward,
and pouring boiling water or ice-cold water on them,
leaving them so till death came; flaying alive; cutting
off arms, feet, nose, ears, and other members, and
leaving them to die; thrusting red-hot wires into and
through their bodies.   They pulled out the eyes of
several Christian pastors, said, "Now dance for
us," poured kerosene on them and burned them to
death.   They put a Bible and a cross before others, and
ordered them to first spit and then trample on both,
and deny Christ; on their refusal they were butchered.
The handsomest girls and young matrons were not
murdered, but worse; each one was kept as a spoil of
some Turk or Kurd, who carried her to his house, and
made a slave and concubine of her.   Many hundreds.

of them are there to this day, enduring the awful fate of having been dragged from happy and virtuous homes, seen their husbands, or parents, or brothers, or all of them horribly murdered, and passing their lives each in doing menial labor and serving the lust of a brutal master, and all the other men he lets have their will of her, without hope, or comfort, or decency, and a long life of shame and misery yet to look forward to. This is another specimen of Mohammedan purity, and it all happens because the Armenians are Christians. If my readers think I am exaggerating, I refer them to the consular reports. All this was done by the barbarians con amore, with relish and delight. They boasted of it, they plumed themselves on it, they praised the Sultan for ordering them to do it, and he praised them for doing it, and decorated all the officers.

The condition of those who were murdered outright was much better than that of those who were imprisoned and tortured. The following was written by an Armenian from one of the prisons:—

" Our condition in prison passes description. Only he who sees can understand it. Most of the occupants of every room are Christians, but many are Moslems. Life would be a shade more tolerable if the subject race were not compelled thus to associate with the dominant race, whose temper, tastes, and habits are so different. Into one small room twenty persons are crowded. Except for a few Moslems, not a single person has room enough on the bare floor to stretch out and lie down. For fully sixteen hours in the night,

the doors of the rooms are all locked. In one of these
small rooms, sometimes twenty cigarettes are smoking
at once. Out of the small amount of food which
reaches us, instead of eating themselves, the Christians are obliged to feed the Moslems confined there.
Moslem oppression continues, even here; it is a tyranny
within a tyranny. In every room there are a few
Aghas or principal Moslems, and every Christian must
contribute money to their lordships. Those who with-
hold such contributions are not allowed to sit down.

"Among the inmates of the prison are twenty or
thirty rowdies and bullies, under whom the Christians must serve as menial slaves. There is no respect,
no pity. The horrible blasphemies cannot be described. There is no book, no Bible, no work, no
sleep. Every man is covered with the swarming vermin with which the unwashed rooms of the prison
teem. To clean ourselves is impossible. Now and
then the rumor sweeps through the prison that we are
all to be put to death, and all our hearts melt like
water.

"The terrible darkness of the night, the curses
and stripes inflicted from time to time, cause us to live
in the valley of the shadow of death. It is a living
grave, a visible hell, a world without God. Out of this
throng of prisoners more than a hundred are in daily
suffering from the gnawing of hunger, and from nakedness, but there is no one to pity. Many praying
men are tempted to cease praying, many are tempted
to change over to the Moslem faith. In truth, all of
us are dumb; what to say we know not. We are
wearied of the long silence; our eyes are strained
with watching, our bones ache, our prayers are despised by the revilers. Night is not night, and day is
not day. Our grief is our food, our sleep is weeping.
for how long a time must we cry ? O Lord, wilt

Thou hide Thyself forever ? How long will Thy anger burn like fire ? And yet some of us are saying: 'Though He slay me, yet will I trust in Him.'

"When will the Christian statesmen and philanthropists of the world find a way to cleanse these Augean stables all over Turkey ? Long centuries cry out for redress. Within a month the following incidents have occurred: A Christian confined in this prison was ordered to receive 400 stripes. After 300 had been inflicted he cried out that he could endure no more or he must die. An officer then presented to him a paper with the names of fifty Christians in the city who were accused therein of sedition. In his great agony he signed it, and this is to be used to incriminate others, wholly regardless of their guilt or innocence. The other victim of unendurable stripes was an old man. When he could endure no more of this inhuman treatment, he also was asked to sign a paper implicating others indiscriminately.

"Can any one living in a free country for a moment understand what it is to live under such a government ? There is a great flourish just at present over the reforms that are being instituted in certain parts of this land. No resident of this country can have confidence in the superficial operations. What will you do with a land where lying is the simplest of mental exercises, and where no one was ever known to blush over it if exposed ? "

I give here the testimony of a gentleman from Sassoun who escaped the atrocities. He is an Armenian from Sassoun, and my personal friend. I quote this from a little pamphlet, entitled " Facts About Armenia."

MASSACRE AT SASSOUN.

ERZEROUM DURING MASSACRE.

THE MASSACRE OF 1894.

" The Armenians of Sassoun were fully aware of the hostile intention of the government, but they could not imagine it to be one of utter extermination.

" The Porte had prepared its plans, Sassoun was doomed. The Kurds were to come in much greater number, the government was to furnish them provision and ammunition, and the regular army was to second them in case of need.

" The various tribes received invitations to take part in the great expedition, and the chiefs, with their men, arrived one after the other. The total number of the Kurds who took part in the campaign may be estimated at 30,000. The Armenians believed in the beginning that they had to do only with the Kurds. They found out later that an Ottoman regular army, with provisions, rifles, cannons, and kerosene oil, was standing at the back of the Kurds.

" The plan was to destroy first Shenig, Semal, Guelliegoozan, Aliantz, etc., and then to proceed toward Dalvorig. The Kurds, notwithstanding their immense number, proved to be unequal to the task. The Armenians held their own, and the Kurds got worsted. After a two weeks' fight between Kurd and Armenian, the regular army entered into an active campaign. Mountain pieces began to thunder. The Armenians, having nearly exhausted their ammunition, took to flight. Kurd and Turk pursued them, and massacred men, women, and children. The houses were searched and then set on fire. From certain villages groups of men, tax receipts in their hands, went to the camp and asked to be protected, but were slaughtered.

" A great number of villages outside of the Dalvorig district, which had in no wise been concerned in the conflicts of the previous years, were also attacked, to the unspeakable horror of the populations. The troops climbed up even the Mount Antok, where a multitude of fugitives had taken refuge, and massacred them. A number of women and girls were taken to the church of Gnelliegoozan, and after being frightfully abused, were tortured to death.

"When the work of destruction was nearly accomplished in the other districts, some of the Kurdish armies were set on Dalvorig. The people defended themselves against the overwhelming number of the barbarians, but after four or five days they saw other tribes and regular Turkish troops marching on them from every side, and they took to flight, but were overtaken and massacred. The scene was most horrible. The enemy took a special delight in butchering the Dalvorig people. An immense crowd of Turkish and Kurdish soldiery fell upon the villages, busily searching the houses and rooting out hidden treasures, and then setting fire to the village. While the troops were so occupied, a number of the fugitives fled wildly to get out of the district, and tried to hide themselves in caves, between rocks, or among bushes. Three days after the complete destruction of Dalvorig villages, the Kurds and the regular soldiers divided among themselves the result of the plunder, and the Kurds returned to their own mountains."

As my use of English is defective, I take the liberty here of quoting from a long letter by E. J. Dillon to the Contemporary Review, January, 1896.

Dr. Dillon is an Englishman who was the special correspondent of the London "Daily Telegraph," a most accurate and conscientious reporter, who writes as an eye-witness:

"If a detailed description were possible of the horrors which our exclusive attention to our own mistaken

interests let loose upon Turkish Armenians, there is
not a man within the kingdom of Great Britain whose
heart-strings would not be touched and thrilled by the
gruesome stories of which it would be composed.

"During all those seventeen years, written law,
traditional custom, the fundamental maxims of human
and divine justice were suspended in favor of a Mohammedan saturnalia.   The Christians, by whose
toil and thrift the empire was held together, were de-
spoiled, beggared, chained, beaten, and banished or
butchered.   First their movable wealth was seized,
then their landed property was confiscated, next the absolute necessaries of life were wrested from them, and
finally honor, liberty, and life were taken with as little ado as if these Christian men and women were
wasps or mosquitoes.   Thousands of Armenians were
thrown into prison by governors like Tahsin Pasha and
Bahri Pasha, and tortured and terrorized till they delivered up the savings of a lifetime, and the support
of the helpless families, to ruffianly parasites.   Whole
villages were attacked in broad daylight by the Imperial Kurdish cavalry without pretext or warning, the male inhabitants turned adrift or killed, and
their wives and daughters transformed into instruments to glut the foul lusts of these bestial murderers.
In a few years the provinces were decimated, Alogh-
kerd, for instance, being almost entirely ' purged '
of Armenians.   Over 20,000 woe-stricken wretches,
once healthy and well-to-do, fled to Russia or Persia
in rags and misery, deformed, diseased, or dying; on
the way they were seized over and over again by the
soldiers of the Sultan, who deprived them of the little
money they possessed, nay, of the clothes they were
wearing, outraged the married women in the presence of their sons and daughters, deflowered the tender
girls before the eyes of their mothers and brothers,

and then drove them over the frontier to starve and die. Those who remained for a time behind were no better off. Kurdish brigands lifted the last cows and goats of the peasants, carried away their carpets and their valuables, raped their daughters and dishonored their wives. Turkish tax-gatherers followed these, gleaning what the brigands had left, and, lest anything should escape their avarice, bound the men, flogged them till their bodies were a bloody, mangled mass, cicatrized the wounds with red-hot ramrods, plucked out their beards hair by hair, tore the flesh from their limbs with pincers, and often, even then, dissatisfied with the financial results of their exertions, hung the men whom they had thus beggared and maltreated from the rafters of the room, and kept them there to witness with burning shame, impotent rage, and incipient madness, the dishonoring of their wives and the deflowering of their daughters, some of whom died miserably during the hellish outrage.

"In accordance with the plan of extermination, which has been carried out with such signal success during these long years of Turkish vigor and English sluggishness, all those Armenians who possessed money, or money's worth were for a time allowed to purchase immunity from prison, and from all that prison life in Asia Minor implies. But as soon as terror and summary confiscation took the place of slow and elaborate extortion, the gloomy dungeons of Erzeroum, Erzinghan, Marsovan, Hassankalch, and Van were filled, till there was no place to sit down, and scarcely sufficient standing room. And this means more than English people can realize, or any person believe who has not actually witnessed it. It would have been a torture for Turkish troopers and Kurdish brigands, but it was worse than death to the educated schoolmasters, missionaries, priests, and physicians who were immured in these noisome hotbeds of infection, and forced to sleep night after night standing on their feet, leaning against the foul, reeking corner of the wall which all the prisoners were compelled to use as . . . . The very worst class of Tartar and Kurdish criminals were turned in here to make these hell-chambers more unbearable to the Christians. And the experiment was everywhere successful. Human hatred and diabolical spite, combined with the most disgusting sights, and sounds, and stenches, with their gnawing hunger and their putrid food, their parching thirst and the slimy water, fit only for sewers, rendered their agony maddening. Yet these were not criminals nor alleged criminals, but upright Christian men, who were never even accused of an infrac-- tion of the law. No man who has not seen these prisons with his own eyes, and heard these prisoners with his own ears, can be expected to conceive, much less realize, the sufferings inflicted and endured. The loathsome diseases, whose terrible ravages were freely displayed; the still more loathsome vices, which were continually and openly practiced; the horrible blasphemies, revolting obscenities, and ribald jests which alternated with cries of pain, songs of vice, and prayers to the unseen God, made these prisons, in some respects, nearly as bad as the Black Hole of Calcutta, and in others infinitely worse. In one corner of this foul fever-nest a man might be heard moaning and groaning with the pain of a shattered arm or leg; in another, a youth is convulsed with the death spasms of cholera or poison; in the center, a knot of Turks, whose dull eyes are fired with bestial lust, surround a Christian boy, who pleads for mercy with heart-harrowing voice while the human fiends actually outrage him to death.

"Into these prisons venerable old ministers of

religion were dragged from their churches, teachers from their schools, missionaries from their meeting-houses, merchants, physicians, and peasants from their firesides. Those among them who refused to denounce their friends, or consent to some atrocious crime, were subjected to horrible agonies. Many a one, for instance, was put into a sentry-box bristling with sharp spikes, and forced to stand there motionless, without food or drink, for twenty-four and even thirty-six hours, was revived with stripes whenever he fell fainting to the prickly floor, and was carried out unconscious at the end. It was thus that hundreds of Armenian Christians, whose names and histories are on record, suffered for refusing to sign addresses to the Sultan accusing their neighbors and relatives of high treason. It was thus that Azo was treated by his judges, the Turkish officials, Talib Effendi, Captain Reshid, and Captain Hadji Fehim Agha, for declining to swear away the lives of the best men of his village. A whole night was spent in torturing him. He was first bastinadoed in a room close to which his female relatives and friends were shut up so that they could hear his cries. Then he was stripped naked, two poles extending from his armpits to his feet were placed on each side of his body and tied tightly. His arms were next stretched out horizontally and poles arranged to support his hands. This living cross was then bound to a pillar, and the flogging began. The whips left livid traces behind. The wretched man was unable to make the slightest movement to ease his pain. His features alone, hideously distorted, revealed the anguish he endured. The louder he cried, the more heavily fell the whip. Over and over again he entreated his tormentors to put him out of pain, saying, ' If you want my death, kill me with a bullet, but for God's sake don't torture me like this !' His

head alone being free, he at last, maddened by ex-
cruciating pain, endeavored to dash out his brains
against the pillar, hoping in this way to end his agony.
But this consummation was hindered by the police.
They questioned him again; but in spite of his condition, Azo replied as before: ' I cannot defile my
soul with the blood of innocent people. I am a Chris-
tion.' Enraged at this obstinacy, Talib Effendi, the
Turkish official, ordered the application of other and
more effective tortures. Pincers were fetched to
pull out his teeth, but, Azo remaining firm, this
method was not long persisted in. Then Talib commanded his servants to pluck out the prisoner's mous-
tachios by the roots, one hair at a time. This order
the gendarmes executed, with roars of infernal laugh-
ter. But this treatment proving equally ineffectual,
Talib instructed the men to cauterize the unfortunate
victim's body. A spit was heated in the fire. Azo's
arms were freed from their supports, and two brawny
policemen approached, one on each side and seized
him. Meanwhile another gendarme held to the middle of the wretched man's hands the glowing spit.
While his flesh was thus burning, the victim shouted
out in agony, ' For the love of God kill me at once ! '

"Then the executioners, removing the red-hot
spit from his hands, applied it to his breast, then to his
back, his face, his feet, and other parts. After this,
they forced open his mouth, and burned his tongue
with red-hot pincers. During these inhuman operations, Azo fainted several times, but on recovering consciousness maintained the same inflexibility of purpose. Meanwhile, in the adjoining apartment, a
heart-rending scene was being enacted. The women and the children, terrified by the groans and
cries of the tortured man, fainted. When they revived, they endeavored to rush out to call for help,

but the gendarmes, stationed at the door, barred their
passage, and brutally pushed them back. *

" Nights were passed in such hellish orgies and
days in inventing new tortures or refining upon the
old, with an ingenuity which reveals unimagined
strata of malignity in the human heart. The results
throw the most sickening horrors of the Middle Ages
into the shade. Some of them cannot be described,
nor even hinted at. The shock to people's sensibilities would be too terrible. And yet they were not
merely described to, but endured by men of education
and refinement, whose sensibilities were as delicate
as ours.

" And when the prisons in which these and analo-
gous doings were carried on had no more room for
new-comers, some of the least obnoxious of its actual
inmates were released for a bribe, or, in case of poverty, were expeditiously poisoned off.

" In the homes of these wretched people the fiend-
ish fanatics were equally active and equally successful.   Family life was poisoned at its very source.
Rape and dishonor, with nameless accompaniments,
menaced almost every girl and woman in the land.
They could not stir out of their houses in broad daylight to visit the bazaars, or to work in the fields,
nor even lie down at night in their own homes, without fearing the fall of that Damocles' sword ever suspended over their heads. Tender youth, childhood
itself, was no guarantee. Children were often married at the age of eleven, even ten, in the vain hope of
lessening this danger. But the protection of a hus-

* The above description is taken literally from a report
of the British Vice-Consul of Erzeroum. Copies are in possession of the diplomatic representatives of the powers at
Constantinople. The scene occurred in the Village of Semal
before the massacres, during the normal condition of things.

band proved unavailing; it merely meant one murder more, and one ' Christian dog ' less.   A bride would be married in church yesterday, and her body would be devoured by the beasts and birds of prey to-morrow,— a band of ruffians, often officials, having within the intervening forty-eight hours seized her and outraged her to death.   Others would be abducted, and, having for weeks been subjected to the loathsome lusts of lawless Kurds, would end by abjuring their God and embracing Islam; not from any vulgar motive of gain, but to escape the burning shame of returning home as pariahs and lepers, to be shunned by those near and dear to them forever.   Little girls of five and six were frequently forced to be present during these horrible scenes of lust, and they, too, were often sacrificed before the eyes of their mothers, who would have gladly, madly accepted death, ay, and damnation, to save their tender offspring from the corroding poison.

" One of the abducted young women who, having been outraged by the son of the Deputy-Governor of Khnouss, Hussein Bey, returned, a pariah, and is now alone in the world, lately appealed to her English sisters for such aid as a heathen would give to a brute, and she besought it in the name of our common God. Lucine Mussegh — this is the name of that outraged young woman whose Protestant education gave her, as she thought, a special claim to act as the spokeswoman of Armenian mothers and daughters — Lucine Mussegh besought, last March, the women of England to obtain for the women of Armenia the ' privilege ' of living a pure and chaste life !   This was the boon which she craved — but did not, could not obtain.   The interests of ' higher politics,' the civilizing missions of the Christian powers, are, it seems, incompatible with it ! ' For the love of the God whom we worship in common,' wrote this outraged, but still hopeful, Armenian lady, ' help us, Christian sisters ! Help us before it is too late, and take the thanks of the mothers, the wives, the sisters, and the daughters of my people, and with them the gratitude of one for whom, in spite of her youth, death would come as a happy release.'

" Neither the Christian sisters nor the Christian brethren in England have seen their way to comply with this strange request. But it may perhaps interest Lucine Mussegh to learn that the six great powers of Europe are quite unanimous, and are manfully resolved, come what will, to shield His Majesty the Sultan from harm, to support his rule, and to guarantee his kingdom from disintegration. These are objects worthy of the attention of the great powers; as for the privilege of leading pure and chaste lives — they cannot be importuned about such private matters.

" In due time they began. Over 60,000 Armenians have been butchered, and the massacres are not quite ended yet. In Trebizond, Erzeroum, Erzinghan, Hassankalek, and numberless other places the Christians were crushed like grapes during the vintage. The frantic mob, seething and surging in the streets of the cities, swept down upon the defenseless Armenians, plundered their shops, gutted their houses, then joked and jested with the terrified victims, as cats play with mice. As rapid, whirling motion produces apparent rest, so the wild frenzy of those fierce fanatical crowds resulted in a condition of seeming calmness, composure, and gentleness which, taken in connection with the unutterable brutality of their acts, was of a nature to freeze men's blood with horror. In many cases they almost caressed their vic-

MASSACRE OF ARMENIANS IN STAMBOUL.

tims, and actually encouraged them to hope, while preparing the instruments of slaughter."

After the horrible scenes at Sassoun, and other places, the Armenian protests shamed the European powers, who signed the treaty of Berlin, to send a commission and investigate the atrocities. It found the stories quite true, laid the facts before the Sultan — and that was the end of it. The Armenians asked, " Since you admit the truth of these things, why do you not punish the criminals, stop the outrages, and compel the payment of indemnity to those who were outraged and who lost their dear ones and their property ? " The powers were deaf to all this. Then the Armenians prepared an appeal (several months ago) and carried it to the Sublime Porte, asking it to do them justice. As soon as the Sultan heard of this, he ordered his soldiers to fire on them if they presented it. The appeal was presented, and before the eyes of the European Ambassadors in Constantinople, the brave soldiers of the kind-hearted Sultan butchered about 3,000 Armenian Christians, several thousand were imprisoned, and several hundred were murdered in the Central Prison. Then the cold, wise, and considerate European powers began to move very slowly, not for the sake of the Armenians, but for their own, their citizens in Constantinople and elsewhere.

They ordered the Sultan to reform Armenia, brought their fleets to the Dardanelles near Constantinople to overawe him, prepared a scheme of reform for Armenia, and made huge threats to the Sultan

17

if he did not accept it. But he knew that this pretended concert of the powers for Armenian reform
was a mere trick and sham, as I have persistently asserted all along in the face of my hopeful European
and American friends; in fact, the Russian government at this very time was secretly urging him to stand
firm and refuse to accept the reforms. He did so,
broached a scheme of his own as a substitute, and the
powers accepted it as such; and then the whole thing
was dropped, the Sultan did nothing whatever about
it, as he had never intended to. The European countries were hoodwinked, and the Armenian massacres
and conflagrations, plundering and deflowering, went
on at a greater pace than ever. Then the powers
dropped the Armenian question, and took up that of
gunboats in the Bosphorus, to protect their citizens
against a rising in Constantinople; that they forced
the Sultan to permit, because their own interests were
concerned in it, — which shows that they could have
forced him to stop exterminating the Armenians if
they had cared. All joined in this except Germany;
the German Emperor is the Sultan's friend, and backs
him up. So now Germany, Russia, and the Sultan
are hand in hand, leagued to prevent any of the miserable victims of his tyranny from escaping his clut-
ches, and the Sultan has the best possible encouragement to go on killing the Armenians. The German
Emperor says, "Better that Armenians be killed
than have a war in Europe and lose the lives of some
of my soldiers." The Czar says, "Time must be

given to the Sultan to reform his country." Lord
Salisbury says, "The Sultan has promised, and we
must wait and see what he will do." And the Sultan,
cursing every Emperor and lord of them all as a set
of Christian hogs, orders the soldiers and the Kurds to
go on with the good work in Armenia. And when we
come to America, the Monroe doctrine obliges it to
quarrel over Venezuela, and not only refuse help
itself, but give Lord Salisbury a good excuse to give
none either.

Such is the situation; the massacres are going on
in Armenia and the Armenians in despair are crying,
"O Lord, how long, how long ! "

Mass meetings are good as far as they go; raising
money and sending it to relieve the Armenians is good
as far as it goes; the Red Cross Society is good as far
as it goes; there are no objections to any of them; they
are all noble and Christian. But, reader, don't you
think all these good movements with good motives
will hurt the Armenian cause, as there is nothing to
aid that cause directly ? All these mass-meetings
merely irritate the Sultan into carrying on the mur-
ders more strenuously, since there is no force back
of them. Don't you think the Armenian question
being discussed in the United States Congress, and
resolutions made without any action, will hurt the
Armenians more than anything else ? If you can't
tread down the Sultan, don't stir him up. Miss Clara
Barton, that noble woman, is in Armenia to help the
Armenians. The Red Cross Society is there and is

feeding the Armenians. I thank her, every Armenian thanks her. But do you think that that will relieve the situation ? Spring has come, and what now ? Will the Armenians have any crops ? Did they, or could they sow any seed ? Is there any farmer left alive ? Has any farmer, if he is alive, any oxen or horses ? If he has, will he dare go to his field, sow, reap, and thresh ? Reader, consider all these things, and reconsider them, and I am sure you will come to the same conclusion I did many years ago, that Turkey does not need a Red Cross Society, but a Red Cross crusade, not like the medieval crusades, but a Protestant American crusade in the nineteenth century. Let me illustrate this Armenian question by the following parable:—

Suppose a lamb is torn by a wolf, and the wolf lies in wait to finish it. You go to the lamb with a bundle of grass in your hand, pat it and say, " Here, poor lamb, I pity you, I give you grass; take it and eat it." Then you leave the lamb and go away. Do you think you have helped the lamb ? As soon as you have gone, the wolf will come and tear the lamb to pieces. If you are going to help the lamb, you must kill the wolf, else no matter how much grass you give the wounded lamb, it will do it no good. You will do no good by sending Red Cross societies to Armenia to feed the Armenians if you have not the power or the will to keep the wild beasts off. You will feed them, and then the wolves will kill them.

Now I will pass in review some of the leading cities

in Armenia where there have been great persecutions. Before beginning, however, I must state that it is impossible to give an accurate census of the population in the Armenian cities, or the number who have been massacred; for the Turkish government never takes a correct census, and never gives or will give the true number of those it has murdered. But I think I can make a fair approximation of both. I will begin with the city of Harpoot. *

HARPOOT AND ITS VICINITY.

This is one of the most important Armenian districts, because the Armenians outnumber the Mohammedans there; in the city the Turks are the more numerous, but there are many Armenian towns and villages which make up. The district has about 150,-000 people, most of them Armenians, and about 40,-000 were killed in the recent massacre. Harpoot is built on three hills, and has a commanding view. Here is located a great American missionary institution, the Euphrates College; it has three departments, the college, the Theological Seminary, and the Girls' Seminary. There were twelve buildings, eight of which were burned in the outrages, a loss of $100,-000.

Almost all the outlying villages were burned, and the movables carried off. Women were made prey, boys and girls were kidnapped; the horrors can never be described. I give here a few words from a private letter, written by a Mohammedan Turk to his brother in this country. I have the letter in my

---

* Extracts from letters are left unsigned for fear of endangering the writers' lives.

possession, written in the Turkish language.   He
says:—

" My dear brother:

All the Christian villages which belong to Harpoot district, we plundered and destroyed, and killed
the inhabitants.   We killed them both with our
swords and with our rifles.   The bullets of our rifles
poured upon them like rain; none of them are left,
neither any dwelling was left, we burnt all their
houses.   We thank God that not a single Mohammedan was killed.   Everywhere throughout Armenia
the Christians were punished in the same manner."

Another testimony from another Mohammedan,
an officer; he says nearly 40,000 were killed in Harpoot province, February 26, 1896:—

" A petition in behalf of the Armenians was given
to the powers in the hope of improving their condition.   An imperial firman was issued for carrying out
the reforms suggested by the powers.   On this account the Turkish population was much excited, and
thought that an Armenian principality was to be established, and they began to show great hostility to
the poor Armenians, who had been obedient to them
and with whom they had lived in peace for more
than 600 years.   To the anger of the people were
added the permission and help of the government;
and so, before the reforms were undertaken, the whole
Turkish population was aroused, with the evil intent
of obliterating the Armenian name; and so the Turks
of the province, joining with the neighboring Kurdish tribes by the thousand, armed with weapons which
are allowed only to the army, and with the help and
under the guidance of Turkish officials, in an open
manner, in the daytime, attacked the Armenian

houses, shops, stores, monasteries, churches, schools, and committed the fearful atrocities set forth in the accompanying table. They killed bishops, priests, teachers, and common people with every kind of torture, and they showed special spite toward ecclesiastics by treating their bodies with extra indignity, and in many cases they did not allow their bodies to be buried. Some they burned, and some they gave as food to dogs and wild beasts.

"They plundered churches and monasteries, and they took all the property of the common people, their flocks and herds, their ornaments and their money, their house furnishings and their food, and even the clothing of the men and women in their flight. Then after plundering them, they burned many houses, churches, monasteries, schools, and markets, sometimes using petroleum, which they had brought with them to hasten the burning; large stone churches which would not burn they ruined in other ways.

"Priests, laymen, women, and even small children were made Moslems by force. They put white turbans on the men and circumcised them in a cruel manner. They cut the hair of the women in bangs, like that of Moslem women, and made them go through the Mohammedan prayers. Married women and girls were defiled, against the sacred law, and some were married by force, and are still detained in Turkish houses. Especially in Palu, Severek, Malatia, Arabkir, and Choonkoosh, many women and girls were taken to the soldiers' barracks and dishonored. Many, to escape, threw themselves into the Euphrates, or committed suicide in other ways.

"It is clear that the majority of those killed in Harpoot, Severek, Husenik, Malatia, and Arabkir were killed by the soldiers, and also that the schools and churches of the missionaries and Gregorians in the

upper quarter of Harpoot City, together with the
houses, were set on fire by cannon balls.

"It is impossible to state the amount of the pecuniary loss. The single city of Egin has given 1,200
(some say 1,500) Turkish pounds as a ransom.

"These events have occurred for the reasons I
have mentioned. I wish to show by this statement,
which I have written from love to humanity, that the
Armenians gave no occasion for these attacks."

The Turk, whose document is thus translated,
figures that the total deaths in the province of Harpoot during the scenes, have been 39,334; the wounded 8,000; houses burned, 28,562; and that the number of the destitutes is 94,870.

"In a letter just received (Jan. 18, 1896) from the
Rev. H. N. Barnum, D.D., of Harpoot, Eastern Turkey, where the property of the American Board was
burned, he says that reports have been secured from
176 villages in the vicinity of Harpoot. These villages contained 15,400 houses belonging to Christians.
Of this number 7,054 have been burned, and 15,845
persons are reported killed. Dr. Barnum adds: 'The
reality, I fear, will prove to be much greater.'"

A letter from an Armenian named Kallajian,
written from Husenik, a town about three miles from
Harpoot, addressed to his brother in this country, says:

"Sunday, November 11, the government came
to our town, Husenik, and asked the Armenians to
give up their arms, and they surrendered all they had;
and in the evening asked them to take the church bell
down. They also obeyed, and by night the Turkish

A PORTION OF HARPOOT.

15,000 Armenians killed in this city and vicinity.

soldiers surrounded the town until the morning, and in the morning early they sounded the bugle.   When they sounded the bugle, about 25,000 Kurds made an attack on the town, and plundered all the houses, killing 700 men, women, and children, besides the wounded.   When the attack was made, we left our house, with two of our neighbors' families and many others from our town, about thirty in all.   One little boy, my nephew, I carried on my shoulders, and the other was carried by its mother, and we ran up the hill toward Harpoot.   The bullets were showering upon us by hundreds, and father fell.   He was shot once in the head and once in the belly, and stabbed with a sword through his chin.   When we reached the top of the hill, about twenty Kurds came down from Harpoot, and took all our clothes and money, and left us naked; and a little after, a band of Turks came down and made so much trouble for us that I am unable to describe it.   They took us to the city, and we finally succeeded in getting to the house of Sadukh Effendi, formerly of our town, but now living in the city.   We went to his house, and this kind man kept us there for two days in his house, and on Tuesday evening he took us to our own town, and as we came near to our house I found that father was dead under a tree.   We went to the house; we saw that our house was open and stripped of everything, and father's trunk was broken open, and his papers were soaked in kerosene and set on fire, and twenty-five houses were destroyed on our street.   We are hungry and in destitute condition; help us if you can.   Our little nephew says: 'O Jesus, keep us afar from such trouble.' "

There are other letters also from Harpoot, but this is enough to show the nature of the scenes there.

PALOO AND WHAT HAPPENED THERE.

Paloo is one of the oldest cities in Armenia. It had 15,000 population, 5,000 Armenians and 10,000 Mohammedans, and there were over forty Armenian villages in the district around. About 5,000 Christians were killed during the recent massacre.

PERSONAL LETTERS FROM PALOO,
December 15, 1895.

"Paloo is in a miserable condition. All the houses and shops have been robbed. About 2,000 persons have perished, and few have survived this great ruin; but we thank God all our family is in safety. Just to-day I received a letter from our home; they write: 'We are alive, but hungry.' They have no bread to eat, and no clothes to wear; our only hope is God. If the country is soon reformed we can get our living, but if not we shall all perish. Turks, Kurds, and soldiers united, plundered, robbed, and burned the houses of Paloo and the neighboring villages. You can guess very well who has given the order."

A personal letter received by the Armenian Relief Association, in this city, under date of Paloo, Armenia, November 24, presents an awful picture of the horrors to which the people there are subjected. The letter is in part as follows:—

"On November 3, the Turks of the town armed themselves, attacked the stores, plundered their contents, and killed those who attempted to defend themselves. A few days later the Turks left the town, joined a band of 10,000 Kurds, and began a general assault upon the surrounding villages, pillaging and burning the houses, and killing all the men. They poured kerosene oil on all the stored grain and set it on fire, and mixed the flour with filth, so that it could not be used. The beautiful women were delivered to the Kurds, who committed the most indescribable outrages. Many were carried off to slavery, and forced to accept Mohammedanism.

"In Habab Village, where the people defended themselves for six days, the government soldiers were called to the aid of the Kurds, and the united forces overpowered the village and burned all except fifteen of their three hundred houses.

"All of the forty-one Armenian villages around Paloo are in ashes, the fields laid waste, and the inhabitants massacred. Nothing is left but death and desolation.

"On November 11, 10,000 armed Kurds fell upon the city of Paloo. They plundered the houses, even pulling down the walls with hooks to discover anything valuable that might be hidden. All the large houses were burned. Ten of the wealthy Armenians, who have always cared for the poor, and sheltered the distressed, are left without a pair of shoes or a blanket, 1,732 men were butchered in cold blood, and of the 10,000 population, two hundred men only are left, saved on condition that they serve the Turks as slaves.

"More than 5,000 women and children are left without any means of living. They are begging from door to door for even a meagre pittance of bran, which is all that is left, and every day death claims more and more of the victims by starvation. All of the more beautiful women have been taken by the Kurds. The Armenian youths who have been forced to accept Mohammedanism are also forced to take Turkish wives to prove their sincerity.

" All of my relations, save two, have been killed
in my presence. Our priests have all been butchered,
except one, who was forced to accept Islamism. Our
churches have been turned into mosques, where the
remaining women and old men are compelled to go
and be taught Islam by the Mohammedan priest."

But here is another letter, from an Armenian
mother to her son in this country, which brings us still
closer to the actual horrors, for this woman was herself
a victim — turned at a blow from a comfortable ma-
tron to a naked beggar, in winter, among the ruins of
her village, her own friends killed, herself foully
abused. Read this, and then talk, if you dare, about
" exaggerated accounts " !

" December 12, 1895.

" My Dear Son:—

" We received your letter dated November 14th,
which we read with great pleasure. You asked for
information about us, as to how we are, etc. Except
your father, we are all still alive, with our relatives,
and long to see you very much. It is very hard to
describe with the pen all the misfortunes that we
have undergone. They cannot be told; but since you
are very eager to know, I will try to write it down
for you very briefly. My dear son, on Tuesday,
November 28th, they took by force the oxen that are
used for ploughing the fields. Until the evening of
that day they gathered all the oxen for ploughing from
Paloo and the neighboring Armenian villages, and
took them for themselves, and gave us notice that they
should attack the village. Wednesday morning all
the people of the surrounding Turkish villages gathered round about our village, and our village was be-

sieged until about noontime. From ten to fifteen persons were killed up to that time from our side, and the village was surrounded by more than twenty-two thousand Turks and Kurds, who bear arms. It was impossible for us to protect our village. We applied to the government, there was no government to hear us; despair reigned in the hearts of all. They fought until evening, and before they had reached us, we, all the villagers, left everything, even not taking bread for one meal with us, went to the monastery and left the village to the Turks. We passed the night in the monastery, hungry and thirsty; the number of the killed reached to thirty by morning. Then we learned that it was not safe, even in the monastery, although they had plundered it two or three times. Thursday, by noontime, the monastery was full of villagers. At noon there was a blow on the door of the monastery. Ravenous Turks, Zazes, and others were besieging the building. Until evening they beat at the iron door to break it; fifteen persons were at it, but it was impossible for them to open it. Within, the shrieks and the cries of the people reached up to heaven. Men, in order to save their lives, dressed themselves in women's clothes, and covered their heads. Your brother wrapped his moustaches so thickly that he should not be known, as the Turks were after him by name. About 3 p. m., when the Turks saw that it was not possible for them to open the gate of the monastery, they broke in one of the stones in the wall, and the plunderers entered. . . . I cannot describe here the sufferings of the people. . . Within one hour they robbed and violated a population of 1,500 people, five times each woman, married or maiden, and then left the monastery. The villagers, every one to save her or his life, left every-

thing, property, cattle, merchandise, and provisions,
and fled, the man leaving his wife, the wife her child,
the son his mother, the brother his sister, and they dispersed in the adjoining mountains, plains, valleys,
and hills, with only their under-garments on, as the
Turks and Kurds had stripped them of everything
else.   Friday morning the number of the killed had
reached about fifty. Your father was shot on the
plain of Sacrat, but the wound was not dangerous.
For three days the people gathered in Sacrat, hungry
and thirsty; from Sacrat they were given over to
the Zazes, to take them to the city. . . . I can
not write down here all the things we endured at the
hands of the Zazes. . Finally, after we had suffered
unmentionable cruelties, being twice plundered in
the city and violated, three brides and maidens were
carried away as slaves by the Kurds, more than one
hundred persons were martyred, among whom were
two priests, and the rest were forced to accept Mohammedanism, and after that the massacre ceased.
For twenty days we remained in the city, naked, hungry, and thirsty, also hopeless. The city was rescued
from the massacre after having suffered the loss of six
hundred houses, together with all the property of the
shops and stores, and the total sum of the martyred
being 2,000. Our village was given over to be burned
for twenty days successively. Out of two hundred
houses, there are hardly thirty left sound; the rest
are all razed to the ground. . . . The rest of
this story will follow by next mail. I wanted to tell
you a little about our hard situation. Saved with only
our undergarments, hungry and thirsty, our whole
family came back from the city, among the ruins. I,
your mother, had to go begging wholly naked and
barefoot to the familiar Kurd neighbors. I had only

one shirt, which I made into a bag to put the things in which I begged from the Kurds. For fifty days I have provided thus for the family; after this I commit it to your care; you know best what to do. We have not got even a head covering; nothing to carry the water home in from the fountain. It is the month of December, and you know well it is the first month of the winter; we have two and a half months yet before coming to the spring. We are all of us very, very, hungry. Those Turks who were so friendly before have turned now not to know us, they don't even give a penny. We have no hope from anywhere else; if you do not come to our help, we shall perish ! perish ! perish ! We, with all the villagers shall die. Behold the description of our misery. Read this to all the villagers that are there with you, and notify them that all of you must be the helpers and deliverers of our people, especially to us who are all helpless and on the verge of starvation. Send us help. I remain

" Your affectionate mother."

MALATIA AND ITS HARDSHIPS.

Malatia is located about midway between Marash and Harpoot, a little distance from the Euphrates river. More fruit is raised in and about there than in any other section of Armenia. The assortment is large, but the apples and pears are especially fine, perhaps better than those of any part of the world. It has about 20,000 population, two-thirds being Mohammedans, and one-third Armenians. The private letters which have been received from there do not state, and cannot state how many Armenians have been killed during the period of the present persecutions, and it is not likely there ever will be any correct estimate of them. The region has suffered immensely, and letters from there reveal a most distressing condition of affairs. The people were plundered and violated in every conceivable way until there was nothing more for the time being for the fiends to wreak their cruelty upon.

LETTERS FROM MALATIA.

Malatia, Dec. 22, 1895.

My Very Dear Son:—

We greet you with the fondest greeting, and it is the desire of our hearts that the good Lord should enable us to see each other again in this mortal flesh. In regard to ourselves, as to how we were, and what we are doing. We are all alive yet with our whole family, no loss of persons from among us. Don't mourn for us. Others are mourning for their loved ones. Though in truth the grief and mourning of others belong to us also because we are all Armenians, one flesh and blood, and we all belong to the same nation.

I did not go to bring up the bride of our neighbor's with the rest, so I was at home when the massacre began. You remember that there was a well in that quarter. The Turks killed the bridegroom, his brother, the priest, together with sixty-five other men, and threw them into that well. In another house they burned seventy-five men, and in still another forty-five men. Finally, I am unable to describe with my pen all that passed in those days and hours.

ARMENIAN PEASANT GIRL.   MOUSA BEG. Kurd chief.

Mousa Beg was specially rewarded for his outrageous and brutal treatment of this girl.   He killed her father by thrusting red-hot wires into his body.

REV. ..... THOUMAIAN (The Armenian Christian Exile), Condemned to Death by the Mohammedan Turks, and Rescued by the intervention of the British Government

May the Lord preserve your dear lives, and give you peace and happiness. · Your father.

Another Letter.

Malatia, Dec. 22, 1895.

My Dear Friend:—

I received your very kind letter about a week ago, for which I thank you very much, and I read it with great pleasure. But we do not get the boys' letters regularly. It is nearly two months since the disaster occurred, and in that time I have received but one letter. The other day an Armenian handed me a letter that was torn into nearly a hundred pieces. I put all the pieces together and read it. It was also from the boys, and I read and was very glad. Now I will try to give you a little information about us. The first Monday I did not go to the market, for from Saturday I got somehow suspicious that there was something impending over the city, and I did not let father go either. My brother.was to accompany those who were going to bring up a bride for my brother's partner in business. While my brother was at the wedding house, they sent him on an errand to go and get a few policemen to accompany them as protection in bringing the bride. Just at the moment when my brother was on his way to the station-house, he sees there was confusion in the market; then he drops the matter of bringing a policeman, but goes to the market and closes the shop, and then turns towards home in a hurry. While on his way, some men fired at him several times, but fortunately he was not hurt. He comes as far as to one of our neighbors, and there drops down exhausted. They came and brought me the news that he was there. Then I plucked up all the courage I could, and went and brought him home. An hour or so after, the Turks came and besieged that

18

same quarter and killed about thirty persons. · On
Tuesday, very early in the morning, we left everything, house, property, and goods, and just to save our
lives we fled to the new church, and I don't know
what became of the rest. We remained there in the
church until Friday; after that we came out of the
church, being a little assured of safety, and have been
living on the provision that the government allowed
us, but that also ceased a few days since. When we
came back home again we did not find a single thing;
they had swept off everything. We brought a mat-
ting from some place, and six of us sleep in one bed.
Some sleep on hay. May you never have to endure
such hardships. This incident seems worse than the
earthquake or the cholera, or the fire. May the good
Lord preserve us from things worse than these. Our
life is not worth the living. We don't know the exact
number of the killed. Malatia is altogether a ruin.
It is a worse ruin than the city of Anni, and even worse
than Sassoun. It is beyond conception, one cannot
keep account of it. May the Lord write it down in
his own account book, so that he should take the account in the day of judgment.

Please excuse all my shortcomings, because I am
out of myself. Our love to all the friends over there.

Yours truly,

P. S. Please tell the boys to know the value of
money, and not waste neither their time nor their money in vain. For we have no one to look for but to
God in heaven, and after Him to them on earth. For
the value of a son is known in the time of adversity,
when he helps his elders or parents. Let them not yet
send any money, for there are no brokers left where
we can change it.

THE CITY OF SIVAS AND THE ATROCITIES.

Sivas is the seat of the vilayet or province of Sivas. The Governor-General of that province resides there. The population is about 30,000; one-third are Christian Armenians, and there are many Armenian Christian towns and villages round about, so that, if the Armenians are not more numerous than the Mohammedans, they equal them in number.   Sivas is a missionary station, and during the atrocities, the Protestant Armenian pastor also was killed.   His name was Garabet-Kilitjiam, one of the most gifted ministers of the gospel, my personal friend and successor.   After I resigned my pastorate at Talas, Cesarea, he succeeded me.   He was offered the choice of accepting Mohammedanism, but refused it, and then he was martyred.

In the city and province of Sivas during the recent atrocities about 10,000 Armenians were killed, and many villages and towns were plundered and destroyed.

The following is a press dispatch:—

London, Nov. 16, 1895.— The representative of the United Press at Constantinople reports, under the date of November 15th, that at six o'clock, on the evening of November 14th, M. A. Jewett, United States consul at Sivas, sent a telegram to United States Minister Terrell informing him that in the disturbances which had taken place at Sivas, eight hundred Armenians and ten Turks had been killed, and that, according to official reports, a large body of Kurds were then approaching the town. Mr. Jewett gave no details of the disorders, but the discrepancy in the figures shows that the Turkish allegations that the Armenians were the aggressors are absolutely untrue, and that the Armenians were deliberately massacred.

From a private letter from Sivas, Nov. 21, 1895.

" The air was full of wild rumors — but we could get at nothing that seemed to have any substantial truthful basis. Dr. Jewett — our consul — was on the alert. He interviewed the Governor-General,— and asked for protection for us, for the U. S. A. vice-consul, for our schools, and for the American Consulate. These were cheerfully promised, and the next day, Tuesday, November 12th, at midday, like a cyclone, Sivas was smitten, as I wrote you last week. Mr. P. and I had steadfastly refused to believe that such violence could take place in our city, and we were totally unprepared for the shock. Our walls had been taken down,— that is, our front wall had been,— a distance of 125 feet. Our girls' school-building had been cut off seven and a half feet on the south-west corner, and both our schools and our dwellings were in an entirely unprotected state. The day of the terrible disaster, the city water was cut off from our street, and for several days the heat was unusual for this time of the year. The dead were buried on Thursday, under the direction of the government, in the Armenian graveyard, a priest of the Gregorian faith being present to offer a prayer.

" Our good native pastor was in the market to attend to the interests of his people, when, at a given signal, a tribe of mountaineers, known as Karsluks suddenly fell upon the Armenians with clubs, and were soon followed by Circassians and local Mussulmen, with knives and pistols; quickly and lastly the police force and regular soldiers joined in with their Martini rifles. It was a combined onslaught of four other races against the Armenians. It has been declared that the Armenians were in armed revolt against the government, and this was done to put down the revolution. When the attack was made against them, we fail to find that there was any armed re-sistance, so far as we can learn. If the Armenians were premeditating an armed attack upon the Mus-sulmen, we never could find it out, but that proves nothing here or there, as missionaries are well known not to sympathize with revolutionists.

"Badveli Garabed died a martyr; his life being offered him three times if he would deny Christ. He bore noble testimony before many witnesses, then fell in their presence, sealing his faith and testimony with his blood.

"Yours affectionately,"

Further Information about Sivas by the Missionaries who wrote to their friends Nov. 12, 1895.

"The cyclone which struck on the 12th reached Marsovan on the 15th. Don't be deceived by any of the silly government statements which attribute all these massacres to the Armenians. It was a deliber-ate plan on the part of the government to punish the Armenians. The Sultan was irritated because he was forced to give them reforms, so he has had 7,000 Armenians killed to show his power since he signed the scheme of reform.

"The killing was permitted to go on here all last week; forty-six were killed Saturday, November 16; sixteen on Sunday, and many more on the follow-ing day. The total number killed is about 1,200 Ar-menians and ten Turks.

"It is a fact that the Kaimakam of Gurun tele-graphed to the Vali at Sivas, saying in effect that there is not an Armenian left at Gurun. The Armenians at Sivas made no resistance, but at Gurun they tried to defend themselves from the butchery, and suffered the worse for it.

"In order to have an excuse for attacking the Armenians at Sivas, the government smashed the windows of Turkish shops and charged it to the Armenians. Food is scarce, and everything was carried off from the Armenian shops. There will be terrible suffering all over this country."

Another letter from Sivas, according to the Constantinople correspondent, gives many details which all go to show that the whole movement against the Armenians is directly traceable to the head of the Turkish government, who proclaimed that his great desire was to keep always in view, "The safeguard of the rights of the people, and the maintenance of public confidence."

"What cruel mockery; Trebizond, Erzeroum, Bitlis, Marash, Harpoot and how many more towns rise up and point the finger of everlasting scorn and indignation to fix on Abdul Hamid Khan the stigma of everlasting infamy! The deliberate murder of thousands of innocent and industrious men, the exposure of ten times that number of women and children and aged persons to absolute degradation and destitution, will justify the name of Kanukiar — the Bloodletter — which has been applied to the head authority of the Empire."

The Riot in Sivas.

"Last week, Monday, November 11, was one of the loveliest days Sivas ever had. Although there were many rumors of trouble afloat, we could get at nothing which seemed to have any greater foundation than the fear that something might happen.

"I went unattended to the boys' school. On my way to school that afternoon, I met a group of excited soldiers. They said nothing to me, but their strangely excited manner impressed me as being out of the usual order. When I began my class work, the boys, instead of answering my questions, broke forth with inquiries. They wanted to know if the soldiers were going to shoot them, and if they were going to be killed. That was the rumor afloat. I hushed them up as best I could, and told them it was not right to speak of such things. I succeeded in quieting the children, but went home full of anxiety.

" The next day, Tuesday, a large gang of Turkish workmen gathered in our street to continue the public work of building up some walls which had been torn down at the Vali's orders, for the purpose of widening the street. Armenian carpenters were employed on our building. Nothing out of the ordinary occurred until the workmen's ' bread time,' about 11 o'clock, was finished.

" Then all the Osmanli (Turkish) gang suddenly raised a hue and cry; each one grabbed a pick or club, anything he could lay his hands on, and a wild rush was made for the market-place. The air was filled with yells of the furious men, who rushed along madly.

" The Protestant pastor remained at home on the day before, but on Tuesday was in a shop when the signal for the raid was given. A perfect cyclone of marauders rushed in and clubbed the unsuspecting men in the stores to death before they could offer any resistance. After the outbreak there was not a single Armenian place of business left in the market.

" No list of the dead was made out, and none could be. The victims were all buried in an immense trench in the Armenian burying-ground two days afterwards. There were between seven and eight hundred bodies thus buried."

MARSOVAN AND THE ATROCITIES THERE.

· Marsovan has 25,000 population, 10,000 being Armenians, and the remainder Mohammedans. Marsovan is one of the greatest stations of the American missionaries. Anatolia College is there; a theological seminary for young men; and a seminary for girls. The writer was the pastor of the Evangelical Armenian church there till he was banished, for the reasons stated in the sketch of him. After this the Turks burned the girls' school; they tried to burn the boys' college building also, but did not succeed. Finally they several times massacred the Armenian Christians, and forced many to accept Mohammedanism.

I have not been able to get exact information about the number of the martyred Christians in Marsovan, but it is believed that in that missionary station about 1,000 were massacred altogether. The richest men among the congregation were murdered, and so thoroughly plundered that their children are left wholly destitute; and the lives of the missionaries are in danger.

CESAREA (KAISERIEH).

The writer is well acquainted with this city, as he was the pastor at Talas, only three miles away, for years. It has about 50,000 population, one-third being Christians; a few hundred Greeks only, but more than 15,000 Armenians. The richest and ablest Armenians live in that city, or in Constantinople, and came from there; its people are the leaders of

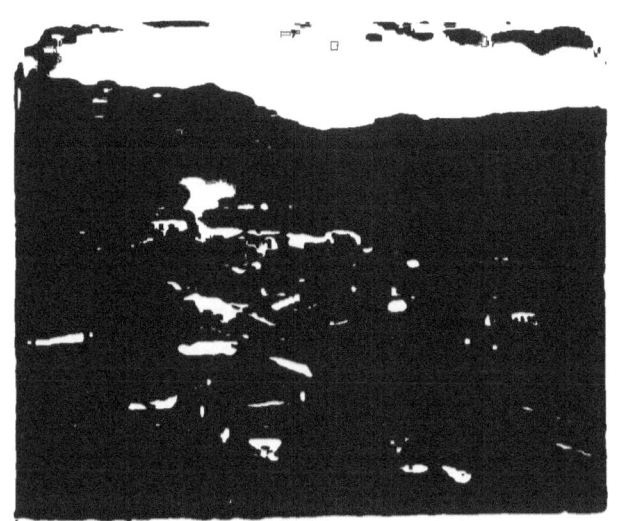

MARSOVAN. (300 Armenians Killed Here.)

WATER PEDDLER.

the Armenian nation, both in business and intellect. For the story of its foundation, see " The Haigazian Dynasty," under King Aram. It is a typical Armenian city; and has several great Armenian churches, with flourishing schools. There is a beautiful evangelical church also, and it is a great missionary station, with several American missionaries, and several missionary schools, both for boys and for girls.

The Rev. Dr. Avedis Yeretzian, one of the greatest of scholars, teachers, and preachers, and my personal friend, was martyred in that city during the recent atrocities. He was shot dead in his own house by a Mohammedan mob, then his wife was shot, then his son, and the remainder of his children were captured by the mob. About 3,000 Armenians were killed and wounded there, besides the loss of property. The Mohammedan population of the city is very savage; side by side in the same city, the Christians are rich, refined, intelligent, and the Mohammedans poor, lazy, sensual, and cruel. I give here two letters from Cesarea.

A Private Letter from a Girl.

Cesarea, Turkey, Dec. 31, 1895.

My Dear Brother:—

Before the massacre, everybody was in fear; several families would gather in one house to protect themselves, and all the Armenian stores were closed for twenty days; but as the government guaranteed that there would be no danger, and told everybody to attend to their business, and open their shops, they did so. It was the 16th of November, on Saturday,

that all opened their shops again, and the transaction
of business commenced in full force.   At 2 p. m., at
the doors of the market, bugles sounded, and several
hundred bashi-bazook [irregular soldiers] were at the
doors of the bazaar, every one of them having in his
hands stilettos, swords, yataghans, guns, revolvers,
hammers, axes, hatchets, sickles, poniards, daggers,
and heavy sticks with twenty or thirty nails fastened
to them.   Then they blew horns, the signal to start
the massacre.   Cries were heard, " First kill, cut, and
butcher the Giavours; the property already belongs
to us; cut, cut, kill, don't care for plundering at present."   Then they rushed into the market and slaughtered all they met.   Oh ! you can imagine what
became of those who fell into the hands of those brutes.
Alas ! alas ! how unspeakable !   They butchered
them like cattle; cut their heads off like onions.   Some
tried to run, but could not, others tried to escape, but
were brought back and killed.   The bazaar was full
of dead bodies.   People hid themselves among the
goods, and in the cellars, and were saved; ten or fifteen
days after, people were found there in a starving condition, not having dared to come out.   They killed in
Avsharaghus factory thirty-eight men; in Kayanjilar
everybody was slain.   After the massacre was over,
the governor, Ferick Pasha, sent soldiers around, and
they discovered many people hiding, and took them
back to the government house (scray), examined their
pockets for revolvers and knives, and not finding any,
the governor sent them to their homes.

They plundered the bazaar of all its goods, and
then, oh, my Lord ! they rushed upon the houses and
upon the women's Turkish baths.   .   .   .   I cannot describe this; when I think of it, my whole body
trembles.   The people in the baths were killed and
wounded, and they carried away the young girls; every

one was killed that they came in contact with. The houses were plundered of all their contents, and buildings were torn down, and houses full of people were burned. Oh, how terrible ! What I say you cannot imagine to be so; you may think it is a dream, because your eyes have not seen nor your ears heard the screams, wailings, weeping, shrieks, and groaning; that even our forefathers have not heard, but of which our ears are full day and night. My brother was in the bazaar, but fortunately he had occupied a private room, where he was safe.

Some of the kidnapped girls were brought back by the government, but most of them were wounded, and half dead from fright. Thank God, we are safe, but we are not better than those girls. We are in Mr. Wingate's house, where many lives were saved. He carried beds and clothing to the people, who were stripped of all. A few Mussulmans also protected in their homes some Armenians; for example, James Imuroglov, Gojaki Ogloo.

Yeretzian Avedis Effendi's house is ruined, himself, his son, and wife are killed, and the rest, five of them, are carried away. Our block and their block is ruined. They butchered Avjinury, Yuzukji, Dirnhitza and carried away her three daughters, but later on brought two of them back. I mentioned them, as you know. They also butchered Yuzikji Apraham and his wife Gaga Haji, Gemerlkli Ohanness, Mustaamelji Gobra, Terrzi Artin, Erzurumli, servant boy. Avedis Ago and his daughter were carried away. Gussi Hamimon's mother is low. Oh, pity the intolerable many, many, I cannot write by my pen, or describe with my tongue the terrible sufferings. O Lord, have mercy upon us ! To my knowledge there were five hundred killed, six hundred wounded; many are dying from their wounds and fright. Eight hundred houses are plundered, and the tenants flocked to the churches. I cannot write one hundredth part of what happened.

We are lost, lost, ruined, no work, no business, every one of us looking for safety. Happy, happy be you that are in America and have nothing to fear. They say to me, you ought to be with your brother in America now. If the way was opened, everybody would like to go.

If you are not in good circumstances there, you must feel satisfied and give the thanks to God always. We also have to thank God that we are still living. It is one month now that we have not been able to go out in the streets. O Lord, help us, Oh! what shall we come to? Oh, my dear brother, if you can help us in any way please do so; make lectures, get some help; everybody is dying of hunger. I cannot write any longer; we leave all to your conscience. I do not write this letter only to you, but to all. Do whatever you can for us, we are in a terrible condition. I thank you, my brother, for the money that you sent to me, thank you very much.

We send our best regards to every one of you. I wrote this letter with the tears in my eyes. We beg of you to write us good letters. Vaham, the little boy, is in good health. We are all well including

Your sister,

Letter from Cesarea.

Cesarea, Nov. 20, 1895.—While the Armenians were engaged in their business, as usual, the Turkish mob fell upon them, killing 600 defenseless men and wounding 1,000 more. The mob divided into four parts. The first part plundered the stores, the second looted the houses, the third secured the maidens and young brides, while the fourth, fiends incarnate, attacked the public baths. These human devils killed six naked women in the presence of the others, snatching their babies from their arms and bayoneting the mothers. The shrieks and agonizing cries of these poor creatures made no impression upon the minds of the savage Turks, who laughed at their death agonies. They then took some of the young girls, who were with their mothers at the bath, and dragged them naked, by their feet, through the streets, followed by a jeering and hooting mob.

The Turks who attacked the houses then killed them and fired the houses. The cries of the women, mingled with the hoarse shouts of the Turks, can never be forgotten. The men who survived the sword were discovered, taken to the magistrate and searched, but no arms were found in their possession, not even a knife. When released, and allowed to return to their homes, they were confronted by a most ghastly picture. Some found their wives dead, others horribly mutilated; daughters were bleeding. My hand almost fails me to write the awful particulars. It took three or four days to remove the bodies of the dead with forty carts. Add to this the want, the desolation. Oh, my God, for how long, how long! Where are those Christian powers who saved African slaves? Where are those Christians who advocated brotherly love and mercy, sending their missionaries to teach us? Are they deaf to our piercing cry?

AINTAB AND ITS HORRORS.

The writer is well acquainted with Aintab, and some of his best friends live there, if they have not been killed. It has about 40,000 population, one-third of it being Armenian. There are great scholars among them. Central Turkey College is there.

It is an American college, but most of the professors are native Armenians, graduates of Yale College. There is also a woman's American College and a hospital. The Evangelical Armenians are the strongest; they have three large churches. They are considered to be the richest Evangelical Armenians in Turkey. But hundreds of them were killed, wounded and plundered; in all about 4,000 of the Armenian population were killed.

A Letter from Aintab, November 23, 1895.

Aintab has had its baptism of blood and fire, and we sit in grief among ruins. We had been hoping that the many things which seemed to combine for our security would save our city from the fury of the storm which is desolating so many places about us. Our Christian community is large (about one-fourth of the whole population), and the Christians, as a class, are exceptionally intelligent and influential; the leading Moslems of the city are intelligent and able men, and have shown themselves to a degree tolerant and even friendly to Christians; the governor has seemed disposed, beyond most Turkish officials, to respect the rights of Christians. There is a considerable number of foreign residents sure to be witnesses of any violence done to Christians. The college and hospital have for years commanded a powerful influence in the city; the hospital especially has the good-will of all classes; the college, its students and teachers were no doubt regarded by many with much suspicion on account of the latent antagonisms inevitably existing between progressive and conservative ideas, but personal relations were, so far as I know, always friendly. Another thing in our

favor has been the fact that the Christians of Aintab
have given very little countenance to the ultra-revo-
lutionists, who have no doubt provoked trouble in
some places. Relying upon all these things, we had
for nearly three weeks been hearing reports of fighting
and massacre at Zeitoon, Marash, and Oorfa, and other
places, with comparatively little anxiety for ourselves.
It is true we were frequently hearing of fearful
threats and warnings of what the Moslems were preparing to do in Aintab, but we had got hardened to
that sort of thing, and regarded it as largely the in-
vention of cowardly roughs to terrify those whom they
did not dare attack. The most alarming thing in the
situation was that the government was disarming the
Christians, and at the same time giving out rifles and
ammunition to Moslems. This, however, was at-
tributed to an exaggerated fear of a Christian rising,
of which they profess to have information.

Meantime the Moslems liable to military service
were called out and equipped and hurried off toward
Zeitoon, where it was reported that the Christians
were in rebellion. This, no doubt, was the occasion
of intense irritation, and both the soldiers and their
friends were saying, " If we must fight Christians we
will begin with those close at hand." Under these
circumstances the native Christians became very
anxious, and made such preparations for defense as
circumstances permitted, at the same time keeping as
quiet as possible, and avoiding all controversy and al-
tercations with the Moslems. The government increased the police force in the city, and held a considerable force of troops at the barracks near the
town, and the governor and principal men seemed to
be making much effort to quiet the people. Several
considerable tumults had occurred and been promptly
suppressed without bloodshed; so day after day

dragged on, each hour increasing the hope that we should tide over the crisis.

Saturday morning, November 16, more than three weeks after the first riot in Marash, at about half past seven, just as we were rising from breakfast, our people came in with white faces saying, " The day of judgment has come in the city." We hastened to the door, and sure enough the mob was at work; all the west and south part of the city seemed to be in an uproar; crowds of people rushing in every direction, roofs covered with excited men, women, and children; the strange mingling of cries of fear, anger, and defiance, with occasional gun and pistol shots, made an exhibition of the most fearful tumult and confusion.

Already troops were hurrying forward, and soon a company of some sixty soldiers were stationed in front of the Girls' Seminary, with pickets out to cover the approaches to the hospital and college. Dr. Shepherd and Mr. Sanders mounted their horses and hastened to the hospital and seminary, where they remained until the rioting ceased. The college is about half a mile west of the seminary and hospital, and commands a full view of these buildings, and of the whole west end of the city, where most of the rioting occurred.

What we, who were looking on, saw from this point was the narrow streets densely crowded with intensely excited people, now and then a rush made upon some house or gate, the rally of defenders on the roofs, among whom women were often foremost, using stones, clubs, and sometimes guns and pistols as best they could. Sometimes the attack is beaten off, and the assailants withdraw to organize a new assault, sometimes a gate or wall is broken down, and then the noise of conflict subsides and the work of massacre and plunder begins.   Later on, long lines of people moving off to their homes laden with plunder, and later still the flames and smoke rising from the burning houses.

What we heard was the indescribable roar of the mob, pierced by the sharp reports of pistols and guns, with now and then shrieks of agony and fear, and shouts of defiance or command, and over all, and most horrible of all, the loud shrill " Zullghat," (wedding cry) very like the cry of our northern loons prolonged and sharpened, raised by Turkish women crowded on their roofs and cheering on their men to attack.   The massacre and pillage began in the markets, and in those parts of the city where Christians' houses, surrounded by Moslem neighbors, offered easy points of attack; these places having been looted, the mob moved on towards what are known as the Christian quarters of the town.   There the resistance became more obstinate; in two of these quarters the old street gates were still in use, by shutting which, the district enclosed becomes a small fortified community capable of making a strong resistance to an organized mob. The assailants were at last beaten off and arrested.

Under such general conditions the storm of mob violence raged on without much abatement till the middle of the afternoon, when the tumult gradually subsided, and night at last brought quiet, except in the vicinity of burning houses, where the uproar went on till near midnight.   By morning, arrangements seemed to have been made which gave us hope that order would be maintained; the guard for our mission premises had been increased, and the soldiers posted at intervals around the Christian quarters of the city.   Very early in the morning of the 17th, crowds, evidently eager to share the plunder, were seen hurrying towards the city from every direction.

19

The soldiers met and turned them back, and even beat some of them and chased them off. They soon returned, however, increased in numbers, and being joined by friends from the city, became very turbulent. About noon we saw through our glass an officer, apparently a captain, ride forward into a mob, and address them at some length; we could not hear what he said, but immediately, without any show of opposition from any one, the whole crowd came pellmell with the soldiers into the city. This was at the southwest corner of the town, and immediately under our eyes. At the same time much the same thing was occurring at the northwest corner; then for an hour chaos was let loose again, and the horrors of the previous day were repeated, only that this time the Christians were prepared, and, being in a strong position, were generally able to beat off their assailants. At one point of the line of defense were a few Moslem houses, and we were delighted to learn that the men heartily and bravely joined in the defense with their neighbors; the gallantry of this act was somewhat marred, however, by the demand which they made the next day for a large sum of money for their service; these men actually demanded and received about $5 apiece for this neighborly help.

When it became apparent that the mob could not force their way into the places held by the besieged, the soldiers, perhaps having received new orders, resumed a show of activity, fired a few shots into the air, and drove the mob out of the city and dispersed them; this is the last serious fighting that has occurred up to the present time, though local tumults have broken out frequently, several houses have been pillaged and burned, and two Christians at least were shot while being conducted through the streets by soldiers. Strict military rule is now established, and special care is taken to safeguard the lives of property of foreigners. We are kept under very close restriction, and not allowed to visit the city except for special objects, and then under a strong guard. The amount of damage we can only estimate; as nearly as we can judge, the figures will be about 200 killed, 400 wounded, nearly all the Christian shops and 250 houses pillaged, and a considerable number burned. Some 1,000 men who in the first panic took refuge in khans and mosques are still held as prisoners, for purposes which we can only surmise.

P. S. Dec. 17. Quiet has for the most part been maintained under strict military rule. No Christian can yet venture out without armed escort, and there are not wanting signs that there is waiting and even expectation of another signal from above. The government, however, seems to be trying to restore order and confidence. We are glad to say that we have heard of no cases of special violence or abuse offered to women.

The above-named prisoners have been gradually released, till now there are only some six of the principal Christians still in confinement. The number of killed just now must be set down at over 400; the butchery in the markets where the first attacks began far exceeded our belief. A great number of bodies were thrown together into some distilleries, and these buildings set on fire and burned to the ground, thus removing for a time much of the terrible evidence of the extent of the massacre. The attack being made in the morning and beginning in the markets, it happened that the killed are about wholly from the " bread-winners " among the Christians. As a result, there are now in Aintab more than 4,000 people dependent on charity for daily bread, and most of those to whom they would naturally look for aid are utterly impovcrished; the outlook for the winter is simply appalling. We appeal for aid speedily in the name of humanity.

THE CITY OF BIRIJIK AND THE ATROCITIES.

The city of Birijik is on the shores of the Euphrates; it has a beautiful appearance from the other side of the river. The Mohammedan population there are very wild and ignorant.

The Massacre at Birijik (Province of Aleppo).

Birijik had about 300 Christian houses, or say about 1,000 souls, in the midst of the Mussulman population of about 9,000 souls. After the massacre at Oorfa on the 27th of October, 1895, the authorities at Birijik told the Armenians that the Muslims were afraid of them, and that therefore they (the Armenians) must surrender to the government any arms that they possessed. This was done, the most rigid search being instituted to assure the authorities that nothing whatever in the way of arms remained in the hands of the Armenians. This disarmament caused no little anxiety to the Armenians, since the Muslim population was very generally armed, and was constantly adding to its arms. In fact, during the months of November and December the Christians have kept within their houses because the danger of appearing upon the streets was very great.

Troops were called out by the government to protect the people. Since the soldiers had come to protect the Christians, the Christians were required to furnish animals for them to carry their goods. Then they were required to furnish them beds and carpets to make them more comfortable. Finally they were required to furnish the soldiers with food, and they

were reduced to a state bordering on destitution by
these increasing demands.

The end came on the first of January, 1896, when
the news of the massacre of several thousands of Christians at Oorfa by the soldiers appointed to guard them
incited the troops at Birijik to imitate this crime.   The
assault on the Christian houses commenced at about
nine o'clock in the morning and continued until night-
fall.   The soldiers were aided by the Muslims of the
city in the terrible work.   The object at first seemed
to be mainly plunder, but after the plunder had been
secured the soldiers seemed to make a systematic
search for men, to kill those who were unwilling to
accept Mohammedanism.   The cruelty used to force
men to become Muslims was terrible.   In one case
the soldiers found some twenty people, men, women,
and children, who had taken refuge in a sort of cave.
They dragged them out and killed all the men and
boys, because they would not become Muslims.   After
cutting down one old man who had thus refused, they
put live coals upon his body, and as he was writhing
in torture, they held a Bible before him, and asked
him mockingly to read them some of the promises in
which he had trusted.   Others were thrown into the
river while still alive, after having been cruelly
wounded.   The women and children of this party
were loaded up like goods upon the backs of porters
and carried off to the houses of Muslims.   Christian
girls were eagerly sought after, and much quarreling
occurred over the question of their division among
their captors.   Every Christian house except two,
claimed to be owned by Turks, was plundered.   Nine-
ty-six men are known to have been killed, or about
half of the adult Christian men.   The others have
become Mussulmans to save their lives, so that there
is not a single Christian left in Birijik to-day.   The

Armenian Church has been made into a mosque, and the Protestant Church into a Medresse Seminary. —[Dr. Dillon.

OORFA AND ITS ATROCITIES.

Oorfa, the old Ur of the Chaldees, where Abraham, the old patriarch of the Bible, was born, was called Edessa in the time of Christ. I have told the story of King Abgar and his conversion in the historical part of this book. It had about 50,000 population, about 20,000 of whom were Armenians before the massacres. Out of that number 8,000 were slaughtered, according to Mr. Fitzmaurice, the British vice-consul who returned from Oorfa to Constantinople on March 21. The Evangelical Armenian pastor, the Rev. Hagop Abuhayatian, was also martyred. I knew him personally. He was educated in Germany, a man of great ability; a great scholar, and a great and forcible preacher.

A Letter from Oorfa, Jan. 28, 1896.

Dear Friend:—

Your only remaining brother sends you a letter, but no letters can begin to explain the sad state of this city. The massacre of Dec. 28 and 29 has left all homes except Catholics and Syrians entirely empty of any comforts. Many families have not one bed even; all cooking utensils, clothing, bedding, carpets, etc., were taken. Most have a little zakhere left, though some have not that. We are feeding about 175 of the most needy, and more will come to us every week. The loss by death is between 4,000 and 5,000. Our pastor, the Rev. Hagop Abouhayatian, Dr. Kivore, and brother Harotoun, Sar-

kis Varjebed Chubukian and brother and son, Garabed
Roumian, Habbourjou Avedis and brother Sarkis, old
sexton Garabed and other sexton Bogos, Majar Kivore and brother Bogos and Berber Monofa and two
sons, Eskejiyan Marderos, Zarman Roomian's three
sons, are some of the dead.   In all, our Protestant
dead are 115.   Some of our people perished in the
Gregorian Church, where 1,500 or 2,000 went for
refuge Saturday night, and on Sunday were murdered or burned, very few escaping.   It was the most
awful of all the terrible events of those two days.

Thank God, two hundred and forty were saved
by coming to me; sixty of them were men.   I could
not keep the men in my house or yard, because it was
forbidden by the guards, but I hid them elsewhere,
and fed them for three or four days.   The government carefully protected me, and killed as many of
my friends as possible.   We have our house and all
the schoolrooms full of the wounded and the most
forlorn.

Our Oorfa redeefs leave to-morrow; we have
new soldiers now for guard of the city, and Christians
especially.   Oorfa redeefs have been poor guards,
and but for them the awful work would not have
been accomplished.   The pastor of Severek, the Rev.
Marderos, was killed.   The Rev. Vartan remains
alive in Adayaman.   Both in Severek and Adavaman
the number of the killed was very great.   In Birijik
about two hundred were killed, and all remaining have
become Moslems; they have been circumcised.

In Aintab about three hundred were killed, 847
shops plundered and 417 houses.

During our first disturbance, six to seven hundred
shops here were plundered, and about 175 houses.
Then the Christians used arms to defend themselves.
Since then all arms have been taken by the govern-

ment from the Christians, and the leaders were forced to sign a paper stating the city as " in peace and harmony, thanks to the rulers," etc.; twenty-five signed it, and now almost all of these have been killed. Our pastor signed for Protestants.

Only two of the Gregorian priests remain, and they are wounded. The bishop is alive, but feeble, and does not work publicly now. Their state is very sad. We desire your prayers, and the aid of all who can give us help by money at this time.

Sincerely your friend,

P. S. Your brother asks you to send a letter to him by me.

DIARBEKIR AND ITS STORY.

Diarbekir (see the historical part for its foundation) has about 40,000 population. Nearly half of them are Christians, but not all of them are Armenians. There are Chaldeans also. The Armenian population numbered about 12,000, of which 5,000 were killed during the recent atrocities.

A Letter from Diarbekir, Nov. 20, 1895.

My Dear Sir:—

After salutation, I offer my thanks to God that after great dangers and tribulation we have reached the present time. God's will be done. How can I describe the horrors in our city to you ? Can any pen or any language tell them ? No, but I shall try to write at least a very short description of them. But who knows if this letter will reach you, because of the letters we write, very few reach you, and very few of your letters reach us, since the government has control of the mail, and it is the government that persecutes us. Our age is a peculiar age. God look at our misery and save us.

How happy were those who were martyred on Nov. 1, and have gone to their reward. The atrocities which happened here on November 1, 2, 3, cannot be matched in the history of the civilized world. I do not think they can be in that of heathen lands, where the people are barbarous.

When I write these lines to you, I hardly know what I am writing; the darkness of Egypt covers all around me. The former millionaires in the city have nothing and are begging bread. Nov. 1 was a black day for the Armenians. Many were separated from their loved ones, even parents from their children. Many merchants and rich people were so thoroughly plundered and stripped that they are literally left naked and hungry, and numbers have been put to unspeakable tortures by the Turks and Kurds. Nov. 1 was Friday; it was about noon when the Mohammedans came out from their mosques. The native Turks, the Kurds who were brought from outside, and the soldiers all united, swords, pistols, guns, axes, and clubs in their hands, fell upon the Armenians in the market place or business place, cut them to pieces, and plundered what they had. If they had been all killed by bullets it would have been a sudden death, and easier. But they cut them to pieces bit by bit with their axes, and made holes in the bodies with their swords.

When they were killing the Armenians, they were repeating the following words, " Bring testimony to prophet Mohammed. Our Sultan ordered us to kill these heathen dogs, the Armenians." The governor of the city, and all other officials, with the commander of the soldiers, during the time of the atrocities were sitting near the great mosque, and while listening to the cries and screams of the martyred Armenians, they were laughing and joking with great pleasure, and ordering the soldiers to carry the most valuable things to their houses.

After they had killed everybody, and plundered everything in the business place, they turned to the residences where Armenians lived, and began to burn and kill. Some of the soldiers went to the tops of the minarets or high towers, and began to shoot the Armenians from there. What a pitiful scene was the condition of the Armenian ladies, who were running from house to house, from street to street, and were shot dead, and their children left orphans. During the three days' massacre 4,000 Armenians were killed, and the burning of the houses and stores continued twenty-four hours. From the gate of the mosque to the place where they make saddles, and from the twin caravansary to the new caravansary, from Sheik Uatad to Melik Ahmed, all the buildings, 1,400 stores, were burnt and turned to ashes. There are other stores also which were not burnt, but everything was taken from them. The stores where goldsmiths worked every article is taken from.

When the Armenians go among the ruins to see if they can find any article, they are forbidden; and if some one manages to find anything, the Mohammedans take it from him, cursing him, and calling him a heathen dog at the same time.

When we come to the residences near your house, from the house of Darakji to the covered place of Sheytan aglou, all are destroyed; from Alo-Pasha bath to the Jemil Pasha Palace, all destroyed. But the church of the Patrees is not destroyed. St. Sarkis's church was plundered and afterwards burned. Before the church was burnt, they killed the priests, and unspeakable violations took place in the church.

In that quarter half of the population were killed, and the other half, who survive, are naked, bare-footed, hungry, and are begging bread.

Now the government pretends to give bread to the hungry, but nothing is given, and those who have a little give to the others who have nothing; but after a few days nothing will be left to eat.   Thank the Lord, the Kurds went out of the city.   But it is twenty days now since the massacre took place, and nobody dares to go out to the streets.

We have no stores, no money, nothing to eat. Though my personal house was not robbed, but I have ten orphans whose fathers and mothers were killed; I am taking care of them.   We have a little; we shall eat that, and see what the Lord will provide.

From the Rev. Dr. Tomy's house to the church of the Evangelical people all the houses were burned. Hovhanness's loss is about $1,000.   Those who hid themselves in Konsol Khan and in the church of the Patrees escaped death.   But every one who escaped was left hungry and thirsty from twelve to fifteen days in their places of confinement, because they were afraid of going out.

All the suburban towns and villages were totally destroyed.   In Sevorag both the Armenian church and the Evangelical Armenian church were destroyed, and only from fifty to one hundred persons were left alive.   The monastery of Argen was destroyed, and the teachers and all the inmates were killed.

They burnt the church of Ali-Punar and killed the priest.   From that place only five or ten persons were left alive.   Your brother at Kitibel with all his family are killed, and both the churches are burned. They forced the ministers to accept the Mohammedan religion; on refusal all three were killed, the Rev. Abosh, the Rev. Khidershap, and the priest.   All who were left alive at Kitibel are only about forty persons. Afram's brother Kisho with all his family were killed. At Renjil nobody is left. At Kara Bash only fifty persons are left alive. The village of Satou is entirely out of existence. In all this province all the towns and villages are destroyed, and the people are killed, except the village of Haziro, which is not destroyed, and the reason is that a Turk, Sevdim Beg, did not permit the Kurds and the Turks to destroy it.

What will become of us hereafter we do not know. We are still in danger, but we trust first in God, then in such friends as you. My personal damage is $5,000 and now is the time to show us sympathy and help us.

If you cannot do it yourself personally, can you not tell the people of the United States of America to help us and relieve our suffering ?

Sincerely yours,

TREBIZOND AND ITS ATROCITIES.

Trebizond is built on the shores of the Black Sea, and is a part of Armenia. The population is estimated at 40,000; only 10,000 are Christians; perhaps about half of them are Armenians, and nearly half of the Armenians were killed and wounded during the recent savageries. Mr. Chelton, who was going to Armenia to organize consulates, was in Trebizond, saw the massacre of Christians, and reported to the government at Washington:—

" Trebizond, Oct. 9, 1895.—Many Armenians were killed here in conflicts yesterday with Turks. No attempt was made to stop the massacre of the Armenians. The Turks were armed, and the number of troops present here is small. It is even stated that

TREBIZOND. THE SCENE OF A GREAT ARMENIAN MASSACRE.

soldiers took part in the slaughter, and in the pillage which accompanied it."

"London, Oct. 17, 1895.—The 'Daily News' publishes a dispatch from Constantinople giving a description by an eye-witness of the rioting at Trebizond. He says that four separate Moslem mobs surrounded the Armenian quarters at eleven o'clock on the morning of Oct. 8, and then began to pillage the shops. Being opposed, they fired on the Armenians, and soon a general massacre began.

"Soldiers joined the mob in firing on the Armenians and in pillaging the shops and houses. The scene continued until 4 o'clock in the afternoon, when nothing was left to pillage and nobody remained to be killed. The mob then began to disperse. The better class of Turks did their best to protect the lives of the Armenians. They sheltered the women and children and many men in their houses. The mob attacked only the orthodox Armenians, leaving Catholics alone."

An Armenian Massacre. Money Cabled to London by the Local Relief Association, Dec. 31, 1895.

"Recent letters telling of the massacres in various Armenian cities contain information that helps to explain many points in the awful outbreak of so-called Mohammedan fanaticism. A letter from Trebizond says:—

"'Bahri Pasha, governor of Van, started to come to Constantinople, and it was learned that he was bringing with him four of the fairest young maidens of Sassoun, who had been spared in the massacre, to make an acceptable present of them to his Sultan. This aroused the Armenian people of Trebizond to a frenzy, and it was impossible to restrain the young

men, the more daring of whom fired upon Bahri
Pasha, wounding him. But he carried out his mission to Constantinople, and was honored with the highest decoration and appointed governor of Adana.

"'Afterward the pasha of Trebizond, calling twelve
of the leading men of the city, demanded that they
should hand over the young men who attacked the
governor, and gave them just a few hours in which to
carry out his orders. The next day they answered him
that the government had no means of finding the men
out.

"'When the mails had arrived, and the people
went toward the postoffice, the trumpet was sounded
three times, and both the soldiers and the mob rushed
upon the people. It is impossible to describe the
horror of the scene — the roar of the murderers, like
that of wild beasts, the shrieks of the women in the
houses from whose arms their husbands and sons were
torn and murdered before their eyes, and universal
tumult, added to the sighs and groans of the dying.
And this we know is only one, and not even the most
terrible of the massacres.'"

BAIBURT.

"Constantinople, Oct. 28, 1895.—Another massacre of Armenians, accompanied by the outraging of
women, is reported to have occurred recently in the
districts of Baiburt, between Erzeroum and Trebizond.
According to the news received here, a mob of about
500 Mussulmans and Lazes, the greater majority of
whom were armed with Martini-Henry rifles, made an
attack upon the Armenians inhabiting several villages
of that vicinity, and set fire to their houses and schools.
As the Armenians fled in terror from their dwellings
they were shot down as they ran, and a number of men

and women who were captured by the rioters, it is added, were fastened to stakes and burned alive.

"The Armenian women who fell into the hands of the mob, it is asserted, were outraged and brutally mutilated. It is also stated that the churches were desecrated and pillaged, the cattle, and all the portable property of any value belonging to the Armenians being carried off by the marauders. During the disturbance 150 Armenians are reported to have been killed. The surviving villages applied for protection to the governor of Baiburt, who, after hearing their complaint, sent three policemen to the scene of the massacre after the slaughter was ended.

"The Turkish officials, it is claimed, know the ringleaders of the outbreak in the Baiburt district; but apparently no steps have been taken to arrest them."

Another Letter from Baiburt.

"The Armenian bishop's vicar was killed, the teachers in the schools and many other men and women were massacred. Women jumped into open wells to escape worse deaths; the villages round about were laid waste.

"Following this was the Erzinghan massacre. On Friday, the 25th of October, 1895, the Moslems finished their noon hour of prayer by pouring out of the mosques and attacking the Armenians in the market, who, taken by surprise, were shot and cut down to the number of 500; their shops being all plundered."

(Signed)   An American Missionary.

ERZEROUM.

This is a large city, almost on the boundary line between Russia and Turkey, in Turkish Armenia. It has about 60,000 people, one-third of whom are Armenians. Several times since the last Turko-Russian war the Christian Armenians have been massacred there by the Turks and the regular soldiers, and during the recent atrocities also there were massacred, and in all about 3,000 Armenians were killed.

Letter from Erzeroum.

"Nov. 27, 1895.—The massacre evidently was pre-arranged. It began all over the city at the same moment. The bugle was sounded, and the soldiers began. They first said, " No harm to women or children," but they soon passed those bounds. A soldier who was on guard says the order was given by the Porte. We made ready for defense, but it soon appeared that the soldiers had cut off the rabble from our section, for no mob passed our street. A few men tried to open the door, but three well-directed shots from our balcony sent them off.

" The soldiers at the head of our street, apparently to guard it, broke open three or four houses within a stone's throw of us, and carried off everything they found. We saw loads of plunder carried away by soldiers. A large number of women engaged in the same work. The affair began shortly after noon and continued about six hours. One Armenian was called to the door by an officer, who professed to be friendly, and was cut down in cold blood. Others were cruelly murdered. The death roll must be towards 300, if not more. Between fifty and sixty wounded are in the hospital.

" Two hundred were gathered in the Armenian cemetery, some horribly mutilated. There must be many wounded in the different houses. The pillaged houses are to be counted by the hundred. No house attacked was left until it was emptied of every movable thing. The next day we went to an Armenian home. In the middle of a small room (the kitchen), lying side by side on a mat, were the bodies of two young women, almost naked, a light covering thrown over their heads. At the other side of the room a grief-stricken woman was trying to make bread from a little flour that had been left. She had to borrow utensils to do it. She left her work, came forward and removed the covering from the bodies. They were those of young women developing into motherhood. The head and face of one was covered with blood, and she was also badly wounded in the hand. The other had a bullet wound through the abdomen from the right side. A companion of these two had been carried off, and was lying dead in another house. Their lives were sacrificed in defense of honor.

"We passed through the ruins to other rooms. Boxes and furniture were in splinters, windows smashed, walls ploughed with bullets. The floor was covered with big patches of blood. The bodies lying in the cemeteries are simply wrecks of human beings. The majority have bullet wounds. Nearly all have bayonet, sword and dagger wounds, some badly mutilated. Two or three were skinned, and some were burned with kerosene. A great many women are missing. Very many dead have been disposed of by the Turks. Hundreds have nothing to eat, and no means of getting anything. The villages of the plain have suffered awfully. No definite news has come; only the news that columns of smoke tell."

MARASH.

The writer became acquainted with many noble Armenians here during his three years in the Theological Seminary, and almost all his friends were killed.

20

Among them were the Rev. Sdepan Jirnazian, a noble Christian minister,— when I was a little boy he was my pastor in the suburbs of Antioch; — Bedros Iskiyan, an American citizen, butchered before his wife and children; Garabed Popalian, another noble man, and the richest among the Armenian Evangelical people; Dr. Kevork Gulizian; Khacher Bayramian and his family; Garabed Salibian, in whose house I used to take my meals. A private letter says that about half the Armenians were killed by the Turks. Marash had about 35,000 population; about 15,000 were Armenians, of whom about 7,000 were killed. It has four Evangelical Armenian churches there, a theological seminary, and a ladies' college. The local governor led the regular soldiers to plunder and kill the people.

Letter from Marash.

London, Nov. 28, 1895.—The correspondent of the United Press in Constantinople telegraphs, under date of November 27, that a second terrible massacre has occurred in Marash, and that the houses there have been pillaged without regard to who their occupants might be. It is reported that thousands of persons were killed and many hundred wounded. The American Theological Seminary was plundered and burned, and two of the students in that institution were shot, one being fatally wounded. The hotels and boarding houses also were plundered. The Christians at Marash, and in that vicinity, thousands of whom are destitute, have appealed for aid.

.. The following letter, under date of November 25, has been received here:

" I will report the events of the 18th in this city. At 7 a. m., almost simultaneously the firing of Martini rifles was heard all over the city, with conflagrations in three Christian quarters.

" We understood the meaning of it. Soldiers began firing against two Christian houses, and their inmates fled into missionary houses, and soon the soldiers were looting their buildings, followed by a mob, who smashed doors and windows, and carried away property.

" Towards noon a squad of soldiers approached the missionary grounds, and it was thought that a guard had been sent in behalf of the missionaries. They entered the grounds of the seminary and academy boarding department. Two seminary students, who had concealed themselves in a cave, were discovered, and one of them fatally shot, while the other was badly wounded.

" The soldiers looted the missionary academy boarding department of all the students' clothing and bedding, and a part of the year's provisions in store. Other soldiers joined and looted the seminary. They repeatedly went to an Armenian house near by, but did not force it.

" Three-quarters of that terrible day the missionaries were left to any chance fate that might befall them. They had been informed by a Moslem of a purpose to burn the Girls' College that day, and a note had been sent to the local governor asking for a special guard. He replied that the barracks near by were charged to care for them. It was soldiers in relays from that very place that were wrecking everything.

" In the afternoon four or five soldiers entered the seminary, and soon after, fire broke out in the rear. As the flames wrapped the building, a trustworthy captain with thirty soldiers appeared at the gate, and the missionaries were assured of safety. The soldiers still continue with the missionaries. We cannot estimate the loss of life. Leaders of society have been struck down everywhere, two missionary academy teachers among them."

AKHISAR.

The valley of the Sakaria (the ancient Sangarius), is, through a part of its course, followed by the Anatolia line of railway. At a spot ninety miles from Constantinople, where the valley broadens out into a considerable plain, is the station and town of Akhisar. This town was, until the tenth of this month, the center of a considerable trade. The plain is dotted with vineyards, olive orchards, mulberry gardens, fields of cotton, wheat, etc. The town consists of about 160 houses of immigrants from Bulgaria, Bosnia, and Rumelia (who, having been concerned in the celebrated Bulgarian massacres, found refuge in Turkish territory), and sixty houses of Armenians.

A Letter Oct. 15, 1895.

Thursday, Oct. 10 (a bright, beautiful day), was market day. Numbers of people from the surrounding villages had come with the fruits of their various industries. The market place consisted of sixty-three permanent shops, and about 150 temporary places of trade, where traders from the surrounding country exposed their wares for sale. The market was almost exclusively in the hands of Armenians, 200 of the shops and trading places being in their hands. Rumors of danger were afloat, but the Armenians anticipated no attack on market-day. They had no arms, or means of defense, and had taken no precautions. They soon began to notice, however, that their Mussulman neighbors had mysterious whisperings among themselves, and that some of them were searching, as with official authority, the persons of Armenian young men, who were supposed to have knives or revolvers about them. Those searching at last found a young Armenian, a seller of calico, who had a knife in his possession. At once they fell upon him, but he escaped in the crowd that gathered, and the Mussulmans turned upon the Armenians, saying, "We must kill them all. Let him who loves his religion join and help." With knives and clubs the work was carried on, the Armenians fleeing, or hiding themselves in or about their shops. Turkish officials encouraged the killers. A herald was sent through the market calling, "Let the Moslems go to the government house." They did go, and immediately returned with rifles and revolvers. Then the slaughter increased in madness. The piteous entreaties of the threatened, the shrieks of the wounded, the groans of the dying, the shouts of the killers, and the hysterical cries of some of the Christians, who, to save their lives were calling out with desperate energy the Mohammedan formula of faith, rose to the deaf heavens. Ten-year-old Turkish boys, as though hunting rats, rushed into holes and corners, and discovering the hiding-places of the merchants and traders, called to their fathers and big brothers, "Here is a Giavour!" and while that one was being dispatched they rushed off to ferret out another. For four hours the slaughter continued. Ropes were attached to the feet of the corpses, which were dragged like the carcasses of dogs through the streets to dry wells, into which they were thrown. An old man, aged 75, was **tumbled in alive, and left to die among the dead bodies** of his friends. The money and watches of the merchants were secured by the ruffians. The notes of hand and account books were torn into shreds (the killers were debtors to the merchants), and the shops were looted. Not so much as a pin or needle was left in the 200 shops. Then the cry was raised, "To the houses!" to complete the destruction of the Christian inhabitants.

Twenty-nine bodies were afterward recovered for burial; thirty-three persons (some of whom afterward died), were found to be wounded, and about forty are still missing. The lieutenant-governor arrived that night on the scene, and sent an official report (by telegram) to Constantinople, to the effect that a row had occurred between Turks and Armenians, in which three Armenians had been killed and two wounded, but that order had been restored! Efforts were made to cover the matter up. Christians were imprisoned for talking about the massacre, or for sending the news to friends. A prominent man, well-known throughout the country, wished to let his circle of friends know that he was still alive, and was permitted to advertise that he had met with an accident, but was quite well.

Great patches of dried blood in the shops presented the appearance of places used for the slaughter of sheep. Groups of people were standing before the houses, statue-like, bewildered and hopeless, while other groups were wailing over the news of the corpses of friends, just recovered from the wells. I saw one of the mutilated corpses, and have seen it night and day since.

An American Missionary.

The above missionary also says not only common people, but also officers of high rank, made free threats of massacre, and ostentatiously sharpened their swords and cleaned their weapons in the presence of their Armenian neighbors. Great care was taken by the authorities to deprive the Armenians of arms; but the Mussulmans were allowed to carry arms freely. The Constantinople demonstration and consequent massacre aggravated the situation. It was pitiable to see the fear that held the Armenians as in a nightmare, and to hear the threats and observe the bearing of the Turks.

A soldier, passing the door of a Christian house and observing a young woman sitting on the doorstep, ground his teeth and called out to her, "You may sit there four days more, and then I will have you on the point of this bayonet." The girl fled in terror into the house.

ZEITOON.

Zeitoon is fifteen miles from Marash. The Zeitoonlis are the bravest of all the Armenians; there are about 15,000 in the city, and no Mohammedans, save a dozen or two Turkish families, and they talk the Armenian language. Until about thirty years ago Zeitoon was a free city; but they were conquered by craft, and became tributary to Turkey. The Sultan garrisoned the place to keep them down, and the troops committed every sort of iniquity. Finally, about two years ago, the Sultan sent physicians there to poison the Armenian boys. These assassins professed to have come to vaccinate the boys; every boy who was vaccinated died. Then the Zeitoonlis revolted, captured the barracks from the soldiers, took all the guns, cannon, and ammunition, and sent the soldiers away. This action enraged the Sultan, and he sent some 20,-000 regular soldiers and 30,000 bashi-bazooks to punish them; but they were repulsed with heavy loss by the Zeitoonlis. It has been reported that during the battle between the Zeitoonlis and Turks about 15,000 of the latter were killed. Finally the Sultan lost hope of conquering them, and asked the European powers to use their good offices to restore peace in Zeitoon, and the consuls of the different powers induced them to resume peaceful work by guaranteeing that the Zeitoonlis shall not be molested. But who believes a word of it ? We know, with horrible clearness, of how much value the powers' "guarantee " is; they say there is no obligation but to keep count of the massacres.

A Few statements from Zeitoon.

" Turkish mendacity is again asserting itself. A few days ago the Sublime Porte set afloat the official report that Zeitoon has fallen, after hard fighting, in which 2,500 Armenians were said to have been killed as against 250 Turks. Now these official reports turn out to have been official lies. News from independent sources shows that Zeitoon has not yet fallen; that its gallant defenders are still holding out their own. To Armenians who understand Ottoman tactics, the alacrity with which Abdul Hamid sent abroad the news of the supposed victory of his troops is a sign of misfortunes and reverses. The Turks control the avenues of communication at Marash, and it is not surprising that they attempt to win victories upon telegraphic despatches — but not at Zeitoon.

The Armenians at Zeitoon are rebels against organized assassination, plunder, and arson. They have been unwilling to submit meekly to Turkish outrages, and are determined to defend their lives, their homes, and their property. They have vanquished Turkish armies before, and strewn the ground with thousands of Turkish carcasses. They need fear nothing but the lack of supplies. Will not Christian nations intervene to save a valiant people who are defending their homes and their liberties, and who cannot be conquered by force of arms, yet who may be compelled to surrender to inexorable hunger ?—[Tigram H. Suni, Dec. 31.

" London, Feb. 3.—A dispatch from Constantinople to the ' Daily News ' says: ' Reports from Turkish sources believed to be fairly accurate state that it is believed that the Zeitoonlis are still holding out. The Turks have made seven different attacks upon the town, but all have failed, and their losses are reported to amount to 10,000. It is alleged that 50,000 troops will be needed to capture Zeitoon.

" It is believed that the Zeitoonlis number from 15,000 to 20,000, well armed, and provisioned for a year. There is a doubtful report that 4,000 Russian Armenians crossed the Persian frontier, and defeated the Turks at Siz, eighteen hours from Zeitoon, and have joined the Zeitoonlis."

MISCELLANEOUS

In the province of Aleppo, the village of Chizek, the Armenian priest was killed for refusing to become a Mohammedan.

In the province of Erzeroum and the district of

Erzinghan, six separate attacks for pillage have been made upon the village of Zimara, and great pressure is being used to force the people of the village to become Mohammedans.

At the village of Gazma the houses have been pillaged, and numbers of the people have become Mohammedans to save their lives.

In the province of Bitlis a considerable number of Armenians at Sert have been forced to become Mohammedans. In the district of Shirvan, out of twenty-two Armenian villages, the inhabitants of four entire villages have become Mohammedans to save their lives. The priests also accepted Mohammedanism, and the churches have been changed into mosques. At a little village at which the inhabitants could not disperse over the mountains a considerable number were killed, and the survivors accepted Mohammedanism. This village is called Kourine. In the district of Chilain, returns from six villages have come in which show a considerable number of persons killed for refusing to accept Islamism.

In the province of Van the stuffed skin of the superior of the monastery of Khizan was still hanging from a tree in front of the monastery three weeks after the massacre took place; that is, at the date of the last news from there, Nov. 27. At Kharkotz in this province three priests accepted Mohammedanism, and were paraded through the streets in the dress of Mohammedan ulema in order to influence the people to follow their example.

In the province of Harpoot in many of the smaller villages, where the people have been supposed by the Turks to be mere peasants, without ideas of their own, the offer of Islamism has not been made, but the people seized without ceremony and circumcised by force, and are considered now as Mohammedans. At Haboosi, in this province, the Christian dead were left unburied in the streets for the dogs to eat. The Armenian church and the Protestant chapel and parsonage were burned.

At Peri, in the same province, 450 Christians were made Mohammedans by threats of death.

At Aivos in the same province, all the buildings were destroyed. The Armenian priest was forced to give the call to prayer, and was then shot for refusing to become a Moslem.

At Garmuri the Christians accepted Mohammedanism at the edge of the sword, and have been circumcised. The Protestant chapel and parsonage were burned, and the Armenian church has been seized and made into a mosque.

At Hokh the Armenian church and Protestant chapel and parsonage were burned.

At Houilu in the province of Harpoot, 266 out of 300 Christian houses were burned, among them the fine new Protestant church. Two priests were killed. Many of the people succeeded in escaping from the village. The rest have been forced to declare themselves Mohammedans.

The events above mentioned took place in the main

between Nov. 6 and Nov. 20. But the process of forced conversion and the murder of individuals who refuse to accept Mohammedanism was still going on as lately as the 20th of December, when the Turkish government was assuring the European Ambassadors that all is quiet in Asiatic Turkey, and that all that is necessary to complete the work of pacification is for Turkey to be let alone.

The nature of the pacification which may be expected if Turkey is left free to carry out its schemes for these provinces may be judged from the following list of educated and influential Protestant ministers, who have been put to death for refusing to embrace Mohammedanism. In every case the offer of life on these terms was made; in several cases time was allowed for consideration of the proposal; and in each case faith in Jesus Christ was the sole crime charged against the victim.

1. Rev. Krikor, pastor at Ichme, killed Nov. 6, 1895.
2. Rev. Krikor Tamzarien.
3. Rev. Boghos Atlasian, killed Nov. 13.
4. Rev. Mardiros Siraganian, of Arabkir, killed Nov. 13.
5. Rev. Garabed Kilijjian of Sivas, killed Nov. 12.
6. Rev. Mr. Stepan, of the Anglican Church at Marash, killed Nov. 18.
7. The preacher of the village of Hajin, killed at Marash Nov. 18.
8. Rev. Krikor Baghdasarian, retired preacher at Harpoot, Nov. 18.

9. Retired preacher at Divrik, killed Nov. 8.
10. Rev. Garabed Resseian, pastor at Cherwouk, Nov. 5.
11. Rev. Metean Minasian, pastor at Sherik, Nov.
12. Pastor at Cutteroul, Nov. 6.
13. Preacher at Cutteroul, Nov. 6.
14. Rev. Sarkis Narkashjian, pastor at Chounkoush, Nov. 14.
15. The pastor of the church at Severek, November.
16. The pastor of the church at Adiyaman.
17. Rev. Hohannes Hachadorian, pastor at Kilisse, Nov. 7.
18. The preacher at Karabesh, near Diarbekir, Nov. 7.
19. Rev. Mardiros Tarzian, pastor at Keserik, near Harpoot, November.

TELEGRAMS FROM HAJIN (ARMENIA).

To the English Consul at Aleppo, and to the English Ambassador of Constantinople.

All the suburban towns of Hajin where Christians live were plundered by Mohammedans, and some of the Christians were killed. The people of Hajin and we are in danger; immediate help is needed.—Nov. 5, 1895.

To the American Minister at Constantinople.

· The Christian villages of Hajin were totally plundered by the Mohammedans. About two thousand, naked and hungry, ran away and came to Hajin. Both the Christian people at Hajin and we are in danger; immediate help is needed.—Nov. 5, 1895.

EXTRACTS FROM A HAJIN LETTER.

My Dear Sir:—   Nov. 25, 1895.

The situation is growing worse here. All the suburban Christian villages were plundered by Mohammedans. Some of the villages which were plundered were as follows:—Shar-Dere, Roumlou, Kokooun, and Dash-olouk. All of them are left naked and hungry. Came here to our city, and we are taking care of them. And the government never punished any of the plunderers. They were encouraged, and surrounded our city, and nobody can go out of the city, and if this continues so, we shall have a famine soon, and die in the city. The government does not protect us, but helps the plunderers, and we are continually threatened to be killed. Our only hope is in God.

ANOTHER EXTRACT FROM A LETTER OF AN ARMENIAN.

Nov. 25, 1895.

My Dear Uncle:—   *

If you ask our condition, thank God that we are alive. But beside life we have nothing, no comfort, no happiness, no property, no church, no religion, all are taken from us. Though we are alive, many of our number were killed, and those who survive are wandering here and there, naked and hungry, and are dying in that manner.

God is angry, and exceedingly angry to us. Perhaps he will hear your prayers; pray for us, or else all of us shall perish. I can never describe the horrible situation in which we are put.

Yours truly,

GROUP OF ARMENIAN CHILDREN.

GROUP OF YOUNG ARMENIAN WOMEN

FROM HADISH VILLAGE, ARMENIA.

My Dear Friend:—   Dec. 2, 1895.

In great sorrow and in despair I am compelled to write to you a few lines to inform you of our most miserable condition.

The Turks and Kurds came to our village, plundered everything we had, killed more than 600 persons, violated the women and girls, tortured the pregnant women, and now we who survive have nothing to live on. Naked, hungry, cold, hopeless, we are crying bitterly. I write these few lines; perhaps you can inform the Christian world and they may help us and relieve our sufferings.   Yours truly,

There are many other cities, towns, and villages in Armenia, where thousands of people were tortured and killed, their houses burned and plundered, their children kidnapped, the women violated. But there is no space to put all here in this book. I am sure the reader will be satisfied with reading this long chapter of Armenian horrors, and the letters on the atrocities from different reliable sources.

To sum up, during these frightful scenes in Armenia more than 100,000 Armenians were killed, and half a million left without food, homes, or clothing; they are dying in heaps; and there is no hope of getting any help from Armenia itself, even when the spring comes, for those who would have supported them are killed, and most of the destitute are women and children. Everything, even to clothes, is taken from them, the head of the family is killed, and they are left hopeless and in despair. How long can the Red

Cross Society help them ? How long can the American people help them ? Not very long; when spring comes they will say, " We have done all we could for the Armenians; let them take care of themselves." But will they stop to think how the Armenians can take care of themselves ? Have they oxen and horses to plough ? No. Is there any man left to support his wife and children ? No. Suppose here and there an Armenian is left (I mean in the country places, not in the cities), dare he go out to his field and work ? No. Were any of those who plundered and killed punished ? No. What guarantee can we have, then, that those who survive will not be killed or plundered in their turn ? None. Will the European powers who signed the Berlin Treaty give any assurance to the Armenians that they will be protected hereafter ? No. Is the Sultan a better man since the massacre ? No. Are the Turks and Kurds better people since the atrocities ? No. They are worse than ever before, because they have a freer hand, and all their passions are roused to greater strength. Well, then, if these are all facts, what is the use of feeding people a few weeks merely to keep them alive for another massacre that will finish the rest of them ?

O reader, do not be cheated. The Armenians need practical aid, not deceptive aid. I mean the Armenians must be liberated from the cruel Sultan; if not, no aid is given to the Armenians. Because the future will be worse than ever before.

Thus far I have continually assumed and tried to

prove that the Sultan of Turkey deliberately ordered all these atrocities committed. But perhaps you will doubt the statement of a native; you will think I am prejudiced. Therefore I will give you American testimonies from reliable sources. Please read the following from the " Review of Reviews " :—

THE MASSACRES IN TURKEY.

From Oct. 1, 1895, to Jan. 1, 1896.

Certain persons in Europe and America, misled by statements of the Turkish government, have ascribed the dreadful massacres which have taken place in Asia Minor to sudden and spontaneous outbreaks of Moslem fanaticism, caused by a revolutionary attitude among the Armenians themselves. The truth is that these massacres, while sudden, have taken place according to a deliberate and preconcerted plan. According to the statement of many persons, French, English, Canadian, American, Turk, Kurd and Armenian, — persons trustworthy and intelligent, who were in the places where the massacres occurred, and who were eye-witnesses of the horrible scenes, — the outbreaks were under careful direction in regard to place, time, nationality of the victims and of the perpetrators, were prompted by a common motive, and their true character has been systematically concealed by Turkish official reports. The following paper is based upon full accounts of the massacres, written on the ground by the parties above referred to. Their names, for obvious reasons, cannot be made public.

I. In Regard to Place.

With only four exceptions of consequence, the massacres have been confined to the territory of the six provinces where reforms were to be instituted.

21

When a band of two thousand Kurdish and Circassian raiders approached the boundary between the provinces of Sivas and Angora, they were turned back by the officials, who told them that they had no authority to pass beyond the province of Sivas. The only large places where outrages occurred outside of the six provinces are Trebizond, Marash, Aintab, and Cesarea, in all of which the Moslems were excited by the nearness of the scenes of massacre, and by the reports of the plunder which other Moslems were securing.

II. In Regard to Time.

The massacre in Trebizond occurred just as the Sultan, after six months of refusal, was about to consent to the scheme of reforms, as if to warn the powers that in case they persisted, the mine was already laid for the destruction of the Armenians. In fact, the massacre of the Armenians is Turkey's real reply to the demands of Europe that she reform. From Trebizond the wave of murder and robbery swept on through almost every city, and town, and village in the six provinces where relief was promised to the Armenians. When the news of the first massacre reached Constantinople, a high Turkish official remarked to one of the Ambassadors that massacre was like the small-pox; they must all have it, but they wouldn't need it the second time.

III. The Nationality of the Victims.

They were exclusively Armenians. In Trebizond there is a large Greek population, but neither there nor elsewhere have the Greeks been molested. Special care has also been taken to avoid injury to the subjects of foreign nations, with the idea of escaping foreign complications and the payment of indemnities. The only marked exceptions were in Marash, where three school buildings belonging to the American Mission were looted, and one building was burned; and in Harpoot, where the school buildings and houses belonging to the American Mission were plundered and eight buildings were burned, the total losses exceeding $100,000, for which no indemnity has yet been paid.

IV. The Method of Killing and Pillaging.

The method in the cities has been to kill within a limited period the largest number of Armenians, — especially men of business, capacity, and intelligence, — and to beggar their families by robbing them, as far as possible, of their property. Hence, in almost every place the massacres have been perpetrated during the business hours, when the Armenians could be caught in their shops. In almost every place, the Moslems made a sudden and simultaneous attack just after their noonday prayer. The surprised and unarmed Armenians made little or no resistance, and where, as at Diarbekir and Gurun, they undertook to defend themselves, they suffered the more. The killing was done with guns, revolvers, swords, clubs, pickaxes, and every conceivable weapon, and many of the dead were horribly mangled. The shops and houses were absolutely gutted.

Upon hundreds of villages the Turks and Kurds came down like the hordes of Tamerlane, robbed the helpless peasants of their flocks and herds, stripped them of their very clothing, and carried away their bedding, cooking utensils, and even the little stores of provisions which they had with infinite care and toil laid up for the severities of a rigorous winter. Worst of all is the bitter cry that comes from every quarter that the Moslems carried off hundreds of Christian women and children.

The number killed in the massacres thus far is estimated at fifty thousand, which includes the majority of the well-to-do, capable, intelligent Armenians in the six provinces that were to have been reformed. The property plundered or destroyed is estimated at $40,000,000. Not less than three hundred and fifty thousand wretched survivors, most of whom are women and children, are in danger of perishing by starvation and exposure unless foreign aid is promptly sent and allowed to reach them.

V. The Perpetrators.

They were the resident Moslem population, reinforced by Kurds, Circassians, and in several cases by the Sultan's soldiers and officers, who began the dreadful work at the sound of a bugle, and desisted when the bugle signaled to them to stop. This was notoriously true in Erzeroum. In Harpoot, also, the soldiers took a prominent part, firing on the buildings of the American Mission with Martini-Henry rifles and Krupp cannon. A shell from one of the cannon burst in the house of the American Missionary, Dr. Barnum. In most places the killing was by the Turks, while the Kurds and Circassians were intent on plunder, and generally killed only to strike terror or when they met with resistance. It is an utter mistake to suppose, as some have, that the local authorities could not have suppressed the "fanatical" Moslem mobs and restrained the Kurds. The fact is that the authorities, after looking on while the massacres were in progress, did generally intervene and stop the slaughter as soon as the limited period during which the Moslems were allowed to kill and rob had expired.

At Marsovan the limit of time was four hours.   In several places the slaughter and pillage continued from noon till sundown, or later.   At Sivas they continued for a whole day.   In every place the carnage stopped as soon as the authorities made an earnest effort, and had it not been for their intervention after the set time of one, two, or three days, the entire Armenian population might have been exterminated.

VI.   THE MOTIVE OF THE TURKS.

This is apparent to the superficial observer.   The scheme of reforms devolved civil officers, judgeships, and police participation on Mohammedans and non-Mohammedans in the six provinces proportionately. This, while simple justice, was a bitter pill to the Mohammedans, who had ruled the Christians with a rod of iron for five hundred years.   All that was needed to make the scheme of reforms inoperative was to alter the proportion of Christians to Mohammedans. This policy was at once relentlessly and thoroughly executed.   The number of the Armenians has been diminished, first by killing at a single blow those most capable of taking a part in any scheme of reconstruction, and secondly by compelling the survivors to die of starvation, exposure, and sickness, or to become Moslems.

It is the very essence of Mohammedanism that the " ghiavour " has no right to live, save in subjection. The abortive scheme of Europe insisting on the rights of Armenians as men, has enraged the Moslems against them.   The arrogant and non-progressive Turks know that in a fair and equal race the Christians will outstrip them in every department of business and industry, and they see in any fair scheme of reforms the handwriting on the wall for themselves.   If the scheme of reforms had applied to regions where

Greeks predominate, the latter would have been killed
and robbed as readily as the Armenians have been.
Are the Greek massacres of 1822 forgotten, when
50,000 were killed, or the slaughter of 12,000 Maron-
ites and Syrians in 1860, and of 15,000 Bulgarians in
1876 ?

VII.   Turkish Official Reports.

The refinement of cruelty appears in this, that the
Turkish government has attempted to cover up its
hideous policy by the most colossal lying and hypoc-
risy.   It is true that on Sept. 30, 1895, some
hot-headed young Armenians, contrary to the entreaties of the Armenian patriarch and the orders of the
police, attempted to take a well-worded petition to
the Grand Vezir, according to a time-honored custom.
It is also true that the oppressed mountaineers of
Zeitoon drove out a small garrison of Turkish soldiers,
whom, however, they treated with humanity; it is likewise true that in various places individual Armenians,
in despair, have advocated violent methods.   But the
universal testimony of impartial foreign eye-witnesses
is that, with the above exceptions, the Armenians have
given no provocation, and that almost, if not quite,
all the telegrams purporting to come from the provincial authorities accusing the Armenians with provoking
the massacres, are sheer fabrications of names and
dates.   If the Armenians made attacks, where are the
Turkish dead ?

And the dreadful alternative of Islam or death
was offered by those who have dazzled and deceived
Europe with Hatti Shereps and Hatti Humayouns, pro-
mulgating civil equality and religious liberty for their
Christian subjects.

Strangest of all, he who is the head of all authority
in Turkey, and responsible above any and all others
for the cold-blooded massacres and plundering of the

past two months, wrote a letter to Lord Salisbury, and pledged his word of honor that the scheme of reforms should be carried out to the letter, at the very moment when he was directing the massacres.   And the six great Christian powers of Europe, as well as the United States, still treat this man with infinite courtesy and deference; their representatives still dine at his tables, and some of them still receive his decorations.

VIII.   The Solution.

If the Armenians are to be left as they are, it is a pity that Europe ever mentioned them in the treaty of Berlin or subsequently; and to intrust reforms in behalf of the Armenians to those who have devoted two months' time to killing and robbing them is simply to abandon the Armenians to destruction, and to put the seal of Europe to the bloody work.   The only way to reform Eastern Turkey is by forcible foreign intervention — not the threat of it, but the intervention itself.

The position and power of Russia give her a unique call to this work.   Should she enter on it at once, the whole civilized world would approve her course.

Russia should have as free a hand in Kurdistan as England has insisted on having in Egypt.   By frankly admitting this, England would gain in the respect and sympathy of the world, and strengthen her own position.

INFERENCES FROM THE ARMENIAN ATROCITIES.

First: That devotion to Christ is not lessened but increased.   Many people think the spirit of unbelief and indifferentism has spread so widely that in this nineteenth century people will no longer die for Christ. But out of 100,000 Armenians massacred, 90,000 were actually martyred because they would not deny Christ. In all lands, Christians praise the old martyrs, the church fathers: let them know that there are as noble church sons and daughters to-day in Armenia as there were church fathers anywhere in the early centuries. Thus these hideous scenes ought to awaken a true Christian spirit both in this country and in Europe.

Second: That it was a religious persecution. Though the false and cruel Sultan gave a political color to it, his universal order was to offer the Armenians the choice of Mohammedanism or death. This is proved by the fact that the leading gospel ministers were specially chosen for martyrdom. And some of the Armenian priests, after having been converted by force, to escape unbearable tortures, were led through the streets, followed by great crowds, as a warning to the remaining Armenians that they must follow the same road. When some of them did it, the Turks forced them to take arms and kill their brothers and sisters for refusing to accept Mohammedanism. To speak of the massacres as political affairs is doing injustice to the cause of Christ.

Third: That whatever a man sows, he shall reap the same. The Sultan and the Turks are sowing, — they are killing, and thousands of the Christians are converted by force to Mohammedanism; but the time is coming when more Mohammedans will be killed than Armenians have been, and thousands, and even millions of the Mohammedans will be converted to

Christianity, and the blood of the Armenian martyrs will be the means of their salvation through Jesus Christ. The time is coming when out of this great persecution a great and happy freedom will proceed. Out of this great darkness a very bright light shall shine.

Fourth: Some of the Turks helped and saved the Armenians. Certainly these were secret converts to Christianity, but their lives being in danger, they cannot confess Christ publicly. All they can do for the present is to help the needy Christians and save them from murder. Another class of Turks who helped is those who were themselves getting a living out of the Armenians. The Armenians gave them employment, and if their employers were killed, how could they get a living? Still another class protected the Armenians, because if the Armenian houses were burned, their houses also would be burned; and they asked and got money from the Armenians as a reward for having saved them. It is a mistake to think that there are good Mohammedans, who, from a good Mohammedan motive helped the Armenians. There cannot be a good Mohammedan motive towards a Christian; if there is a good motive, it is not a Mohammedan motive.

Fifth: That the time has come when American and European Christians should trust no longer in the promises of the Sultan and the European governments, but as Christian people must use something more than " moral principle " before all the Armenians and American missionaries are killed. Moral influence is very good as far as it goes; being a Christian minister, I also believe in it. But as far as the Turks are concerned it can do nothing, because they do not know what morals are, or what moral character is. All the Turks are morally corrupt. They know only two things: one is the sword, the other is moral corruption. They came and captured that country by the sword, and they must go by the sword; there is no other way. Europe tried the experiment century after century, but could find no other way. Moral advice, wise counsel have never moved the Turks, and will never move them hereafter. Europe and a part of Armenia were taken from them by the sword, and the only way Armenia and the Armenians can be saved is by using the sword. When Christ comes again He will never yield; He will never be crucified, but he will judge and condemn. The time has come when Christians have suffered enough; they must unite and remove that great curse, the Mohammedan power, and make free that happy and beautiful Bible Land, Armenia and Palestine.

Reader, you cannot go and visit to-day the places where man was created, where Noah's ark rested. You cannot go in safety to visit the places where Christ was born and walked. Why? Simply because a corrupt Mohammedan power wills there, and will not permit you. Is it not a shame to mighty Christian nations and powers that this is so? Will not the Christian nations be aroused with great indignation and give the last blow to such a cruel Mohammedan tyranny ?

Sixth: That Turkey is a mere barbarism; it is not to be considered or treated as a nation, for it is not one in any sense. International law cannot be applied to Turkey. The Sultan must be considered as a brigand, a mere lawless oppressor, and the Turks as mere murderers, and dealt with accordingly. The powers must give up the farce of treating the Sultan as a national sovereign, who speaks for his people, and may govern, therefore, much as he pleases. As Mr. W. W. Howard says, " The blackest spot in the round world is the heart of the Sultan of Turkey."

A FAREWELL LETTER FROM A PROMINENT ARMENIAN.
MARCH 24, 1896.

" We are evidently a doomed people. A hundred thousand of us have been butchered, and more than a million of us are in extreme suffering from hunger, and cold, and nakedness. Multitudes beyond the reach of foreign aid must inevitably perish before spring. As to the rest of us, our supplies of food and money are rapidly diminishing. We can prosecute no business, we are not at liberty to earn our daily bread, and for even the most fortunate, the future has only the prospect of starvation a little later than our poor brethren.

" We hear the announcement that order and peace are being restored, but to us these are empty words. The terrible and wholesale massacre at Oorfa and Biridjik occurred long subsequent to the most solemn and emphatic assurances that nothing more of the kind was to be apprehended, — long after the commission sent out from Constantinople to carry the message of peace and reform to Armenia had reached its field of labor.

"Massacres are not now so frequent as they were a few months ago, but the attitude of relentless hostility on the part of the government towards us, the ferocious aspect of our Moslem neighbors, has not a whit improved. They seem to be eagerly watching for an opportune moment in which to finish their bloody work, and rid themselves forever of this troublesome demand for reform.

"May we not then rightfully offer our farewell message to our fellow men ?

"First — To our Moslem fellow countrymen:

"We desire to express our deepest gratitude to those of you who have sympathized with and helped us in these days of calamity and bloodshed. Towards those who have robbed and massacred us, and plundered and burned our houses, we have chiefly feelings of compassion. You have perhaps done these terrible things in what has seemed to you the service of your religion and government.

"Second — To our Sultan — most dread and potent sovereign:

"Apparently you have been persuaded that we are a rebellious people deserving only utter and speedy extermination. For such as you, this work of destruction is no doubt an easy one, the more so as we have had neither the means nor the disposition to resist it.

"Third — To the European powers:

"We have not been an importunate nor a turbulent people. We did not incite the Crimean War, nor any of the subsequent wars which have stricken this empire. It is not of our will that we were begotten to a new political life by the treaty of 1856. Our complaints and appeals have been based solely on

the sentiment of humanity and the common rights of
man.   It was you who arranged the " scheme of reforms," and urged it upon our Sultan till he was irritated to the extent that he seems to have adopted
the plan of ridding himself finally of this annoyance
by exterminating us as a people; and now, while he
is relentlessly carrying out this plan, you are standing
by as spectators and witnesses of this bloody work.

" We wonder if sympathy and the brotherhood of
man and chivalry are wholly things of the past, or
are the material and political interests dividing you
so great that the massacre of the whole people is a
secondary thing ?   In either case " We who are about
to die salute you."

" Fourth — To the Christians of America:

" Although we have cherished strong prejudice
against your mission work among us, recent events
have proved that our Protestant brethren are one with
us, and have shared fully our anxieties and our perils.
You have labored through them to promote among us
the peace and prosperity of the gospel.   It is not your
fault that one result of their teaching and example
has been to excite our masters against us.   The Turkish government dreads and dislikes nothing so much as
the ideas of progress which you have sent us."

VIII.

THE ARMENIANS OF TO-DAY.

There are about five millions of Armenians in the world at present: three millions in the Turkish Empire, a million and a half in Russian Armenia, and half a million more scattered through Persia, India, and Burmah, Egypt, Europe (there are two or three hundred thousand in the Austrian Empire), and America. There are poor and ignorant people among them, as among every people; the majority, however, are (or were before the late horrors) well off, and many of them rich, educated, refined, and, in a word, modern Christian people. Of all the impudent inversions of truth ever perpetrated, the most outrageously impudent and shamelessly the exact contrary of fact is the assertion of Mavroyeni Bey, the Turkish minister at Washington, that the case of the Turks against the Armenians is like that of the whites against the Indians in this country; that the American whites must be allowed to keep the Indians down, and the Turks must be allowed to keep the Armenians down. If the Indians possessed all the money, all the intelligence, all the cultivation, and all the morals in America, and the whites were a mob of ignorant, cruel, lustful ruffians holding them down by the organized

AN ARMENIAN FAMILY.

ANATOLIA COLLEGE AT MARSOVAN.

power of the sword, the comparison would be just. As it is, the Turks correspond fairly enough with the Indians, and the Armenians to the whites, in every other respect than military power. Does a Turk — a true Turk — ever write a book ? Does he ever publish a newspaper, or read one ? Does he ever build a church, or pay attention to the moral precepts taught in one ? Does he ever found or manage a business, or even an estate ? In a word, does he have any more intellectual, moral, or business part in the life of modern civilization than a Hottentot or a Matabele ? And do not the Armenians do and have all these things ? Are they not in the stream of the same kind of cultivated Christian life led by Americans ? Nowhere else on earth, but in the Turkish Empire, can one find millions of gentlemen and ladies and civilized modern citizens ruled over, oppressed, and massacred in hundreds of thousands by a gang of mediaeval Asiatic barbarians, not advanced from the time of Timour or Jenghiz Khan. It is the greatest anachronism and monstrosity of modern times.

If my work is thought prejudiced, listen to what is said of them by men of the first authority, — the greatest statesmen, the best informed special correspondent, and one of the chief historians of England at the present time. First the statesman:—

" The Armenians are the representatives of one of the oldest civilized Christian races, and beyond all doubt one of the most pacific, one of the most industrious, and one of the most intelligent races in the world."
—[Gladstone.

Next the special correspondent:—

"The Armenians constitute the whole civilizing element in Anatolia (Asia Minor); peaceful to the degree of self-sacrifice, law-abiding to their own undoing, and industrious and hopeful under conditions which would appall the majority of mankind. At their best, they are the stuff of which heroes and martyrs are moulded."—[E. J. Dillon.

Lastly the historian:—

"The best chance for the future of the Asiatic provinces of Turkey lies in the uprising of a progressive Christian people, which may ultimately grow into an independent Christian state. The Armenians have, alone among the races of Western Asia, the gifts that can enable them to aspire to this mission. They are keen-witted, energetic, industrious, apt to learn, and quick in assimilating western ideas."—[James Bryce.

IN THE TURKISH EMPIRE.

There are about two millions of Armenians in Armenia Proper, and another million scattered through the rest of the empire. The absurd figures given by some writers, making them greatly less than this (one magazine editor got it down to 300,000 ! It is significant that he was a strong apologist for the massacre, and laid all the blame to the Armenians) result mostly from taking the official statistics of the Turkish government. Now, there are three reasons why these are always grossly wrong; of no more value than the weather predictions in an almanac, and always wrong in the direction of understating the numbers.

One is that it is the Sultan's interest to make them as small as possible, that the Armenians may not be considered to have the right to autonomy as a nation; the fewer they are, and the more outnumbered by the Turks, the less right they seem to have. " An independent Armenia ? " shriek the Turkish ministers and officers. " Why, there are only a few hundred thousand Armenians in their so-called country, and even so, there are three Turks to one Armenian in that very district ! "

The second is that in an Oriental country a census is not a means of knowledge but an engine of taxation. The ruler has no care for information on the subject for his own sake, as Western governments have. What he wants is to see how many people and in what places he can screw more taxes out of. The people know this as well as he, and use every effort to outwit his agents, and prevent them from knowing their numbers. This is why even civilized governments ruling over Oriental nations can rarely get any nearer than a rough guess at the numbers of the nation; the inhabitants are suspicious, and resort to falsehood. In the case of the Armenians, remember what I said in the first chapter about an Armenian being taxed for every male child he has, every year as long as the child lives; naturally, he will not tell the number of his children unless he has to. Here is a practical illustration. Some years ago I was in an Armenian village when the Sultan's officers came to take the census. There were about 300 persons in the village; the officer wrote 200, because only a few names of boys were given him out of the whole. The tax is based on

22

the registration, and if you can keep off the registers you can escape the tax.

The third is the gross incompetence, the corruption, and the drunkenness of the officers. The Turkish officials, governors, mayors, clerks, generals, soldiers, all drink any sort of liquor they can lay hands on, and are drunk as often and as long as sober; they are so ignorant that they cannot do their work decently even when they are sober; and they are utterly venal, without the least sense of official obligation. What sort of a census is likely to be taken by these ignorant, whiskey-swilling, venal barbarians? One of these officials, whom I know well, once came to a village to take the census. The Armenians got him so drunk that he barked like a dog, bribed him, and he put down about half the number of the population.

How, then, do I know the correct number? From a knowledge of the districts, the numbers of villages, and statistics resting on a better foundation than the above. I do not pretend that the number is exact; but it is near enough for practical purposes.

The Armenians in Turkey are divided into four classes. The first comprises merchants and bankers. The second is the professional class: physicians, professors, teachers, and preachers. The third is that of artisans: weavers, blacksmiths, copper, silver, and gold smiths, tailors, shoemakers, etc. The finest Oriental rugs are made by the Armenians, and there are weavers of silk and cotton goods, and all kinds of hand-made embroidery. There are no factories in

Armenia. The fourth class is that of farmers, a pure, simple, industrious class, with beautiful farms, vineyards, and orchards, whose products I have described.

One-tenth of all the Armenians in Turkey are in Constantinople. Many of them are poor, in the nature of things; but the leading bankers, merchants, and capitalists there are Armenians, surpassing even the Greeks and Jews. I give a few representative names: Gulbenkian, Essayian, Azarian, Mosditchian, Manougian, Ooujian. The physicians in largest practice are Armenians: Khorassanjian, Mateosian, Dobrashian, Vartanian, etc. The Sultan's personal treasurer is an Armenian, Portukalian Pasha. The chief counselor in the foreign office in Constantinople is an Armenian, Haroutiune Dadian Pasha. The greatest lawyers are Armenians: Mosditchian, Tinguerian, etc. The chief photographers of the Sultan are Armenians, Abdullah Brothers and Sebah, the former considered one of the best photographic firms in the world. The personal jeweler of the Sultan is an Armenian, Mr. Chiboukjian. For all his hate of the Armenians, he has to employ them, for no others are competent or trustworthy. The best musicians are Armenians: Chonkhajian Surenian, Doevletian, and an Armenian young lady named Nartoss, who often plays the piano before the Sultan. The greatest orator in Constantinople is an Armenian and a professor in Robert College, Prof. H. Jejizian, to my thinking, superior to either Beecher, Wendell Phillips, or Robert Ingersoll, all of whom I have heard. Finally, the Ar-

menians, as a whole, form the best " society " in Constantinople, and their modes of living, dress, houses,
and ways are precisely like those of Americans or
Europeans. These are Mavroyeni Bey's " Indians " !

Smyrna is a city of 150,000 or more population.
About 80,000 are Greeks; you may call it a Greek
city. The Armenians there number about 8,000, or
one-tenth of the Greeks, but are ten times richer than
all the Greeks together. The principal buildings are
owned by Armenians; the business is in the hands of
the Armenians. The chief business men are well-
known in Europe. Mr. Balyivzian owns many steam-
ers which ply on the Mediterranean. Mr. Spartalian is
another very rich and very benevolent man; he built
a magnificent hospital at Smyrna. In Samsoun, Marsovan, Cesarea, Adana, Amassia, Tocat, Sivas, Harpoot, Mesere, Malatia, Diarbekir, Arabkir, Oorfa, Aintab, Marash, Tarsus, Angora, Erzeroum, Erzinghan,
Moosh, Bitlis, Baiburt, Trebizond, — in a word, everywhere it is the same. Go where you like in Turkey,
you find the Armenians at the top.

When I say they are the richest, I mean until
early in 1894 they were the richest. But now, in
many cities of Armenia proper, since the recent atrocities, they have become the poorest.

Leading citizens, and the fathers of families, for
the reasons I have mentioned, were specially singled
out for vengeance. Their stores, banks, and houses
were plundered and then burnt, their money and
jewelry taken from them, and then they were mur-

dered wholesale. Now the Turks and the Kurds for a time are rich with Armenian property; wearing the gold watches of Armenian gentlemen, their women wearing the jewelry of Armenian ladies.

IN RUSSIA.

The Armenians in Russia are the richest and the most cultivated of any in the world, and have great influence. Mr. Kasbarian, an Armenian, is considered the richest even of them. The rich city of Tiflis is practically an Armenian city.

There are about 50,000 regular Armenian soldiers in the Russian army, and some of its greatest generals have always been Armenians.

If the Czar would permit this force and the capitalists to settle the Armenian question, they would do it in a month, and make Armenia free. The Armenians have so far been treated very kindly and have prospered exceedingly in Russia, but I do not believe it will last. In my opinion, the young Czar is only waiting for his coronation to oppress the Armenians as he has the Jews. Yet the Czar's ablest servants and advisers have been Armenians. The body-guard of Nicholas' grandfather Alexander was the Armenian Count Loris Melikoff, universally known; three times wounded by Nihilists on account of his position. During the last Turko-Russian war some of the generals who accomplished the most with the least sacrifice were Armenians: Der, Lucasoff, Lazareff, Melikoff. There are now no less than eighteen Armenian generals in the Russian service. I will mention a part: General Sdepan Kishmishian, commander of Caucasus; General Hagop Alkhazian, General Alexander Lalayian, General Demedr Der Asadoorian, General Ishkhan Manuelian, General Alexander Gorganian, General Ishkhan Gochaminassian, General Khosros Touloukhanian, General Arakel Khantamirian, General H. Dikranian.   There are many other prominent Armenian officers.

In Moscow, St. Petersburg, and other great cities in Russia there are many Armenian professors in the universities, mayors of cities, judges of courts, and high civil officers.   I will give a few of their names, to show that I am not talking blindly:

Count Hovhannes Telyanian, minister of education, etc.

Gamazian, minister of foreign affairs in Asia.

Muguerditch Emin, counselor of education.

Nerses Nersessian, professor in Moscow in the Royal University.

Dr. Shilantz, professor in the medical college at Kharcof.

Boghos Gamparian, superintendent of the Royal army of Riza.

Melikian, professor of natural sciences in the University at Odessa.

A. Madinian, mayor of Tiflis.

V. Keghamian, mayor of Erevan.

H. Moutaffian, mayor of Akheltzka.

Hundreds and thousands are high officers in different departments of the Russian government, but there is no space to give a roll of them.

One, however, a personal friend, I must write a few words of, namely, Professor John Ayvazovski, of the council of the St. Petersburg Academy of Fine Arts, a marine painter of the first rank. He is now 79, but looks scarcely 60, with beautiful large, bright eyes. He came to the World's Fair, where fifteen of his pictures were exhibited in the Russian section; and he presented two other fine ones to the American people in recognition of their help to the Russian famine sufferers, — one showing the arrival in port of a steamer with its cargo of grain, the other the advent of a drosky at a village of starving people, with a man in front waving an American flag. He visited and painted an excellent picture of Niagara. He had seven pictures at the Philadelphia Exposition of 1876. His paintings are mostly in royal palaces: there are 120 in that of the Russian imperial family, and 34 in the Sultan's. His own gallery, at Theodosia, Russia, has 84. He has received many prizes from expositions. He is also a great scholar and a good Christian. His brother, who lately died, was one of the greatest bishops of the Armenian church.

There is a very interesting story about Professor Ayvazovski's boyhood which I will give here:

His parents were Armenian peasants, living in a village not far from Moscow. One day Nicholas I was passing by the hamlet on horseback, and dropped his whip. The Emperor beckoned to young Ayvazovski, and told him to pick it up.   The boy approached boldly and asked, " Who are you ? "   Nicholas replied, " I am the Emperor."   The boy rejoined, " If you cannot take care of your whip, how can you take care of your subjects ? "   The Emperor was pleased at this remark, and ordered him to be educated at his own expense, and in any profession he chose.   He took to the brush, and is the pride of his nation.

IN PERSIA, INDIA, ETC.

The Armenians of Persia are great merchants, and high civil officers of the Shah.   I name only a few:

Chahanguir Khan is minister of arts and superintendent of the arsenal.

Nirza Melkoum Khan was the former ambassador of the Shah at London; a man of great wealth and learning, and an able diplomat.   He retired on account of age, and lives in London.

Nazar Agha was ambassador of the Shah at Paris.

General Sharl Bezirganian is the general superintendent of the telegraph service in Persia.

In India and Burmah there are great Armenian merchants, who are millionaires, and respected by the governments and the peoples.

In Egypt, though few in number, they are the ruling element.   Nubar Pasha was the prime minister of the Egyptian government until a few weeks ago; one of the richest men in Egypt, and the greatest statesman in Africa.   He speaks several languages, and spends his summers in France, owning property in

Paris.   Dikran Pasha is another rich and very gifted Armenian, and Boghos Pasha another man of power.

IN EUROPE.

There are very rich merchants among the Armenians at Vienna, Paris, Marseilles, London, and Manchester.   There is a strong Armenian colony at Manchester.   All of them are merchants, and some of them millionaires.   Almost the whole clothing trade between England and Turkey is in their hands. They have a beautiful Armenian church there, and always a learned Armenian bishop; I speak from knowledge and observation.   They are much respected by the English.   Some of the Armenian gentlemen are married to English ladies of good family, and their domestic life is very happy.   Prince Loosinian, an Armenian, a very great scholar, and much respected by the French, lives in Paris; he is descended from the last Armenian dynasty.   His brother Khoren Nar-Bey Loosinian was one of the foremost Armenian bishops; the Sultan of course hated him, and it is said had him poisoned while imprisoned in Constantinople.

The Armenian scholars in Europe are well-known, and on a level with the best of any country.   There is not an institution of learning in Europe where they are not to be found, either as students or professors; and the prizes and medals they win are many.

There are two great centers in Europe for the Armenian scholars and authors: one at Vienna and the other at Venice.   They have colleges and printing presses in these places; and they write, translate, and

publish themselves in nearly all languages all sorts
of valuable books. So the Armenian people are well
supplied with the best modern books. But it must
be remembered that these valuable books are forbidden
by the Sultan to go into Turkish Armenia; he wants
the people kept ignorant. Some of their great scholars came home from Europe to preach and teach in
Armenia, to elevate their nation; but some were killed
and some banished during the recent atrocities.

IN AMERICA.

The Armenians are a new people in America.
Seventeen years ago, when the writer first came to
this country, there were not more than a hundred in
the United States; since then about 10,000 have come,
most of them within ten years. The first ones came
about forty-five years ago, among them Mr. Minasian
and Mr. Sahagian, — both poor young men, now both
rich. Mr. Minasian lives at Brooklyn; Mr. Sahagian
at Yonkers, N. Y. Those who have come lately are
mostly the poorer class; they fled from the " order " of
the Sultan, and not being allowed to leave Turkey,
bribed the police and ran away. Not knowing the
English language, they work in factories in various
States. There are some well-to-do merchants, however, doing business in New York, Boston, and elsewhere, handling Oriental rugs, dry-goods, etc. Some
of the New York names are Gulbenkian, Topakian,
Tavshandjian, Yardimian, Chaderdjian, Telfeyian,
Kostikian. In Boston are Ateshian, Bogigian, etc.
Mr. Kebabian is in New Haven; Mr. Enfiyedjian in

Denver.   There are many others also in other large cities.

Besides merchants, there are many professional men among them, about a dozen physicians in New York city alone: Dr. Dadirian, Dr. Gabrielian, Dr. Ayvazian, Dr. Apkarian, Dr. Altarian, Dr. Koutoojian.   Some of them are engravers and photographers. In New York city there are Hagopian, Kasparian, Matigian, and others, very skillful engravers.   In Boston there is the New England Engraving Co., who are Armenians; the manager is Mr. G. Papazian.

There are about half a dozen Armenians who are pastors of American churches in different states. About a dozen are special lecturers on the Armenian atrocities: Mr. H. Kiretchjian, the secretary of the American Relief Association, Mr. Samuelian, Rev. A. Bulgurgian, Rev. S. Deviryian, Mr. S. Yenovkian, etc.

There are hundreds of Armenian students distributed among nearly all the universities, colleges, and theological seminaries in America, and most of them are of a superior sort.   The greatest physicians in Turkey are Armenians, who were graduated from different medical colleges in this country.   Some of the leading pastors and professors in Armenia, who were banished and killed during the recent atrocities, were graduated in this country.

Of the factory hands mentioned, there are about 1,000 in Worcester, Mass.; about 800 in New York and Brooklyn; about 400 in Boston, and the remainder are scattered everywhere from New York to California, from Maine to Florida.

A number of Armenian young men have married American women; I believe ninety per cent. are happy. After forty or fifty years, there will be a large class of American citizens of Armenian blood, and many millionaires among them. They are gifted in business, and they are a sober, honest, and faithful people. I do not think that there is a single criminal among the 10,000 Armenians in this country.

Some of the Armenian daily and weekly newspapers are as follows:

In Constantinople: Arevelk, Avedaper, Puragn, Dyaghig, Hayrenik, Masis, Pounch.

In Smyrna: Arevlian Mamoul.

In Etchmiazin: Ararat.

In Tiflis: Aghpour, Artzakank, Mishag, Murj, Nor-Tar, Darak.

In Venice: Pazmaveb.

In Vienna: Hantes Arnsoria.

In Marseilles: Armenia.

In London: L'Armenie.

In New York: Haik.

Wherever the Armenians go they carry with themselves the church, the school, and the press.

THE ARMENIAN RELIEF ASSOCIATION.

This association is putting forth every effort to alleviate the sufferings of needy Armenians wherever they may be found; their work has already resulted in untold blessings and it deserves the hearty support and contributions of the benevolent public. The officers of the association are the following well-known American and Armenian gentlemen:

Right Rev. Bishop H. Y. Satterlee, D.D., president.

Hon. Levi P. Morton, first vice-president.

Right Rev. Bishop Potter, D.D., second vice-president.

Charles H. Stout, Esq., treasurer.

J. Bleecker Miller, Esq., chairman executive committee.

Nicholas R. Mersereau, Esq., secretary.

Herant M. Kiretchjian, general secretary.

Rev. J. B. Haygooni, A.M., organizing secretary.

Mr. H. K. Samuelian, agent.

The headquarters of the association is in New York.

IX

THE FUTURE OF ARMENIA AND THE BATTLE OF ARMAGEDDON.

I am going to predict the future of Armenia. Not in the usual sense of guessing at it, but in the literal sense of foretelling the truth. I am not a prophet of God, yet my prediction is based on facts, and its accuracy should be given some credit from the way my predictions two or three years ago about the recent atrocities that have already taken place, have come true to the letter. At that time no American or European could be made to believe that such horrors would be perpetrated; but I said they would be, and they were. And even now the Western peoples are nearly as blind as ever; they cannot see the future of Armenia even with all the facts before them. Many have lost hope in it altogether; they think Turkey will exist forever, and exterminate the last of the Armenians. Doubtless I should in their place, but I was born in Turkey and know the situation.

This, then, is the truth as I forecast it:—

Till the end of next year the Armenians will suffer more than ever before. Perhaps a million will be massacred yet, not only in Turkey, but in Russia.

The Jews, also, in great numbers, and not only the Jews and the Armenians, but the Americans and Englishmen too. The key rests in the character of the present Czar. Nicholas II is not like his father or grandfather, a strong man. I will not discuss the moral character of the two Alexanders, but I allow their powerful intellects and strong wills. They favored the Armenians. But the present Czar has no strength of character at all; he is weak both in intellect and morals. The Sultan is called the sick man of Turkey, but the Czar is the sick man of Russia. His short-sightedness in upholding Turkey is one proof. Up to the time of the coronation next May you will see no more massacres, for the Czar has ordered the Sultan to hold his hand, that there may be a peaceful ceremony, not clouded with horrors; that over, he will not only give the Sultan leave to unchain his dogs, but he will unchain his own. The atrocities in Turkish Armenia will be redoubled, and the Czar himself inflict on the Armenians all that has been inflicted on the Jews. Even this is not all: The Czar will instruct the Sultan to get rid of all American missionaries, either banishing them as breeders of sedition, or, if they refuse to go, requiring the United States government to order them back. Probably the government will obey. Probably, also, the missionaries will not obey the government; they will stay where they are. Then the Sultan will say he is not responsible for their lives, and will issue secret orders to kill them, which will be carried out. Further, the Czar will begin a fresh persecution of the Jews, and order the Sultan to follow suit on the Jews in Turkey, which will be done; no fear of the Sultan's refusing an order to butcher anybody.   Still more, the Czar will command him in secret to banish the English missionaries from Turkey; the Sultan will request the English government to call them back, and there is little doubt that Lord Salisbury will comply; but they, like the Americans, will refuse to go.   Then they will be murdered by secret orders from the Sultan, who will say he is not responsible for it.   These massacres will continue for two years more.   The victims will cry aloud, the Americans and English will have greater mass-meetings, but the governments of both will do nothing.   And Germany, Austria, and Italy will look calmly on; if they act it will be with the Czar, and not against him. Meantime both in Europe and America the war preparations will continue with greater zeal and energy, until the cup is full, until the crisis comes; then the noble blood of the Anglo-Saxon race will begin to boil, and the English and American people at once will be aroused like one man, and the governments will have to yield.   The wrathful Jews will contribute Jewish capital for the war expenses; the wrathful Armenians throughout the world will give both money and soldiers to the governments fighting their battles. And a fierce battle will be fought between Russia, Turkey, and France on one side; America, England, the Jews, and the Armenians on the other.   The former alliance will be beaten: the Czar's Greek

Church bigotry, the Sultan's Mohammedan fanaticism, and France's infidelity together will be crushed; Russia will go to pieces, Turkey will go pieces, France will go to pieces; Armenia will be free, Judea will be free. The scattered Armenians will return to Armenia, the scattered Jews will return to Judea. Both the Armenians and the Jews will have their separate governments; not kings, not princes, but a clean republican form of government. Russia and Turkey will be opened to the gospel work. Where now hundreds of missionaries are going from England and America to other lands, then thousands of them will go; and Christian America and England will open their hearts and purses together to send as many missionaries as they can to Russia, to Turkey, and to France. They will hasten the coming of the Lord Jesus Christ. They will prepare the way for the coming King, who has the power both in heaven and on the earth.

What will become of Germany, Austria, and Italy, who form the Triple Alliance ? That alliance will be dissolved. The German Emperor is trying hard to maintain it, but he will fail. France will once in a while threaten Germany with vengeance, but she will never be able to carry it out, and there is no need for it, because the German people during this century will get rid of their Emperor. There will be a great civil war in Germany, between the people and the army. If the German emperor could do it, he would begin to crush the Socialists now. He will order his soldiers to kill their brothers and fathers,

23

but they will not, — they are not as foolish as the Emperor; the only result will be the break-up of the German Union, and the division of Germany into small republican governments. Italy, Austria, and Spain will all have the same fate: civil war, and splitting into small republics. No czars, no emperors, no princes, no lords will remain. Government will be for the people, of the people, by the people. The time has come; this century will purify the whole world. But until it is purified, a great deal of fire will burn, very great battles will be fought, until freedom and peace shall reign. And the Armenian blood, now continually pouring like a river in Armenia, will be the cause and the foundation of the coming freedom of the world. For the present, the world is not free; it is not civilized. It cannot be with such rulers. To be free and happy, the people must be aroused, and get rid of them. The United States must be the example to the older nations; they must embrace Washington's principles.

It is true that England and America will never go regularly to work to give freedom to Judea and Armenia, nor with that intention. Their immediate motive will be to punish Russia and Turkey for the murder of the missionaries, and after the victory is won, by the help of Jewish and Armenian purses and swords, the Armenians and Jews will be rewarded by giving them their original homes and mother-lands.

This will be laughed at by many, perhaps most, as a romantic and pleasant dream. They will say it can never be accomplished during this century; perhaps in the future, after a century or two, but not now. I am used to this incredulity; my predictions are never believed at the time: but after they come true they are. This century is not like the other centuries; a day in this century is equal to a year of those which have passed away. We may expect from a year of it as much as from a century in the ancient times. This world is a wonderful world now, and will be more wonderful hereafter. The future of the world is bright, and the world will be brighter and happier.

Why do I keep repeating " two years " ? Why do I not say one year or three years, or a few years ? I have reasons for it: one is the political situation in Europe, and the other is the Bible prophecy in the Book of Revelation.

THE POLITICAL SITUATION IN EUROPE.

The Europeans have already made great preparations for battle. Every one of them preaches peace and prepares for war; and none of them have finished their preparations yet, — if they had, they would be in the thick of it by this time. Each of them declares that its preparations will be finished about the end of 1897. Russia is building war-ships, England is building war-ships, France is building war-ships, and all will be finished about the end of 1897. All preparations converge on the end of 1897. When all are ready, they will begin. When newspapers write about an immediate European war, I do not believe it. There will be no European war for two years; but after that there is no escape from it, — they have to fight, and will fight. The war-ships will be ready, the cannon will be ready, the guns will be ready, the ammunition will be ready, the soldiers will be ready.

The cunning Sultan knows all this, and is in a hurry to exterminate the Armenians, so that when they start in earnest with guns to reform Armenia, he can say there is no Armenia or Armenians to reform. But that makes no difference for the European powers: Turkey is doomed, and the Turkish Empire will come to an end forever within this century. There will never be any more Turkish Empire or Mohammedan government; all the Mohammedan powers will be under Christian rule.

The second reason is my belief in the Bible prophecies. The close resemblance of the Jews and Armenians will be observed by the reader: both the chosen people of God. The children of Israel were the chosen people before Christ, and as the Armenians became the first Christian nation after Christ, they became the chosen people after Christ. And these chosen people have suffered more than any other nations on the globe; they have had more martyrs than any other nation, and have been carried into captivity, and finally scattered throughout the world. The Bible lands are Palestine and Armenia, where the first man, Adam, was created, and where Christ was born and was crucified; and so these lands after Christ, becoming the first Christian lands, became the Temple of God.

We have a prophecy in the eleventh chapter of Revelation that the court of the Temple will be given unto the Gentiles, and the Holy City shall they tread under foot forty and two months; "and I will give power unto my two witnesses, and they shall prophecy a thousand two hundred and three score days, clothed in sackcloth." (Rev. xi, 2-3.)

Forty and two months and a thousand two hundred and three score days are just the same thing. Each day in the Bible prophecy is one year. According to this interpretation, which I consider correct, the Holy City will be trampled by the Gentiles one thousand, two hundred and sixty years. Now the question is this, Where is the Holy City, and who are the Gentiles who will trample the Holy City? First, the Holy City is both literally the Holy City before Christ, and spiritually the Holy City after Christ.

Literally, the Holy City is Jerusalem, where the Temple of God was; this is very clear. Spiritually, the Holy City is Christianity; wherever there are Christians, there is the Holy City. But this is very general, and takes the whole world after it is Christian. But before we come to that general Holy City, we find in the third verse of the same chapter the following words: "I will give power unto my two witnesses, and they shall prophesy a thousand, two hundred and three score days, clothed in sackcloth." So from these statements we find that two especial witnesses in that Holy City, clothed in sackcloth, will testify. Who are these two witnesses? My interpretation is that they are the two chosen peoples of God and Christ. And the two chosen peoples are the Jews and the Armenians. The Jews were the chosen people before Christ, and the Armenians became the chosen people after Christ, as King Abgarus, the Armenian king, believed in Christ before Christ was crucified, and afterwards, in the time of Gregory the Illuminator, the whole Armenian nation became a Christian nation, in 310 A. D. Before Palestine was considered a holy country, Armenia was considered a holy land, because the first man was created there, and Noah's ark rested on Mount Ararat. And as the Armenians became the first Christian nation on the globe, Palestine and Armenia were the holy countries or the Holy City. Although this is so, after all the literal Holy City, Jerusalem, remains a holy city; and she will be after Christ, under the rule of Gentiles one thousand two hundred and sixty years, while the two witnesses will testify there under sackcloth for one thousand two hundred and sixty years.

Now the question is this, How long is it since the city of Jerusalem was captured by the Gentiles, or more correctly by the " beast that ascendeth out of the bottomless pit " (Rev. ii. 7), which is the Mohammedan power ? The Mohammedan power in different places in Revelation is called the Beast, the Dragon, the Whore or Harlot, and the False Prophet, and it is the Gentile kingdom after Christ. And the time which is given to the Mohammedan power to rule, to destroy, and to kill the Jews and the Christians in Jerusalem or in the Bible lands, is only one thousand two hundred and sixty years. Since the city of Jerusalem was captured by the Mohammedans is 1258 years, and when this present year and the next come to an end in 1897, the Mohammedan power will also come to an end, and the city of Jerusalem will be restored to the Jews, and Armenia to the Armenians.

Towards the end of the Mohammedan power, Mohammedans will begin to kill both the Jews and the Armenians for three and a half years (see Rev. xi, 7, 8, 9). Now, for a year and a half the Mohammedans have been killing the Christians, — which the author predicted two or three years ago; and they will kill two years more. "And the sixth Angel poured out his vial upon the Great River Euphrates and the water thereof was dried up." (See Rev. xvi, 12.) That means that the people on the shores of the Euphrates were killed, namely the Armenians.

I am not writing a commentary on Revelation, but simply bringing in a few passages to enlighten the mind of the reader about the future of Armenia and the battle of Armageddon.

THE BATTLE OF ARMAGEDDON.

(SEE REV. xvi, 13–16.)

The battle of Armageddon is the final and the greatest battle. All the nations will take part in it; but the leaders in the battle will be the ones I have said, and the other will be their followers on the one side or the other. And this battle will settle all the questions which are not settled now. The great Eastern question will be settled, the great question between capital and labor will be settled, all the emperors and czars, kings, and princes will come down from their thrones, and permanent international arbitration will be established. The questions which are asked now will never be asked: What do the emperors say? What do the czars say? What do the Sultans say? Men will ask then, What do the people say? What is the wish of the people?

Then the question comes, where is Armageddon? Armageddon is Armenia. Of course this is entirely a new interpretation to European and American scholars; no one has ever been certain where Armageddon is, but it is generally thought to be somewhere near Jerusalem, a little hill called Mount Megiddo. In the time of Judges, " The kings came and fought, then fought the kings of Canaan in Taanach by the waters of Megiddo." (Judges v, 19.) But as a native of the Bible lands, and as a native minister, I am positive about it. The first question is, What does Armageddon mean? It means the High Lands. Is there any higher land in the Bible lands than Armenia? The main land is from 4,000 to 7,000 feet above the level of the sea, and Mount Ararat is about 18,000 feet high. Another question is, What does Armenia mean? It means precisely the high lands, as Armageddon does. Armenia took her name from King Aram or Armenag; both mean high lands, or the possessors of high lands; and Armenia also means the high lands.

Again, what does Ararat mean, which is just in the center of Armenia proper ? It means the holy or high land. Now bring all together, Armageddon, Armenia, Ararat, all mean just the same: high lands. Not only high lands, but holy high lands. Long before Palestine was called a holy land, Armenia had the name of Holy land, and the Armenians were called the Highlanders.

In a word, Armageddon is the combination of three different words, Armenia - Garden - Eden: Armageddon.

So the final battle will be fought in Armenia. The nation with the greatest part will have the greatest future. As man fell from grace in Armenia, man will be restored to peace and holiness in Armenia. And before that peace, holiness, and restoration come, the greatest battle will be fought in Armenia. After the fall of man, disgrace and curse went forth from Armenia; so prosperity and blessings will come forth from Armenia. As the first battle in the world was fought in Armenia, between Cain and Abel, and the other battles followed, so the last battle will be fought in Armenia, and the universal peace will come out of it. As the first martyrdom in the world was in Armenia, so the last and greatest martyrdom will be in Armenia. And from the blood of Armenian martyrs everlasting happiness will follow to all nations. And the kingdom of Christ will be established throughout the world.

X.

POEMS ON THE ARMENIAN QUESTION.

[From the New York Independent, by special permission.]

LORD SALISBURY.

By the Rev. T. S. Perry.

" *Oh! for a year, a month, a day of Oliver Cromwell.*" — *The Independent.*

" *What Lord Salisbury seems to lack is a little Cromwellian courage.*" — *A Speaker in City Temple, London.*

1.

Oh! for an hour of Cromwell,
   For a leader brave and grand
To guide the wrath, and point the path,
   Of a mighty Christian land !
To heed the cry of innocent blood,
   To blush for the world's disgrace,
With hand to deal a blow of steel
   In the murderous Moslem's face !

2.

Alas ! for a leader heedless
   While massacred villages flame,
Unmoved by shrieks of maidenhood
   At wrong too foul for name !
Strong to throttle the feeble,
   Feeble to beard the strong,
With eye o'er-meek, and blanching cheek,—
   How long, O Lord, how long ?

(362)

3.

And women cover their faces,
   And men are fain to hiss.
Cromwell's head upon Temple Bar
   Were a leader better than this !
And heaven grows black with horror,
   And earth grows red with wrong,
And martyrs cry from earth and sky,
   How long, O Lord, how long ?

Orange Park, Florida.

DEUS VULT.

By ALLEN EASTMAN CROSS.

*" It is time that one general shout of execration — not of men,
but of deeds — one general shout of execration, directed against deeds
of wickedness, should rise from outraged humanity." — Gladstone's
Armenian address at Chester.*

No tomb of death shall be our guest
Wherein the Lord of Life may rest.

No empty sepulcher of stone
Across the world makes bitter moan,

But Christian hearts that break and bleed
For our avenging pity plead.

O brothers, for our brothers' sake
Let the crusading spirit wake !

O Christian England, 'tis the Christ
By Moslem hands is sacrificed !

Away, away with hollow words,
Now sheath our speech, unsheath our sword !

God wills: The guns of Christendom
Proclaim the tyrant's doom has come !

Manchester, N. H.

SONNETS.

By HENRY VAN DYKE.

I.

The Turk's Way.

"S'and back, ye messengers of mercy ! Stand
 Far off, for I will save my troubled folk
 In my own way." So the false Sultan spoke;
And Europe, harkening to his base command,
Stood still to see him heal his wounded land.
 Through blinding snows of winter and through
  smoke
 Of burning towns she saw him deal the stroke
Of cruel mercy that his hate had planned.
 Unto the prisoners and the sick he gave
New tortures, horrible, without a name;
 Unto the thirsty, blood to drink; a sword
Unto the hungry; with a robe of shame
 He clad the naked, making life abhorred.
He saved by slaughter, but denied a grave.

II.

America's Way.

But thou, my country, tho' no fault be thine
 For that red horror far across the sea;
 Tho' not a tortured wretch can point to thee,
And curse thee for the selfishness supine
Of those great powers who cowardly combine
 To shield the Turk in his iniquity;
 Yet, since thy hand is innocent and free,
Rise, thou, and show the world the way divine.
Thou canst not break the oppressor's iron rod,
 But thou canst minister to the oppressed;
Thou canst not loose the captive's heavy chain,
But thou canst bind his wounds and soothe his pain.
 Armenia calls thee, Empire of the West,
To play the Good Samaritan for God.

New York City.

TO THOSE WHO DIED FOR THEIR FAITH.

Armenia, 1894 to 189—?

By Mrs. Merrill E. Gates.

"These loved their lives not, to the death!"
  But we at ease to-day, who claim
  Allegiance to the One great Name,
Could we as nobly die for Faith?

We challenge not the crucial test!
  Self cannot prove to self its power
  If e'er should come that testing hour
God give us grace to choose the Best!

But these have overcome! Their Lord
  In bitter death have not denied!
  Have chosen still the Crucified
In face of bayonet and sword!

Our age heroic looms! Our eyes
  Behold white martyr brows! Still hears
  Our sin-gray world with unthrilled ears
Once more the martyr-chorus rise!

Come Thou to succor the great need!
  Thy judgment shall not long delay!
  God doeth his strange work to-day!
The Judge is at the door! Take heed!

Amherst, Mass.

ARMENIA.

By Willimina L. Armstrong.

Out of storms and peace light, out of confusing things,
Bound in mysterious fashion by the bindings of blood
   and hate,
    Lo, are the Nations assembled now
    At the Twentieth Century Gate.
Leaning beside the portal: Close! in the name of God!
Over the Garden of Eden, in the evening of this our Day.
    Over the breast of the Mountain old
    Where the Ark of deliverance lay.

Leaning beside the portal: Hark to the clashing arms!
Hark to the voice in the Garden, to the Nations of Earth
   it calls,
        "Bid! for the Woman is Christian blood;
        And the sword and the bayonet falls!"
Sold! A Christian Woman! Sold in the name of Christ!
Sold to her death in the Eden with its soil by her blood
   made damp!
        Sold in the eve of our Mighty Age!
        With the light of our Age for a lamp!
New York City.

ARMENIA'S BITTER CRY.

By Hetta Lord Hayes Ward.

I.

World, world, hear our prayer
Oh where is Russia, where?
  A fearful deed is done,
  Its glare affronts the sun.
Smoke! Flame! Fire!
Rouse thee, great Russian Sire!
  When Christian homes are ablaze,
  Hast thou no voice to raise?
Thy neighbor to thee has cried,
Pass not on the other side.
  Look on our dire despair!
  Where art thou, Czar, oh, where?

II.

Land of the sun and sea,
Wake, Rome and Italy!
  Our ancient Church in vain
  Calls thee to break her chain.
Shame! Shame! Shame!
Where sleeps thy early fame?
  To death our priests are led,
  Their flocks lie slaughtered, dead.
Awake, good Pope of Rome!
Our saints through blood go home;
  Hear thou their dying plea,
  Where, where is Italy?

III.

Land of Fraternite,
Brave France, turn not away!
  Shall blood thy lilies stain?
  Wilt bear the curse of Cain?
Wake! Wake! Wake!
For God and glory's sake!
  On a ghastly funeral pyre,
  Brave men are burned with fire;
God calls to France, the free,
"Thy brother, where is he?"
  Lest God in wrath requite,
  Awake, befriend the right!

IV.

Where is good Frederick's son
When evil deeds are done?
  Shall prisons reek and rot,
  His mother's blood speak not?
Haste! Haste! Haste!
Time runs too long to waste.
  If halts the Kaiser dumb,
  Let all the people come.
Your oath must sacred stand,
Treaties of Fatherland;
  Victims of Turk and Kurd,
  Rest on your plighted word.

V.

Your sisters' shame and blood
Cry out to England's God.
  Slain on the church's floor,
  Their blood flowed out the door.
Speak! Speak! Speak!
The strong must help the weak.
  Leave Turkish bonds unsold;
  Betray not Christ for gold.
Let the Moslem dragon feel
Once more Saint George's heel.
  England, awake, awake!
  World, hear, for Jesus' sake!

Newark, N. J.

ARMENIA.

By Geo. W. Crofts.

Tune: "Maryland, My Maryland."

Where'er thy martyr blood has run
    Armenia !
Shed by the fierce Mohammedan,
    Armenia !
There nations gather in their grief —
There would they bring in swift relief —
Oh, may thy agony be brief,
    Armenia !

God's eye of pity glances down,
    Armenia !
He sees thy rudely broken crown,
    Armenia !
His heart is touched with all thy woes,
His mighty arm will interpose,
He'll save thee from thy cruel foes,
    Armenia !

All o'er thy verdant plains shall spread,
    Armenia !
The golden grain where thou hast bled,
    Armenia !
Thy harvest song shall yet arise
To him who rules in yonder skies,
Whose ear has heard thy bitter cries,
    Armenia !

America extends to thee,
    Armenia !
The cordial of her sympathy,
    Armenia !
And every soul in this free land
Would give to thee the helping hand,
And near thee in thy sorrow stand,
    Armenia !

In this dark hour be brave and strong,
 Armenia !
The right shall triumph over wrong,
 Armenia !
'Twill not be long till thou shalt see
The glorious dawn of liberty,
When thou shalt be forever free,
 Armenia !

ARMENIAN HYMN.

By Alice Stone Blackwell.

[From the Armenian of Nerses the Graceful ; born 1102, died 1172.]

O Dayspring, Sun of righteousness, shine forth with light
 for me !
Treasure of mercy, let my soul thy hidden riches see !
Thou before whom the thoughts of men lie open in thy
 sight,
Unto my soul, now dark and dim, grant thoughts that
 shine with light !
O Father, Son, and Holy Ghost, Almighty One in Three,
Care-taker of all creatures, have pity upon me !
Awake, O Lord, awake to help, with grace and power
 divine;
Awaken those who slumber now, like Heaven's host to
 shine !
O Lord and Saviour, life-giver, unto the dead give life,
And raise up those that have grown weak and stumbled
 in the strife !
O Skillful Pilot ! Lamp of light, that burneth bright
 and clear !
Strength and assurance grant to me, now hid away in
 fear.
O Thou that makest old things new, renew me and adorn;
Rejoice we with salvation, Lord, for which I inly mourn.
Giver of good, unto my sins be thy forgiveness given !
Lead Thy disciples, Heavenly King, unto the flocks of
 Heaven.

24

Defeat the evil husbandman that soweth tares and weeds;
Wither and kill in me the fruits of all his evil seeds !

O Lord, grant water to my eyes, that they may shed
warm tears

To cleanse and wash away the sin that in my soul appears !

On me, now hid in shadow deep, shine forth, O glory
bright !

Sweet juice, quench thou my soul's keen thirst ! Show
me the path of light !

Jesus, whose name is love, with love crush thou my
stony heart;

Bedew my spirit with thy blood, and bid my griefs depart !

O thou that even in fancy art so sweet, Lord Jesus Christ,
Grant that with Thy reality my soul may be sufficed !

When thou shalt come again to earth, and all thy glory
see,

Upon that dread and awful day, O Christ, remember me!

Thou that redeemest men from sin, O Saviour, I implore,
Redeem him who now praiseth Thee, to praise Thee ever-
more.

Dorchester, Mass.

Miss Alice Stone Blackwell is a noble Boston
woman who is greatly interested in the Armenians.
She has written many articles and poems, and done
much toward arousing public sentiment throughout
the United States in behalf of the Armenians.

The author of this book esteems it a privilege to
offer his personal thanks, as well as those of his persecuted nation, to Miss Blackwell, by whose kind permission the following poems from her book, "Armenian Poems," are here reprinted.

THE LAMENT OF MOTHER ARMENIA.

I.

In alien lands they roam, my children dear;
Where shall I make appeal, with none to hear?
Where shall I find them? Far away from me
My sons serve others, thralls in slavery.

Chorus.

Oh, come, my children, back to me!
Come home, your motherland to see!

II.

Ages have passed, no news of them I hear;
Dead, dead are they, my sons that knew not fear.
I weep, the blood is frozen in my veins;
No one will cure my sorrows and my pains.

Chorus.

III.

My blood is failing and my heart outworn,
My face forever mournful and forlorn;
To my dark grave with grief I shall descend,
Longing to see my children to the end.

Chorus.

IV.

O wandering shepherd, you whose mournful song
Rings through the valleys as you pass along!
Come, let us both, with many a bitter tear,
Weep for the sad death of our children dear!

Chorus.

V.

Crane of the fatherland, fly far away,
Fly out of sight, beyond the setting day;
My last sad greetings to my children bear,
For my life's hope has died into despair!

Chorus.

LIBERTY.

Michael Ghazarian Nalbandian was born in Russian Armenia in 1830; graduated at the University of St. Petersburg with the title of Professor ; was active as a teacher, author, and journalist ; fell under suspicion for his political opinions, and underwent a rigorous imprisonment of three years, after which he was exiled to the province of Sarakov, and died there, in 1866, of lung disease contracted in prison. It is forbidden in Russia to possess a picture of Nalbandian ; but portraits of him, with his poem on "Liberty" printed around the margin, are circulated secretly.

I.

When God, who is forever free,
  Breathed life into my earthly frame, —
From that first day, by his free will
  When I a living soul became, —
A babe upon my mother's breast,
  Ere power of speech was given to me,
Even then I stretched my feeble arms
  Forth to embrace thee, Liberty!

II.

Wrapped round with many swaddling bands,
  All night I did not cease to weep,
And in the cradle, restless still,
  My cries disturbed my mother's sleep.
"O mother!" in my heart I prayed,
  "Unbind my arms and leave me free!"
And even from that hour I vowed
  To love thee ever, Liberty!

III.

When first my faltering tongue was freed,
  And when my parents' hearts were stirred
With thrilling joy to hear their son
  Pronounce his first clear-spoken word,
"Papa, mamma," as children use,
  Were not the names first said by me;
The first word on my childish lips
  Was thy great name, O Liberty!

IV.

Liberty answered from on high
  The sovereign voice of Destiny:
" Wilt thou enroll thyself henceforth
  A soldier true of Liberty ?
The path is thorny all the way,
  And many trials wait for thee;
Too strait and narrow is this world
  For him who loveth Liberty. "

V.

" Freedom ! " ¯I answered, " on my head
  Let fire descend and thunder burst;
Let foes against my life conspire,
  Let all who hate thee do their worst:
I will be true to thee till death;
  Yea, even upon the gallows tree
The last breath of a death of shame
  Shall shout thy name, O Liberty ! "

THE WANDERING ARMENIAN TO THE SWALLOW.

By C. A. Totochian.

I.

O swallow, gentle swallow,
  Thou lovely bird of spring !
Say, whither art thou flying
  So swift on gleaming wing ?

II.

Fly to my birthplace, Ashdarag,
  The spot I love the best;
Beneath my father's roof-tree,
  O swallow, build thy nest.

III.

There dwells afar my father,
  A mournful man and gray,
Who for his only son's return
  Waits vainly, day by day.

IV.

If thou shouldst chance to see him,
  Greet him with love from me;
Bid him sit down and mourn with tears
  His son's sad destiny.

V.

In poverty and loneliness,
  Tell him, my days are passed:
My life is only half a life,
  My tears are falling fast.

VI.

To me, amid bright daylight,
  The sun is dark at noon;
To my wet eyes at midnight
  Sleep comes not, late or soon.

VII.

Tell him that, like a beauteous flower
  Smit by a cruel doom,
Uprooted from my native soil,
  I wither ere my bloom.

VIII.

Fly on swift wing, dear swallow,
  Across the quickening earth,
And seek in fair Armenia
  The village of my birth.

NOTICE.

The author of this book delivers lectures on the following subjects :

ARMENIA, ARMENIANS, AND THE RECENT ATROCITIES.

THE SULTAN OF TURKEY, HAMID THE II.

AMERICAN MISSIONS IN TURKEY.

SOCIAL AND POLITICAL LIFE IN TURKEY.

About 400 stereopticon views, as well as large maps, and costumes are used to illustrate the various lectures, which are highly instructive and entertaining, and never fail of interesting the most critical audiences.

The lectures are delivered upon very reasonable terms. For particulars address,   REV. GEO. H. FILIAN,

Cor. Eastern Parkway and Cresent St., Brooklyn, N. Y.

From the testimonials of prominent clergymen, authors, and secretaries of Y. M. C. A.'s, the following few are selected.

From Dr. R. S. Storrs, President of the American Board of Foreign Missions.

Your address to my congregation was admirable in its tone, and its entire impression upon those who heard it. Your knowledge of the facts presented is, of course, accurate and complete ; and your method of presenting the facts is clear, impressive, and leaves the minds instructed and the hearts quickened.

From the Faculty of Chicago Theological Seminary.

This will introduce to you Rev. George H. Filian, a graduate of this Seminary, a man of true character and devotion. He has been obliged to suspend work for a time in Turkey, owing to his faithfulness in preaching the truth, and is recommended to the consideration of Christians throughout America.

By order of the Faculty, H. N. SCOTT, Secretary.

From Prof. G. B. Wilcox, D.D., Chicago Theological Seminary.

Rev. G. H. Filian, a graduate of this Seminary in 1882, and since pastor of Armenian Evangelical Church, Marsovan, Turkey, is lecturing on Turkish missions and Turkish manners and customs. He is *an exceptionally able speaker*, and may with all confidence be introduced by any pastor to his congregation. I speak from long and intimate acquaintance.   G. B. WILCOX.

(375)

From Rev. John H. Barrows, D.D., Pastor First Presbyterian Church.

Rev. Geo. H. Filian, of Syria, lectured on Constantinople to my people last night, greatly interesting them. His illustrations are excellent, and he speaks with great enthusiasm. The evening's entertainment was very wholesome, and I cordially commend his worthy lecture. My people have heard him also with pleasure on "Social Life in Turkey."

From the Department Secretary Y. M. C. A. of Chicago, Illinois.

Rev. Geo. H. Filian delivered before one of our meetings his interesting lecture on "Missions in Turkey." I have never heard a speaker more interesting, and that held the attention of the audience in a greater measure than Mr. Filian. He is intelligent upon such a subject. He is versatile in expression, enthusiastic in delivery, and certainly very devout in heart. DANIEL SLOAN.

From the Secretary in charge Central Building, Y. M. C. A., Brooklyn, N. Y.

Rev. Geo. H. Filian gave his stereopticon lecture on "Constantinople" before our young men last night, and I am pleased to say that it is a lecture of rare interest and enjoyment. The views are beautiful and very instructive, as they are rarely thrown upon a screen. Mr. Filian has the advantage of speaking from actual experience, and his eloquent words, devoted spirit, and fund of humor quickly win the attention and sympathy of any audience.

ARTHUR B. WOOD.

From Rev. Henry Van Dyke, D.D., Pastor of the Brick Church, New York.

Your lecture before our Young Men's Society on Monday was a decided success. Every one was interested in what you had to say, and the pictures were excellent. We shall be glad when the time comes to have you with us again.

From Rev. George M. Stone, D.D., Hartford.

Mr. Filian is thoroughly intelligent on the whole Eastern question, and gives a view of Armenia and its present trial which is exceedingly valuable.

From A. C. Dixon, D.D., Pastor Hanson Place Baptist Church, Brooklyn, N. Y.

Rev. George H. Filian has lectured twice in the Hanson Place Baptist church, and it gives me pleasure to say that his lectures are interesting and instructive. They stir the heart to work and pray for the relief of persecuted Armenia.

From Louis Albert Banks, D.D., Pastor of Hanson Place M. E. Church, Brooklyn, N. Y.

I take great pleasure in saying that the Rev. Geo. H. Filian, who has spoken from the platform at Hanson Place M. E. church in behalf of the Armenian Christians, and also lectured in our church on Constantinople, is a very eloquent and earnest speaker, who will attract attention and arouse interest anywhere.

www.ingramcontent.com/pod-product-compliance
Lightning Source LLC
Chambersburg PA
CBHW030816110726
47900CB00006B/1635